OUT OF THE STARS

JAKE BIBLE

aethonbooks.com

OUT OF THE STARS
©2022 JAKE BIBLE

ALSO IN SERIES

ONE

"So, I know you're pregnant, but..." National Intelligence Director Gordon Miles says as he approaches Adrianna VanderVoort, also known as the "Spook," while she stands, stunned, and watches insanity unfold on the many screens set on the White House underground bunker's Situation Room. He offers her a glass. "Seems like a time for a mojito."

"I wish," VanderVoort says. She absentmindedly pats her pregnant belly then points up at the main screen. "Would someone care to tell me what the actual fuck I'm looking at?"

She turns to face the rest of the Situation Room, but no one offers her an answer. Not the Joint Chiefs of Staff. Not the Cabinet. Not any of the White House advisors or techs. Especially not President Charles Nance, who is seated at the head of the huge conference table, his eyes glued to the screen.

"Are they fighting or dancing?" Director Miles asks.

"Neither," Dr. Blane Hall says from his seat at one of the many computer stations in the Situation Room. "In my professional opinion, which I'm not sure even applies anymore considering..." He waves a hand at the screen. "It appears that the Yellowstone kaiju is—"

"The what?" National Security Advisor Joan Milligan asks.

"Kaiju," Dr. Hall replies. "It is the Japanese word for giant monster, and since Japan's kaiju has perished, I thought we should honor it by calling these creatures by a more accurate name."

Everyone stares at Dr. Hall, then looks to VanderVoort.

"I don't give ten shits what we call these things," VanderVoort says. "Someone tell me why the Yellowstone monster, er…kaiju, is running away from Australia!"

And that is exactly what's happening on the monitor. One gigantic monster is clearly running away from the other.

With all four massive arms waving frantically over its head, the Yellowstone kaiju is dashing and dodging, zigging and zagging, doing everything it can to keep the gargantuan version of a Komodo dragon from sinking its deadly teeth into its two huge legs that never stop with the dashing and dodging, the zigging and zagging.

"It could be tired," Secret Service Agent Paulo Alvarez says. "It has been fighting non-stop."

"Does that look tired to you, Agent Alvarez?" VanderVoort shouts. "Does it?"

"Looks like slapstick," Director Miles says and sips from the mojito he offered VanderVoort. "Vaudeville."

"I'm not finding it funny," VanderVoort says. "Dr. Hall?"

"Yes, Ms. VanderVoort?" Dr. Hall responds.

"Figure this out," VanderVoort snaps.

"I, uh, well, uh…" Dr. Hall stammers.

"You, uh, well, uh, figure this out," VanderVoort says in a mocking tone.

She sighs and shakes her head, turning from the monitor to take in all the personnel in the Situation Room.

"Does anyone have any news from Sergeants Bolton and Holt?" she asks. When no one responds, she throws her hands up in the air and stalks off. "I'm gonna take a long-needed piss. When I come back, I want someone to have an answer to something. Under-fucking-stood?"

All eyes watch her storm off. Then all eyes turn back to the screen.

"Huh," Director Miles says, taking another sip. "Is it me, or is the Yellowstone kikkoman—"

"Kaiju," Dr. Hall interrupts.

"Bless you," Director Miles says. "Is the Yellowstone *kaiju*... talking to itself?"

———

"WHAT THE FUCK?" Anson Lowell screams as he races around the landscape that had been part of Wyoming. Or Montana? Idaho maybe? Lowell isn't quite sure what state he's stomping on.

Which is the problem. He's so huge that it only takes a few dozen strides and he's crossing state borders.

"WHAT THE FUCK? WHAT THE FUCK? WHAT THE FUCK? WHAT THE FUCK?"

Lowell doesn't have time to worry about his interstate crossings. He's too busy freaking out over what has happened to him. And too busy trying to stay alive as a gargantuan Komodo dragon dogs his every massive step.

"Back off, you fucking butt-ugly, oversized gecko!" Lowell screams. "Don't you have a GEICO commercial to go shoot?"

That's what it sounds like in Lowell's head. But externally, his new mouth bellows only shrieks and roars, not words of sarcasm. Although Lowell suspects the shrieks and roars do have a sarcastic tinge to them.

The Australian monster ignores every shriek and roar and continues its chase of Lowell, its teeth dripping with saliva, the ground below sizzling and smoking with each drop.

"You should get that looked at!" Lowell shouts, still moving, never able to stop.

Lowell, having spent most of his life in prisons, is not averse to fighting. Even if he has suddenly found himself as the consciousness of a nightmare. His first instinct was to throw up his fists and get to punching. But…

But that isn't as easily done as he thought. Mainly because he has four fists instead of two, and so far he hasn't figured out how to independently control them. When he thinks of moving his left arm, both arms on that shoulder move. They shadow each other and throw him off-balance. Something he cannot afford while being pursued by what he's being pursued by.

Lowell's left foot hits a soft spot in the ground, and he stumbles. He tries to recover from the stumble, but his brain is too confused by the new body, so he just keeps falling, falling, and crashes into a hillside that no longer stays a hillside but becomes an explosion of dirt, rock, and ash.

Australia is on him instantly.

"NO!" Lowell screams and manages to box the huge lizard's earholes, sending Australia scrambling backward, its head shaking back and forth in agony.

Lowell pushes up onto all four hands then manages to stand, his eyes locked on Australia.

"Can you back the fuck off?" Lowell yells.

The air vibrates from the roar that comes out of his mouth. Lowell senses something there, but Australia doesn't back off, regroups instead, and rushes at Lowell before he can finish the thought.

"Front right fist smash!" Lowell yells.

And to his surprise, his front right fist obeys and slams down onto Australia's muzzle just as the giant lizard reaches him.

The monster isn't expecting the blow, not after the pitiful show Lowell has made so far, and it collapses to the ground, steaming blood gushing from its mouth. Tips of teeth poke up through its upper lip. It screeches with pain and anger.

"Oh, yeah? Well, fuck you too!" Lowell roars. He kicks Australia in the forehead then goes in for the coup de grace. "Both right fists smash!"

They do. But not on Australia.

The giant lizard throws itself to the side and Lowell's fists hit the ground and shatter the earth, sending fissures shooting out in all directions.

"Little shit," Lowell mumbles while his mouth makes grunting noises. "Get back here."

Lowell straightens and takes one gigantic step, then freezes. He glances down at his huge foot and grimaces.

"Well…shit," he says just as the fissures widen and the ground opens up beneath him, swallowing him whole. "SHIT!"

———

"The tremors are getting worse," Sergeant Connor Bolton says as he watches the sun rise over the far-off horizon. "We may have company soon."

The man he's addressing, Mark Halpern, only shrugs, his eyes on the satellite phone resting in his lap, a cord snaking from the bottom to a small solar panel that's propped up on an overturned cooler a couple feet away, aimed so the first rays of sunlight will activate the panel and get juice flowing into the dead battery.

On the other side of Halpern, resting against his thigh, is an AR15 semi-automatic assault rifle. Bolton makes sure his eyes don't stray to the rifle. The last thing he wants is for Halpern to worry that Bolton is going to make a move. Which, considering Bolton's injuries and exhaustion, isn't his plan. But he has no idea who Halpern really is, so he plays it cool.

"What's your story, Halpern?" Bolton asks.

"Little of this, little of that," Halpern replies. "I've been around."

"But not military?" Bolton presses. "Right?"

"No. Never got a chance to serve," Halpern says. He lifts his right leg. "Car accident when I was a teenager. Too much beer, too much speed. Missing most of the muscle in my calf, and my knee is more metal and plastic than flesh."

"I'm surprised they didn't take it off," Bolton says. "I've

known more than a few men and women who didn't get to keep theirs."

"Yeah, but they had Uncle Sam paying for the prosthetics," Halpern says and lowers his leg. "I was just a regular citizen with parents who had poor health insurance. So the doctor made a choice and did what he could."

"Does it hurt?"

"Sometimes. Not as much anymore. I've kept up my own physical therapy routine. What's left is pretty strong. Won't be running any marathons, but I guess no one will anymore."

"Unless they's running from the monsters," Jeremy, one of Halpern's people, says as he walks up to the two of them and hands Halpern a canteen. "Bet you'd be running then, right, Mark?"

"I'd rather not find out," Halpern says. A wave of tremors shakes them then subsides. "That doesn't feel like footfalls. More like the earthquakes that happened right before the eruption. Ol' Yellowstone may be fixing to blow again."

Jeremy cackles. "I'd think it's already blown all its wad."

Halpern gives the man a weak smile, then points his chin across the road to the rows of semi-intact trailers.

"Sun's coming up, Jeremy," Halpern says. "How about you scrounge us some breakfast? See what's left in those trailers."

"Ain't nothing left," Jeremy says. "Haley and me already looked."

"Take Ginevra with you and check again," Halpern says. "You probably missed something. Double-check the junkies' trailer. They always have shit stuffed in the walls."

"Really?" Jeremy asks, obviously annoyed at being sent away.

"Really," Halpern replies.

Bolton can feel the tension between the two and he tucks that little observance away for future use. A couple of rays of fresh sunlight hit Bolton in the face and he shields his eyes as Halpern grins and claps his hands together.

"Now we can get things going," Halpern says. He stands and

sets the sat phone next to the solar panel on the upended cooler. He takes a deep breath, returns to his seat to fetch the AR15, and starts walking, motioning for Bolton to follow. "Come on."

"Where are we going?" Bolton asks.

"Just need to stretch my legs," Halpern says. "Get a little space from my compatriots. They're good people, but maybe not…"

Halpern lets the thought drop, but Bolton picks it up.

"Maybe not the brightest?" Bolton suggests, making sure to keep his tone light as he stands too and does his best to hurry and catch up to Halpern. Every muscle in his body protests, but he makes it and is soon walking right beside Halpern as they leave the trailer park behind. "No offense."

"None taken, Sergeant," Halpern says. "I'm no rocket scientist myself. But I have the sense not to stick my hand in the fire. Not all of them have that same sense."

They walk for a couple of minutes, both watching the sun rise over the carnage that the world has suffered. Halpern sets the pace, but Bolton can tell he's taking it slow, making sure Bolton doesn't tire out.

"Anything on your mind?" Bolton asks.

"Why do you ask that?" Halpern replies.

"Gut instinct," Bolton says. "And we're also now out of earshot of your friends."

"Compatriots," Halpern says. "We're all in it together, but I wouldn't call them my friends."

"You didn't know each other before everything went to shit?" Bolton asks.

"No, we did, but we've been joined in a common cause, not a common friendship."

"And that common cause was…?"

"Is. The common cause still exists. Probably more so now than ever. Especially since we found you, Sergeant Bolton."

Halpern doesn't offer an explanation and Bolton knows not to push. They keep walking a few more yards before Bolton lets out a long exhale.

"Okay, I gotta sit my ass down," Bolton says. "I've been pushing hard for days now on almost no sleep and no food. Then I had a building dropped on me, so…"

"We can sit over there," Halpern says and points to an ash-covered kids' plastic picnic table that sits alone in an empty yard. The house behind it is a shattered foundation. No walls anywhere, standing or collapsed. Just a foundation.

Bolton makes for the picnic table and eases himself awkwardly down onto the low, plastic bench.

"Better than nothing," Bolton says.

Halpern doesn't sit. He stands with his back to the sun, shielding the light from Bolton's face.

"This place you're heading to…" Halpern starts.

"Colorado Springs," Bolton says.

"You mentioned Schriever or Fort Carson," Halpern says. "You said you could get us in there?"

"I can try," Bolton says. "With how things are, I don't know if I'll succeed, but I will try."

"Say you can get us on one of those bases, then where are you going?" Halpern asks.

Bolton shakes his head. "Nowhere. My mission is to get to Colorado Springs."

"Nah," Halpern says and points a finger at Bolton. The man's silhouette against the sunlight stiffens. "Your mission is something else. You want us to help you get down there safe and sound, then you're going to ditch us at whatever government facility is still standing. Where are you going after you ditch us, Sergeant?"

"My mission is… fluid," Bolton says. "I'm to go to whatever facility is still standing."

"You already mentioned Schriever and Fort Carson," Halpern says, giving Bolton a pointed, knowing look. "What other facility is there?"

"What does it matter?" Bolton asks. "You and your…compatriots will be all set."

"I know, I know," Halpern says. "Almost sounds too good to be true."

"Everything sounds too good to be true in this Hell," Bolton says and gestures at the destruction around them. "Look, Halpern, I don't know what you want from me. I just watched a good frogman bleed out and I have to keep the mission on track by myself in this shit. I could use your help. You can probably use my help."

There's a huge crash from one of the trailers. Then Jeremy starts shouting and cursing. Bolton smiles.

"Yeah. You could definitely use my help," Bolton continues. "We cover each other's backs and I get you and your compatriots to safety while I finish my mission."

Ginevra begins shouting and Jeremy shouts back.

"They need to shut up," Bolton says. "They're gonna bring the monsters down on us."

"True. True," Halpern says. He lets out a low whistle and in seconds a woman comes jogging up, holding a decent-looking .300 WinMag sniper rifle. "Haley. Tell them to be quiet."

Haley—short, pudgy, with a cute, affable face—snorts and jogs over to the trailer. She shoves the door open, barks a couple of words, then leaves the trailer and disappears into the park. Jeremy and Ginevra are silent.

"Two tours in Iraq," Halpern says as he watches Haley disappear. "Crazy as a shit-house rat, but a damn fine shot."

"Two tours?" Bolton asks. He has his doubts. She didn't give off a "having served" vibe to him. "Where was she stationed?"

"Kabul or something," Halpern replies.

Bolton sighs inwardly. Kabul is not in Iraq. He highly doubts Haley served anywhere other than maybe Burger King. Most likely it was her father or another relative who served and she picked up enough to fool Halpern.

That puts Halpern as a bad reader of people, which makes Halpern's group more dangerous than before. If Halpern doesn't have a handle on his compatriots, then they might be more of a liability to Bolton than an asset.

"I tell you what," Halpern says and starts pacing, "you level with me and if I believe you, we'll help get you down to Colorado Springs."

"You know what?" Bolton says and stands up. Halpern instantly stops pacing and grips his AR15 harder than he has been. "Calm down. I'm not making a move. But I do think I've changed my mind. I'm going to take my sat phone and solar charger, my .45 and ammo, and all the rest of my stuff, and be on my way."

"That so?" Halpern asks, and the barrel of the AR15 comes level with Bolton's chest. "I believe I have to argue against that."

"Do whatever you want," Bolton says with a shrug, "but you gain nothing by killing me."

"I gain a sat phone," Halpern responds.

"And no way to operate it," Bolton says. "You need the code."

"Then how about you give me the code?"

"That would be pretty stupid of me."

"You standing there with an AR15 pointed at you and acting like you're in control of this situation is pretty stupid of you."

"I am in control of this situation."

"How do you figure?"

Bolton glances over Halpern's shoulder.

"I lied about my partner being dead."

Halpern instantly takes the bait and spins around.

Of course, there's no one there.

Bolton slams his fist into the back of Halpern's neck and the man crumples. Bolton has the AR15 out of Halpern's hands and into his before the man fully hits the ground.

"Jesus…" Halpern gasps and puts a hand to the back of his neck. "That fucking hurts…"

"Not as much as a bullet to your knee," Bolton says. He charges the weapon and takes aim. "Right or left?"

Halpern holds his hands up, pleading. "Wait! Wait!"

"Why should I?" Bolton asks, his finger slowly moving from the outside of the trigger guard to the trigger itself.

"So Haley can come up behind you," Halpern says with a grin.

Bolton realizes an instant too late that the grin on Halpern's face is real.

Then he feels the butt of that .300 WinMag connect with the back of his head and the lights go out.

———

Excruciating pain. Blinding pain. Unbearable pain.

None of the three descriptors even touch the agony that rages through Lu's head. If she could open her eyes, which she isn't going to even attempt, and look into a mirror, she wouldn't be surprised to see a bullet wound right in the middle of her forehead.

"Mom…?" Kyle's voice croaks from the dark.

"Shhhh… no talking," Dr. Probst mumbles. "Silence is golden…"

"What the fuck happened?" Lu asks.

She makes the hard decision and opens her eyes.

Total darkness.

She doesn't have to wave her hand in front of her face to know the darkness is complete. She's been in situations where light isn't even a concept, let alone a reality, and she knows for a fact that there isn't a light source anywhere near them.

"No, no, no," Dr. Probst says. "That's talking. Stop."

"You're talking," Kyle counters.

"In order to get the both of you to stop," Dr. Probst says.

"How's that working out for you?" Lu asks and realizes she sounds just like Lowell.

Lowell…

"Lowell?" Lu says. "You awake?"

No answer.

"Lowell?" she tries again. "Wake the fuck up, asshole."

Still no answer.

Lu doesn't want to, but she knows she has to crawl around until she finds Lowell just to make sure he's not dead. She shifts her position and the world falls away.

Or she falls away as she tumbles off the cart she was lying on.

"Fuck!" she growls.

"Talking…" Dr. Probst snarls. "Don't."

"Be careful," Lu warns. "You aren't on the—"

"Ow!" Dr. Probst cries out as Lu hears a thump. "Why were we in a cart?"

"Cart?" Kyle asks, then there's another thump. "Oh. Cart. Shit…"

"Lowell?" Lu calls again. "Lowell, you awake?"

"Is he dead?" Kyle asks. "What happened anyway?"

"The Substance," Dr. Probst answers. "It got into our heads…" She takes a deep breath. "It may have killed Lowell."

"No," Lu says. "He hasn't been affected by it like everyone else."

"Why is that?" Kyle asks.

"I have no idea," Lu says. "Dr. Probst?"

"Your guess is as good as mine," Dr. Probst says. "Maybe it didn't kill Lowell. Maybe he's only unconscious."

"Which means we crawl around and try to find him in here," Lu says. "If he's in here."

"Kyle and I can crawl," Dr. Probst says. "I'd rather not move again, but we can do that while you find the door and see if you can get us out of here."

"Where are we?" Kyle asks.

"Good question," Lu says. "We were going down to see the Substance, then…"

All three are silent as they try to figure out what happened to them.

"My laptop!" Dr. Probst exclaims, then moans. "I remember something…"

Silence.

"Yeah? What?" Kyle asks.

"Oh, sorry," Dr. Probst says. "We were at the doors to the Substance. We made it that far and the doors opened, then my laptop fell and…"

Dr. Probst groans.

"That voice," Lu says. "There was a voice in my head."

"Yes," Dr. Probst said. "There was a voice."

"I remember the voice," Kyle said. "It was so fucking loud."

"And wrong," Dr. Probst says. "There was something wrong with the voice. What was wrong?"

"It wasn't speaking English," Lu answers. "I don't know what the language was, but it wasn't English."

"Right… right…" Dr. Probst mutters. "I don't think it was human either."

"Is the voice what drove everyone insane?" Kyle asks. "Maybe the surges in the Substance were the voice breaking free and screaming into people's minds, making them go bug-fuck nuts."

"That's an extremely reasonable hypothesis," Dr. Probst says. "Well done, Kyle."

"Thanks," Kyle says. "But it doesn't get us out of here."

"Take the compliment, Kyle," Lu snaps then sighs. "Sorry. I didn't mean to snap. Let's get back to it. You two see if you can find Lowell in here and I'll see if I can find the door."

No one moves.

"I have no idea which way the door is," Lu says.

"We each need to go in a different direction until we reach a wall," Dr. Probst says. "Then we crawl clockwise until we find Lowell and/or the door."

"Good plan," Lu says. "I'll go this way."

"We can't see you, Mom," Kyle says.

"Shit. Okay," Lu says. She crawls to their voices and reaches out. "There. We're together. Kyle, you go this way." She pats him on his right shoulder. "Cheryl, you go this way." She taps Dr. Probst on the left shoulder. "I'll go straight ahead. Good luck."

They move off in different directions and all that can be heard is the shuffling of their hands and knees on the concrete. Then a thump and an oof.

"Found the wall," Dr. Probst says.

Another thump and oof.

"Found my wall," Kyle says.

"Hold on," Lu calls to both. "Still crawling."

It takes her a couple of extra seconds, but then she reaches the end of her journey.

And the doors.

"Yes," she says. "I guessed right. I'm at the doors."

"Can you open them?" Kyle asks.

"Want to hold on and give me a second?" Lu snaps.

"Sorry."

"No, I'm sorry. Again," Lu says.

Carefully, slowly, Lu stands up, her hands on the doors the entire time. She's almost afraid that if she stops touching them, the doors will just disappear.

"Ow," Dr. Probst says. "What'd I run into?"

"Probably a cart," Kyle says. "I just bumped into one. We must be in the cart hold."

Lu shuffles to the side and pats around the wall until she finds a keypad. There are only two buttons. She presses one of them.

"In the cart hold?" Dr. Probst asks.

A loud grinding then an even louder buzzing fills the space, followed by silence.

"Wrong button," Lu says. She presses the other one.

The grinding picks up again, then a grating noise joins it as the doors split apart.

"Wait!" Dr. Probst cries. "That thing's behind those doors!"

Lu mashes her hand against the close button over and over, but it's too late. The doors have opened.

"There's nothing there," Lu says.

"No monster thing?" Kyle asks.

"No...nothing," Lu says. "No light or anything. I don't hear anything either."

"It's gone?" Dr. Probst asks. "Where'd it go? You don't think it took Lowell and is off eating him somewhere, do you?"

"Jesus," Kyle says.

"Sorry," Dr. Probst says.

"The ground is slick," Lu says as she slides one foot forward then the next, shuffle stepping her way through the doors and toward where she hopes is the elevator. She pauses, crouches, and wipes a finger across the floor. She brings the finger to her nose. "Stinks. Smells like rancid blood."

"Maybe you shouldn't go that way," Dr. Probst says. "We should try a different direction."

"Only other direction is toward the Substance," Lu says. "You really want a replay of that shit?"

"No, no, of course not," Dr. Probst says. "You're right. I'm off my game at the moment."

"We're all off our games," Lu says.

"We don't even have games," Kyle says.

"The carts!" Lu exclaims.

"Too loud," Dr. Probst says. "What about the carts?"

"They have headlights," Lu says. "One of you crawl up into one and turn on the lights."

There's a pause, some bumping noises, then the pitch darkness explodes with light.

"Jesus!"

"My eyes!"

"Fuck, that hurts!"

It takes Lu a couple of seconds to adjust to the light. It hurts like hell to keep her eyes open, but she forces her lids not to close. She's staring directly at the elevator doors only a few feet from her.

"What do you see?" Dr. Probst asks.

"There's something smeared on the ground, but that's it," Lu says. "It's clear."

"We sure we want to risk using the elevator?" Kyle asks.

"No choice," Lu says. "None of us are in any shape to climb

any stairs."

"There are no stairs," Dr. Probst says.

"No, I mean, the levels above were purged, right?" Kyle says. "That may have damaged the elevator shaft."

The three of them remain silent for a few seconds.

"That thing fell onto the elevator," Lu says as the memory hits her. "Then it came after us."

Dr. Probst walks slowly to Lu's side. Kyle joins her. All three stare at the elevator.

And the slime trail that leads to it.

"You think it went back in?" Kyle asks.

"Fuck," Lu says.

They're silent for a few seconds more.

"It's the only way up," Dr. Probst says. "I don't have my laptop, so I don't know if any of the levels are safe. But if we're going to find out, then we have to use the elevator."

"We could stay down here," Kyle says just as his stomach growls.

"Only for a couple of days," Lu says. "Then we'll slowly start to die of thirst."

She sighs and steps up to the elevator doors. She stares at the control buttons on the wall.

Then she presses a button and the doors begin to slide apart.

———

Surrounded by a week's rations worth of empty juice boxes, Tony glares daggers at his radio rig.

"They're not answering," he says, the anger in his voice bordering on rage.

"Calm down," Krissy says and picks up the last full juice box. "Have some grape."

"I don't want grape!" Tony shouts and smacks the juice box from her hand.

He turns on his stool, the rage twisting his features.

Krissy slaps him across the cheek.

Tony blinks a few times and the rage is gone. He rubs his cheek, tears welling in his eyes.

"Ow," he says. "You struck me."

"You ever turn on me like that again and I'll do more than fucking strike you, freak," Krissy snarls. "I'll beat your ass until—"

"Everything alright in here?" Terrie asks from the doorway, supported by a pair of crutches. She points one at Krissy. "What just happened? Are you two fighting? Physically fighting?"

"She slapped me," Tony says. "But I deserved it."

The admission causes Krissy to raise her eyebrows in surprise. She looks at Terrie and sees a mirrored expression.

"Okay…" Terrie says, then carefully walks to the radio bench.

"You need to be lying down," Krissy says.

"I'm fine," Terrie insists. Krissy lets it drop. "Are you sure you're on the correct channel?"

"Yes," Tony replies curtly. "I know the channel I connected to the White House with. I wouldn't forget something like that."

"No, no, of course not," Terrie says. "So, you're calling them on the correct channel, but they just aren't answering? Or is there static like maybe something went wrong on their end?"

"It's static no matter what scenario you propose," Tony says. "There's always static until someone answers. See?"

"You mean hear," Krissy says with a sly grin.

Tony frowns at her, but a very, very slight smile plays at the corners of his mouth.

He twists a knob.

"Static," Tony says as the sound of static fills the air. He flips a switch and the static is gone. "I can filter it out, but it's only a masking tool. The static still exists, but we can't hear it. Doesn't change anything, really. They're not answering."

He picks up the handset, puts it to his mouth, and depresses the button.

"Why aren't you answering?" he shouts, then flings the

handset onto the bench.

Tony's shoulders slump and his chin hits his chest. Then he begins to cry.

Krissy and Terrie exchange a look. Krissy sighs and reaches out to Tony, taking him in her arms as he cries. Tony clings to her and buries his face in her chest.

"Are you fucking joking?" Krissy snaps and shoves his head away from between her breasts. "Fucking little perv."

"What? I wasn't! No!" Tony yells and stands up quickly, tears still streaming down his face, snot running from his nose.

"Ugh. Gross," Krissy says as she stares down at the wet marks on her shirt. "I'm going to go change."

She storms off, leaving a still-blubbering Tony and a weak Terrie behind her.

As she hurries down the short hallway, she feels the earth tremble.

"Terrie!" Krissy yells when she stumbles her way into the main room of the bunker. "Terrie!"

Despite being on crutches, Terrie nearly barrels into Krissy's back as she stutters to a stop and stares at the main room.

"Don't just stand there!" Terrie shouts. "We need to stop it up!"

Terrie shoves around Krissy and hobbles straight for the far wall. The far wall where water is slowly, but not too slowly, seeping in between the bottom of the wall and the floor.

"Grab towels!" Terrie yells.

"Towels?" Krissy laughs. "Are you shitting me?"

She sighs and shakes her head. Instead of walking over to Terrie and the water issue, Krissy stomps over to Roy.

"Hey!" Krissy shouts at Roy. "Roy! The bunker is leaking! Wake up so you can tell us how to fix it!"

Krissy gives Roy a shove. He only slumps further into the chair, his head lolling at an uncomfortable angle.

"Oh… Shit…" Krissy says. "Terrie?"

"I'm five seconds away from cursing a blue streak at you,

Krissy. God will not be pleased, so do not put me in that position," Terrie snaps. "Come help me!"

"Terrie…I think Roy's dead," Krissy says. She glances at Terrie and the older woman stares back at her, then looks to Roy. "Before you ask, yes, I'm pretty fucking sure."

"Check his pulse," Terrie says.

"No fucking way!" Krissy snaps. "I'm not touching a corpse!"

"Corpse?" Tony asks from the doorway. "Is Roy dead?"

The two women pause, look at each other, look at Tony, then look away.

Krissy clears her throat. "I think so. Sorry."

"You have to be sure," Tony says and walks causally over to Roy. He leans down, presses two fingers to Roy's neck, and waits. His lips move slightly as he counts, then he pulls his fingers away. "He's dead."

"I'm so sorry, Tony," Terrie says.

"There's nothing to be done now," Tony says. "Everyone dies. We'll die too."

Tony looks to Terrie, the wall, and then the water seeping in at the base of the wall.

"At the rate the water's coming in, we'll drown in approximately fifteen hours," Tony says.

"Yeah, I'm not drowning in a fucking bunker," Krissy says. "How do we stop it?"

"We'll need to pump the water out, then seal the gap between the wall and the floor," Tony says.

"Is there sealant?" Terrie asks. "And a pump?"

"Yes," Tony says. "Follow me."

Terrie gives Krissy a sharp look.

"Right. I'll go," Krissy says.

Tony walks off without waiting and enters one of the doors that Krissy still hasn't explored. She's seen a few of the supply tunnels and rooms, but not all of them. Obviously.

"In here," Tony says as he opens the door, walks down the tunnel to the door at the end, and opens this door too. "A lot of redundant supplies. But the sealant is in here. So are some rolls of sheet metal."

"What do we need sheet metal for?" Krissy asks as she inspects a five-gallon bucket of industrial sealant.

"You can't just slap sealant onto the wall and floor," Tony replies, his tone nothing but sharpened contempt. "You must put a strip of the sheet metal down, bend it into an L-shape, press it against the gap between the wall and the floor, then seal around the sheet metal."

He abruptly turns and leaves.

"Hey!" Krissy yells and takes off after him.

Tony hurries quickly into the main room, then heads directly for his room.

"Stop!" Krissy shouts.

Tony slows then stops. He turns and looks at Krissy, his expression one of boredom and annoyance.

"What?" he asks.

"Where the fuck are you going?" Krissy asks. "We need your help with—"

"I'm going back to my conversation," Tony says.

"Conversation?" Krissy and Terrie ask in unison.

"You reached the White House?" Terrie asks.

"Why didn't you say that right away?" Krissy snarls.

"I haven't reached the White House," Tony says. "I've reached someone else. A different party entirely."

Tony doesn't elaborate, turns quickly, and is gone.

Krissy balls her fists and slams them against her thighs, then grunts in pain. She faces Terrie.

"I'll be able to patch the wall faster than you," Krissy says, waving a hand at Terrie, indicating her condition. "After I take Roy out of here…"

"I'll find out who Tony is speaking with," Terrie says. "Maybe we can get someone to come help us."

"Help? I don't want help," Krissy says as her eyes shift toward Roy. "I want the fuck out of here."

TWO

It's dark, but not really.

That is the extent of a description Lowell can come up with while he lies on his back and stares up at the huge hole above him.

Well, as he lies on the back of the giant monster he's trapped inside.

Or has become.

Or…

"Whatever," Lowell mumbles. His monster mouth lets out a low growl. "Shut up." Another growl. "I said shut up." A third growl. "Fucking hell…"

A fourth growl that is responded to from above.

Lowell can just make out the shadow of Australia at the edge of the hole. Or he assumes it's Australia. Lowell really hopes the monster hasn't found a friend.

Australia shrieks down at him but stays up top, pacing back and forth.

"Left hands flip the fucker off," Lowell commands, and the hands do as he says.

He thinks the same command without saying it and the hands flip their middle fingers once more.

Progress.

Lowell manages to think his behemoth body up and onto its knees. The pain is rough, but Lowell shakes it off, takes a deep breath into his monster lungs, and lets it out slowly.

Which causes a good amount of dirt, dust, and ash to swirl all about him.

"Big boy's got some lungs," Lowell says. He ignores the weird noises his monster mouth makes.

Lowell gets to his feet, steadies himself, then takes a look around.

The space he's in is massive. It'd have to be for his monster body to stand fully upright and still have a few thousand feet of hole towering above him. However, the space isn't just over him, but all around him. For as far as his monster eyes can see, which it turns out is pretty far, a gigantic cavern extends.

"I guess I get to choose my own adventure," Lowell says, and his monster mouth echoes in its strange tongue.

Australia shrieks once more and without even thinking this time, Lowell flips it off again.

More progress.

"This way," Lowell says to himself. Australia shrieks down at him. "Fuck off! Jesus…"

Feeling surprisingly spry on his giant feet, especially after taking a bit of a tumble that had to be close to a mile down into the Earth, Lowell moves off in his randomly chosen direction.

It takes Lowell a few minutes to realize a couple of things: that his monster eyes are pretty damn strong in the dark, and that the gigantic cavern isn't completely dark.

Striations of blue crystal spur this way and that throughout the cavern's walls.

The crystals are a color blue that Lowell recognizes instantly. It's the hue of the diesel-drinking junkie monsters' tongues. Lowell chuckles. No way that's a coincidence.

He trudges along until a noise stops him in his tracks.

A low rumbling is close by then gone. Lowell waits a few

seconds but doesn't hear it again.

As soon as he starts walking once more though, the rumbling occurs a second time. Lowell stops; he doesn't need a third time charm to figure out where the rumbling is coming from.

Both of his right arms pat his hungry belly. The second he realizes the source of the rumbling is the second he recognizes a gnawing pain in his guts.

He's fucking hungry. Hungrier than he's ever been in his life.

Lowell focuses on the hunger and is surprised that the pain isn't centralized to one location. He glances his monster head down at his monster abdomen, confused.

Then it hits him that his monster body must have more than one stomach. Or maybe no stomach at all, but some weird stomachless digestive tract.

Whatever the anatomy, the monster rumbly in his monster tumbly increases with each step he takes.

"Fuck me," Lowell says, suddenly lightheaded.

He puts two hands out against the cavern wall to steady himself. His palms come in contact with the blue crystal striations and a million-mile-an-hour montage of images slams through his brain.

Lowell screams and yanks his hand away from the crystal.

The montage stops, but the images remain, swirling in his brain until he forces them away. He's too damn hungry to rationally process what his mind's eye is seeing.

Then the ground actually shakes.

"Great. More eruptions," Lowell mutters. "Probably too much to ask to not get roasted alive by hot lava, but then the world is what it is and being roasted alive by hot lava while inside some giant monster body is sorta how things go now, right?"

His growls echo off the cavern's walls and are responded to by Australia's echoing shrieks.

"Shit," Lowell says.

He gets himself together, stands up straight, and turns to face back the way he'd just come.

Australia. Coming at him fast.

"What part of fuck off don't you understand, you fucking fuck?" Lowell roars.

Australia's shrieks nearly shatter Lowell's ears. If he has ears. He isn't too sure he does. What he is sure of is that he doesn't have time to check as Australia closes the distance with lightning speed.

For a moment, Lowell is frozen. He can't fight a giant lizard. Especially not while confined in close quarters like the massive cavern he's in. He needs room to run, to dodge, to get away from…

Then it hits Lowell. Not a thought, but an instinct that has been honed over years upon years of confinement in prisons, in jails, in the backs of police cars, in basements, in closets…

Lowell's body language changes as his entire being fills the massive monster he's been forced to inhabit. He raises his four fists.

He totally knows how to fight in close quarters.

"Bitch," he snarls, "you are about to fuck with the wrong convict."

Australia lunges at Lowell and is stopped dead in its tracks as two fists slam down on the beast's snout, pushing the monster's mouth into the dirt and rock of the cavern.

"How's that, motherfucker?" Lowell roars. He doesn't notice the guttural sound that his mouth emits. To his mind, it's all the same: rage.

Australia thrashes away as Lowell brings his other two fists down.

"Yeah, you better run, you fuck!" Lowell rages. "I get a hold of you and you'll be the biggest set of boots this planet has ever fucking seen!"

Australia leaps. But not at Lowell.

Instead, the monster leaps against the cavern's wall and bounces off, rocketing directly at Lowell's chest. Lowell twists at the waist and ducks down, using two arms to brace himself against the ground and two to wrap around the neck of a very surprised Australia.

Without missing a beat, Lowell keeps twisting and uses his momentum to fling Australia against the opposite wall. Hunks of rock and shards of blue crystal spray everywhere as Australia drops hard.

"What the fuck am I worried about?" Lowell asks himself. "I've broken psychos a billion times scarier than your lizard ass."

Lowell doesn't allow Australia to recover and lets loose with a brutal kick to Australia's midsection. The monster shrieks, but with pain, not anger. Another kick and Australia struggles like mad to get away, but Lowell isn't allowing escape to be part of the script.

Two hands grip Australia's tail and pull back, dragging the monster's belly across the jagged rock and blue crystal shards. Blood begins to pool under Australia as it continues its desperate fight to be free of the rage-drunk Lowell.

"You ever heard your own leg get dislocated?" Lowell asks, the voice in his head casual, calm—the voice externally almost taunting.

Grip, twist, pull.

Pop.

Australia's painful shrieks increase in volume exponentially.

The monster's left rear leg is a useless stick of flesh and bone—a gargantuan stick, but useless nonetheless as it hangs from only muscle and tendon, the ball and socket no longer joined together.

Lowell laughs and the cavern shakes.

"Now we're talking," he says as he grips, twists, pulls at the other rear leg.

Pain explodes in a forearm.

Australia has bent itself in half and its jaws are clamped onto Lowell's arm.

Burning agony, like liquid fire, rushes up Lowell's arm and straight into his head. He feels sick, he feels stunned, he feels like he's...dying?

Then he sees the poison dripping from around Australia's muzzle.

Shit.

The rage in him erupts with as much force as the Yellowstone supervolcano.

Without realizing it, Lowell unleashes a sonic wave blast from his mouth that not only dislodges Australia from his forearm but sends the beast tumbling away. Australia rolls dozens and dozens of yards before coming to a broken rest against a giant boulder.

Lowell staggers and struggles to keep upright, but the venom coursing through his veins quickly turns his muscles stiff and his nerves into hot, sparking wires.

"Fuck me," he mumbles and tries to turn around so he can get out of the cavern that is about to become his tomb.

Australia hisses.

Lowell sighs.

He turns back, wobbles over to Australia, grabs a smaller boulder, lifts it with barely controllable muscles, and brings the rock down hard and fast onto Australia's head.

Blood and brains, bone and skin explode everywhere.

Lowell sighs again and collapses onto his monster ass.

He leans back against the wall and comes in contact with the veins of blue crystal once more. A trillion images slam into his head, but as his consciousness, and life, fades away, one image stands out.

Lowell reaches for that image, knowing it's the most important thing in his life.

What little life he has left…

———

"Where the fuck did they go?" VanderVoort shouts. "I step away to piss and you lose the kaiju?"

"Thank you," Dr. Hall says. "Using the proper terminology is key—"

"Shut up," VanderVoort says. Dr. Hall doesn't argue and closes his mouth, but the look in his eyes tells VanderVoort he has something important to say. "Spit it out, Dr. Hall."

"They were fighting, then Yellowstone fell through the Earth's crust," Dr. Hall said. "It was weird. It was like…"

"Like it didn't know its own strength," Alvarez finishes.

"Gonna agree with the doctor and the agent," Director Miles says, still sipping from a mojito. "That thing is acting weird."

"Acting weird?" VanderVoort asks in a way that states she doesn't expect an answer. "How should a creature that's over a thousand feet tall act? Is there a specific script it's supposed to follow?"

"Play the footage back, Hall," Director Miles says.

Dr. Hall does and VanderVoort catches up on what she'd missed when desperate to relieve her pregnancy-battered bladder.

"Am I wrong?" Director Miles asks.

"No," VanderVoort admits. "Its behavior has changed." She points at Dr. Hall. "I want to know why."

"I would also like to know why," President Nance says from his seat at the head of the Situation Room conference table. "In fact, Ms. VanderVoort, I believe it's time I took the reins again. There's no word from Bolton or Holt, which means your supervenom plan cannot be implemented, and now all the monsters have disappeared below ground. You've tried your best, but you're failing mis—"

"Primary monsters," Dr. Hall says and clears his throat. "I mean, kaiju. The primary kaiju have disappeared, Mr. President. We still have the kaiju in Mexico City and Africa."

"And there is something in Antarctica," a tech says.

"Exactly," Dr. Hall agrees. "In my professional opinion, Ms. VanderVoort has responded more appropriately than this entire table." Dr. Hall waves a dismissive hand at the conference table and all seated around it. "She certainly hasn't tried to turn the planet into a radioactive wasteland."

Voices explode in protest, all of their anger directed at Dr. Hall.

VanderVoort smiles at the indignation being flung from the Joint Chiefs and Cabinet. Her eyes shift from Dr. Hall to President Nance.

"I would have put it a bit more diplomatically," VanderVoort says.

"No, you wouldn't have," Director Miles mutters.

"But," VanderVoort continues, "Dr. Hall is correct. The nuclear option failed, and considering that's the Hail Mary weapon in your arsenal, President Nance, I'm afraid your presence here is more of a hierarchical distraction than a legal necessity."

The angry, indignant voices all come to an abrupt silence. Eyes shift from Dr. Hall, turn to VanderVoort, then slowly light upon President Nance.

"Ms. VanderVoort, I'm going to give you the benefit of the doubt," President Nance says, "and assume you're not suggesting I remove myself from my own Situation Room. Please help dissuade me from that notion."

VanderVoort gives President Nance a kind but patronizing look and shakes her head.

"I wish I could put your mind at ease, Charles," is all Vander-Voort says.

The two titans of the apocalypse lock eyes. No one in the Situation Room moves a muscle or bats an eyelash. Breaths are held until all at once there's a flurry of motion and the personnel quickly take sides.

Firearms are up, voices are raised, and violence is ready to erupt.

"Stop," President Nance orders in a calm voice. "Stand down."

The few men and women, and they are few, who rallied to the President's side try to argue.

"Stand down!" President Nance shouts. "Ms. VanderVoort is correct. My choices have only worsened the catastrophe."

"Sir!" Joan protests. "You are President of the United—"

"No need to finish, Joan," President Nance interrupts. "There is no United States of America anymore. And it would be idiotic of me to think there ever will be again."

President Nance points at the main monitor showing a smoking Yellowstone caldera. His eyes stay locked on Vander-Voort's.

"Wherever they've gone, it's their world now," President Nance continues. "Borders are meaningless when monsters can stride across them with only a few dozen steps. I'm not sure how Ms. VanderVoort achieved her position, but it's a position that is responsible for the entire planet, not just our neck of it."

He sighs, straightens up, and finally breaks eye contact with VanderVoort. President Nance smooths out his wrinkled clothes and smirks.

"I'm going to take a shower and get some sleep," he announces. "Call me if you need me."

With back straight and eyes clear, President Nance walks from the Situation Room and into the corridor that leads to the Presidential Suite. Every eye in the room follows him until he's lost from sight. Then those eyes turn to VanderVoort.

"You sure about this?" Director Miles asks. VanderVoort nods. "Alright. I've got your back."

VanderVoort smiles.

"I hate to ask it, but does anyone have a problem with me being in charge?" she asks the room.

VanderVoort has been at the game long enough to recognize that more than a few people staring at her have a serious problem with her being in charge despite not voicing the fact explicitly. She takes note of those she should be worried about, especially the Joint Chiefs and a couple of Cabinet Secretaries, but doesn't act on her worries. They'll come for her, but she'll be ready.

She's always ready.

"Alright. Now that we're one happy, harmonious family, how about everyone figure out where in the fuck the kaiju went!" VanderVoort announces. "And for God's sake, someone track down Bolton and Holt!"

———

Bolton has to give it to the woman called Haley—she knows how to crack a skull and put a man down fast.

He's been awake for a few minutes, and Bolton uses the time to study his surroundings and the rag-tag posse that knocked him unconscious and took him captive. The room is dank and dark, most likely a basement. Industrial by the size and smell, but not huge. Other than Bolton, there's only Mark Halpern, the guy Jeremy, and the two women, Haley and Ginevra.

Overriding the agony in his head, Bolton concentrates and tries to listen for others outside the room.

Nothing.

"How's the head? I'd offer some Tylenol, but we're rationing all painkillers," Halpern says when he sees Bolton staring at him.

"I've had worse," Bolton says from his spot in the far corner of the room where he's zip-tied to a metal folding chair. He pulls at the plastic restraints. "You could loosen these, though. They're cutting into my skin."

"Yeah, right!" Jeremy barks. "We loosen them straps and you'll come at us faster than a fat lady after a chocolate cake!" Laughter explodes from his mouth at his own joke. No one else joins in.

"While I can't get behind the humor," Halpern says, "I can agree with what Jeremy here is saying. Can't exactly risk it, Sergeant Bolton. You'll have to live with the discomfort. But as you said about your head, you've probably experienced worse."

"What's your endgame, Halpern?" Bolton asks.

The pain in his head, and nausea in his stomach, are almost overpowering, but it's 100% true that Bolton has experienced worse. He's trained for the unfortunate situation he's found himself in. The key is to stay alive until circumstances change. When they do, he'll strike with everything he's capable of mustering.

He has no plan on mustering mercy.

"Getting this working," Halpern admits, holding up the satellite phone. "We tried placing your thumb against this circle, thinking it'd activate like an iPhone, but that did nothing. Get me in touch with the White House so they can come and rescue us, and my endgame is over. That's it, Sergeant. We just want to be rescued."

"You kinda blew that chance when you knocked me cold," Bolton responds. "The United States government frowns on attacking its military personnel, Halpern. The reality is, even if I get that phone working for you, no one is coming."

"We're going to them, right?" Jeremey says. "Down to one of them bases? They'll let us in since we got you."

Bolton grins at Jeremy, then returns his attention to Halpern. "That opportunity passed with a rifle butt to the back of my head. If they were to let you in, it'd be inside a very small, very dark cell for the rest of your life."

Halpern chuckles and sets the phone down on a card table. Right next to a pile of everything Bolton had had in his pockets. Including the disc needed to activate the sat phone. Bolton makes sure he keeps his eyes averted from the disc.

"My turn to ask what your endgame is," Halpern says. "All you're doing when you talk like that is tell me that you have no worth. You're just another mouth that needs the food and water we have short supply of. Why make yourself useless?"

"Never said I was useless," Bolton replies. "I just said that your current plan isn't going to work. We need to start over and come to a mutually beneficial understanding before any calls are made to the White House."

Ginevra snarls. "Bullshit. They ain't gonna let some SEAL die out—"

"Green Beret," Bolton says. "Army Special Forces. Not a SEAL."

"So fucking what?" Ginevra snaps.

"That's enough," Halpern says and pats Ginevra's shoulder. "I'd like to hear Bolton out and see where this is going." He chuckles again. "Let me guess. It's going to Colorado Springs?"

Despite the pain it causes, Bolton chuckles too.

"I have a mission assignment," Bolton says, "and I plan on completing that mission assignment. Let me go and I'll forget all about you."

"Single-minded military man," Halpern says. "Still thinking there's order in this world. I hate to break it to you, Bolton, but order is long gone."

Bolton begins to respond, then closes his mouth. He is very aware of how much order is left in the world. Zip. Zilch. Zero. He's seen things he doubts the yokels before him can even comprehend. He's watched it all fall apart as good men died.

He knows that the mission he's trying to complete is a long shot. But that's all that's left. Long shots. The idiots in the room somehow believe they can be rescued just by making a phone call. They have no idea that he, Bolton, is trying to rescue the entire world, not just this dank, dark basement.

Before he can try once more to force just a sliver of reason on Halpern, a radio squawks from the opposite corner. The surprise on Bolton's face must be blatantly obvious, because Halpern chuckles harder.

"Didn't notice Joshua over there, did ya?" Halpern says to Bolton. "We sometimes forget he's there too. Only time he moves from that radio is when he has to piss."

"When we have to remind him to piss," Haley says.

"He don't talk much," Jeremy says in a less than quiet whisper. "But he knows stuff. Weird stuff. Like how to fix that radio and guns and—"

"Shut up," Halpern says. Jeremy shuts up.

Two voices can be distinctly heard from the corner: one is in the room, one is coming from the radio.

"Who's he talking to?" Bolton asks. "How do you have a working radio?"

"Dumb luck," Halpern says. "Dumb luck named Joshua. Jeremy is right. Joshua knows a lot about certain things. He had enough spare parts to put his radio back together after the first

EMP. We're shielded enough down here that the last one didn't fry the circuits."

"Okay, but who's he talking to?" Bolton asks.

Halpern glances at the corner then shrugs.

"Guess it won't do no harm to tell you," Halpern says with an undertone that Bolton translates into, *You're probably going to be dead soon anyway.*

"Some kid," Jeremy says before Halpern can continue. "Out by Seattle or someplace up there."

"Kid? Or is it some young soldier or sailor?" Bolton asks. "Maybe the Navy was able to hold Everett after all and—"

"That's all gone," Halpern says. "The kid is a teenager in a bunker on some island in Puget Sound. From what he says, everything even close to Seattle, including the Everett Naval Base, is destroyed."

"Jesus Christ," Bolton says as he thinks about all the personnel and the civilians who had converged on Everett for rescue. Not to mention the Seattle-area population. Millions were gone like that.

Everyone goes quiet as they listen in on the radio conversation. It's fairly innocuous, just Joshua trying to get information from a teenage boy who's not giving up much. Bolton smiles. The kid would probably survive some serious interrogation.

Then another voice comes on the radio and Bolton's blood turns to ice then suddenly to fire.

He knows that voice. He knows it like he knows his own.

Bolton is thankful that all attention is on Joshua and the radio. Otherwise, Halpern may question why Bolton's eyes are nearly bugged out of his head as a small smile plays across his lips.

———

"Hello? With whom am I speaking?" Terrie asks, taking the radio handset from Tony. The boy protests, but Terrie ignores him. "My name is Terrie Morgan, retired U.S. Marshal. Who is this and how many of you are there?"

Only crackling silence responds.

"You scared him off," Tony says with exasperation.

He tries to take the handset back again, but Terrie refuses to let it go. Tony huffs and crosses his arms over his chest, but he doesn't storm off or leave the room.

"Hello? If there's someone in charge, may I please speak with them?" Terrie says and waits. "Hello?"

"U.S. Marshal, retired?" a new voice asks. "Then you have access to the government."

Terrie laughs and closes her eyes. She heard the disdain and desperation mixed in equal measures in the voice. Unless whoever is on the other end of the transmission has vast resources, there isn't much point in continuing the conversation.

She made a mistake by announcing she was a former U.S. Marshal.

Before, when the world was normal, that announcement would have carried weight. But now, after, it only sows seeds of distrust. It was a mistake borne of exhaustion, pain, and stress, but it was a mistake.

Terrie may have blown any chance of being rescued.

"What?" the voice on the radio asks. "What do you mean?"

"He's not speaking to us," Tony says and uncrosses his arms, a look of interest on his face.

"Hello?" Terrie calls. "Hello!"

"Hey, Terrie."

Terrie staggers, and Tony barely catches her before she can collapse, her knees suddenly weak. She repositions the crutches and takes a deep breath.

"What's wrong?" Tony asks. "Are you sick?"

Still gripping the handset, Terrie brings the mouthpiece to her lips.

"Connor?" she whispers.

"Yep," Bolton responds. "Wow. You're alive."

"I'm alive? You're alive!" she nearly shouts. "What are…? Who is…? Where is…?"

"I understand all of your questions," Bolton says. "I'm not in a place to answer everything, but, yes, Lu and Kyle are alive and well."

"They are?" Terrie nearly shouts. "Where?"

"Just safe," Bolton says.

"Right. Good," Terrie replies, understanding immediately that Bolton is not in a position to reveal Lu and Kyle's location. Either for their safety or for the safety of wherever they are. She prays they're in a secure government facility. And if they are, then why is Bolton where he is and in the situation he's in? "Are you safe?"

"For the moment," Bolton says.

No. He's not safe. Terrie hears that plain as day.

"You're on an island in Puget Sound?" Bolton asks.

"Yes. In a bunker," Terrie replies. "I have no idea how long the bunker will hold out though. There are some horrible beasts outside that would like to get inside."

"That's the narrative of the day," Bolton says with a sad laugh. "How much time do you think you have? Can you hold out?"

Before Terrie answers, she looks at Tony. The teenager shrugs, closes one eye, then says, "A couple of weeks. Maybe."

"A couple of weeks. Maybe," Terrie relays into the handset. "You?"

"My time is short," Bolton says. "I need to be somewhere soon. But I believe once I've taken care of what I need to do, then I'll be free to come get you."

The sounds of protests, a scuffle, then crackly silence fill the air.

"What happened?" Terrie asks Tony. "Did we lose the signal?"

"No," Tony states and checks the radio. He shakes his head. "It sounds like a disagreement. They're disagreeing."

"Disagreeing? What does that mean?" Terrie asks, praying she hasn't caused any harm to come to Connor Bolton. "Get him back. Get him back! He knows where my daughter and my grandson are!"

Tony only blinks at Terrie.

"I said get him back!" she snaps.

"How?" Tony asks. "They're not talking." He cups a hand to his ear. "Nope. No talking."

Before Terrie can get more worked up, the second voice returns.

"Ms. Morgan, my name is Mark Halpern," the voice says. "How much room do you have in that bunker?"

"Room…? What are you talking about?" Terrie replies. "We need to leave here. We're not looking for others to join us."

"And where are you going to go when you leave there?" Halpern asks. "An island in the middle of a large body of water sounds about as secure a location as you can get." He clears his throat. "Trust me."

"I don't trust you, Mr. Halpern, because I don't know you," Terrie says. "I do know Connor Bolton. Put him back on."

"That won't be happening," Halpern says. "Sergeant Bolton will no longer be speaking to you."

"If you've harmed him—!" Terrie shouts

"Calm down, Ms. Morgan," Halpern interrupts. "Sergeant Bolton is fine. A little banged up, but fine. And if you would like him to stay fine, then you will need to tell me exactly where you are so we can come join you."

Tony snorts and rolls his eyes, then mouths, "Crazy and dumb."

Terrie nods. Crazy and dumb. A nightmare combination.

"How many of you are there?" Terrie asks.

"Five," Halpern says. "Six with Bolton."

"Yes. We have room," Terrie says and waves off Tony's look of protest. "If you arrive with Connor unharmed, then you and your friends can share the bunker with us."

Tony opens his mouth and Terrie holds up a warning finger. Tony closes his mouth.

"I'll put Tony back on and he can help guide you to us," Terrie says. "Is your radio portable?"

"Not easily, but yes," Halpern says. "Our batteries should last the trip."

"Good," Terrie says and closes her eyes. "Good. Here's Tony."

She places the handset in Tony's hand but doesn't let go.

"Figure out how to get them here as fast as possible," Terrie says.

"Why? So we can run out of supplies sooner?" Tony scoffs. "We don't have room for them. And there's flooding."

"I know!" Terrie snaps. "They can have the damn bunker! I just need Connor here so he can take me to my daughter and grandson!"

"Oh," Tony says and his whole body deflates. "Okay."

"Hey," Terrie says and catches Tony's eye. "You and Krissy are coming with us. I won't leave you here."

"And Biscuit," Tony says. "He comes too."

"Well, yes, he is my dog," Terrie says and smiles. "Now, get back on that radio and do whatever you can to get them here, understood?"

"Understood," Tony says.

"But do not tell them we're leaving when they get here," Terrie says. "Make them feel like they'll be welcomed into the family and can stay here with us forever."

Tony frowns. "That's a lot of lying. I'm not very good at lying."

Terrie's face hardens. "I think you're better at it than you admit, Tony. No more BS."

Tony pauses, and Terrie can't quite figure out the look on his face.

"Except for them," Tony says finally, placing the handset to his mouth. "They get the BS."

"Exactly."

"Hello?" Tony says into the handset.

"Hey, Tony," Joshua's voice replies. "You gonna help with coordinates?"

He casts one last look at Terrie, then nods and says, "Are you familiar with the state of Washington?"

"Some," Joshua says.

Terrie finds a stool and plops down onto it while Tony and Joshua converse about travel logistics.

Lu and Kyle are alive. That's all she can think about. They're alive.

And not even God himself will stop her from getting back to them.

———

The elevator opens onto an apocalyptic scene of a scorched hallway.

What were once white walls are now nothing but several layers of soot.

Lu, Dr. Probst, and Kyle stare at the destruction but do not leave the elevator.

"Well, we know which way not to go," Dr. Probst says as she points down at the corridor floor.

"Gross," Kyle says at the sight of the fluid trail that leads from the elevator doors and down the corridor, lost around the corner.

"No footprints," Lu says and claps her son on the shoulder.

"So?" Kyle says.

"Lowell didn't come up here," Lu says.

"He's got to be somewhere," Dr. Probst says. "Who else got us onto that cart and left us in the cart hold?"

"Maybe he stopped on another level," Kyle says.

"The elevator wouldn't stop at any other level," Lu says and steps from the elevator. "Come on."

"Whoa," Dr. Probst hisses out. "Are you about to follow the trail of gross?"

Kyle snorts. "Trail of gross."

"Yes," Lu says. "That's the way to the control room, right?"

"Yeah, but... the, uh..." Dr. Probst stammers.

"Gross trail," Kyle finishes for her.

"That," Dr. Probst says. "Look at it. That's slime. Guess what made that slime?"

"The doctor blob thing," Kyle says.

"The doctor blob thing!" Dr. Probst says. "Although, I wouldn't quite put it that way…"

"Control room is that way," Lu says. "As well as the central elevator."

"So?" Dr. Probst replies.

"The central elevator that goes up into the warehouse," Lu says. "A warehouse full of weapons. Weapons we can use to kill the doctor blob thing."

Dr. Probst winces. "That name's going to stick, isn't it?"

"Yep," Kyle says.

"We get some weapons, then we hit the control room," Lu says. "And we take it back. Then we get in contact with Vander-Voort and figure out what the fuck is going on."

"The figuring out what the fuck is going on is the most ambitious part of your plan," Dr. Probst says. "Because we'll probably die before we do find out."

"Doctor blob thing," Kyle says.

Dr. Probst points at Kyle and nods.

"Would you rather go back down?" Lu asks. "How long will it take for the Substance to fry our brains?"

"I have no idea," Dr. Probst says.

"What *do* you know?" Lu presses.

Dr. Probst struggles to respond, then shakes her head.

"We're fucked anyway you look at it," Lu says. "How about we at least fight to survive instead of laying down to die?"

"Jesus Christ," Dr. Probst says. "Fine. Let's get some guns and take the control room. Or die trying."

"Can we not die trying?" Kyle asks. "Maybe not die at all?"

"That's the goal," Lu says. "But it won't be easy."

They all glance at the slime trail that leads away from the elevator.

"No shit," Kyle and Dr. Probst say.

THREE

Lowell is unceremoniously vomited out of the Substance and flung against the shield doors separating it from the concrete tunnel beyond.

"Home again, home again…" Lowell mutters as he lies naked and piled up against the bottom of the shield doors.

Sweat coats his body in a thick sheen and he shivers. Which hurts like hell.

But the pain means he's alive, and Lowell doesn't take that for granted.

After several long minutes, Lowell picks himself up off the ground and checks his naked body for wounds. Other than the injuries he's already sustained, his body only has a few new bruises, probably from his less than graceful ejection from the Substance.

The Substance…

Lowell faces the glowing, swirling anomaly and smiles. To him, it isn't an anomaly anymore. He knows exactly what it is and how it works.

He also knows that it's only a small part of a larger whole.

Lowell needs to find the others and tell them.

The others…

He left them in the cart hold. Unconscious and unprotected.

Unprotected against the Ebony Man.

Hold on…the Ebony Man?

Lowell dimly remembers switching places with the strange being. A strange being that emitted nothing but pure evil. Although, that doesn't feel quite right…

The being has another name, but Lowell's brain can't translate it. Not yet, at least. He has a feeling that eventually he'll be able to. But until then, Ebony Man it is.

Even though Lowell has checked his body over and it seems to be in good order, he knows instinctually he's no longer the Anson Lowell who existed before entering the Substance.

He's something more.

And something less.

None of it exactly makes sense, but then most of his life hasn't made sense, so nothing new there.

First part, though, is getting into the concrete tunnel.

There doesn't appear to be any shield door controls on the wall or anywhere else he can see.

"Shit," Lowell says, his voice a raspy, dry croak.

He swallows what little spit he can muster, but it isn't much. He's so thirsty.

And still very hungry.

In fact, his hunger has grown even worse as soon as he's back being just-human Lowell instead of Yellowstone-monster Lowell.

His stomach growls with an aggression that startles Lowell.

"Yeah, yeah, fucking hold on," Lowell says. "You know how to get out of here?" Silence from his stomach. "I didn't fucking think so."

He suddenly realizes he does know how to get out.

A flash of memory before dying…

That thought gets Lowell's attention.

He died. Despite being alive and kicking at the moment,

Lowell knows he died as the Yellowstone monster. He actually died.

And when he did, he connected to something greater than everything. He connected to the planetary whole and was shown a truth that should have turned his mind to mush, the weight of the truth so heavy.

But Lowell has suffered through truths and lies a million times worse than what was revealed to him. He's carried pain and torture within himself so great, for so long, that even an impossible truth can't destroy his mind.

Lowell takes a few deep breaths, steps to the shield doors, places both hands on their surface, and says, "Open up, motherfuckers."

There's a brief, bright-blue flash, and the doors begin to open.

Lowell knows next time he won't have to use words. His mind and body are now attuned to the facility. With that attenuation comes realization that his friends are about to be in a lot of fucking trouble.

"Shit," he mutters as soon as the doors are wide enough for him to squeeze through. "Shit fucking shit."

The tunnel is pitch-black, but Lowell can see almost as clearly as if it were early dawn or late evening. The tunnel walls and floor are shrouded in shadow, but they're easy to make out.

Lowell breaks into a run. The hunger in his belly grows exponentially with each step. As does the dread that he may be too late to help Lu, Kyle, and Dr. Probst.

His legs pick up speed until he's running faster than he's ever has in his life. So fast that when he reaches the end of the tunnel, he isn't sure how to stop.

Lowell plants his feet, leans back, and slides to a halt just as he's about to slam into the elevator doors. He doesn't quite execute the maneuver as smoothly as he'd like, and he has to throw his arms out to stop his final momentum.

The elevator doors crumple slightly and Lowell growls. He's

not surprised that the growl sounds like a miniature version of the Yellowstone monster's growl.

"You better fucking open," he says as he presses the button and waits.

The doors protest from their damage but slide open.

No elevator.

A wicked grin spreads across Lowell's face.

The Ebony Man.

Lowell felt him when he touched the shield doors by the Substance. The being is inside the facility and has taken control. Lowell steps into the empty elevator shaft and looks up. In a second, he hears the squeal of brakes then the rapid fall of the elevator car.

Without hurrying, Lowell steps back out of the shaft and waits. In three seconds, the elevator car slams into the ground, sending bits of concrete and metal exploding out at Lowell. He covers his eyes, but that's about all the precaution he takes against the shrapnel.

After the dust settles, Lowell checks his body, sees nothing but superficial cuts and gashes, and climbs onto the top of the crushed elevator car. There's a service ladder directly in front of him, and Lowell grabs the rungs.

Hand over hand he climbs, and doesn't stop climbing until he reaches the floor he needs.

Of course, the doors to the floor are closed and on the opposite side of the service ladder, but that only annoys Lowell.

"You can open up or you can let me smash through them," Lowell shouts, his voice echoing up and down the elevator shaft. "Your choice, asshole!"

Nothing.

Lowell waits. He knows he's been heard.

The doors finally open and Lowell flings himself backward through the opening and slides on his ass and back across the corridor's slick floor before coming to a stop against the far wall.

The elevator shaft doors close and Lowell picks himself up. He tries to wipe the gunk off himself but only smears it around.

His belly growls even louder and the smell of the gunk, the slime from the doctor blob thing, begins to have an appetizing odor.

"Oh, fuck no," Lowell says to himself.

He turns toward the control room. Then he turns the opposite way and faces the direction the cafeteria is in.

"Nope. Gotta save friends first," Lowell says, turning back toward the direction of the control room. "Lunch second."

He tries to whistle, but his mouth is too dry and his lips too cracked for any sound other than a raspy hiss to come out.

Lowell shrugs, then strolls casually toward the control room.

———

The satellite phone beeps twice then lets out a loud squawking that is half ring and half klaxon.

Halpern stops his haphazard packing, picks the sat phone up, and stares at it.

"You gonna answer that?" Bolton asks from his chair.

Bolton's left eye is swollen shut and his bottom lip is split, but he looks better than the rest of Halpern's group. It took all of them to get Bolton strapped back to his chair after he tried to fight them off so he could keep speaking with Terrie.

"How'd you get it to work?" Jeremy asks through swollen lips.

"I didn't," Halpern says, his eyes shifting to Bolton. "How'd it turn on by itself?"

"You charged it," Bolton replies. "That means it can take incoming calls."

"Without your code?" Halpern asks.

"It'd be a shitty configuration if I have to psychically know when to activate the code so I can receive calls," Bolton replies. "Answer it."

Halpern hesitates.

"It's a little overwhelming, isn't it?" Bolton asks. "Knowing you're one phone communication away from speaking to the President of the United States. What do you say? What's he going to say? Will there actually be help on the other end of that phone? Or will you give away your location as soon as you answer it?"

Halpern's head whips around to face Bolton, his eyes wide with panic.

"Oh, shit!" Jeremy exclaims. "They can track us with that? Get rid of it, Mark!"

"Don't be stupid," Haley says, a wet rag pressed to the gash over her right eyebrow. "Even if they can track it, how are they going to get here? This Bolton guy said he had to use a bike to get to Colorado Springs."

"Yeah, if the government could get here, then they would have given Bolton a ride," Ginevra says.

"Shut up!" Halpern barks as the phone continues to ring. "Let me think!"

"No time to think, Halpern," Bolton says. "You're in the big leagues now. You wanted to mess with government business and now that mess is yours to take care of. What are you going to do? You wanted the sat phone working. You wanted to use it to be rescued. Here's your chance."

"I said shut up!" Halpern shouts.

"I can shut him up," Haley says and produces a long knife from a sheath on her leg. "Take that tongue right out."

"Stick to snipering," Bolton replies. "You don't want to get close enough to me to use that pig sticker."

"No," Halpern says to Haley, and she slowly puts the knife away.

"Come on, Halpern," Bolton taunts. "Answer it."

Halpern puts the phone to his ear then pulls it away. He shakes his head. Bolton tries not to smirk.

"How are we getting to Puget Sound?" Bolton asks. "It's

hundreds and hundreds of miles away. You think you'll really make it there? Answering that phone is your only real choice. There's true safety on the other end of that line."

"We can get there," Joshua says from the corner. He stands up and shakes a piece of paper at the entire room. "I have their coordinates. We can use the Crawler to get us there."

"That thing? It's slow as molasses," Jeremy complains.

"And cramped as hell," Ginevra adds.

"Leave him here," Joshua says to Halpern, the paper flapping in Bolton's direction. "We don't need him now that I know where we're going."

Bolton laughs. The phone continues to ring. Halpern shakes his head.

"That woman won't let us in without Bolton," Halpern says. "He's our ticket."

"Or you answer the phone and get rescued by the U.S. government," Bolton says. "That was the original plan, Mark. Always stick with your first instinct. Answer the phone."

Halpern screams and throws the phone full strength at Bolton. It misses Bolton by a foot and slams into the wall, then clatters to the floor, still ringing.

Then it stops.

"What the fuck?" Bolton snaps. "You want to break it?"

Halpern grunts then retrieves the sat phone. It's scratched, but nothing is broken as far as he can tell.

"It's fine," Halpern says with some relief.

Bolton grins to himself. He'll wear Halpern down. He can tell the man's bravado is weakening by the minute. Too many choices to make. Halpern isn't an experienced leader. The decisions are paralyzing him.

"Load the radio and gear into the Crawler," Halpern says as he tucks the phone into a cargo pocket on his pants. "And gag this asshole. I don't want to have to listen to him the whole trip."

"Gladly," Haley says and takes a stained bandana from out of her pocket as she stands up and walks toward Bolton.

"Oh, come on," Bolton protests, seeing the state of the bandana. "At least use something clean!"

Everyone ignores him, and Bolton ends up with the soiled bandana stuffed into his mouth. He gags and coughs the material into a better position but can't spit it out.

Bolton glares at his captors, but they ignore him as each of them gets to work gathering their belongings.

———

"Nothing?" VanderVoort asks. "No one can tell me what happened to either of those kaiju? That's it? One falls underground, the other follows, and poof, nothing left?"

"Ma'am?" a tech says.

"What? Tell me you have something," VanderVoort says, turning to the tech.

"Um, I don't know if it's good news," the tech says, "but one of the satellites that came back online was able to grab some thermal footage. I think it shows the two kaijus fighting underground."

"Kaiju," Dr. Hall says. "Kaiju is also plural. No need to—"

VanderVoort points a finger at Dr. Hall and he shuts up.

"Keep talking," VanderVoort tells the tech.

"Yes, ma'am," the tech replies and clacks at his keyboard. The image on the main monitor changes. "This is what I was able to find."

It's hard to make out, but there's definite thermal movement under the ground. Significant thermal movement when considering the scale.

"There they are," VanderVoort says. "They took the fight to the sewers."

The thermal images approximate the Yellowstone kaiju and the Australia kaiju, and all eyes watch the jumbled, confusing battle unfold.

Then slowly, both thermal images fade out and the show is

over.

"What happened?" VanderVoort asks. "Where'd they fucking go now?"

"I believe," Dr. Hall says after clearing his throat. "I believe they're dead."

He looks about the Situation Room then at VanderVoort.

"They killed each other," Dr. Hall finishes.

"That's what a kill looks like on thermal," Director Miles confirms. "Seen thousands of them from drone footage over the years. Stop, then slow fade."

"They're dead?" VanderVoort asks. "Are you shitting me? They killed each other?"

"It appears so," Dr. Hall says.

"Well, fuck yes then!" VanderVoort cheers. "Come on, people! Let's hear some happy in this room!"

Slowly, cautiously, everyone in the Situation Room begins to clap, then cheer, then simply shout with delight.

"There's still Mexico City, Africa, and Antarctica," Director Miles says to VanderVoort.

"I know, Gordon," VanderVoort says. "But we'll let everyone have a moment before we get back to work."

VanderVoort allows the jubilation to continue for a few minutes, then pats the air with her hands until everyone quiets down.

"There are still other kaiju to deal with," she says. "Luckily, none of them are tearing up the planet at the moment. Everyone back to work on how we take out the others. Got it?"

The room gets it and is back to work trying to figure out how to save the world. But this time, there's considerable more hope and enthusiasm than just minutes before.

"We need confirmation," Joan says from the conference table. "We don't know for sure if they're dead."

"We have people still in the Wyoming bunker," Director Miles says. "We could send someone from there to recon and get us visuals, boots-on-the-ground confirmation."

"Call them," VanderVoort says. "Let's see who's up for a hike."

A tech jumps into action without being told.

"Has anyone reached Bolton or Holt yet?" VanderVoort asks as she waits for the uplink to connect to the Wyoming bunker.

"I've been trying, ma'am," a tech replies. "The sat phone is charged. It rang for several minutes, but neither Sergeant Bolton nor Sergeant Holt answered."

"Why wouldn't they answer?" VanderVoort wonders aloud. "They take the trouble to charge the phone, but they don't answer?"

"Ma'am, I have Wyoming on the—AAAAAAAAAA!"

The tech collapses to the floor, his hands gripping his head as his eyes bulge from their sockets.

The image on the main monitor is replaced by a blank, black face.

The face of the Ebony Man.

"Hello, humans," the Ebony Man says as everyone in the Situation Room begins to scream and writhe in pain. "It's time I speak to the person in charge. Could that person please make themselves known?"

VanderVoort hears the Ebony Man's words, not with her ears, but deep in her mind. The voice tears at her brain, shredding synapses with every word. But despite the agonizing onslaught, VanderVoort manages to raise a hand and open her eyes so she can stare straight at the bizarre apparition on the main monitor.

"Hello, person in charge," the Ebony Man says. He snaps his fingers. "That should be better."

While the rest of the personnel in the room continue to suffer through their pain, VanderVoort's agony is instantly lifted. She feels like hammered shit, but she no longer wants to pull her brain out of her ear and throw it against the wall.

Her hands go to her belly, and she sighs with relief as she feels the child inside her kick several times.

"What...?" VanderVoort gasps, trying to get to her feet. She gives up and settles onto her ass right there on the floor. "What are you?"

"What, you ask? Not who am I?" the Ebony Man responds. "Do I not look like you?"

The Ebony Man's visage shifts a thousand times, the deep black replaced by face after face after face before settling back into its ebony nightmare form.

"I suppose I do not look like you," the Ebony Man states. "I have adopted a humanoid form, but that does not satisfy those tiny primate brains. Oh well, I do not have the patience to decide on an appearance." He waves at his face. "This will have to suffice."

"What do you want? Where are the doctors?" VanderVoort asks.

"I shall answer your second question first," the Ebony Man says.

The view on the monitor widens to show the entire Wyoming bunker control room. Directly behind and to the side of the Ebony Man is the blob of doctors.

"Although there are others about this facility," the Ebony Man says. He pauses and lifts his nose to the air. "And something… else. I shall meet this new one soon."

VanderVoort doesn't know what to make of that last statement. She pushes it aside for later review. Instead, she asks, "What did you do to the doctors?"

Before the Ebony Man can answer, the screams and shrieks and cries around her intensify. VanderVoort looks about in alarm and sees that her colleagues are dying. Blood pours from ears and nostrils in rivers.

"Stop! You're killing them!" she shouts.

"They are already dead," the Ebony Man says, the image on the monitor tightening back onto only him. "All of humanity is already dead. Your species will not survive this planetary ordeal. Perhaps I should simply put them out of their misery now to save time."

"No!" VanderVoort screams as the Ebony Man lifts his fingers, ready for another snap. "Please!"

The pitch-black mouth widens on the Ebony Man's face, but VanderVoort isn't fooled into thinking it's a smile.

"Very well," the Ebony Man says.

He snaps his fingers and VanderVoort cries out. She scrambles onto her hands and knees, careful of her belly, and manages to get shakily to her feet as all the screams and cries stop. She is relieved to hear them replaced by moans instead. Most of them, anyway.

As VanderVoort turns about, she sees that close to two-thirds of the personnel are still down and not making any sounds. She suspects most are dead, but she hopes that a few are only unconscious.

"May we return to business?" the Ebony Man asks. "As unlikely as it is, I fear I am in need of assistance. I require transport."

VanderVoort's attention is instantly back on the main monitor.

"Transport…?" she responds. "To where?"

"Ah, let me access that information," the Ebony Man says. He pauses. "Yes. I am to be taken to what you call Antarctica. How soon can you arrange transport?"

"I… I can't," VanderVoort says. "We don't have vehicles. None of them work."

"You do," the Ebony Man says. "There is a vehicle here that is operational. The irony is that it is so primitive I cannot operate it. My influence on the technology would obliterate it instantly. I need a simple primate mind to operate the vehicle."

VanderVoort realizes what the Ebony Man is talking about. There's a vehicle in each bunker. One large enough for all personnel to escape in if needed.

"I know what you're referring to," VanderVoort says. "But the vehicle is programmed to a static location. A rescue point where it can be recovered after launch."

"Yes. Correct," the Ebony Man says. "That's the vehicle I speak of. You will use that to transport me to my destination."

"No," VanderVoort says. "I can't. It only goes to one destination."

"Yes. Antarctica," the Ebony Man says.

"No, not Antarctica," VanderVoort replies. "It only goes to—"

"Change its destination to Antarctica," the Ebony Man says. "You have one of your hours."

"Hold on!" VanderVoort shouts. "Even if I could do that, which I can't, who will operate it for you?"

"One of the primates here in this facility," the Ebony Man says, and his head tilts upward. "I will retrieve one and position ourselves in the vehicle. You will have the destination programmed for Antarctica by then."

The screen goes blank.

No one speaks. All eyes turn to VanderVoort.

"Anyone know how to remotely reprogram the escape shuttle?" VanderVoort asks. No one responds. "Well, fuck."

———

"We are so dead. We are so dead. We are so dead," Dr. Probst mumbles under her breath.

"We are not dead," Lu says as the elevator lifts up into the warehouse and the doors slide open. "So shut the fuck up."

"Uh... Mom?" Kyle says, staring into the warehouse as the overhead lights slowly buzz to life. "What is that?"

Lu takes a tentative step out into the warehouse, then covers her nose with the back of a hand.

Everywhere they look, the crates and floor are smeared with a black slime that seems to absorb the light from above. And the smell is atrocious, burning everyone's eyes and nostrils.

But that isn't the worst part.

"It's moving," Dr. Probst says, one step behind Lu as the marshal slowly makes her way into the rows of gunk-coated crates. "Undulating."

"Is this from the doctor blob thing?" Kyle asks, choking as the fumes coat his throat and burn, burn, burn.

"I have no answers," Lu says. "But we're not here for answers. We're here for weapons. Cheryl? You've been in this warehouse more than us. Which crates are the weapons?"

"I don't know," Dr. Probst replies and waves a hand in a vague direction. "That way?"

Lu grunts. "Great. Start reading stencils."

The three move quickly, or as quickly as they can without slipping on the black slime, and begin reading what stencils they can make out on the stacked crates.

It takes them at least thirty minutes before Kyle calls out.

"Here!" Kyle shouts. "M4s!"

"Perfect," Lu says and starts looking along the sides of crates until she finds what she needs.

A pry bar.

"How are you going to open it?" Dr. Probst asks. "All the other crates are stacked on top of it."

Then Lu stares up at the top of the stacked crates.

"One thing about government work," Lu says as she tucks the pry bar into a belt loop, "is that it's always predictable. If there are M4s on the bottom, then there are M4s on the top."

She starts to climb the crates.

"Mom!" Kyle exclaims. "Be careful!"

"I wasn't planning on hot-dogging it," Lu replies.

"I don't know what hot-dogging means," Kyle says.

"She'll be careful," Dr. Probst says.

Lu makes it three crates up before things get dicey. The slime is thicker and stickier the further up the stack she goes. It undulates faster and faster until it fairly vibrates around Lu's hands as she reaches past the gunk for non-slime handholds.

It takes close to twenty minutes for her to make it all the way to the top crate. Lu can barely make out the stenciled letters through the slime, but she confirms that the top crate holds the same inventory as the bottom crate.

With her balance on the crate perilous, Lu removes the pry bar from her belt loop, places it to the crate's lid, and shoves hard. It takes thoughtful movement to leverage the lid up while keeping herself from falling, but she manages.

The lid gives way with a pop then a slither as it tumbles slowly away, the black slime slowing its fall to the ground on the other side of the stack. Lu tucks the pry bar back into her belt loop and grins at the crate's contents.

Dozens of neatly rowed M4 carbines looking like they're brand new off the factory line.

"This is the hard part!" Lu shouts down at Kyle and Dr. Probst. "You're going to have to catch them as I throw them down!"

"What? That's crazy!" Kyle yells. "We miss and they'll brain us!"

Lu considers this for a moment. She glances down at the two and realizes Kyle is right. Dr. Probst is no athlete, and Kyle is just a teenager with zero experience handling weapons the way Lu needs him to.

"I have an idea!" Dr. Probst shouts, then takes off jogging. Or semi-jogging as she avoids the pools and puddles of black slime.

In minutes, she returns with a hand jack. On the jack is an open crate of MREs.

"Toss them into here!" Dr. Probst yells. "The meals will cushion their fall!"

"Great idea," Lu says and waits until Kyle and Dr. Probst have the crate of MREs positioned directly under her. "Look out below!"

Lu lets an M4 drop and it falls right into the crate with a whump. Kyle quickly pulls it out, checks it over, and grins up at his mother.

"Not a scratch!" he calls.

Lu drops five more, giving them each two M4s to carry.

Then she slowly climbs down and nods approvingly at Kyle and Dr. Probst.

"Ammo," she says.

"That I know," Dr. Probst says. "Ammo is up front."

Dr. Probst leads the way, and they eventually come to the stack of crates filled with ammo boxes of 5.56mm rounds.

"Magazines," Lu says. "Each M4 has one, but we need extras for reloading. Cheryl?"

"I just saw these here," Dr. Probst replies. "I don't know where magazines are."

"I'll look," Lu says and points at Kyle. "Go back, dump out those MREs, and bring that hand jack and crate back here. We're stockpiling."

"Can we eat some of the MREs?" Kyle asks and shivers. "I don't want to, but I'm fucking hungry."

Lu frowns and is about to say they don't have time, but Dr. Probst stares intently at her. Lu nods.

"Yes. Bring some back," Lu says. "We'll take a minute, refuel, then start loading magazines."

"They may be over this way," Dr. Probst says, relief in her eyes. "I don't know for sure though."

Dr. Probst chooses a direction and leads Lu to another stack of crates. Magazines, but for small arms, not the M4s. It takes them a while to finally track down the correct crates, and once again Lu scales the tower, pops open the top-most crate, and finds the treasure. She drops them down one by one since they're empty metal shells and light enough for Dr. Probst to catch by hand. Which Dr. Probst does with semi-decent accuracy.

"Sorry," Dr. Probst says, nodding at a small stack of dropped magazines. "I separated those out. I figured they may be damaged from the fall."

"Good thinking," Lu says. "Kyle!"

"Coming!" Kyle responds and joins them with the hand jack and a crate filled with boxes of ammunition. And a few MREs. "Only chicken lasagna."

"It'll do," Lu says. "Let's pull out some ammo boxes and get to work while we eat. I want every one of these magazines loaded."

"All of them?" Kyle says, eyeing the pile of good magazines. "That's gonna take forever."

"Bullshit," Lu says. "You know how to load ammo. Once we get in a rhythm, time will fly by."

Kyle gives her a look that says he has zero confidence in that statement but doesn't complain verbally.

They take a few minutes to organize their assembly line, then dive into the job.

Loading the magazines with cartridges is the easy part. Keeping the chicken lasagna MREs down is the hard part. Through burps and close calls, the three manage to get every viable magazine loaded and stacked in the empty crate. There are plenty of full ammo boxes too, so they can reload magazines as needed.

"That comes with," Lu says, nodding at the hand jack as she works, rubbing her hands together to keep them from stiffening up after the repetitive work of loading magazines.

"Where?" Dr. Probst asks.

"The control room," Lu says. "That's the goal."

Lu slaps a fresh magazine into her M4, charges the carbine, and smiles.

"Back to the elevator," she says.

Dr. Probst doesn't move.

"What's wrong?" Lu asks.

Dr. Probst glances at the end of the rows of crates.

"We could just leave," she says. "We might be able to get the doors open, and if it isn't too bad out there, we could walk away from this place."

Lu gives her a curious look. "Are you feeling okay?"

"Yeah, yeah," Dr. Probst says and shakes her head. "Weird. I, um, hadn't even thought of leaving until the words came out of my mouth. We have to stay here and figure this shit out."

"You sure you're okay?" Lu asks.

"Yes. I'm good," Dr. Probst says.

Lu sees the uncertainty in the woman's eyes, but she doesn't push.

"To the elevator?" Kyle asks, his eyes flitting back and forth between Dr. Probst and his mother. "Time to go blob hunting?"

"Time to go blob hunting," Lu says.

They make their way back to the elevator in silence, load the hand jack and crate inside, cram around it, then descend.

The ride down feels like an eternity, but as soon as the doors open, everything moves at lightning speed.

"Hello, primates," the Ebony Man says and yanks Dr. Probst from the elevator.

He grips her by her neck and lifts her up off her feet. Then he throws her down the corridor and turns his attention to Lu and Kyle.

"Your turns," the Ebony Man says and reaches for Kyle.

Lu empties her M4's magazine into the Ebony Man's chest, sending the being stumbling back from the elevator and up against the far wall.

"Cheryl!" Lu calls as she rushes out of the elevator, her hands automatically changing out the spent magazine for a fresh one. "Cheryl!"

"Alive," Dr. Probst croaks from down the corridor.

Lu takes aim at the Ebony Man again and unloads a second full magazine.

The Ebony Man dances and jitters against the corridor's wall until Lu's M4 clicks empty.

Then he straightens himself and laughs.

"So predictable," the Ebony Man says, taking a step toward Lu. "There was no need for me to watch you primates complete your little task up above since I knew what you were going to do, but it was amusing watching the stunted industriousness your tiny brains can produce."

Lu Morgan is a trained law enforcement professional and has spent thousands of hours honing her skills so she'd never freeze in the field. But the sight of the Ebony Man unharmed, and flippant to boot, causes Lu's hands to shake as she tries to switch out for a fresh magazine.

"All that fear," the Ebony Man says as he inches closer to Lu. "If only it could be harnessed. Your human power needs would be over." His approximation of a mouth spreads across his approximation of a face into an approximation of a smile. "Not that your insignificant species has any time left on this planet."

The Ebony Man puts his fingers together in snap formation.

"Goodbye, monkey," he says, and his pitch-black fingers twitch.

Then the Ebony Man goes stiff and spins about so fast that Lu isn't sure she sees him move.

But even as fast as the Ebony Man is, he isn't faster than Anson Lowell's fist.

"There you are, you weird freaky fuck," Lowell says as he cold-cocks the Ebony Man.

There's a flash of bright-blue light and the Ebony Man flies off his feet, his body flung through the air down the corridor in the opposite direction of Dr. Probst.

"Hey," Lowell says to Lu. "You okay?"

Lu blinks at Lowell a couple of times.

"You're naked," she finally says.

"Yeah, well, that's the most normal part of everything right now," Lowell says. He looks in the direction of the Ebony Man. "Hold on. The asshole is getting back up."

Lowell sprints down the corridor directly at the Ebony Man.

Lu turns to look at her son. Kyle stands just inside the elevator doors, keeping them from closing.

"Are you hurt?" Lu asks. Kyle shakes his head. "Good. Get that crate out here into the corridor. There's still a—"

Two noises cut Lu off: the roar of rage from the Ebony Man and the scream of terror from Dr. Probst.

Lu instinctively turns toward Dr. Probst. And just in time.

"Lu! Kyle!" Dr. Probst screams as the doctor blob thing drags her around the corner and out of sight.

"Fuck!" Lu shouts. She grabs a couple of magazines, shoves them into her pockets, and stares hard at Kyle. "Keep up!"

Then she's off chasing after Dr. Probst, leaving Kyle to do as ordered: keep up.

FOUR

Krissy sits in the middle of the main room, freshly showered and with cleanish clothes on. They're Belle's clothes and baggy, but they're warm and not caked with mud, so Krissy ignores the hint of cheap perfume and the fact that she's wearing a dead woman's shirt and sweats.

"My daughter and grandson are alive," Terrie says as she limps into the main room, heads for Roy's empty recliner, then switches directions and settles onto a couch against the wall. "I just spoke with my grandson's father. Lu and Kyle are alive."

"You spoke with your grandson's father?" Krissy asks. "How the fuck is that possible?"

Terrie openly ignores the curse and replies, "God's Will."

"No, really, how the fuck did you find him?" Krissy asks. "The odds—"

"There are no odds when the Divine is involved," Terrie says, her voice harsh and unforgiving.

Krissy holds up both hands in mock defense. They're blistered and bleeding.

Terrie sighs.

"You need to wrap those," Terrie says.

"I cleaned them," Krissy says then gestures at her head. "I'm saving the gauze for my pretty face."

"It is pretty," Tony says from the doorway. Krissy's head whips in his direction and he flinches. "It is…"

"What is it, Tony?" Terrie asks. "What did they say?"

"They're leaving soon," Tony says, his eyes looking everywhere but at Krissy. They land on Biscuit and he walks over to the huge wolf-dog, drops into a cross-legged sitting position, and begins stroking Biscuit's fur. "They have a vehicle Joshua calls the Crawler. I don't know what it is, but he says it has wheels and tracks and can get through any terrain. It's also armed and armored."

"Probably some military surplus vehicle they snagged from local law enforcement," Terrie says. "If it's what I think it is, then at its top speed it'll be a week before they get here."

"That's what Joshua says," Tony responds. He clears his throat and finally looks in Krissy's direction. "Roy?"

"I buried him," Krissy says. "The things out there are gone for now, but I could hear them moving around the forest, snapping trees and shit. They'll be back."

"They will," Terrie says. "And we have a lot of work to do before they return. And even more work before Connor gets here."

"I don't think Joshua and his people like Connor," Tony says. "He's their prisoner."

"Hostage," Terrie corrects. "That Halpern man is holding Connor hostage and using him as leverage so we let them in the bunker."

"Sounds like we have some great company on the way," Krissy says. "We aren't letting them in, are we?"

"We are, but they won't be a threat," Terrie says. "I'll make sure we're fully prepared for that moment."

"How?" Krissy asks.

"We should have a week," Terrie says. "But I'm going to assume we only have about four or five days. In those days, I'll make sure both of you can shoot the whiskers off a squirrel at one hundred yards."

"There are no more squirrels," Tony says. "We need a different target."

"We're not actually shooting at squirrels, moron," Krissy says then sighs. "Sorry."

"Figure of speech, Tony," Terrie says. "What I mean is I'll make sure you can hit what you're aiming for."

"Then we kill Joshua and his people?" Tony asks, his voice wary.

"We do what we need to in order for us to stay safe, for Connor to be safe, and so we can get to my daughter and grandson," Terrie says. "I do not want to kill Mr. Halpern or Joshua or anyone else."

"But we'll blow heads off if we have to, right?" Krissy says.

"Only if we have to," Terrie says. "Ideally, Connor will take control of the situation well before they arrive here and we won't have to deal with Mr. Halpern or any of his people."

"We don't live in an ideal world anymore," Krissy says.

"No, we don't," Terrie agrees. "Which is why you two need some training."

"I can shoot," Tony says. "I think I can. Roy showed me when I was younger. He stopped letting me shoot when he decided I wasn't normal."

"Can you take orders and not argue?" Terrie asks.

"I don't know," Tony says.

"At least he's honest about it," Krissy says. "I'm hungry. What are we eating?"

"Depends on what you're making," Terrie says.

"I would like hamburgers," Tony says.

"Do we have burgers?" Krissy asks.

"Space burgers," Tony says. "Dehydrated beef patties that can be reconstituted with water."

"Yum yum yummy yum," Krissy says.

"Burgers sound great," Terrie says, eyeing Krissy.

Krissy glares and holds Terrie's gaze, then her shoulders slump and she gets up from the floor.

"Fine. I'll make the burgers," Krissy says. "Wanna help me, Tony? You know where everything is."

"I'm busy," Tony says. "Tell me when they're ready."

He turns and walks back to his radio room.

"No problem!" Krissy shouts after him.

There's a far-off, muffled shriek from outside and the bunker shudders slightly.

"Keep your voice low," Terrie says. "I'm not getting eaten just before my chance to reunite with my daughter and grandson."

"Whatever," Krissy says and moves into the kitchen area.

Biscuit whines but doesn't lift his head or move to get up.

"The dog's not too worried," Krissy says.

"The dog is exhausted," Terrie replies. "As am I."

She eases her legs up and lays out on the couch.

"Wake me when the food is ready," Terrie says and closes her eyes.

Krissy mumbles her annoyances as she preps the meal and Terrie slowly drifts off to the grumpy sounds of the surly teenager while thoughts of Lu and Kyle drift through her fading consciousness.

———

"Mom!" Kyle yells as he struggles to keep up with his mother.

He can hear Dr. Probst's screams and pleas for help, but he doesn't hear any responses from Lu.

Kyle rounds a second then a third corner and comes to a full stop.

There's no sign of Dr. Probst, his mother, or the doctor blob thing.

"Shit," Kyle says, realizing he took a wrong turn somewhere. "I should have followed the slime."

He looks down at the semi-clean floor beneath his feet. No slime.

Kyle spins about and screams, nearly dropping his M4 as terror fills his every cell.

There, at the end of the corridor, stands a being. It's not the Ebony Man. Not the doctor blob thing, that's for sure. And it's not Dr. Probst or his mother.

The being is maybe humanoid? It's hard for Kyle to tell. The outlines are fuzzy. Or is that Kyle's head? He doesn't exactly feel right when he looks at the being.

"Hello?" Kyle manages to utter.

The being tilts what Kyle thinks is its head.

"Where'd you come from?" Kyle asks.

More head tilting.

Then a step forward.

"No, no, you can stay right there," Kyle says, taking a step back. "Totally cool if we keep our distance."

Two steps. Kyle matches them with two backward steps.

Three steps, four steps. An arm reaches for Kyle.

"Nope," Kyle says and slings his M4 to his back. "Big nope."

He turns and runs.

This time, Kyle doesn't care where he's going. He isn't trying to find anyone, only trying to stay as far away from the new wrinkle in life inside the facility.

Kyle has no idea how many corridors he's sprinted down, how many corners he's turned, how many closed and sealed doors he's passed before he finally finds a door that isn't locked tight.

Activating the door, Kyle jumps inside, his hand mashing the door's controls as soon as his legs are clear of the threshold. The door slides shut and Kyle tries to find a lock. But a tingling sensation at the back of Kyle's neck sends him down to his knees, his head just under the small porthole window in the door.

A shadow occludes the light coming in from the corridor through the porthole window, and Kyle knows the mystery being has caught up with him. He carefully, silently, brings the M4 around from his back. He grips the weapon tightly, realizes he hasn't charged the carbine, and gently pulls on the bolt, desperate to chamber a round.

None of those movements are as silent as Kyle would like, and he cringes at the metal on metal sounds the M4 makes.

There's a knock at the door. Kyle freezes, his breath caught in his throat.

Another knock, then the door slides open and Kyle is forced to scramble away on his hands and knees. He spins around when he reaches a row of cabinets he can put his back against. The M4 is up and waving back and forth.

At nothing.

There's no weird being in the doorway. There's no weird being anywhere that Kyle can see.

Then Kyle catches a shadow out of the corner of his eye and doesn't even have time to scream before a long finger touches Kyle's left temple.

Pain more powerful than even the waves of agony caused by the Substance and the Ebony Man course through Kyle's body. His limbs go rigid and he barely recognizes that his bladder has loosed. The M4 clatters harmlessly to the floor.

Stimuli in volumes that no human brain is meant to endure at one time fills Kyle's mind.

Knowledge rolls over Kyle like an avalanche. He understands none of it. There's no way he can. His human brain isn't capable of comprehending the data that is shoving its way into Kyle's skull.

Eons pass.

The agony waves crash over and over against the rocks of Kyle's mind.

Then the finger withdraws and the agony stops.

Kyle turns and vomits. It's the only response he can manage.

There's a voice in Kyle's head asking him questions. He answers and doesn't answer.

Then vomits again.

When Kyle is finished vomiting and stable enough that he thinks he can get to his feet, he realizes the weird being is gone. The event is fading from his memory already.

"No fun," Kyle mumbles as he gets to his feet. He reaches down for his M4, picks it up, and checks the weapon. "Find Mom…"

Kyle stumbles from the room, looks both ways down the corridor, then chooses a direction and stumble-walks as fast as he can.

———

"Cheryl!" Lu shouts as she tries to keep up with the doctor blob thing and its captive. "Cheryl! Answer me!"

"Fucking help!" Dr. Probst replies, her voice far off but not too far off that Lu worries she won't catch up.

"I'm coming!" Lu yells. "Keep up, Kyle!"

It takes Lu two more corridors before she realizes her son hasn't been responding to her orders to stay close and keep up.

Lu risks a glance over her shoulder and fear stabs her deep inside when she sees only an empty corridor and no Kyle.

Motherly instinct wants to bring Lu to a halt so she can turn back and find her son. Dr. Probst's screams for her to "Fucking come get me, Lu!" are all that keep Lu from reversing directions. She has to consciously force herself to continue running toward the doctor's shouts though.

Lu's eyes return to the slime trail that coats the corridor's floor. She can see Dr. Probst's finger marks smearing the slime. They're random, chaotic, desperate.

"Hold on, Cheryl!" Lu shouts, putting on an extra burst of speed that she knows she'll pay for later. Her body feels rough; she's getting close to her limit. "I'm almost to you!"

Lu has no idea if this is correct or not. Dr. Probst's screams always seem to be two corridors away no matter how fast Lu runs.

Then the running is over.

A tentacle strikes out at Lu as she rounds a corner. Decades of training kick in and Lu instinctively slides under the tentacle, landing hard on her right hip as she slides around the corner, her M4 up and finger closing on the trigger.

But Lu holds her fire.

The doctor blob thing retracts the offending tentacle and adds it to the many others that envelop Dr. Probst, suspending the doctor in the air, keeping Lu from squeezing the M4's trigger.

"Don't shoot me!" Dr. Probst shouts.

"Not going to!" Lu shouts back.

"Lower your weapon," the doctor blob thing says.

Or Lu thinks it says. She's not sure if she's hearing the words with her ears or with her mind.

"I don't think I will," Lu responds.

Tentacles tighten and Dr. Probst squeaks.

"Lower the fucking weapon!" Dr. Probst cries.

"I do that and we're both dead," Lu says.

"Master needs you," the doctor blob thing says.

Again, Lu has no idea if she's physically hearing the words.

"You let her go and I'll lower the weapon," Lu says.

"Leverage," the doctor blob thing replies.

"Same here," Lu says and gestures with the M4.

The tentacles tighten even more.

"Getting…hard…to…breathe," Dr. Probst says.

"Let her go," Lu says.

She relaxes her shoulders and sights down the M4's short barrel.

"Your body language is aggressive," the doctor blob thing says. "You seek to harm us."

"No shit," Lu says. "I've got some pretty good reasons."

"A truce is suggested," the doctor blob thing says. "Master needs you."

"Fuck your master," Lu says.

The doctor blob thing roars and Lu watches the tentacles constrict with lightning speed.

Lu fires with equal speed and black blood spurts everywhere, coating the corridor's walls, the floor, the ceiling.

Dr. Probst falls to the ground and slip-slide-scurries her way to Lu as the doctor blob thing writhes with pain and rage, most of its tentacles turned into flailing chunks of flabby flesh.

"You alright?" Lu asks when Dr. Probst reaches her.

"No, I am not fucking alright!" Dr. Probst shouts. "You shot at me!"

"I shot around you," Lu says and helps Dr. Probst to her feet.

"Master doesn't need you in one piece," the doctor blob thing says, done writhing. "Only alive."

"Fuck," Lu says and grabs Dr. Probst by the shoulder, turning her toward the way to the elevator. "Run!"

"Run? I can't—" Dr. Probst begins to say, but the sight of the doctor blob thing suddenly racing right for them shuts her up and gets her feet moving. "Running!"

Lu leads the way, but she doesn't make the mistake she'd made with Kyle. Lu's hand stays gripped to Dr. Probst, pulling her along after her, making sure they stay together.

"Master doesn't need you in one piece!" the doctor blob thing shouts.

That time, Lu knows it's in her head and not out loud.

She's really fucking sick of words, pain, thoughts being shoved inside her mind without her consent. Really fucking sick of it.

———

"You cannot defeat me," the Ebony Man says as he picks himself up yet again after suffering another one of Lowell's punches. "Pitiful human."

"Yeah, not thinking that word applies to me anymore," Lowell says. He pauses. "Either of those words, really. You made a big fucking mistake switching places with me."

"It allowed my release from the Substance and the shackles of that terrestrial prison," the Ebony Man says as he begins to pace back and forth like a leopard in a cage, his blank face directed at Lowell. "Know that there is no stopping me."

Lowell laughs. Laughs hard.

The Ebony Man's face scrunches up in annoyance. Even without features, it's easy to tell that Lowell's laughter has hit a nerve.

"You will suffer for you hubris," the Ebony Man says and snaps his fingers.

Nothing happens. Except for Lowell's continued laughter.

The Ebony Man snaps again and lets out a low growl when once more the gesture fails to provide the results intended.

"Stop that!" the Ebony Man roars.

Lowell slowly stops laughing, wipes at his eyes, and gives the Ebony Man a shit-eating grin so brilliant it could have been used to light up a film set.

"You did this, asshole," Lowell says and waves his hands over his naked body. "You sent me in there and shit happened."

"You should have been killed!" the Ebony Man shouts.

"By what? The Substance?" Lowell asks. "Or by that fucking giant lizard I ended up fighting? Now, that was some wild shit. I've been in brawls before, but never with four arms of my own and an opponent the size of Rhode Island."

"Your human body and mind should have been consumed by the Substance," the Ebony Man says.

Lowell tilts his head. He heard the word the Ebony Man said and his mind instantly translated it into "Substance." But Lowell knows that the true name is much more ancient and cannot be comprehended fully by a human brain.

Good thing Lowell no longer feels he has a human brain.

No, what he feels is an ever-expanding consciousness that's allowing impossible images and thoughts to become known.

"Kinda tickles," Lowell says.

"Tickles...?" the Ebony man responds. "You make no sense."

"Wrong there, Mr. Licorice," Lowell says and smiles at his joke. "Mr. Licorice. That's your new name."

"My name is—"

"Don't care," Lowell interrupts. "Really. I don't. What I do care about is what's in Antarctica."

"There's nothing of importance there for you," the Ebony Man says.

"Wrong again, Mr. Licorice."

"Do not call me that."

"Or what? You'll destroy me?" Lowell shakes his head, then closes the space between them. He gets right up in the Ebony Man's blank face. "You said the Substance should have consumed me. I think it did. The thing is, Mr. Licorice, that me and the Substance kinda dug each other. I shit my britches when I ended up a thousand feet tall with some serious dental work and a couple more appendages than I'm used to, but in the end, even after getting my ass handed to me by the GEICO lizard on steroids, the Substance looked out for me."

"No," the Ebony Man says. "You're not worthy."

"And you are?" Lowell laughs even louder. "Pal, you can't hide your shit from me. I know about Antarctica and what's waiting down there. I know who you are and how you ended up on my planet. I also know there's a lot of scrapping still to do before the real fight begins."

The Ebony Man stiffens.

"You don't like that, do you?" Lowell asks. "You don't like that the Substance likes me and hates every molecule in your being. That really pisses you off."

"Primitive creature," the Ebony Man spits.

"Maybe, but primitive can mean simple, and sometimes simple is good," Lowell responds. "You had a job to do when you were sent to Earth. You'd made a deal. Bring the Substance to this planet, let it do its thing, and you could walk away free once everything was complete."

Lowell shudders and takes a step back.

"I'm not happy about what the purpose of the Substance is or why it was sent here," Lowell continues. "Terraform the planet so it can be an outpost for this sector of the galaxy? That's some fucked up sci-fi shit right there."

The Ebony Man is stone-still, like a slice of obsidian standing in the middle of the corridor. Now it's Lowell's turn to pace back and forth like a caged animal.

"When you hid within the Substance and refused to leave, shit went south," Lowell says. He jams a finger in the Ebony Man's direction. "Naughty Mr. Licorice. You brought the monsters here. This should have been the only facility. But because you were obviously milking the Substance for your own gain, more monsters were sent. They burrowed. They built. They connected. Connected to each other but not to here. And not to one other place."

Lowell stops pacing.

"Antarctica," Lowell says. "How'd you do that? How'd you make a backup without being in Antarctica?"

"Willpower," the Ebony Man says.

"Damn, man," Lowell says. "Golf clap for that. Not even the progenitors of the Substance thought you had it in you."

"You know nothing of the Substance or those that created it," the Ebony Man says. "You know nothing at all. Your mind is tricking you into beliefs simply to keep you from going insane. You are already a prisoner of your own madness and you don't even know it."

Lowell smiles, then slams a fist into the Ebony Man's face. The being rockets back against the wall then slides to the floor.

"How's that for a belief?" Lowell asks. "As for being a prisoner, I think you hit on something there. I have been a prisoner most of my life. Kinda like you. The Substance saw that and realized I'm a better candidate at achieving the end goal than you. Sorry, Mr. Licorice, but you've been fired."

"Impossible," the Ebony Man says, slowly getting back to his feet.

Lowell slams a closed fist into the top of the Ebony Man's skull before he's fully upright, dropping him back down to the floor.

"Impossible? Then how the fuck am I kicking your ass so easily?" Lowell asks.

"Because I'm letting you," the Ebony Man says and launches at Lowell.

Ebony fingers grasp and constrict around Lowell's neck, shutting off the oxygen to his brain instantly. Lowell grabs at the ebony fingers, clutches at the ebony wrists, but fails to remove the hands from his throat. Lights dance around the edges of his vision and his lungs start to burn as his throat closes, closes, closes, shuts.

"Goodbye, primate," the Ebony Man says.

A whistle echoes down the corridor.

The Ebony Man glances from Lowell's slack body to the source of the whistle.

"Boy," the Ebony Man says. "I will be with you shortly. Enjoy your last few seconds of life."

"I talked to your bosses," Kyle says from the end of the corridor. "They're not happy. Not at all. Looks like they're calling in your debt."

"No," the Ebony Man says. "You lie."

"Nut punch!" Lowell squeaks as his fist connects with the Ebony Man's crotch.

Nothing happens.

"No genitalia," the Ebony Man says then pauses. "Wait..."

Lowell's fists continue punching, a blur of violence directed at the spot right between the Ebony Man's legs. He keeps punching until the Ebony Man's lower half loses its humanoid form and melts into a puddle of ebony goo.

Lowell extracts himself from the Ebony Man's warped body and gets to his feet. He rolls his shoulders and checks himself over.

"Not a fucking scratch," he says, then looks at Kyle. "Thanks, kid. That distraction was exactly what I needed."

"What are we going to do with him?" Kyle asks, pointing at the Ebony Man as the being squirms about on the ground. "Can we put it down?"

"You tell me," Lowell says. "Sounds like you just had a conference call with the galactic brass. What'd they say?"

"You believe that?" Kyle asks.

Lowell taps his temple. "Kid, I believe all kinds of shit now." He looks Kyle up and down. "And you ain't looking so hot. I think you had an accident."

"See what happens to you when you get more info than you can handle shoved into your brain," Kyle snaps.

"Not judging, man," Lowell says. "Been there. I mean it. I was lucky when it all hit me. I was in a giant monster body. I'm sure that lizard dick pissed all over the place before I died."

"Uh…" Kyle says.

"Never mind. Talk to me," Lowell says.

Kyle does and Lowell frowns. The frown grows deeper and deeper until he holds up a hand.

"Stop. Just fucking stop," Lowell says. "That shit I didn't know. How much time do we have?"

"A week? Maybe more?" Kyle says, shaking his head. "I don't know for sure. I can't quite convert time from them to us."

"Totally understand that," Lowell replies. "A week…"

"Maybe more," Kyle adds.

"Maybe more. Right," Lowell says. "Not much time."

Lowell turns to the Ebony Man.

"Hey! Licorice prick!" Lowell shouts. "Quit your crying and get yourself together!"

The Ebony Man continues to squirm about. Lowell's fist snaps out and grabs the Ebony Man by the top of his ebony skull, stopping the squirming instantly.

"I said quit it," Lowell says and lifts the Ebony Man off the ground. He shakes the being over and over until legs form once again, then he sets the being on its feet. But he keeps his grip on the top of the Ebony Man's skull. "Time to talk."

"Words are useless to—" the Ebony Man begins.

Lowell squeezes and the Ebony Man cries out.

"I said time to talk," Lowell snarls. "Antarctica. How were you going to get there? It's a long way from Wyoming, pal. Even with your almighty E.T. powers, you'd still have to hoof it."

"I refuse to assist you," the Ebony Man says.

"No problem," Lowell says and starts to pull the Ebony Man by his head down the corridor. "Let's go chat with the Substance."

"No! Wait!" the Ebony Man screams.

Lowell pauses. "I thought that might get your attention. Talk."

Before the Ebony Man can say a word, more screams are heard.

"Kyle! Lowell!"

"Mom? Mom!" Kyle yells then turns and runs off toward the screams.

"Damnit," Lowell says and stalks off after Kyle, dragging the Ebony Man with him. "Can't the drama be over already? I have so much shit to do…"

———

"That's a Stryker," Bolton says, completely surprised by the vehicle standing in front of him. "How in the hell did you get a Stryker?"

"We have our sources," Halpern responds as the group gathers around the armored vehicle. "And we got lucky. It still works even after the EMP."

"The electrical system is shielded," Bolton says. "And wherever we are looks like it's underground."

"We're deep, yeah," Jeremy says. He unlatches a back hatch and he and Ginevra load crates and duffels into the back. "Still fried most of our shit though."

"Have you double-checked everything?" Bolton asks. "It would suck to get halfway to our target location and break down."

"It'll work," Joshua says. He climbs into the driver's seat with his radio, shuts the door, and just sits and waits.

"Joshua has a way with tech," Haley says, shoving Bolton out of the way so she can get to the rear of the vehicle and add her gear to the pile Jeremy and Ginevra are loading. "If he says it'll work, it'll work."

"Gonna be close quarters," Bolton says to Haley. "Just like the VWRAPS back in Iraq, right, Haley?"

Haley glances from Bolton to Halpern and back to Bolton.

"Yeah, right," Haley says to Bolton.

Bolton smiles his most disarming smile.

"No such thing as a VWRAP," Bolton says. "But since you didn't serve, you wouldn't know that."

"She served two tours!" Jeremy snaps.

"Three," Ginevra corrects.

"None," Bolton says and holds his hands up. He frowns at the double serving of zip ties but continues. "Calm down. Not trying to start a fight. I just want everyone here to know that I'm the professional soldier. And I'm also the guy who's gone from Wyoming to Idaho and back during all this shit. If we're going to make it to Puget Sound, then you need to take these cuffs off me and start paying attention when I talk."

"Uh oh, Mark," Jeremy says with mock worry, "sounds like this guy is gunning for your job."

"I'm not worried," Halpern says. "Sergeant Bolton knows we hold all the cards. If he wants to see his family, then he better play nice."

"You need me to get into that bunker," Bolton says. "Harm me and Terrie will eat you alive."

"The old woman doesn't worry me," Halpern says.

"She should," Bolton counters.

"Yet she doesn't," Halpern says.

Bolton shrugs.

"I just wanted to make sure all of you know I gave you a chance," Bolton says. "Not a lot of those being handed out in the world right now. My advice is you take the chance I'm offering and get your heads straight. Do that, and we'll forget all about this bullshit."

He holds up his bound hands.

"Keep pushing your luck though, and I will put all of you down well before we get to Puget Sound."

"Tough talk," Halpern says. "Get in the back, Sergeant Bolton."

"You're making a mistake, Mark," Bolton says.

He sees the punch coming, adjusts his footing slightly so he can absorb the hit better, then collapses to the ground as if the strike is ten times stronger than it was.

"See, Sergeant Bolton," Halpern says. "Not worried about you, and definitely not worried about the old woman. Behave yourself on this trip. I took the gag from your mouth after Joshua said we may need you to help navigate. But that's my last warning. You keep pushing your luck and I won't need a gag. I'll just take your tongue. Understood?"

"Loud and clear," Bolton says. He bites the inside of his cheek to produce a little more blood and spits onto the ground. "Didn't even see that hit coming. Nice work on not telegraphing your punch. If you can do that, then maybe I'm a little bit more over my head than I thought."

"I have some training too," Halpern says, then twirls his hand in the air. "Load up and let's move!"

Halpern limps around to the passenger's side door and climbs in.

Joshua turns his head and gives Bolton a cold look. Like a shark zeroing in on its prey. Bolton takes a moment to reassess his opinion of Joshua. And a moment is all he gets as Jeremy and Ginevra grab him and drag-push-shove him to the back of the vehicle.

"Get your ass in," Jeremy says.

Bolton tries to climb up through the hatch, but his bound hands slip and he falls backward. Jeremy and Ginevra catch him, keep him from knocking all three of them down, and shove him up and inside the vehicle.

The hatch slams shut.

Bolton is crammed in with the gear in a back space that has been cordoned off from the rest of the vehicle's interior by chicken wire.

Chicken wire…

Bolton shakes his head and tries not to laugh.

He also slips the knife he'd snagged from Jeremy's belt into his right boot.

"Comfy?" Jeremy asks as he gets in through a side hatch with Ginevra and Haley.

"I've ridden in worse," Bolton says.

Jeremey and Ginevra laugh. Haley glares. Halpern glances back over his shoulder and fixes Bolton with a stern look. Joshua starts the vehicle.

Halpern returns his attention to the windshield and reaches up to push a button.

A bay door slides open and Joshua drives the vehicle up out of the subterranean space, slowly corkscrewing up a long, concrete ramp until they reach another bay door that's already opening.

Bolton has no idea what type of facility it is they leave, but he knows it's not military. Looks industrial from the demolished equipment that's strewn here and there over the grounds. It's hard for him to see clearly from his vantage point. That, and the sun has already set and the only illumination is from the vehicle's floodlights.

Riding in a Stryker with a bunch of fools is not how he thought the mission would end. Then again, he honestly wasn't sure he'd get as far as he has.

Bolton leans back into the gear, struggles to get comfortable, and closes his eyes. He'll sleep for as long as he can, maybe eat a meal or two if they give him food, then make his move once they've gotten used to him.

———

"Ma'am?" a tech calls out.

"What is it?" VanderVoort asks with a sigh. She's seated in a chair at the end of the conference table, her red, bleary, sleep-deprived eyes flitting back and forth from monitor to monitor while those still alive continue to clear the room of corpses. "What do you have for me?"

"That boy is back," the tech says. "The one I spoke to before."

"The one in Puget Sound?" VanderVoort asks. "So?"

"He had said before that he has a way to get communications back up and running with all of our assets," the tech says.

"Great. Have him explain the tech to you, you explain it to everyone else, then get to building that shit," VanderVoort replies.

"He's cagey about giving us his, uh, secrets, as he says," the tech says.

"Then why are you talking to him? Why the fuck are you talking to me?" VanderVoort snaps.

"He mentioned a Connor Bolton," the tech says.

All attention is now on the tech. He blanches.

"How is that possible?" Director Miles asks.

"Who cares?" VanderVoort says. "Does he know what the status of Sergeant Bolton is?"

"He says the sergeant has been captured by a militia group and the group is bringing Sergeant Bolton to them so they can take over the bunker," the tech answers.

"Shit," VanderVoort says. "They didn't make it to Diamond-back. Shit!"

"It was a long shot," Director Miles says.

"Fine. Great. Whatever," VanderVoort says. "Get the tech from him then. At least maybe we can contact the ships in the gulf or whoever is still out there."

"He wants to make a trade," the tech says.

"What? Let me talk to the little shit," VanderVoort says.

"He refuses to speak to anyone in authority because you're

trained to lie to him and steal his work," the tech says and holds up his hands. "His words, not mine."

"What does he want to trade?" VanderVoort asks.

"He wants sanctuary for him and the people he's with," the tech says. "He wants to be brought here."

"Oh, is that all he wants?" VanderVoort says with a laugh. "No problem. Tell him he gets his wish."

"Ma'am?"

"Do it. Tell him that if his tech works and we can establish communications with everyone, then he and his friends will be allowed sanctuary here in the White House's ultra-secure Situation Room," VanderVoort says. "And he can have all the ice cream he wants to eat too."

"Ice cream, ma'am?"

"It's a joke. I don't give a shit what you tell him. Get that tech and keep him happy until we have comms back up."

"Yes, ma'am."

"This should be interesting," Director Miles says. "You hungry?"

"Starving," VanderVoort replies.

"I'll rustle up something. Stay put," Director Miles says.

VanderVoort looks at the chair she's in, at her huge belly, and laughs.

"Staying put," she says and sighs.

FIVE

The hunger in Lowell's stomach rises to a crescendo so intense he fears that the organ will crawl right out of his mouth.

The cause of the intensity?

The sight of the doctor blob thing pursuing Lu and Dr. Probst as the two women sprint up to him.

"Get behind me," Lowell says in a low, barely audible voice. He clears his throat. "Better yet. Just keep running. I don't think you want to see this."

"He's right, Mom," Kyle says.

Lu doesn't argue. She doesn't say a word. She reaches Kyle, wraps her arms around him, then hurries her son ahead of her as she and Dr. Probst keep moving.

Dr. Probst does pause to look at the Ebony Man that's in Lowell's grip. Lowell acknowledges the look with a shrug and jerks his head toward the way he came.

"You're still naked, by the way," Dr. Probst says, then nods and dashes after Lu and Kyle.

"I'll throw some pants on after I take care of something," Lowell says, even though he's now alone in the corridor.

Lowell takes a deep breath and faces off with the doctor blob thing.

"What's with the hunger?" Lowell asks the Ebony Man as he lets go of the being's skull. "This shit is rough."

The Ebony Man doesn't answer, only laughs weakly.

"Release our master," the doctor blob thing says.

"Okay," Lowell says and flings the Ebony Man at the doctor blob thing.

The two monstrosities collide in a tangle of nightmarish limbs, slide all the way down the corridor, and slam into the far wall.

Lowell takes his time getting to them.

"Destroy the little ape," the Ebony Man says, getting to his feet.

Lowell smirks at the sight of the Ebony Man wobbling on his newly formed legs.

"We will devour with pleasure," the doctor blob thing says.

"I have a feeling that's my line," Lowell says.

"Do not hesitate!" the Ebony Man roars.

Lowell twitches and sticks a finger in his ear.

"Tone it down, Mr. Licorice," Lowell says. "You're done for, dude. Give it up."

A tentacle shoots out at Lowell, but he easily grabs it. With a shit-eating grin, Lowell rips the tentacle free from its fleshy mooring on the doctor blob thing's grotesque body. The monster shrieks in agony and black blood spurts from the fresh stump.

"Oh...damn," Lowell says. "That smells like sushi."

He stares down at the still-wriggling tentacle in his hand. He sniffs appreciatively, then takes a bite.

As soon as the monster juices fill his mouth, Lowell is lost in his hunger.

The Ebony Man cackles in triumph.

"You see, primate?" the Ebony Man says. "The baser urges rule your kind. You do not have the capacity to control that hunger. It will be your downfall."

The Ebony Man snaps his fingers and the doctor blob thing rockets down the corridor, straight at Lowell.

Lowell doesn't stop his devouring of the severed tentacle. Instead, while his left hand holds the meal, his right arm cocks back in anticipation, then strikes hard and fast as soon as the doctor blob thing is on him. Lowell's right hand pierces the doctor blob thing's body, stopping the monster dead.

Literally.

Lowell yanks his hand free and a trail of innards and organs come with it. The doctor blob thing deflates to the floor like a popped balloon.

Tossing the remnants of the tentacle aside, Lowell eyes the feast before him. Then he looks past the abominable corpse at the stunned Ebony Man.

"I'm guessing you've never had to eat three meals a day in prison," Lowell says. "You get good at not getting shanked while eating."

"I will not be humbled by a monkey!" the Ebony Man shouts.

He launches himself at Lowell, giving Lowell just enough time to sigh with exasperation before twisting his body so he can grab the Ebony Man by both arms and flip him head over heels down the corridor. The pitch-black being tumbles over and over until the wall stops his momentum and he comes to an unceremonious stop.

"I'd say I could do this all day, but that might encourage you to try," Lowell says. He grabs the doctor-blob-thing corpse and drags it with him as he stalks over to the Ebony Man. "You gonna be cool, or do I have to kick your ass some more?"

The Ebony Man rolls over onto his back. His entire body shudders, turning from solid to liquid then back to solid in the blink of an eye.

"How?" is all the being manages to croak out.

"How what?" Lowell asks.

"You're insignificant gnats of a species," the Ebony Man says.

"Yeah, please keep talking, Mr. Licorice," Lowell responds. "Can't wait to hear where this is going."

"My kind are superior in all ways," the Ebony Man continues.

"Uh huh, sure. And?"

"You should be a splatter of blood under my boot."

"You aren't wearing boots."

"You understand my meaning."

"You bet. You think you're hot shit, but you aren't. Want to know why? Of course you do! You asked 'how,' which is like 'whys' cousin."

Lowell bends down and gets his face right up against the Ebony Man's blank face.

"This is my planet, bitch," Lowell says. "You forgot about home advantage, Mr. Licorice." He straightens back up. "Now, you stay put while I try to do something about this fucking hunger. Twitch a licorice nib and I'll tear you down into molecules. Got it?"

The Ebony Man nods and places his back firmly against the wall.

"Good," Lowell says. He eyes the monster corpse. "I wonder where the bacon is on this thing."

———

Lu and Dr. Probst collapse into chairs the second they enter the facility's main control room. They're both white as ghosts and shaking hard from fear and adrenaline. Lu's eyes go wide and she opens her mouth to scream some of the fear away, but closes it as her son walks into the control room after them.

"What's going on?" Dr. Probst asks, beating Lu to the question.

"I wish I didn't know," Kyle says, his face haggard and his shoulders so slumped they look to be carrying the weight of a million worlds on them. "Really, Mom. This sucks."

"What sucks? What do you wish you didn't know?" Lu asks.

She gets to her feet and checks her son over, her hands

smoothing his hair, patting his cheeks and arms, her eyes staring into his.

"Everything," Kyle says. He gently removes himself from Lu's maternal ministrations and collapses into his own chair.

Lu looks to Dr. Probst, but she only shrugs.

"Kyle? What's going on?" Lu asks, returning to her chair.

"Everything," Kyle says and taps at his temple. "The alien shoved everything in here and it fucking hurts, Mom."

"Uh... did you say alien?" Dr. Probst asks.

"It's not from our planet, so yeah, I said alien," Kyle replies.

"Your head. You must have hit it, Kyle," Lu says and is about to get out of her seat once again, but Kyle waves a hand at her to stay seated.

"I didn't hit my head," Kyle says. "The alien touched my head and downloaded way too much shit into my brain. The ultimate TMI."

Lu starts to say something, but Dr. Probst makes eye contact with a look that says, *Let him speak.*

Lu waits for Kyle to continue.

Kyle shakes his head, then sits forward, his eyes on the control panels.

"How do we contact the White House?" he asks.

"Why do we need to contact the White House?" Dr. Probst asks.

"Because they're coming," Kyle says.

"They?" Dr. Probst asks.

"I... I don't know what to call them," Kyle says and taps his temple again. "There isn't a translation."

"More aliens?" Dr. Probst prods.

"Different," Kyle says. "Huge. Like the monsters stomping around our planet. But not... they aren't shells." Kyle shakes his head, obviously confused. "Whatever they are, they're coming here and are going to destroy Earth."

"Destroy Earth? Why?" Dr. Probst asks.

"It's what they do," Kyle says with a shrug. "They destroy

worlds, take them over, and shape them into forts or bases or outposts or whatever."

"It's a war," Lu says. "We're stuck in the middle of a war."

"A war? Like an alien war?" Dr. Probst asks. "Jesus Christ…"

"That's why I have to talk to the White House," Kyle says. "I was told there's a way for humanity to survive. But we've only got a week at the most."

"A week at the most to save humanity?" Dr. Probst scoffs. "Well, humanity's dead. Bureaucracy will see to that."

"We don't have a choice," Kyle says. "There's one shot at us living through this and we have to act now."

"I don't understand," Dr. Probst says.

"Ya think?" Lu snorts.

"Right there with you," Kyle says.

"Why save us if they're coming to destroy us? Why bother with us at all?" Dr. Probst asks.

"Get me in touch with the White House," Kyle says. "I don't have the energy to explain it twice. Do you know how to contact them?"

Dr. Probst looks about the control room. "Yeah… I think so."

"Good," Kyle says. He closes his eyes. "Jesus, I'm tired…"

"Hey!" Lu snaps. "Don't fade yet. You say what you have to say to get this ball rolling, then you can nap."

"Sounds good," Kyle says.

Dr. Probst works at the consoles for a couple of minutes while Lu struggles to keep Kyle awake.

"There. That should do it," Dr. Probst says finally and taps at one last key.

The large, main monitor flickers to life, displaying the White House's seal. But that's it. No answer from the other end, just an official graphic they're forced to stare at with frustration.

"They aren't picking up," Dr. Probst says and looks about in panic. "What do we do?"

"Wake me when they pick up," Kyle says and his eyes close tight.

"Keep trying," Lu says, her attention divided between the White House seal and her sleeping son.

"Not like I can do anything else," Dr. Probst says.

———

"It's the Wyoming facility," a tech announces. "It's trying to make contact again."

"Yeah, not answering that call," VanderVoort says. "Let that freak thing go to voicemail." She snorts at the thought. "I just sent you to voicemail, you out-of-this-world piece of shit. Fuck you."

"Why not just snap its fingers?" Dr. Hall asks. "It called us that way before…" He looks about the Situation Room. "And it killed that way before. I don't think voicemail will hold it back."

"He's probably right," Director Miles says.

For once, VanderVoort can use some other opinions, but those are in short supply. Most of the Joint Chiefs are dead, as are most of the Cabinet. There are a few capable techs, a few Secret Service agents, and some other support personnel left. It comes to a paltry two dozen as opposed to the close to one hundred who had been maintaining the Situation Room.

"Ma'am?" Joan asks from the conference table, where she's shoved together a couple of chairs and is trying to stretch out and rest. "If I may?"

"Fucking please do," VanderVoort says.

"This is a fluid situation," Joan says. "We have to respond in kind. By not answering, we could make the situation worse."

"Or we could avoid getting our heads torn open from the goddamn inside out," General Azoul snarls.

"Gordon?" VanderVoort asks.

"I already agreed with Dr. Hall," Director Miles says. "I doubt we can ghost that thing."

"Fuck," VanderVoort says. "Where are we with reprogramming the shuttle to go to Antarctica?"

None of the techs answer. Most avoid VanderVoort's eye completely.

"Shit," she says. "If I answer and that thing wants to know when he gets to take a joyride to the South Pole, what should I tell him? Anyone?"

"The truth?" Dr. Hall suggests.

"Cute," VanderVoort says. "I'm serious, people!"

"Just answer the call," President Nance says, emerging from the corridor to the Presidential suite. "This is a 'damned if we do, damned if we don't' scenario, Ms. VanderVoort. You play the cards you're dealt and keep playing until the game is over."

"That's a lot of folksy wisdom there, Charles," VanderVoort replies. "But it's the only wisdom anyone has, so fuck it, right? Let's play cards."

Nothing happens.

"That means answer the damn call," VanderVoort explains.

The main monitor goes live, and gasps of surprise are only overshadowed by the sighs of relief.

Dr. Probst's face fills the screen.

"Finally!" Dr. Probst shouts. "What's happening there? Why'd it take so long to answer?"

"Is it only you, Dr. Probst?" VanderVoort asks with caution.

"No," Dr. Probst replies. "Lu and Kyle Morgan are here with me."

"No one else? No *thing* else?" VanderVoort asks.

"Oh, you mean the Ebony Man," Dr. Probst says. "No, it's not here. Lowell is handling that guy."

"Lowell? Anson Lowell? The convict?" General Azoul asks. "What's going on in that facility?"

"Well, I'll tell you if you all shut up and let me talk," Dr. Probst snaps.

"Please do, Doctor," VanderVoort says.

"I… uh…" Dr. Probst stammers. "I got nothing. Kyle is the one with all the info."

"Wonderful," VanderVoort says. "Please put the teenager on so he can make his report."

VanderVoort puts a finger gun to her temple and drops the thumb. More than a few heads nod in agreement.

Kyle's sleepy face replaces Dr. Probst's on the screen.

"Hey," Kyle says. "So, yeah, uh, I got a whole bunch of shit jammed into my brain by an alien."

Stunned silence is an understatement.

VanderVoort looks about, shakes her head, then focuses back on Kyle.

"Uh…are you alright?" she asks.

There's a voice off-screen and Kyle nods.

"Right. Thanks, Mom," Kyle says. "I'll explain that part first so you have context. My Mom is big into context."

Kyle explains his encounter and how he came to receive way too much information. VanderVoort and the others listen with skepticism, but that skepticism quickly becomes fear as Kyle gets to the new information.

"My mom nailed it," Kyle explains. "We're in the middle of a war between two galactic factions. Maybe more than two factions, but two sides, for sure. It's a little fuzzy."

"Take your time," VanderVoort says, her hands wrapped protectively around her belly. "Be thorough. Don't leave any intel out."

"I'll try," Kyle says. He takes a deep breath. "The Ebony Man was sent here millions and millions of years ago. If the pictures in my head are right, his arrival is what wiped out the dinosaurs. He was the asteroid that hit Earth. Except it wasn't an asteroid, it was a ship or something."

Kyle looks about his surroundings and holds out his arms.

"This facility, or at least the part holding the Substance, was his ship and his prison," Kyle says.

"Prison?" VanderVoort asks. "What does that mean?"

"I think he was a criminal given a chance to turn Earth into a new outpost for one of the sides. Our side? It's still hazy," Kyle says. "But the arrival of the Substance changed things here. It may be the reason humans evolved. Like a spark or something. That spark was supposed to use the animal life at the time and form it into, well, organic fighting machines?"

"Are you asking me or telling me?" VanderVoort asks.

"I said it's a little hazy," Kyle continues. "The Substance did grab onto the DNA of the current animal life, specifically the dinosaur DNA. But the Substance also got mixed in with mammals and the seeds of humanity were born. When that happened, the Ebony Man was told to hibernate and wait out the new intelligent species. Once humanity was extinct, he could begin terraforming our planet and turn it into an outpost."

"I'm sorry, son, but are you saying that thing was supposed to wait millions and millions of years, then wipe us out?" General Azoul asks. "Why wait at all? Makes no sense."

"No, he wasn't supposed to wipe us out," Kyle responds.

"Coulda fooled me," General Azoul replies.

"Let the boy speak," President Nance says. "Go on, son."

"Yeah, so the Ebony Man went rogue," Kyle says. "He wasn't supposed to do his work until humanity became extinct. But he's been plotting while in hibernation. Somehow manipulating the Substance while asleep? I can't figure that part out. But the beings in charge realized what he was doing and they sent more of their kind here. That's where all the other facilities came from. They were set up to fight the Ebony Man if he woke up his...vessel? I can't translate the word!"

Kyle slams a fist down and starts rubbing his forehead over and over.

"Hey, how about we take a break?" Lu says, shoving her way into view. "We can call you back in—"

"No!" Kyle yells. "I'm forgetting! I have to tell it all before it's gone to make room for more!"

"Kyle, no," Lu says.

"MOM!" Kyle yells, then shakes his head in apology.

Lu retreats and Kyle continues.

"The Ebony Man technically shouldn't have been able to activate his monster until extinction was assured," Kyle says. "He found a loophole: global warming. Humanity will be extinct in a little over a century because of climate destruction. He used that fact to trigger his release. That's how the Yellowstone supervolcano became active. It was him circumventing the system and waking up early."

"And that woke up the others," VanderVoort interrupts. "They were sent to stop him if he pulled any shit. He pulled shit, and now our planet is done."

"The planet as we know it," Kyle says. "But humanity can still survive."

"How?" VanderVoort asks.

"The facilities," Kyle says. "They're all over the world and they can be used to save us. We just have to get the people there."

"Hold up, hold up," VanderVoort says. "You want millions of people to hide in alien bunkers?"

"I don't want anything except a fucking nap," Kyle says and shakes his head again. "Sorry. Sorry."

"No, it's fine, son," President Nance says. "You keep talking."

"All I know is the alien that touched my head showed me that people can survive in the facilities," Kyle continues. "If we can get everyone to their closest facility, then somehow humanity won't become extinct."

"Somehow?" General Azoul says with a scoff. "Is everyone listening to this? Aliens coming to kill us. Giant monsters sleeping for millions of years underground without being detected. A galactic war? This kid has obviously been concussed."

"An intergalactic war," Kyle says. "It's everywhere."

"Is anyone believing this bullshit?" General Azoul shouts.

"Oh, fuck off," a voice snaps. "Move, kid."

Kyle doesn't hesitate and gladly cedes his seat to a still naked, although now coated in black slime, Lowell.

"Howdy," Lowell says. He smiles wide, and the entire Situation Room draws back involuntarily. "I haven't looked in a mirror, but, yeah, I'd probably cringe too."

"Anson Lowell," VanderVoort says, keeping her gorge at bay while she tries to continue looking at the slime-coated convict. "Are you part of this too?"

"Part of this?" Lowell asks and laughs. "Lady, I am this. Do I have a story for you."

"Does your story include clothes?" VanderVoort asks.

"Nope, so deal with it," Lowell says. "I'm here to tell you all the tale of how I became a thousand-foot monster..."

———

Once Lowell is finished with his story, he leans back in the chair and puts his arms behind his head.

"Any questions?" he asks.

Dr. Probst's hand shoots up. Lowell glances over and frowns.

"From them, not you," Lowell says. He looks from Dr. Probst to Lu, then at Kyle, whose eyes are closed once more. Lowell ignores the being collapsed at his feet. "Kid, wake up. You aren't done yet."

"Fuck," Kyle says, his voice thick and sleepy. "I don't think I have anything left."

"You do and you know it," Lowell says.

Lu starts to protest, but Kyle holds up a hand. "It's okay, Mom. I gotta do this."

"Tell them the last part, then I'll tell them about Antarctica," Lowell says.

Kyle scoots his chair over to Lowell so he's in the camera frame too. He looks up at the main monitor and VanderVoort's extremely agitated and terrified face.

"Whoever the aliens are, they've opened up all the facilities," Kyle says. "All we have to do is get people to them, then lock them down before the big beings get here. If we lock them down, then we have a chance. If we don't, then humanity goes extinct."

"But the facilities are dangerous," VanderVoort says. "I watched all of my scientists die."

"That was the Ebony Man," Kyle says. "But Lowell has him under control."

"Mr. Licorice have nappy time," Lowell says.

"I don't know what the fuck that means…" VanderVoort replies. "Anyway. So we have to get everyone to the facility. Right when global communications are out and…" VanderVoort pauses.

"Oh, she has something," Lowell says, seeing the look on VanderVoort's face. "What ya got?"

"There's a kid in Puget Sound who has tech he says will reconnect comms across the globe," VanderVoort says.

"How are you talking to him?" Lowell asks.

"He has a shortwave radio that's modified with some device he created," VanderVoort says. "He got through White House security protocols like they don't exist and contacted us, so I believe the device will work."

"Perfect. That's how you start coordinating the migration to the facilities," Lowell says. He studies the look on VanderVoort's face. "What's the problem?"

"We've told him we'll come get him once he gives us the tech, but he isn't being too cooperative," VanderVoort says. "He wants to know specifically how we'll get him and the others with him to the White House and we don't have an answer."

Someone says something to VanderVoort off-screen.

"We can't figure out how to modify the shuttle to get to Antarctica," VanderVoort snaps. "How will we modify it to fly to Puget Sound, pick them up, then fly to DC?"

"Hold that thought," Lowell says. "Antarctica. That's where I need to go."

VanderVoort blinks a few times, then sighs. "I knew this was too good to be true. That thing got to you."

VanderVoort gestures to kill the feed, but Lowell shouts, "Hold the fuck on!" and the screen stays active.

Lowell reaches down and grabs the Ebony Man by the head and lifts him up again.

"Say hi, Mr. Licorice," Lowell says. The Ebony Man only groans. "He's a little under the weather after I beat his ass."

"Beat his ass…?" VanderVoort asks. "How…?"

"I told you the Substance changed me," Lowell says. "Get me to Antarctica, and instead of using the monster—"

"Kaiju!" Dr. Hall can be heard shouting from off-screen.

"Kaiju? Like the Japanese monster movies?" Lowell asks. "Of course!"

He laughs and claps his hands together.

"Perfect! So, there's a giant kaiju down in Antarctica that Mr. Licorice was going to use to conquer Earth with so it's ready for his overlords or whatever they are," Lowell says. The Ebony Man groans something and Lowell gives him a shake. "Yes, they are your overlords. Now shut up, Mr. Licorice. Anyway, the kaiju in Antarctica is one of the really big ones. Like twice the size of Yellowstone. It's been grown to be used not only for kicking ass, but for like long-range space travel. I shit you not, folks. It's a space kaiju!"

"Like the others coming to destroy us," Kyle says.

"Instead of flying off like a little scared bitch, which is what Mr. Licorice was going to do just in case his overlords try to pull a fast one on him," Lowell says and lets Ebony Man fall back to the ground with an audible thud, "I'm going to use the space kaiju to fight off the other space kaiju coming to shred this planet to its core. Which, by the way, is a type of organic machine powered by the Substance and controlled by the other facilities. Not this one, since it isn't connected due to Ebony Man's indiscretions, but the rest are part of a network that basically is the bones and arteries of Earth."

"Earth is an organic, interstellar base," Kyle says. "I can't explain it. You'll see once everyone is inside the facilities and we hit the reset button."

"Is there actually a reset button?" Lowell asks and rubs his temples. "That feels more metaphorical."

"I don't know anymore," Kyle says and yawns. "I gotta sleep. I'm done."

"Sleep? Done?" VanderVoort says. "You're just getting started."

"No, he is not!" Lu snaps and crosses the control room to Kyle. She helps him to his feet and turns him away from the camera. "Come on. You can sleep now, baby."

Kyle is pretty much already asleep on his feet as Lu helps lead him out of the control room.

"So, everyone know their assignments?" Lowell asks with a smirk. "While you all get that kid to fix the world's communication issues, I'll be here getting the shuttle reworked so it will send me down south to good ol' Antarctica."

"How will you get the shuttle to work?" VanderVoort asks.

"It's connected to this facility, right?" Lowell asks.

"Yes," VanderVoort says.

"Great," Lowell says and holds up a hand. "I kinda have a connection to the place now. Sorta. It's a work in progress. Still figuring out what I can and can't do. But, send me all the information on the shuttle, and between Dr. Probst and I, we'll get it working."

"Wait, what?" Dr. Probst asks. "I'm a geologist, not a shuttle technician! Why won't anyone listen to me?"

"Don't sell yourself short, Cheryl," Lowell says. "You didn't become the geologist you are by being stupid. With your brain and my magic touch, we can get the shuttle reprogrammed and ready to take me down to Antarctica." He glances down at his feet. "Me and Mr. Licorice here."

"You're taking…that with you?" Dr. Probst asks.

"He's the keys to the front door," Lowell says and returns his attention to VanderVoort. "We good here?"

"Good? Hardly," VanderVoort says, "but we have no choice. You do what you need to in order to save this planet. We'll do what we can to coordinate communication with the survivors across the world and start the migration into the facilities."

"Great," Lowell says. "Then we'll sign off and get to work. Good luck!"

He kills the comm and smiles at Dr. Probst. She does not smile back.

"Why so glum, Cheryl?" Lowell asks.

"This is fucking insane," Dr. Probst says.

"I know," Lowell replies, a grin stretching from ear to ear. "Wait until they find out that some of the facilities might still have aliens in them. That's gonna be really fun."

"Get that goddamn kid with the radio back on the comms!" VanderVoort shouts.

"Yes, ma'am!" the tech in charge of communicating with Tony replies.

VanderVoort turns her chair about to face everyone left. It isn't many.

President Charles Nance, National Security Advisor Joan Milligan, General Lawrence Azoul, National Intelligence Director Gordon Miles, Dr. Blane Hall, Special Agent Paulo Alvarez, a few assorted aides, and a few techs.

That's it.

"Can we do it?" VanderVoort asks. "If we can get comms reconnected, can we move millions and millions of people into these facilities?"

"Most Americans are already on ships," Joan says. "We can divide the ships up and send them in different directions so we spread the load across a few of the facilities."

"If the ships are operational," Director Miles says.

"We'll deal with that once we have comms up," VanderVoort says.

"How many people can the Wyoming facility hold?" General Azoul asks VanderVoort.

"At most, three hundred thousand," VanderVoort says.

"Seriously?" Joan asks. "That many?"

"It has levels and areas that have never been opened before," VanderVoort says. "We've barely scratched the surface of the facilities. All focus has been on the Substance."

"Okay," Joan says. "But even if there are ten viable facilities, and they all can hold the same amount of survivors, then that's only three million people. And we don't know if all the facilities are viable. Millions will still die."

"Billions," General Azoul says. "Millions have already died because of the eruptions. Once those doors to the facilities close, the total will be in the billions."

"Are you willing to make that call, Ms. VanderVoort?" President Nance asks. "Are you willing to choose who lives and who dies?"

"Honestly? Yes," VanderVoort says. "I've been called the Spook for most of my career. Know what else I've been called? The Ghoul. I don't plan on letting anyone die, but I don't get to make that choice. Simple math does. There's X amount of space for Y amount of people. Once X is full, what's left of Y is shit out of luck."

"Good Lord," Joan says. "You're a monster like those things."

"Hey!" Director Mile shouts. "Stop acting like your shit doesn't stink, Joan! You're the fucking National Security Advisor. You may not have the numbers VanderVoort does, but you have plenty of innocent blood on your own hands. We all do."

"Gordon is right," President Nance says. "This has now become a numbers game. We get as many people to safety as we can now, then we pray to the good Lord above for forgiveness later."

"Uh, has anyone figured out how we get us to the Wyoming facility?" Dr. Hall asks. "It's the closest one, right? That's where we'll want to go?"

Stunned realization hits everyone like a ton of bricks. They look at Dr. Hall and he winces.

"We are going to try to get to a facility, yeah?" he asks. "Because if not, then I think I want to resign and start walking now. Alvarez can come with me. We make a good cross-country team."

"We barely survived getting across DC," Alvarez says.

"We'll be secure down here," General Azoul states. "No need to leave."

"I highly doubt that," Dr. Hall says. "That Kyle kid said in order to survive we have to get to a facility. I can see the skepticism in your eyes regarding the alien aspect of this scenario, but I'm going to err on the side of caution and believe him. If he says we have to get to a facility, then we have to get to a facility."

An argument breaks out, and VanderVoort rubs her eyes until she can't take it anymore.

"Shut the ever-loving fuck up!" she bellows.

The argument quiets down.

"Nothing happens until we have comms," she says. She points at the tech burdened with that duty. "Talk to me!"

"I have him on the line, ma'am," the tech says. "He still wants a guarantee of rescue."

"Give it to him," VanderVoort says. "I already said that. Do not make me repeat myself again."

"He wants proof, ma'am," the tech says.

"Let me talk to him," VanderVoort says.

"He refuses—"

"Let me fucking talk to him!" she roars.

"Yes, ma'am," the tech says. "Comms open."

"Hello? Who am I speaking with?" VanderVoort asks.

"I said I didn't want to talk to anyone in charge," Tony's voice responds. "You lie to get your way."

"Everyone lies to get their way," VanderVoort says. "Are you telling me you don't lie to get your way? Ever?"

There's a long pause, and VanderVoort looks at the tech. He shrugs his shoulders.

"I'm not very good at lying," Tony says finally.

"That's not the same as never lying," VanderVoort says. "So I'm going to assume your moral objection to speaking to me is bullshit. But what I'm about to tell you is not bullshit, okay? It's very, very hard to believe, but I think due to the circumstances we have all been forced to witness, the unbelievable isn't the same as the impossible. Do you agree?"

"I don't know," Tony says.

"I think you do," VanderVoort says. "Let's begin again. What's your name?"

A long pause.

"Tony."

"Hello, Tony," VanderVoort says with a smile. "You may call me Adrianna. It's a pleasure to meet you."

"We haven't really met," Tony says. "We're talking to each other, but we haven't met in person."

"This one is a winner," General Azoul says.

VanderVoort shoots him a look that almost knocks him out of his seat.

"My apologies for that, Tony," VanderVoort says. "Some people in charge are not just liars, but they're also assholes."

This causes Tony to laugh. VanderVoort's smile returns.

"Are you ready for one hell of a story, Tony?" VanderVoort asks.

"Is it a science fiction story?" Tony asks. "I like those the most."

"You have no fucking idea," VanderVoort says before launching into an abbreviated version of what she was told by Lowell and Kyle.

SIX

The sat phone rings for the twelfth time since the Stryker has set out on its journey.

Bolton comes awake quickly at the sound, instantly orients himself to where he's at, then leans his forehead against the chicken wire.

"Answer the damn phone," Bolton says once more. "It doesn't matter if they track us with the phone. Planes are grounded. Drones are stuck in Colorado Springs. We're traveling in a fucking Stryker, which can take a missile hit and still survive. Answer! The! Phone!"

"Don't do it," Jeremy says.

"Yeah, don't do it," Haley says.

"I have zero intention of answering the phone," Halpern says. "So stop asking or the gag goes back in."

"I thought you was gonna take his tongue?" Ginevra asks. "Do it. Just cut it out and shut him up."

"We need him talking," Joshua says from the driver's seat. Those are the first words he's spoken since the journey first began. "Leave his tongue."

"I'd like to second that," Bolton says. "Mark? I'm not trying to make trouble, but they are calling for a reason. Please, I beg you, answer the sat phone."

The radio suddenly crackles to life.

"Hello?"

"That's the kid," Halpern says to Joshua. "What does he want?"

Joshua looks over at Halpern. The look says it all.

"Right," Halpern says. "How would you know. I'll find out."

He grabs the handset and clears his voice.

"Hello? Is this Tony?" Halpern asks. "This is Mark Halpern."

"Where's Joshua?" Tony asks.

"He's busy driving, but you can talk to me," Halpern says. "I'm in charge here."

"I don't care about you," Tony says. "I need to talk to Sergeant Bolton."

"I'm afraid that isn't going to happen," Halpern says. "He's unavailable."

"I don't believe you," Tony says. "Put him on."

"I can't do that, kid," Halpern says. "We're on the road and the radio handset won't reach where he's riding."

"You're lying," Tony says.

Bolton chuckles, and Haley reaches back with her rifle and slams the butt against the chicken wire.

"Shut it," she snarls.

"Tony, right?" Halpern asks.

"I need to speak to Bolton," Tony says.

"Listen, Tony—"

"I hear the satellite phone ringing," Tony says. "That's the White House trying to reach Sergeant Bolton. Everything has changed. We can't stay here. We're leaving the bunker."

"What?" Bolton exclaims. "God damnit, Mark! Let me talk to him!"

"How has everything changed?" Halpern asks. "Why would you leave the bunker?"

"I'm not allowed to tell you," Tony says. "On orders from the White House."

Halpern laughs. "Kid, I wasn't born yesterday. Stop messing around. If you're leaving the bunker, then there's no reason to keep Sergeant Bolton. He's alive because you want him to be. No bunker, no Bolton."

There's a long pause.

"I lost him," Halpern says.

"No, he's still there," Joshua says. "He does that."

"Aliens are coming to destroy the world," Tony says. "Or what's left of it."

Silence. Then uproarious laughter from Halpern, Jeremy, Ginevra, and Haley.

Joshua and Bolton stay silent.

"I don't know what he's high on, but it sounds great!" Jeremy exclaims. "Tell him to save some for us."

"You high, kid?" Halpern asks.

"I am not high," Tony says.

"Let the kid speak," Joshua says.

"You're getting a little pushy, bud," Jeremy says. "You don't boss Mark around."

Joshua turns his head slowly and glares at Jeremy.

"Uh, watch the road," Jeremy says. "You're gonna crash us."

Joshua doesn't look back at the road but keeps his eyes on Jeremy.

"Jesus," Jeremy says. "Sorry…"

Joshua turns back to the road.

Bolton really wants to know who the fuck Joshua is. He's seen that look in Joshua's eyes before. Plenty of times. By killers and operators.

"Let the kid speak," Joshua says again.

Halpern sighs, then says into the handset, "Aliens? Did you say aliens?"

"I said aliens," Tony replies. "Please pay attention so I'm not forced to repeat myself. Time is limited, and you're wasting that limited time. If you would like to survive, then you will let me speak to Sergeant Bolton."

"No can do, kid," Halpern says. "As amusing as this talk is, and it is very amusing…. Aliens… ha…. As amusing as this is, I don't plan on wasting time with your fantasies. Can I speak to an adult?"

"Why?' Tony asks.

"So I can get actual, real information," Halpern says with exasperation. "Not some stoned kid and his talk of aliens. Let me speak to Terrie."

"I called you," Tony says.

"Yes, you did," Halpern agrees.

"I called you, so you have to speak to me," Tony says. There's a long pause. "I still hear the sat phone ringing. Please answer that."

"Oh, I should answer the sat phone *and* let you speak to Sergeant Bolton?" Halpern chuckles. "Are you in charge now?"

"Put Joshua on," Tony says. "He's reasonable."

"Guess he don't know you too well, eh, Joshua?" Jeremy mutters.

"Kid, listen—" Halpern begins.

"You're an idiot," Tony says. "I prefer speaking to the government people. They may be liars, but they're reasonable. And intelligent."

Joshua snorts. Halpern glares at him.

Halpern looks back over his shoulder at Bolton.

"You've been talking to government people?" he asks, his eyes on Bolton. "Why would you do that? Like you said, kid, they're liars."

"But not idiots," Tony says. "Unlike you."

This time, Bolton snorts and Haley slams the butt of her rifle against the chicken wire again.

"Soon I'll have that WinMag in my hands," Bolton states.

Haley blanches at his tone but tries to sneer and play it off. Bolton can see he got to her though.

"I'm done playing, kid," Halpern says. "We'll talk more when I see you face to face. You can try your aliens story again then and we'll see how that goes for you."

"Three rings, two rings, three rings, one ring," Tony says, and the radio goes to static.

"What the hell does that mean?" Halpern asks. He looks about the interior of the Stryker. "Anyone know what that means?"

Bolton does, and by the way Joshua stiffened when Tony said that, Bolton believes Joshua does too. Again, Bolton really wishes he knew who the hell Joshua was.

"I'm sure Haley can tell you what it means," Bolton says. "She served."

"If you don't know, then I ain't gonna tell ya," Haley snaps at Bolton.

The sat phone stops ringing.

"Finally," Ginevra says. "That was starting to give me a head—"

The sat phone rings three times. Silence.

Bolton waits, his eyes on Joshua.

"Weird," Halpern says.

The sat phone rings twice. Silence.

"Uh, Mark?" Jeremy says. "Maybe we should let Bolton answer it."

"You going chicken now?" Ginevra snaps at him.

The sat phone rings three times. Silence.

"Last chance," Bolton says, his eyes never leaving Joshua.

"Last chance?" Halpern does his little chuckle and eases back into his seat. "Says the man locked in the back."

The sat phone rings one single time. Silence.

The Stryker slows to a stop.

"What's wrong?" Halpern asks, leaning forward to peer out of the windshield. "Road looks good. Why'd you stop?"

"Give me the sat phone," Joshua says.

Bolton is transfixed.

"What? No," Halpern replies. "The sat phone stays in my hands."

"Give me the sat phone," Joshua says again. Same tone, same inflection.

"What's going on?" Haley asks.

"Yeah, what's your deal, Joshua?" Jeremy asks.

"Three, two, three, one," Bolton says.

Joshua holds up a single finger. "I have this, Sergeant."

"Understood," Bolton says.

"Have this? Have what?" Halpern snarls. "What's wrong with you? Get this vehicle moving so we can make our date with a safe life in a bunker."

"You will give me the sat phone now, Mark," Joshua says. "I won't ask again."

"Who the fuck do you—?" Halpern starts but can't finish because he's too busy choking on his crushed trachea.

Bolton didn't even see Joshua move. No one did. That's why it takes a couple seconds for Jeremy, Ginevra, and Haley to catch on to what just happened. By the time they do, it's too late.

Joshua opens the driver's door and jumps out.

"Mark?" Jeremy calls. "Oh, shit, he can't breathe!"

The Stryker's side door is yanked open and Joshua grabs Jeremy by the leg and pulls him straight out of the vehicle. It's not a graceful exit, and Jeremy's head makes contact with every hard surface on his way to the road.

There's a sickening *thunk,* then Joshua climbs inside the Stryker and reaches for Ginevra. She tries to scoot away from him, but there's nowhere to go. Ginevra kicks and kicks, but Joshua gets her ankle and repeats the same rough removal he performed on Jeremy.

"I'll fucking shoot you!" Haley says, trying to get her long rifle up to her shoulder and aimed at Joshua.

Bolton whistles.

Haley, not being the trained soldier she lied about being, turns and looks at Bolton. All she ends up seeing is the blade of a knife shoved through her right eye as Bolton slams his body against the chicken wire hard enough to bend it the distance needed to get to the woman.

"Chicken wire," Bolton mutters before looking at the side door.

Joshua is standing there, his eyes on Bolton.

"Can you get out, or do I need to open the back hatch?" Joshua asks as he leans in, grabs Haley's corpse, and pulls it from the vehicle.

"I got it," Bolton says and shoves against the chicken wire. It pops free after a couple of seconds and Bolton crawls through the gap and into the main part of the vehicle. He scrambles up front to the passenger's seat just as Joshua hops back into the driver's seat.

Halpern is still in the passenger's seat, his eyes bulging as he slowly suffocates.

"This could have gone a lot differently," Bolton says to Halpern before reaching across him to open the passenger's door.

Bolton shoves the still-choking Halpern out onto the road, takes his place, and pulls the door shut.

"Sergeant Connor Bolton, United States Army," Bolton says as Joshua starts the vehicle up and gets it moving again. "And you are?"

"Off the books," Joshua states.

"Which agency?" Bolton asks.

"Off the books," Joshua states again.

"Got it," Bolton says. "Except, the books don't exist anymore, which makes us all off the books. You killed three people just now, and one is still choking to death, so I'd like to know who I'm riding with."

Joshua doesn't respond.

"Come on, man," Bolton says. "The old ways are gone."

"All of them," Joshua says.

"Agencies? All of them?"

"All of them."

"Is your name really Joshua?"

"It is."

"Good. Call me Connor."

"I prefer Bolton."

"Bolton works just as well."

"You'll want to call Tony back and find out why they're leaving."

"He said aliens."

"He did."

They sit quietly for a few seconds.

"I don't think he's joking," Bolton says.

"I know he's not joking," Joshua responds. "The kid isn't a joker."

"I should check in with the White House first," Bolton says.

"They'll slow us down," Joshua says. "Tony first."

"I know you're used to working off the books, but I'm not," Bolton says. "I have a duty to the President of the United States."

"You have a duty to your family," Joshua says. "Terrie Morgan is part of your family, right? And she's in the bunker with Tony. Call Tony."

"Not the response I was expecting," Bolton says and looks at the radio, then the sat phone, then back to the radio.

He picks up the handset.

———

"Hello, Sergeant Bolton," Tony says. "I'm glad Mark Halpern let you speak to me."

"Halpern isn't with us anymore," Bolton replies, his voice crackly with static. "It's just me and Joshua."

"Good," Tony says instantly. "Mark Halpern was in the way of ours and your safety. Please say hello to Joshua for me."

"He says hi back," Bolton says.

"Joshua does not say hi," Tony says.

"Okay, he says hello Tony," Bolton says.

"That sounds more like Joshua," Tony says.

"Listen, Tony, you were talking about…aliens?" Bolton asks.

"I was," Tony says. "But Terrie is here and would like to speak to you."

"Uh, yeah, maybe that's a good idea," Bolton says.

Terrie hobbles over to the workbench and takes the handset from Tony. She gives Tony a look and he frowns.

"May I use your stool?" she asks.

"Yes," Tony says and gets up.

But he doesn't go far. He moves to the other stool at the workbench and starts checking his device.

"Connor?" Terrie asks.

"Here, Terrie," Bolton replies. "Are you alright?"

"We're fine, Connor," Terrie says and rests her forehead in her free palm. "Or as well as people can be when faced with the possibility of extraterrestrial life and the extinction of the human race."

"I'm thinking you start at the beginning," Bolton says with a laugh.

Tony looks over and sees Terrie smiling widely. He thinks it's the first true smile he's seen on the woman's face.

While Terrie fills Bolton in on everything they've been told, Tony focuses on his work. It's a better device than the one connected to the radio Terrie is using. That one allowed him to contact others with working shortwave radios even though his radio isn't shortwave. But the device he's working on now can contact anyone or anything with a communication device.

He's tested all the circuits and now all he has to do is load in the operating system.

"Hand me that phone," Tony says to Terrie, who's still busy speaking to Bolton. "I asked you nicely, so please hand me that phone."

"Hold on," Terrie says. "What do you need, Tony?"

"That phone," Tony says and points at a disassembled iPhone that looks like it's seen better days. "Now, please."

Terrie hesitates, then hands the phone to Tony.

"Thank you," Tony says after a pause.

"You're welcome, Tony," Terrie says, then returns to her conversation with Bolton.

Tony does a couple more tests, then he connects the phone to the device by a convoluted tangle of wires.

The phone powers up and a single icon appears on the screen.

Tony presses his finger to the icon and the device before him powers up and starts to hum almost imperceptibly. Tony smiles.

"It works," Tony says.

"Hold on," Terrie says and lowers the handset. "What works?"

"My communication device," Tony says. "I've combined my innovative hardware design with the app I was supposed to build for Herschel Industries."

Tony gestures at the walls around them.

"It uses the bunker's metal walls as a booster for transmission," Tony says. "It can do this with any significant amount of metal. Like a vehicle."

Terrie stares at him for a second, then places the handset to her mouth. "Hold on, Connor."

"Why are you looking at me like that?" Tony asks. "I've done nothing wrong. This is a good creation. This is ingenious. My mother used to say I was a genius and I create ingenious devices. This is one of them."

"Are you telling me that you didn't know this would work for sure before you told the White House you already had a working device?" Terrie asks.

"I knew it would work," Tony says. "I wasn't lying."

"I'm not so sure about that," Terrie says with a smile. "Good job, Tony."

"Thank you," Tony says. "You may return to your conversation with Sergeant Bolton."

Terrie smirks and does just that.

After a few more tests, Tony gets up and leaves the room. He finds Krissy dozing on the couch. He glances over at the far wall and frowns.

"The wall is leaking again," Tony says.

Krissy opens her eyes, fixes them on Tony, then pushes up to her feet with more than a few exhausted grunts and curses. She shuffles over to the wall, looks at the water pooling here and there, shrugs, curses some more, and shuffles back to the couch.

"You didn't dry the seam area properly before applying the sealant," Tony says. "You should do it over."

"Why?" Krissy asks. "Aren't we leaving soon? Hiking our asses to Wyoming so we can live the rest of our lives in a giant bunker instead of a tiny bunker? All because aliens are not just coming to destroy Earth, but because aliens already fucking live here!"

"Yes, but you didn't do the job correctly and you should do it again," Tony says.

"Bro, you need to fuck off and let me rest," Krissy says.

"I was going to tell you that I can now communicate with the world, but I won't tell you that anymore," Tony says.

"You just did, genius," Krissy says.

Tony opens his mouth to speak, closes it, scrunches up his face, then sighs.

"Yes. I did," Tony says.

"Is Terrie talking to the soldier guy?" Krissy asks.

"Yes, she is," Tony replies. "I'm hungry."

"Then go get yourself—"

Krissy is interrupted by Biscuit suddenly barking at full, furious volume in the direction of the bunker's main hatch.

Tony and Krissy freeze.

Then they're a flurry of motion as the sound of wrenching metal echoes through the bunker.

"One of them has opened the outside hatch!" Tony shouts.

"Terrie!" Krissy screams.

"Well…that's a big fucking shuttle," Dr. Probst says as she and Lowell, with the Ebony Man perpetually in tow, stand at an observation window and look down at a shuttle set into an upright launch position within a massive launch bay. "How many people do you think that holds?"

Lowell, cleaned up and dressed in a generic facility jumpsuit, wipes away years of dust on the observation window and presses his forehead against the thick glass.

"Only needs to hold one person and one dipshit alien," Lowell says, shaking Ebony Man by the head. The being groans. "What's that, Mr. Licorice? You can't wait to fly the friendly skies and go see some fucking penguins? Me too!"

"You enjoy tormenting it, don't you?" Dr. Probst asks.

Lowell steps back from the window and starts to argue, then shuts his mouth. He looks down at the helpless being.

"More than I should," Lowell says. "Yeah. Fuck…"

Lowell drops the being and Dr. Probst gasps.

"Don't let it go!" Dr. Probst cries. "It's still a monster!"

"Right," Lowell says and takes hold of the Ebony Man's skull again. "So, keep a firm grip, but stop being a bully?"

"I wouldn't call you a bully. The thing is evil," Dr. Probst says. "But don't lose your humanity."

"Doc, that got lost a long time ago," Lowell says. "It wasn't until all this shit went down that I started to find it again."

"Jesus, that's sad," Dr. Probst says.

"I like how you don't sugarcoat things, Cheryl," Lowell says.

They continue to stare at the shuttle.

"Where do we start?" Dr. Probst asks.

"Right here," Lowell says. He frowns at Dr. Probst. "I swear this isn't bullying. It's kinda the only way I can extract accurate info from this asshole."

Lowell shoves his hand deep inside the Ebony Man's head.

"Don't worry, he doesn't feel it," Lowell says. The Ebony Man moans. "Much."

Lowell's eyes roll back in his skull and he hums to himself for several seconds. Then his eyes return to normal, his hand withdraws from the Ebony Man's head, and he gives Dr. Probst a big smile.

"Alright, so I have the exact coordinates up here now," Lowell says and taps his temple. "Now, let's see if I can reprogram the shuttle to go where I need it to go."

"One of us should go with you," Dr. Probst says.

Lowell gives her a surprised look. One that is only matched by Dr. Probst's own surprised look.

"Volunteering?" Lowell asks.

"I, uh, I..." Dr. Probst stammers.

"Just messing with you, Doc," Lowell says. "This trip is meant for only me and Mr. Licorice."

"Stop calling me that..." the Ebony Man whispers. "You disgusting freak..."

"Oh, we're gonna have the best road trip ever, Mr. Licorice," Lowell says. "Don't you worry."

"I'm still fuzzy on the purpose of this trip," Dr. Probst says. "You're going to find a monster bigger than the Yellowstone monster?"

"Kaiju," Lowell says, holding up a finger. "Gotta be scientific, Doc, and call them by the proper name."

"I don't know if Japanese monster movies count as science," Dr. Probst says.

"You got any other science that explains the giant brutes?" Lowell asks. Dr. Probst only blinks. "Exactly."

They turn back to the shuttle.

"How do we get down there?" Dr. Probst asks.

"Follow me," Lowell says and leads the way, dragging the Ebony Man behind him.

They leave the observation area and Lowell shoves a door open to a stairwell.

"It's gonna be a hike," Lowell says and starts down the stairs.

At first he lets the Ebony Man's body slam against every single stair, until Dr. Probst gives him a look of disapproval.

"Sorry," Lowell says.

He lifts the Ebony Man up enough that the impacts on the stairs aren't so brutal.

"That's as good as it gets," Lowell says. "I'm not playing sack of potatoes with this asshole, so you can forget me carrying him."

"I give up," Dr. Probst says.

"Do you...?" the Ebony Man mutters. "Surrender to me, primate, and I will show you—"

Slam.

"Oops," Lowell says after letting the Ebony Man's head impact with the stairwell's railing. "Clumsy me."

They reach the end of the stairs and the only door other than the one they entered through above.

Lowell opens the door and drags the Ebony Man out onto a massive catwalk that connects directly to a hatch set in the side of the shuttle. Dr. Probst follows, her eyes wide as she takes in the huge launch chamber.

"Did the government build this?" Dr. Probst asks. "It's more advanced than anything I've seen from NASA or the private rocket and space exploration companies."

"The government did build it," Lowell says. "But they had a little help from some schematics stored in the facility's database. Some of this tech they leaked to NASA, the stuff they could fully understand and control, but there's a good amount of this ship that's just straight up out of this world."

"And you can fly it?" Dr. Probst asks, mimicking Lowell's tap of the temple. "Because of what's in your head?"

"Fly it? Fuck no," Lowell says. "I may have alien knowledge, but that doesn't mean I suddenly became the right stuff. The shuttle is on autopilot. Once we get the coordinates switched to Antarctica, then that's where it'll take us and nowhere else."

"How are you going to get back?" Dr. Probst asks.

"That part is no problemo," Lowell says. "I'll walk."

"Oh," Dr. Probst responds.

"Don't worry, Doc, I got it under control," Lowell says. "This guy will get me inside the facility, then I take it from there."

"What will you do with it?" Dr. Probst asks.

"Not sure yet," Lowell says. "I do like the taste of licorice."

"Dear God…" Dr. Probst gasps.

"Kidding!" Lowell says. "I sure as shit won't be eating this guy. There're plenty of the flying things and the cattle out there to snack on once I'm Mr. Big. No need to chomp on Mr. Licorice."

"Please tell me you aren't going to call yourself Mr. Big," Dr. Probst says.

They reach the shuttle's hatch and Lowell presses a hand against the metal. The hatch pops inward and slides to the side. Without hesitation, Lowell steps inside. Dr. Probst follows him.

"I'm not Mr. Big," Lowell explains as they orient themselves to the shuttle's vertical position. "The kaiju is Mr. Big."

Everything is on end, but there are plenty of handholds and footholds set into the walls that the two can make their way up to the cockpit.

"The kaiju is Mr. Big, but you aren't? How is that possible?" Dr. Probst asks. "Does it have its own consciousness too?"

"What? No, nothing like that," Lowell answers. "Think of the kaiju more as flesh vehicles than actual living creatures. Yeah, sure, they are living creatures too, but empty living creatures just waiting for a consciousness to fill their big, bad, kaiju brains and take over."

"What if they don't want to be taken over?" Dr. Probst asks.

"Jesus Christ, Doc, don't jinx things," Lowell says when they finally reach the cockpit. "I'm kinda playing it by ear, so let's not add to the insanity of this shit, okay?"

"Sorry," Dr. Probst says. She looks at the four seats set into two rows in the cockpit, all oriented on their backs, facing up. "Now what?"

"Now I need you to find navigation," Lowell says.

"You don't know which station is navigation?" Dr. Probst asks with alarm.

"Playing it by ear, Doc," Lowell responds.

"Okay..." Dr. Probst says and starts looking at the different sets of controls next to each seat.

Lowell drags the Ebony Man to the rear-most seat, tosses him into it, and straps him down. Tight.

"I know you can slime melt your way out of that," Lowell says to the Ebony Man, "but don't. I'd hate to have to ground you from TV privileges for a week, Mr. Licorice. So behave, okay?"

"I will destroy you," the Ebony Man croaks.

"Right. You be you," Lowell says and gives the straps one more hard tug.

"I think this is it," Dr. Probst says, her hands hovering over a control console. "Should I try to turn the instruments on?"

"Nope," Lowell says and gently moves Dr. Probst out of his way.

He places both hands on the console and the station comes to life. As does the entire shuttle.

Dr. Probst grips a seat's armrest and steadies herself as the shuttle shudders with power.

"Alright. Let's see," Lowell mutters as he keeps his hands pressed to the navigation console. "If I think this, then think that, then think this again..."

The console lights up and a detailed map of the planet comes to life on the monitor. Lowell taps at the monitor until the image dials in tight to Antarctica. But as soon as he lifts his finger, the image switches to a small island in the South Pacific.

"Shit," Lowell says. "The stupid thing wants to default to its original coordinates."

"How are you doing that?" Dr. Probst asks. "Interfacing with the shuttle?"

"No fucking clue," Lowell replies. "I just am."

He tries again, but the second he lifts his finger, the default location returns.

"You may have to stay in contact with it the entire journey," Dr. Probst says.

"Shit," Lowell responds. He wants to look over his shoulder at the Ebony Man, but he restrains himself. "That's going to make things tricky."

"Can you maintain control of the shuttle and…it?" Dr. Probst asks.

"Don't really have much of a choice," Lowell says. "I'll sit right here and just keep hanging on."

"What if he makes a move on you?" Dr. Probst asks.

"What did I say about not jinxing me, Doc? Fucking A," Lowell snaps.

"You brought me with you to help," Dr. Probst snaps back, "so I'm helping. You have to think this through, Lowell."

"I'm trying!" Lowell shouts.

"Try harder!" Dr. Probst shouts back.

Anger fills Lowell's eyes, but he takes a deep breath and calms himself.

"You're right," he says. "Thanks for keeping it real."

"I don't know what else I can do," Dr. Probst says. "I'm a geologist, not a rocket scientist."

Lowell grins. "Speaking of being a geologist. There's another reason I wanted you here. We need to talk."

"Aren't we talking now?" Dr. Probst says.

"Yeah," Lowell says. "But we need to talk talk. I have something to show you."

"Where?" Dr. Probst asks.

Lowell's grin turns apologetic as he holds up a single finger.

"I promise it won't hurt," he says.

"No you do not, sir!" Dr. Probst snaps. "You're not putting thoughts in my head!"

"Trust me," Lowell responds. "When I show this to you, you'll know what you need to do. After I leave, it will be the main mission for you and Lu and Kyle in this facility."

Dr. Probst glares at Lowell.

"Please," Lowell says. "Trust me."

"Shit," Dr. Probst says. "What are you going to show me?"

"What else would I show a geologist?" Lowell responds. "Rocks."

"I hate you," Dr. Probst says and closes her eyes.

"No, you don't," Lowell says and presses his finger to Dr. Probst's forehead.

She gasps, goes stiff, then slowly relaxes.

"Oh, my," she whispers as her eyes open. "I see what you mean."

"So you understand how important this is?" Lowell asks.

"Yes," she says. "I'm sorry I doubted you."

A smile plays at her lips as she rubs her eyes then looks directly at Lowell.

"You were right," she says. "You need a geologist. Bad."

"Told ya," Lowell says and takes a deep breath. "Well… kinda time for me to go."

"What? Now?" Dr. Probst responds.

"No time to waste," Lowell says. "I mean, I could really use a fucking nap, but I guess I'll sleep when I'm dead."

"Who's the jinx now?" Dr. Probst says.

"Okay. Get out," Lowell says but with his trademark smirk firmly in place.

Dr. Probst hesitates, then gives Lowell a hug. She quickly pulls away and smiles sheepishly.

"Never hugged a murderer before," she says, making sure she puts a smirk on her face too.

"That you know of," Lowell says and gives Dr. Probst a pat on the shoulder. "They're everywhere, you know."

"Jesus, Lowell…" she says and shakes her head. "Good luck."

"Thanks."

Lowell waits for the sound of the shuttle hatch closing tightly before he turns and looks at the Ebony Man.

"You might survive this," Lowell says, "if you do exactly what I tell you to do. One slip, and I put you down. Are we clear?"

"We're clear, primate," the Ebony Man says.

"Right…" Lowell says.

He takes a seat, gets himself strapped in tight, then reaches out and places a hand on the navigation console. Once the Antarctica coordinates are displayed, Lowell places his other hand against the shuttle's floor, orienting his body in a weird sci-fi approximation of the game Twister.

The shuttle's engines roar to life.

"I really hope I don't shit my pants on takeoff," he says.

———

A countdown blares facility-wide, and Dr. Probst makes it back to the main control room just before the computerized voice hits three.

"Where's Kyle?" Dr. Probst asks Lu as she takes a seat in the control room and stares up at the main monitor. The shuttle bay fills the screen.

"Sleeping like a baby," Lu says. "I doubt even this launch will wake him up."

"I've only had a taste of something shoved in my head, so I can only imagine what he's going through," Dr. Probst says.

The facility shakes and rumbles as the countdown hits zero and the shuttle's engines come fully to life. The screen is filled with fire and smoke and the outline of the shuttle lifting off.

Then like that it's gone, and the rumbling and shaking stop.

"Did you say you had something put into your head too?" Lu asks, wary.

"Yep. Lowell shared something with me," Dr. Probst says, "and for the first time since I was forced to jump out of a jet over what turned out to be a monster nest, I actually feel like my skills will be put to good use."

The view on the main monitor switches from the shuttle bay to corridor after corridor, tunnel after tunnel, chamber after chamber of concrete.

"Jesus, this place is way bigger than I thought," Lu says.

"You have no idea," Dr. Probst responds, still searching.

"What are you looking for?" Lu asks. She rolls her chair up next to Dr. Probst's. "Where is that?"

"Deep," Dr. Probst responds. "These are chambers and tunnels under the Substance."

"Under? This facility actually goes under the Substance?" Lu asks.

"I'll say it again, you have no idea," Dr. Probst says. "Technically, this facility should be connected to all of the other facilities. But it's not because of the Ebony Man."

"Connected to the other facilities? That'd mean some tunnels are thousands of miles long," Lu says.

"Not exactly. It's complicated," Dr. Probst replies. "Luckily, we won't have to travel far. As long as I can find the right tunnel, we can get things back the way they're supposed to be."

"And how do we do that?" Lu asks.

Dr. Probst stops scrolling through video feeds of the many, many tunnels, chambers, and corridors that make up the Wyoming facility.

"Here we are," she says and smiles at Lu. "Any chance you know how to work a jackhammer?"

"Um… yeah, I do," Lu says. "Why?"

"We've got a vein to find," Dr. Probst says and points at the monitor. "And it's behind a few dozen feet of concrete."

"Great," Lu says.

"It will be if Lowell's plan works," Dr. Probst says and gets up. "We better get started. This could take a while."

————

"At full speed, with us taking turns to drive and stops to refuel, it'll take us," Bolton says from the passenger seat, "three days minimum to reach the coast. Better than a week but still slow. We have to go faster."

Joshua's response is to raise an eyebrow. That eyebrow raise says it all. Bolton slumps back in his seat.

"Exactly. How do we go faster?" Bolton says. "Gotta work the problem…"

"Let me know when you figure it out," Joshua says, his eyes on the demolished roadway before them.

The Stryker they're in was designed to crawl up over anything, which it proves time and time again as it climbs massive hunks of asphalt and crunches over fallen tree after fallen tree. Bolton knows that if they could keep a sixty-mile-per-hour pace, which is the top speed of the vehicle, they could make up some time.

But the apocalyptic landscape is not cooperating with their wishes, so they only manage to average about thirty miles per hour at the most.

"We need aircraft," Bolton says.

Joshua snorts.

"Stop the vehicle," Bolton orders.

Joshua gives him a questioning look but doesn't stop the vehicle.

"I'm not kidding," Bolton snaps. "Stop!"

Joshua rolls his eyes and slows the vehicle to a stop.

"Explain," Joshua says.

"My original mission was to head to Colorado Springs," Bolton says.

"I know," Joshua replies.

"There are military facilities there," Bolton says.

"I know," Joshua repeats.

"One of them is the Diamondback facility," Bolton says. "I was supposed to get down to Colorado Springs, hopefully meet up with survivors, and maybe get armed drones into the air."

"Armed drones? To kill the monsters with," Joshua says.

"In theory," Bolton responds. "Lasers. But if we skip the bases and head straight to Diamondback, they may have something. They might have experimental tech in development that can help us."

"And you want to go down there instead of going to Puget

Sound?" Joshua asks, looking skeptical. "The radio the kid has is more important."

"I'm not saying we abandon that mission," Bolton says. "I'm saying that Diamondback has lots of different tech in development, not just weapons."

"Aircraft," Joshua says.

"Aircraft," Bolton says.

"Understood," Joshua says and begins the tedious process of turning the massive vehicle around on a surface that was once a highway and is now a ghost of a road.

It takes them close to thirty minutes just to get the Stryker pointing the way they want.

"Do you think Diamondback will be manned?" Joshua asks.

"I hope so," Bolton says. "We won't know until we get there."

"Big risk," Joshua says.

"I know," Bolton replies, "but it's a risk we need to take."

"We'll be wasting time if we get to Diamondback and there's no aircraft," Joshua states. "Your family will be left stranded."

"I know," Bolton says with a sigh. "I know…"

SEVEN

"Tony, get the rifles!" Terrie yells over the deafening impacts against the bunker's internal hatch. "Krissy, gather as much gear as possible! We're getting out of here!"

"How?" Krissy shouts.

"I don't know!" Terrie yells.

"I need my device!" Tony shouts.

Terrie starts to argue but knows how important that device is.

"Get it!" she shouts. "I'll get the rifles!"

"What gear am I getting?" Krissy asks.

"Food, water, clothes, respirators, sleeping bags, tents, anything we need to survive out there!" Terrie responds.

"*It* is out there!"

"Well, *it* is about to be in here, so less arguing and more gathering, young lady!" Terrie yells. "Tony!"

"I'll hurry!" Tony shouts from the corridor to his room.

Terrie flinches at the booming thuds coming from the main hatch, then races as fast as she's able to the armory.

Small arms are useless against the monsters. But the monsters aren't the only threat, so she chooses three Beretta 9mm semiautomatic handguns. Terrie grabs several boxes of 9mm ammunition and four extra magazines per handgun.

For the monsters, she snags two crates of grenades and a Barrett .50 caliber sniper rifle with plenty of ammunition. She also takes an assortment of knives, paracord, zip ties, a hatchet, three machetes, three first aid kits, three gun belts with holsters, and a collapsible shovel.

All of it gets stored in three duffel bags except for the Barrett, which she straps to her back. She doesn't like the weight it puts on her legs, but she has no choice. It won't fit in a duffel unless collapsed and she knows it'll be just a pointless hunk of metal and plastic in that state. So on her back it goes.

Of course, there's no way for Terrie to carry the three duffel bags by herself. She moves quickly from the armory to one of the supply rooms and hunts desperately for a cart or wheelbarrow or something with wheels.

She finds exactly what she needs in a collapsible cart with four huge rubber tires. It takes only the release of three latches and the push of a button and the cart is fully formed and useable.

Terrie is about to leave the supply room when something catches her attention on a shelf by the door. She pauses, opens the translucent plastic crate, and almost cries.

A self-inflating life raft with four folding oars.

In the cart it goes. It could literally be the life raft that saves them from a horrible death at the tentacles of the monsters above.

Monsters that are still knocking at the hatch.

Using the cart as support, Terrie tosses the crutches on top of the raft and wheels the cart back to the armory. She struggles to get the duffels inside, manages the job, and wheels the cart back to the main room.

Biscuit is barking his dog-wolf head off while Krissy hurries around gathering anything and everything that looks useful.

"I'm ready to depart," Tony says. His hands are empty but there's a large backpack on his back. "It's a dry bag, so the radio and device will be safe."

"Help me, you moron," Krissy snaps. She has an armful of food boxes that are quickly on the floor as Biscuit lets out a howl so loud it almost overpowers the sounds of menace coming from outside the hatch. "Motherfucker!"

"Language!" Terrie snaps. "Tony, help her load supplies into this cart."

"That was Roy's hunting cart," Tony says.

"Roy won't be needing it anymore," Terrie says. It's gruff and unkind, but she doesn't have time to soothe his feelings right now. "Speaking of Roy, your grandfather said there was another way out of this bunker. Where, Tony?"

"Another way out?" Tony replies. "I do not believe we can go that way."

"We don't have a choice, Tony," Terrie snaps. "How do we get out of here?"

The thudding at the door grows in intensity and Biscuit's barks, growls, and warning howls intensify with the attacks.

"We don't have much time, Tony," Terrie says. "How do we get out of here?"

"That way," Tony says and points to the far wall of the main room.

The far wall that is still leaking water through the seams.

"You have to be fucking kidding me," Krissy says.

"Zip your profane lips, miss," Terrie says.

Krissy holds up her hands in surrender, but her eyes burn with defiance and fear.

"That way?" Terrie asks. "How far is it before the exit?"

"I don't know how far," Tony says. "I've never measured it."

"Have you walked it before?" Terrie asks.

"Yes."

"How long did it take you to walk it?"

"Fifteen minutes."

"Slow or fast walk?"

"Normal walk."

"Then with gear and the state my legs are in, it'll probably take us thirty minutes," Terrie says. She eyes the hatch, sees the dents that have started to appear in the metal. "It'll be close. Come on."

"Come on? That's it? Come on?" Krissy says. "Where are we going to go, Terrie?"

"Somewhere else," Terrie says. "We were leaving the bunker anyway. The timeframe has been moved up is all."

"And if the things are on the other side of this secret exit?" Krissy asks.

Terrie pats the cart. "Then they'll want to get out of our way."

Krissy glares for a second, then shakes her head and laughs.

"Might have been easier if that shark had eaten me too," Krissy says.

"We have to cross open water," Tony says. "I can push you in. I'm certain a shark will be willing to finish the job."

Terrie and Krissy both stare at Tony for a moment, then burst out laughing.

"What did I say?" Tony asks.

"Show us the way out, Tony," Terrie says.

Tony shrugs and walks to the far wall. He kneels down and hunts along the base of the wall. When he finds what he's looking for, he gives the wall a hard smack and a slim panel pops free. Tony opens the panel and grabs a handle, then yanks hard.

The sound of metal on metal joins the cacophony of the monster attacks and Biscuit's never-ending barking. A third of the wall is shifting to the side.

But before the wall is even an inch of the way open, water starts streaming into the main room.

"Shit!" Terrie shouts.

"Language!" Krissy responds.

"Help me get this open!" Terrie yells and starts shoving supplies out of the way in the cart to get to the raft. "Now!"

"We need that stuff!" Krissy shouts.

"And we'll take it, but we need this first!" Terrie yells and smacks the plastic crate at the bottom of the cart. "And we need it now!"

The wall continues to open, although it struggles against the weight and volume of water pressing against it from the other side. In seconds, Terrie, Tony, and Krissy are standing ankle-deep in salt water. Biscuit, without missing a bark, leaps onto the couch.

Krissy and Tony cram supplies into their arms, keeping everything from getting wet from the continually rising water. As soon as it's clear, Terrie yanks the top of the crate off and pulls out the raft. She turns it this way and that until she finds the pull tab.

Terrie pulls the tab and tosses the raft toward the wall.

The raft is already inflating by the time it splashes into the water.

"Everything in the raft!" Terrie orders. "Keep the duffel bags dry!"

Krissy shakes her head but doesn't argue and throws the supplies she's holding into the raft, then turns quickly and fetches a duffel.

"Shit, what's in this?" Krissy asks.

"Probably grenades," Terrie replies, "so don't be rough."

Krissy gulps and places the duffel carefully into the almost fully inflated raft. Tony follows suit, and by the time the water is halfway up their calves, they have everything loaded.

"How deep is it going to get?" Krissy asks.

"Deep," Terrie says as a rush of salt water flows into the main room.

They're now thigh-deep in water and Biscuit is no longer barking at the hatch, but barking at the water that has come up over the couch cushions and is swirling around his furry legs.

Terrie grabs the cart and shoves it through the water.

"That's gonna slow us down," Krissy says.

"If I don't have something to hang onto, then I'm never going to make it," Terrie says. "The water is too deep for me to wade on my own."

"Grab the raft," Krissy says.

"No, you two need to hang onto the raft and get it moving," Terrie says. "If I fall behind, just keep going. I'll try to catch up."

Krissy gives Terrie a suspicious look.

"I'm not sacrificing myself or anything like that," Terrie says. "But I won't be the reason we all drown. Now start pushing that raft!"

Krissy and Tony do just that.

"Biscuit!" Terrie yells. "In! Now!"

Biscuit continues to bark at the imploding hatch.

"BISCUIT!" Terrie roars.

The hybrid shakes its head, growls low, then jumps into the water and paddles over to Terrie. She struggles to help the dog-wolf climb into the cart, but she manages it, and Biscuit ends up sitting in several inches of seawater at the bottom of the cart while Terrie starts shoving.

Terrie follows Krissy, Tony, and the raft through the opening in the wall and down a pitch-dark tunnel. The tunnel is just an extension of the Quonset hut-style corrugated metal, same as the main bunker, only slightly narrower.

It's slow going for sure.

Terrie is out of breath after only a few yards and she leans more and more on the cart, her legs draining of strength with each step. But she can't quit. She has two teenagers, a still-barking dog-wolf, and herself to save.

Quitting is not an option.

"How much farther?" Krissy shouts. "The water's still rising."

She isn't wrong. The water level slowly reaches Terrie's hips then up over her waist. Biscuit is basically clinging to the top of the crate and staring hard at Terrie.

"I know, boy," Terrie says between gasps of air. "We'll get you out of the water soon."

On they trudge, and on the water rises.

"I can't keep going," Terrie calls out. "I'll rest a minute. You two go on and I'll be right behind."

Krissy looks back over her shoulder and shakes her head.

"Jesus Christ," she says and lets go of the raft. She wades up to Terrie. "Come on. I got you."

"I don't appreciate you taking the Lord's name in vain," Terrie says.

"Do you appreciate drowning?" Krissy asks. Terrie doesn't answer. "Then shut it and move."

Terrie starts to reply but purses her lips, nods, and allows Krissy to help her over to the raft. She gratefully grabs onto a side handle and lets the flow of the water and the buoyancy of the raft take the weight off her legs.

"Now you, you crazy mutt," Krissy says as she power-shoves the cart right next to the raft.

It takes Biscuit a couple tries, but he manages to scramble up into the raft where he looks considerably more comfortable. So comfortable that he starts his thunderous barks all over again.

"Damn, he's loud," Krissy says.

Terrie glances at her then frowns.

"Where's the cart?" Terrie asks.

"I broke it down," Krissy says.

"We'll need it when we hit land!" Terrie exclaims.

"I didn't leave it behind," Krissy replies. "It's too bulky to shove through chest-deep water. Guess what? Broken down, the tires float."

Terrie is a good deal taller than Krissy, and while the water is only past her stomach now, it's hit Krissy's chest. Terrie looks back over the top of Krissy's head to see the cart flat and floating, pulled along by the string that should be holding Krissy's sweats up.

"Just my undies," Krissy says when Terrie's attention returns to her.

"Alright," Terrie says. "Speed is what's important now. Pants later."

"And living," Tony says.

"That's why we need speed," Terrie says. "The water is high enough that we can probably climb in and paddle."

"We should wait," Tony says. "The exit is close, and we cannot be inside the raft when we reach it."

"Why?" Krissy asks.

"It's a hatch like in the bunker," Tony says. "It'll be hard to get the raft through while inflated, so we'll need to—"

His words are cut off by Biscuit's increased barking, which is in turn overpowered by a nightmarish wrenching noise that echoes from the bunker's main room.

"Oh, no," Terrie says. "It's in! Push faster!"

Krissy and Tony both make an exhausted grunting noise, but neither complain.

They all push faster.

———

"Do we have comms yet?" VanderVoort shouts. No one responds. "I guess that's my answer."

"We lost contact with the Puget Sound bunker," a tech says.

"Christ," VanderVoort says as she studies the monitors connected to the other facilities. All are either static or fixed on blank walls.

Or not quite blank walls. Some walls have smears of blood across them from the deaths of the facility doctors after the surge through the Substance.

"How'd he do that?" VanderVoort mutters.

"Do what?" Director Miles asks. He hands VanderVoort a cup of tea. He has yet another mojito in his hand.

"The Ebony Man," VanderVoort replies, taking a sip of the tea. "Thank you. This hits the spot."

"The Ebony Man, what? Kill everyone?" Director Miles asks. "Did he?"

"What do you mean? Who else did it?" VanderVoort responds. "You heard Lowell."

"Maybe no one did it," Director Miles says. "You've seen surges through the Substance before. It's deadly on its own. The Ebony Man's escape from his neck of the Substance may have caused a chain reaction through the rest of the Substance, which ended up killing everyone even remotely close to it. Wrong place, wrong time."

"Wrong place…" VanderVoort thinks for a minute. "Dr. Hall?"

"Yes, Ms. VanderVoort?" Dr. Hall says.

"Lowell said that the Wyoming bunker and the Antarctica bunker aren't connected to the rest of the bunkers," VanderVoort says.

"That's what he said, yes," Dr. Hall agrees.

"But I know for a fact that the Substance does connect to all facilities," VanderVoort continues. "This can't be disputed. I've seen it with my own eyes."

"If you say so," Dr. Hall replies. "What do you need from me?"

"If the Substance is connected, then what does Lowell mean when he says the two facilities aren't connected?" VanderVoort asks.

Dr. Hall looks about the Situation Room. All eyes are on him. He sighs.

"I have no idea," Dr. Hall says. "Maybe there's a different type of connection he's talking about."

"Ya think?" VanderVoort says and shakes her head at Dr. Hall. "Sorry. Let's work on what connection he could mean."

"Comms?" Alvarez suggests. "I assume each facility has our comms tech, but what about alien comms tech? The Wyoming and Antarctica facilities might be on a different channel or totally different tech or just disconnected altogether."

"That," VanderVoort says. "I like that. Continue."

"That's all I've got," Alvarez says.

"Going off his supposition, it could be possible that when the other facilities were created, they instituted a type of firewall against the Wyoming and Antarctica facilities," Dr. Hall adds, "in order to isolate them and keep the Ebony Man from exerting control over the other kaiju."

"That could be," VanderVoort says. "Which we could further suppose that if the other facilities have their full array of communications capabilities intact, then maybe they have a way to talk to others of their kind…out there."

VanderVoort points up, and everyone follows the gesture to the ceiling, then they turn their attention back to VanderVoort.

"Keep thinking on that," VanderVoort says, her eyes on Dr. Hall. "You're the SETI guy here."

Dr. Hall opens and closes his mouth like a gasping fish, then clamps his lips shut tight, nods, and turns back to his workstation where he begins typing furiously at a keyboard.

"Where are you going with this?" President Nance asks.

"We have threats here on Earth, but both Lowell and the Kyle kid say that a bigger threat is coming," VanderVoort says. "Maybe we should consider contacting them ourselves."

"To what ends?" President Nance asks.

"I haven't figured that out yet. Negotiations?" VanderVoort says. She turns to the remaining members of President Nance's inner circle. "That's your jobs, folks. You're the politicians and diplomats. Let's suppose we can get communications established with the extraterrestrials heading this way."

"If they actually are," Director Miles says. He gets an angry look from VanderVoort. "What? Just playing Devil's advocate here."

"Don't," VanderVoort says.

"No problem," Director Miles responds and nods at her cup. "More tea?"

"Please."

"I'll be right back."

"What would we say to aliens?" Joan asks.

"How the fuck should I know?' VanderVoort responds. "All of you sitting at that table get to figure that out. We also need to figure out how to get people into the empty facilities. They may be on foreign soil, but I'd like our people to take control, or we could end up just fighting amongst ourselves."

"I'll see what I can do about that," General Azoul says. "If we can get good ol' fashioned terrestrial comms back up."

"Still no word from the boy or Terrie Morgan?" VanderVoort asks. A tech shakes his head. "Great. In the meantime, I need to talk to Dr. Probst. Someone see if you can find her. She's obviously not in the main control room of the Wyoming facility."

———

"What are we doing again?" Lu asks as she puts a pair of safety goggles over her eyes and sets a hard hat on top of her head. "Rock hunting?"

"There's a vein of blue crystals somewhere behind this wall," Dr. Probst says as the two women stand in a very dark, except for the cart's halogen floodlights, concrete tunnel. "We need to expose that vein of crystals."

"Yep, that's why we have the jackhammer," Lu says, hooking a thumb over her shoulder at the huge power tool that's weighing down the back of the cart they rode in. "Why does that help us?"

"The other facilities have security measures in place to block all connections to this facility," Dr. Probst says. "But if I can connect to the vein, I may be able to study the harmonics of the blue crystal and see if we can override the security measures."

"You really think you can do that?" Lu asks.

"I have no clue," Dr. Probst says. "I won't know until I see the vein."

"This isn't going to be easy," Lu says. She turns to the jackhammer then turns back to the wall. "And it might bring this entire facility down on our heads."

"I doubt that," Dr. Probst says. "There are so many tunnels and load-bearing walls that I don't believe that..."

Dr. Probst stops talking when she sees the look on Lu's face.

"Considering all that's gone wrong? Then yes, it could bring the whole place down on us," Dr. Probst admits.

"As long as we're on the same page," Lu says. "Now, give me a hand with this jackhammer and the tripod."

The two women wrestle the jackhammer out of the cart and

walk-drag it over to the tunnel wall. They return and grab out a huge, iron tripod from the cart too. That's what was really weighing the cart down, and the small vehicle bounces upward slightly when the weight is removed.

They drag that over and take several minutes to get the tripod set up so they can then lift the jackhammer on top. Lu locks the power tool in place, sets the blade against the wall, and looks at Dr. Probst.

"Say when, Cheryl," Lu says.

"I don't know," Dr. Probst says. "I guess go for it."

Just before Lu starts the jackhammer up, there's a squawking from the cart.

"What's that?" Dr. Probst asks.

"Radio," Lu says and lets go of the jackhammer. It stays put in the tripod as she hurries over to the cart. She picks up the handset to the cart's small radio. "Yes?"

"Please hold for Ms. VanderVoort," a tech says from the radio.

"Please hold? I'm not some Hollywood douchebag producer," VanderVoort says over the tech. "Give me that. Who am I speaking with?"

"Lu Morgan," Lu replies. "Is this Ms. VanderVoort?"

"It is. May I speak with Dr. Probst?" VanderVoort asks.

"Hold on," Lu says and holds out the handset.

Dr. Probst takes it and frowns. Lu shrugs.

"This is Dr. Probst," Dr. Probst says.

"Good. I finally found you," VanderVoort says. "We tried every channel connected to that facility and I was starting to think you'd been eaten."

"Eaten?" Dr. Probst asks.

"A valid concern, considering," VanderVoort replies.

"We're down in one of the sub-level tunnels," Dr. Probst says.

"You are? What for?" VanderVoort asks.

Dr. Probst explains as much as she can of what Lowell showed her. VanderVoort laughs.

"It may sound funny, but I believe it'll work," Dr. Probst says, annoyed.

"No, no, sorry, Doctor," VanderVoort says. "I'm not laughing at the notion, but at the timing. It's exactly why I am calling. The information you gave us just confirms our theories. How certain are you that it will work, Dr. Probst?"

"I'm not certain at all," Dr. Probst says. "But while Lowell travels to Antarctica, there's nothing else for us to do here."

"Oh, I can find you some task if you need busy work," Vander-Voort says with a chuckle. "Just kidding. You stay on that task and report back as soon as you have something for me."

"Uh, yes, ma'am," Dr. Probst says. "Anything else?"

"Do you want something else?" VanderVoort replies.

"I do not," Dr. Probst says.

"Then get to work," VanderVoort says, and the radio goes quiet.

"She is something," Lu says. "Let's get to work like she said."

Lu grabs the jackhammer once more, starts it up, and takes aim at the wall. She shoves forward and concrete chips begin to fly. After several minutes, they've only made a few inches of progress.

"We should have brought food!" Dr. Probst shouts.

"What?" Lu yells back.

"Food! We should have brought food!" Dr. Probst shouts. "We're going to be down here for a while!"

"I left a note for Kyle!" Lu yells. "He can bring us something when we take a break!"

"Good thinking!" Dr. Probst says and stands back from the shower of concrete, her hand shielding her eyes even though she's wearing protective goggles too.

Kyle tosses and turns then finally gives up on sleep. He'd managed an hour or so, but then his subconscious kicked in and he was basically dreaming what he should be thinking while awake.

So he wakes up.

Kyle sighs and swings his legs over the edge of the medical bed he's sleeping on. Way more comfortable than a cot. He hasn't even put a foot on the ground before he sees the very large note from his mother taped to some equipment directly next to the bed.

Reading the note, Kyle nods and stands up. He could use something to eat too. He's starving. The feeling causes some panic in him considering Lowell's voracious and unorthodox appetite, but he calms down quickly. He's not like Lowell. He hasn't been inside the Substance.

In bare feet, Kyle leaves the med bay and walks to the elevator, where he rides it to the cafeteria floor.

The room is a mess, but Kyle ignores the debris and hunts down enough food for himself, his mother, and Dr. Probst. He loads the food and water he's going to transport into a supply box, then takes his own food and finds a seat.

Images rush and race through Kyle's mind, and he struggles to make full sense of them. He knows that if he simply opens his mind and doesn't think too hard, then realization will hit him, but he's too tired to let the flow just happen. He wants to understand it all, not just be a semi-participant standing on the outside, watching.

With food done, Kyle throws his trash away and grabs the supply box.

Next stop is hunting down some new clothes and getting clean.

Kyle sets the supply box next to the elevator, then shuffles off to the personnel locker room.

It takes him a few tries to find the locker room, but after a couple of wrong turns, he gets there and is grateful to find clean towels and more than a few generic jumpsuits in his size.

Kyle strips down, grabs a towel, starts the hot water in one of the shower stalls, and steps into heaven.

He gets right to work soaping up and rinsing off, then takes several minutes to just soak in the hot water, letting the soothing steam fill his pours.

Kyle is about to step out of the shower when an image slams into his brain. He staggers and nearly slips, only avoiding a nasty fall in the shower by grabbing onto a soap holder recessed into the wall. He takes a few deep breaths, then hurries out of the shower.

He's barely dried off when he slides into his jumpsuit, finds a pair of white ankle socks, throws on some boots he finds that fit, and runs out of the locker room to the elevator.

"Come on, come on," he growls as he waits for the elevator doors to open.

When they do, he gets on and jams the button for the floor the control room is on.

The doors barely slide open before he's running down the corridor and into the control room.

"Where are you?" he says as he hunts around the stations for the communications console.

Finally finding it, he stares at the handset and at the interface it's connected to.

"I don't know how to call him," Kyle snaps. "Fuck!"

He remembers the channel his mother said they'd be on and tries that. No answer.

"Damnit!"

Out the control room he runs, back into the elevator, to the cafeteria floor where he pauses only long enough to snag the supply box he'd left there, then down, down, down he goes.

When the elevator opens, Kyle shudders. Being down this low and this close to the Substance gives him the creeps, even though he knows a ton more now than he did before about the facility and the Substance it's built around.

"Mom!" Kyle yells.

Of course, there's no cart hold for him to snag a vehicle from. He's going to have to hoof it. He pulls a flashlight from a cargo pocket in his jumpsuit and turns it on. The tunnel goes on forever and all he sees is darkness at the edge of the flashlight's beam.

He sighs.

Kyle debates tossing the supply box aside but knows he's probably going to be hungry again after the walk he's about to take. So he holds the box tight and starts off at a slow jog.

But as the image from the shower replays in his head, Kyle's jog becomes a run then a sprint, even with the weight of the supply box in his arms.

After a few minutes, Kyle can hear the distinct sound of the jackhammer. After a few more minutes, he can see a small circle of light.

"MOM!" Kyle yells, but there's no response. He doubted there would be.

On he runs, his legs getting more and more tired with every step. He's annoyed as hell that he's soaked in sweat after taking a shower. The annoyance is shoved aside by the image again.

"MOM!" Kyle yells when he reaches the circle of light being put off by the floodlights on top of the cart.

Lu doesn't hear him, but Dr. Probst does and turns to look at Kyle. She smiles at the box in his hands, then frowns once he enters all the way into the circle of light. Dr. Probst reaches out and taps Lu's shoulder.

Lu stops the jackhammer and takes off her ear protection.

"What?" she asks Dr. Probst, then sees Kyle. "Oh good, food... Kyle? What's wrong?"

"Lowell doesn't know," Kyle says. "I saw something that I think he doesn't know about."

"How's that possible?" Lu asks. "You know what he knows, right?" She looks to Dr. Probst. "Right?"

"I would think so," Dr. Probst says.

"No, Lowell got his information by touching the blue crystal directly and by being exposed to the Substance," Kyle says. "I got touched by the alien thing. Or its image or whatever it was." Kyle waves his hands around. "Some representation of this facility, I think."

"And you're just now realizing this new information?" Dr. Probst asks.

"There's too much to sift through all at once," Kyle says. "I have more information in my head than I can comprehend. It wasn't until I was taking a shower that something hit me."

"What? Hit you? Is there another monster down here?" Dr. Probst cries, spinning in circles in alarm.

"I'm not being literal," Kyle says. "I was taking a shower and I think the water triggered an image."

"Of…?" Lu asks, her patience thinning by the look on her face. "Out with it, Kyle."

"There's another facility," Kyle says. "One that even Vander-Voort doesn't know exists."

"Another facility? Where?" Dr. Probst asks.

"Uh…" Kyle closes his eyes. "The ocean. Deep. It's at the bottom somewhere."

"Which ocean, Kyle?" Lu asks.

"Technically, it's all one ocean," Dr. Probst says.

"Really?" Lu snaps.

"Sorry," Dr. Probst says. "Kyle? Can you figure out where the facility is?"

"Um… the Pacific Ocean," Kyle says and nods. "Yeah, that feels right. It's deep. Really deep. A…trench?"

"A trench?" Dr. Probst snaps her fingers. "The shuttle kept trying to default to an island in the South Pacific, like it knew where it needed to go."

"Yeah. There," Kyle says.

"The Mariana Trench," Dr. Probst says. "It could be a different one, but that's the deepest. The Tonga Trench is close to as deep, as is the Philippine, but Mariana is the deepest of the three."

"So… what does this mean?" Lu asks.

"I don't know," Kyle says. "I almost have it. The Earth's core…? No…"

"We need to tell Lowell," Dr. Probst says. "He's planning based on what we know now. This could change things."

"That's what I'm saying!" Kyle exclaims. "How do we call him?"

"We don't," Dr. Probst says. "He's in the air. He'll contact us once he reaches Antarctica and starts his plan."

"Should we tell VanderVoort?" Kyle asks.

Dr. Probst and Lu exchange looks.

"No," Lu says. "We should talk to Lowell first. This will only complicate things. Lowell, then VanderVoort."

"If Lowell thinks we need to tell her," Dr. Probst says.

"Why wouldn't we tell her?" Kyle asks.

"VanderVoort is in charge," Lu says. "But Lowell knows what's going on."

"Or did," Dr. Probst says.

"He knows more than VanderVoort," Lu continues. "We speak to Lowell and see how he wants to play this."

"Hold on," Dr. Probst says. "VanderVoort doesn't know about the underwater facility. That means it isn't connected either. Is it another of the Ebony Man's creations?"

Kyle shakes his head. "No, it's different."

"How do you know?" Dr. Probst asks.

"It's different, trust me," Kyle says. "It doesn't feel like the Ebony Man." He closes his eyes again, then opens them. "It doesn't feel like the other facilities either. I mean, it does, but it doesn't…"

"Then what is it?" Lu asks.

"I don't know," Kyle says. "Ugh!"

They stand there in silence.

"We need to keep working," Dr. Probst says.

"Kyle? You go back to the control room and wait for Lowell to contact us," Lu says. "When he does, you tell him what you told us. Hopefully, we'll have cracked this wall and found the vein by then."

"The blue crystal," Kyle says and nods. "Yeah. That will work.

We might even be able to tap into the ocean facility and see what it's all about."

"Hopefully," Dr. Probst says.

"Get going," Lu says. "He could be calling any minute."

Kyle grins sheepishly.

"What?" Lu asks.

"Can I take the cart?" he replies. "I'll bring it back and come get you guys once Lowell calls."

"Yes, take the cart," Lu says. "We'll be here for a while."

Kyle smiles and hops in the cart, then pauses. He sighs and shakes his head.

"You won't have light," he says, shoulders slumped.

"Oh, right," Dr. Probst says. "Sorry."

Kyle takes a deep breath and begins his long walk back to the elevator.

———

Lowell can see the Antarctic continent below as the shuttle rockets over the ice-and-snow-covered landscape. His gut tells him the facility is near, but he doesn't know the exact location. He's hoping the shuttle does.

Ten minutes later, the shuttle begins to whine and slow down. Then the nose dives.

Lights flash on every single console and a klaxon blares.

"Time to land this baby," Lowell says. He places a hand on the console in front of him and frowns. "Um… hello, shuttle? I'm touching you. You're supposed to do what I tell… you…"

Reality hits him. He's no longer in the Wyoming facility. He knows he has control over that facility, but the shuttle isn't connected anymore and wasn't built by ancient aliens. It was built by people, and he's not as connected to people anymore as he used to be.

"Well, this is gonna suck," Lowell says as the nose pitches downward even more. "Shiiiiiiit!"

The snow-and ice-covered landscape races up toward Lowell and the shuttle, then they become one.

And despite Lowell's newfound knowledge and abilities, it turns out he's not immune to the consequences of being inside a shuttle when it hits ground at an alarming speed.

Everything shatters around Lowell, and then an intense cold he's never felt before envelopes him.

He lays there for several minutes before he takes the risk of moving.

Legs work. Arms work. Eyes work. Ears work. Skin definitely works, as the subzero temperatures of Antarctica threaten to freeze him in place.

"Probably should have brought a parka," Lowell says.

He hauls himself out of the shuttle, which isn't hard since most of the cockpit is exposed to the elements. He just climbs right out the front.

Lowell orients himself as best he can, chooses a direction, and starts hiking through the snow. Then he stops, smacks his head, and backtracks to the shuttle.

Lowell climbs inside and finds his target. He grabs the Ebony Man by the skull again and drags him out of the broken cockpit.

"You wouldn't happen to have one of those hand warmer gel pack things, would ya?" he asks the dazed Ebony Man. "No? Would have been way cooler if ya did."

Once more, Lowell starts to trudge through the frozen landscape, his body already shivering.

EIGHT

Bolton and Joshua have been pushing the Stryker hard, navigating the broken interstate system at reckless speeds and without regard for the dangers that could come for them at any second. They have a destination to reach and a schedule to keep, and Joshua is dead set on getting them there as fast as possible.

Which Bolton is grateful for but also slightly wary of, since Joshua is more a "go through it" driver than a "go around it" driver.

"We need to refuel," Joshua says. "Let's hope it's safer than last time."

Bolton nods, thinking about the last refueling stop. They'd barely gotten out of the rest stop before some scared locals tried to take the Stryker from them. Bolton talked them down, but it almost came to him opening fire with the turret-mounted .50 caliber machine gun. He knew they only wanted safety, but he has a mission to complete and a family to save.

"This exit should work," Bolton says, pointing at a half-demolished "Gas" sign that advertises the many different oil and gas companies just waiting to provide quality service and heart-clogging snacks at inflated prices.

Joshua sees a semi-intact truck stop from the highway and takes an exit without any discernible ramp. The Stryker navigates the rubble as designed and they pull into the truck stop, drive past the useless pumps, and over to the fuel tank access hatches.

"We used diesel last time," Joshua says, jumping down from the Stryker to join Bolton, who's busy removing debris so they can tell the difference between the hatches. "The vehicle is multi-fuel rated, but we need to stay consistent or we could blow the engine."

"I know," Bolton replies.

"Reminders are good," Joshua states, a rifle to his shoulder as he surveys the area, looking for the next threat.

"This is the one," Bolton says and smacks the hatch painted bright green. "I'll get the pump."

Bolton walks back to the Stryker and opens the rear hatch. He frowns at the space that had been his brief holding cell. He grabs the handle of a hatch set into the floor of the Stryker, pops open the compartment, and pulls out a long, industrial siphon hose, then a heavy-duty hand pump.

"Let's hope the tank hasn't been compromised," Joshua says as he slings his rifle, lifts the hatch, and reaches out for the siphon hose. Bolton hands him an end and Joshua drops it through the hatch and feeds it down until they both hear a slight splash. "I'll take the first turn at—"

A cry fills the air and both men freeze.

"It's one of those blue-tongued assholes," Bolton says. "Shit."

Several more cries join the first one.

"They smell the diesel," Joshua says and stands up. "You pump, I'll hold them off."

"Don't bother," Bolton says. "Even using the turret, you'll only make them angry."

"Then we should both pump and get refueled as fast as possible," Joshua says.

"No, grab out the .50 cal ammo," Bolton says. "And a roll of duct tape."

Joshua blinks at Bolton a few times.

"Trust me," Bolton says. "Start taping a dozen rounds together. Make as many bundles as you can. I'll pump the diesel into the Stryker."

Joshua's skeptical look returns.

"I know how to kill them," Bolton says. "So fucking hurry, will ya?"

Joshua shakes his head and rushes back to the Stryker's side hatch, yanks it open, and gets to work.

Bolton gets to work too and attaches the siphon hose to the pump, then unravels the fill hose and places the nozzle into the Stryker's fuel tank. He primes the hand pump and begins the siphoning process.

All while several monsters cry and call to each other from somewhere out in the destroyed landscape.

"They're getting closer," Joshua yells from the Stryker.

"I know," Bolton says. "How're the bundles coming?"

"I have a dozen done," Joshua replies.

"Perfect. Keep making them," Bolton says.

Bolton works the hand pump until his arms feel like they're going to fall off. The cries are even closer and the sounds of trees snapping begins to accompany them.

"That's gonna have to do," Bolton says and stops pumping. He pulls the nozzle out of the fuel tank and grabs a gas can from inside the Stryker. He catches Joshua's eye. "Put the bundles by the turret, then get ready to drive. We need to go."

A thunderous roar punctuates Bolton's statement.

Joshua moves lightning quick and is back in the driver's seat and has the Stryker started up and the engine revving before Bolton has the extra gas can filled. Bolton tops the can off, gathers up the siphon gear, stows it and the gas can, and hops into the Stryker.

Instead of taking the passenger's seat, Bolton climbs into the turret platform, opens the top hatch, and removes the .50 caliber machine gun that the turret was designed for. Now with space to move, Bolton sets up the gas can and the bundles of taped-together ammo so they're in easy reach.

Then he waits.

"See anything?" Joshua calls as he drives them away from the truck stop and back up to the mangled highway. Despite the road's state, it's the easiest path forward. "We're clear ahead."

Before Bolton can reply, all hell breaks loose.

Three of the diesel junkies sprint in their disjointed way across an empty field, straight for the Stryker.

"Three on our eight!" Bolton yells. "Punch it!"

Joshua laughs and the Stryker moves faster, tossing Bolton this way and that in the turret's opening. Bolton braces his legs against the turret cage, reaches for the gas can, opens it up, then dowses the taped bundles of ammo in diesel.

"I smell diesel," Joshua shouts from below.

"It's on purpose," Bolton says. "Bait."

Bolton doesn't hear Joshua's response, if there is one.

His eyes tracking the incoming monsters, Bolton hefts a diesel-soaked ammo bundle in each hand, counts down in his head, ignores his exhausted muscles, and throws both out behind the Stryker. He repeats the motion five more times, sending a total of ten bundles rolling across the destroyed asphalt.

Half the bundles are lost between the cracks and crevices, but the other half lay out in the open, wet and waiting.

Two of the monsters hit the road and go straight for the bundles, while a third ignores the bait and heads straight for the Stryker.

"Shit," Bolton says and grabs up two more bundles.

This time he doesn't toss them, but waits and watches as the beast moves in fast. Bolton lets the monster get closer and closer.

The diesel junkie is about twenty yards behind the vehicle when it opens its snaggle-toothed maw and sends its blue tongue directly for Bolton.

Knowing the creature is going to attack that way and experiencing the attack are two different things, but Bolton's training holds him steady, and at the very last moment he ducks down inside the vehicle while simultaneously throwing two bundles up into the air. Bolton watches with satisfaction as the tongue snatches the diesel-soaked bundles and is yanked back out of view.

"That seems to be effective," Joshua says as Bolton clambers toward the rear of the vehicle and the porthole window in the rear hatch. "I can see them in the side view. Two are down and the third doesn't look happy."

Bolton confirms Joshua's report and sees one, then a second monster burst open as gray foam spills out of their bodies. The third monster staggers in pursuit of the Stryker but falls behind quickly, then drops too.

"That all of them?" Joshua yells back.

"I'll check," Bolton says and makes his way back up top.

To the east, he thinks he hears more cries and calls, but they're far off.

Then the vehicle rocks to the side and Bolton cries out as his hip slams into the edge of the turret opening. He ignores the pain and spins around to see a fourth monster attacking from the other side, its massive head down and ready to slam into the Stryker a second time.

Bolton grabs for the bundles, manages to snag four, and drops down into the Stryker as the monster's head impacts with the vehicle again.

"It's gonna break us apart!" Joshua says. "Feed the thing!"

Bolton takes a deep breath and shoves back up through the opening. He throws a bundle at the monster's head, but it only bounces off its warped lips and falls harmlessly to the ground. The beast doesn't even try to snatch for the bundle, its eyes locked onto Bolton and the vehicle.

"Fuck," Bolton growls. "They learn."

He whips about, desperate for a solution, and spies the gas can wedged between two buckled plates of armor. Bolton pushes halfway up out of the turret and reaches for the gas can, only to be forced back inside the Stryker as the monster's blue tongue nearly snatches his arm off.

"How's it going?" Joshua asks with a laugh.

Bolton glares at the back of the man's head but doesn't respond.

He picks himself up, launches up through the turret opening, reaches as far as he can, snags the gas can, and falls back into the vehicle just before the blue tongue can grab him.

It does get a little of Bolton though, as the man feels the hair on the back of his head sizzle and burn from the monster's caustic saliva. Bolton slaps at his head but doesn't slow down as he grabs a .50 cal ammo box. He carries both the gas can and the ammo box to the rear hatch.

"When I tell you to," Bolton shouts, "you floor this thing."

"As opposed to what I'm doing now?" Joshua responds.

"Like you have the Devil on your tail, floor it," Bolton says.

"You asked for it," Joshua says with a little more mischief in his voice than Bolton likes.

Bolton sets the ammo box next to the rear hatch, fills it with diesel, then opens the hatch. A blue tongue nails the hatch, suctions tight, then yanks it free from the Stryker.

"Fuck!" Bolton shouts and scrambles back as the Stryker fishtails for a moment before Joshua regains control.

"Do what you're planning to do already!" Joshua shouts.

With a swift kick, Bolton sends the ammo box out of the hatch and tosses the gas can with it. Diesel and ammo fly everywhere as the box and can hit the cracked pavement.

Bolton says a quick prayer that the amount of diesel will be too much for the monster to resist. For a second, Bolton is sure his prayer has gone unanswered when the beast slams into the Stryker once more, but then it falls back and whips its massive head around to the tantalizing treat Bolton has left for it.

"You learn, but just like any junkie," Bolton says, "you can't help yourself."

"What?" Joshua shouts.

"Nothing," Bolton calls back.

Bolton watches the monster sniff at the diesel on the ground. Then its tongue darts down over and over again to lap up the fuel. When that's gone, the monster turns its attention to the scattered ammo that's coated in diesel. With a satisfied grin, Bolton watches the monster gobble up the ammo.

Then the grin leaves Bolton's face as he witnesses the beast spit the ammo back out, the diesel having been sucked right off the cartridges.

"No, no, no," Bolton mutters.

The monster shifts its position and faces the retreating Stryker. Then it races straight for the vehicle.

"It's coming in hard!" Bolton yells.

One hundred yards. Fifty yards. Ten yards and the monster fills the view out of the rear hatch. Then a shriek echoes over the land and the monster stops in its tracks, letting the Stryker gain distance once more. Bolton is puzzled until he sees the monster lift its head to the sky and roar.

Two wings and six claws slam down onto the monster, and Bolton doesn't know whether to scream or cheer as the diesel junkie and a winged monster roll over and over across the destroyed highway, both nothing but teeth and talons, violence and rage.

"Now!" Bolton yells. "Floor it now!"

"Bolton, I have been flooring it," Joshua says. "Get your ass up here and sit down. You can't do much more than watch."

The statement irks Bolton, but he knows Joshua is right. He clambers back into the passenger's seat, straps in, and watches the brutal battle unfold in the side view mirror.

The diesel junkie looks like it's about to win when three more winged monsters land next to the skirmish and join in.

Within seconds, the diesel junkie is ripped to shreds.

"Don't do it," Bolton says, hoping the winged beasts won't get curious about the Stryker.

He holds his breath, then lets it out when he sees two of the winged monsters begin to feast on the dead diesel junkie while the other two scramble about for the remnants of the spilled diesel.

"We'll need to refuel twice more before we hit Colorado Springs," Joshua states. "We're going to need a solid defense plan before then, or we're not going to complete the mission."

"I know," Bolton replies. "I know…"

———

Terrie shivers in her wet clothes despite being huddled tight with Tony, Krissy, and Biscuit in a small rocky cave they found. A day has passed since they escaped the flooding bunker and the monster that had breached it.

As much as Terrie would love to get moving and put the raft into the water, they simply can't risk it. There are at least three of the monsters stomping about the island from what she can tell. If they expose themselves, then they could easily be snatched up and eaten in an instant.

Yet that's not the worst part.

A gray dawn breaks the horizon and weak light starts to fill the tiny cave. Terrie squints at the craft filled with gear that is about ten yards from the cave mouth, then she looks to the shoreline that's only about one hundred yards past the raft.

A shoreline teeming with warped life.

Dozens of ooze creatures flop about in the tide. Fish, birds, mammals, crustaceans, all shuffle about, their bodies being battered by the incoming waves, yet not seeming to notice or care.

There's a stirring against Terrie's side and she looks down at Biscuit's open eyes. The dog-wolf lets out a quiet whine and Terrie strokes his matted, damp fur.

"I know, I know, boy," she whispers. "I have to pee too."

Krissy and Tony come awake and instantly stare out at the shoreline.

"They're still there," Krissy says, shivering too, her naked legs dangerously white.

"Trapped," Tony states.

"Keep your voices down," Terrie warns. "We'll really be trapped if they hear us and decide to attack."

"What do we do?" Krissy whispers. "How do we get out of this shit?"

Terrie frowns at the curse but says nothing. She's too exhausted to admonish the girl for her language.

"I don't know," Terrie says. "We can't get to the water." She watches the things move about in the surf. "And I'm not sure we want to. It's a long way in a rubber raft from this island to the mainland."

"There's a better boat," Tony says. "But it's on the other side of the island."

"Doesn't help much then, does it?" Krissy snaps.

"Just like you," Tony retorts.

"Stop it," Terrie says before the two teenagers start bickering in full. "Working together is the only way we survive this."

Terrie takes a deep breath, closes her eyes, and mentally works through different scenarios. No matter how much she tries, she can't figure out how to get them out of the cave without being spotted.

"We're going to have to wait until night," Terrie says. "They'll see us otherwise."

"Wait until night?" Krissy gasps. "I'm not going to be able to wait until night."

"Me either," Tony states.

"I'm there with you both," Terrie says. She cranes her neck and looks toward the sloped back of the small cave. "I'm afraid we'll have to use the cave to do our business until the sun goes down."

"If you haven't noticed, Terrie, the sun is just coming up," Krissy says. "That means we're going to be sitting in this cave with piss smell all day long."

"I have to poop," Tony says.

"Filter much?" Krissy snaps.

"Stop it, both of you," Terrie says. "Tony, you're out of luck. Hold it. Krissy? Deal with it. This is a matter of survival, not comfort. When this is all over, when we're safe, then you can say how bad you had it, but until then, you suck it up. Am I understood?"

"Are you understood?" Krissy asks, pointing out at the ooze creatures. "Should we ask them if they understand too? Maybe we can ask them to suck it up and just go away."

"You know exactly what I'm saying, young lady," Terrie says. "Do not play dumb. And stop fighting me when all I'm trying to do is keep us alive."

"Do better," Krissy says.

Terrie holds her temper in check despite the almost uncontrollable urge to throttle the girl.

"Tony? Relieve yourself first," Terrie says. "Then Krissy, then I will go and try to get Biscuit to go as well."

"What if Biscuit has to poop?" Tony asks. "Will he be told to hold it?"

Terrie sighs and laughs, covering her mouth to stifle the sound.

"You two are impossible," Terrie says. "Just go do your business."

"I will try my best," Tony says, extricating himself from their huddle and crouch-walking to the back of the cave.

Krissy frowns at Terrie the entire time they listen to Tony's splashes against the cave wall.

"We should change your bandages," Terrie says, seeing the state the gauze and tape wrapped about Krissy's face are in. "Can't have you dying of infection right before our rescue."

Krissy opens her mouth a few times, but the sarcastic comments don't come. She finally shakes her head and looks out at the raft with all the supplies.

"How do we get the first aid kit?" Krissy asks. "And maybe some pants for me."

"Very carefully," Terrie says.

Tony returns and smiles. "There's a hole back there. It's convenient."

"I bet," Krissy says, and shifts her body around Tony as he settles back down. "Be right back. You keep working out how we get fresh bandages for my face and pants for my ass. Oh, and also how we don't die in this shithole."

"Not a shithole, since we aren't allowed to poop in it," Tony says. "Just a peehole."

Krissy rolls her eyes and crouch-walks her way to the back of the cave.

"Did I hear you say you are going to try to retrieve supplies from the raft?" Tony asks. "If that's the case, then I would like my radio."

"We need bandages and pants for Krissy and food and water for all of us first," Terrie says. "If we're able, then we can try to grab your radio."

"It would be best to have," Tony says. "We can alert the White House to our situation. We may be able to contact Sergeant Bolton and get a report on his travel progress. Even if we do get off this island and to the mainland, we'll have to travel a good distance before we meet up with him and Joshua."

"Yes, Tony, I'm well aware of the issues before us," Terrie says.

Terrie studies the terrain between the cave and the raft. It's mostly sandy soil and tumbled rocks from millennia of incoming and outgoing tides.

Could they use the rocks as distractions? Toss a few off to the side or into the water as misdirection? Terrie doesn't know if that will fool the ooze creatures or not, but the reality is they do need food and water. And if Krissy's bandages aren't changed, then infection will set in and she will most certainly die.

Biscuit whines, and Terrie strokes his fur until Krissy returns.

"It is a good hole to pee in," Krissy says, smirking at Tony.

"I told you," Tony says.

"You going next?" Krissy asks.

Terrie doesn't respond.

"Terrie?" Krissy asks.

"What? Oh, yes," Terrie says. "You two think on how we get from here to the raft and back without being noticed while I relieve myself."

"Sure. No problem," Krissy says. "Should be super easy to figure out."

But there's nothing to figure out.

The second Terrie gets up to crouch-crawl her way to the back of the cave, Biscuit springs to his feet and, instead of following Terrie, he bolts out of the cave to lift a leg.

Terrie freezes in place, still crouched, and watches in horror as slowly, one by one, the ooze creatures turn toward the new activity.

"Oh, no," Krissy says. "Biscuit…"

Done with his business, Biscuit lifts his canine snout and wafts the air, then he turns and faces the slowly moving horde of ooze monsters making its way toward the cave. The hybrid's hackles rise and a primal growl builds from the dog-wolf's chest to his throat, then out between lifted, snarling lips.

"Biscuit, no," Terrie hisses, but the dog-wolf is not listening. A threat too big to ignore is coming for them.

"That's our distraction," Tony says, and he's out of the cave, crawling on hands and knees to the raft before Terrie can stop him.

"Boys are so smart," Krissy says and turns to face Terrie. "What's the call?"

Terrie doesn't know. They can use Biscuit's distraction to gather supplies from the raft, but then what? They'll be trapped back in the cave again in minutes and surrounded or worse by ooze creatures.

Or they can unfold and pop open the cart that was stowed on top of the raft, toss the supplies in there, leave the raft behind, and try to go find the better boat Tony had hinted at.

If there is a better boat.

"Terrie!" Krissy calls, snapping Terrie from her thoughts.

The scene outside the cave is not ideal.

The ooze creatures are only about twenty yards from Biscuit, and Tony is almost at the raft. The second he starts digging for his radio amongst the supplies, the ooze creatures will spot him.

"We fill the cart," Terrie says. "Then we run."

"You think we can do either of those things before we get eaten?" Krissy asks. There's no sarcasm in her voice or attitude, only fear that's matched by the desperate look in her eyes.

"Do we have a choice?" Terrie responds.

Krissy shakes her head.

"We do this," Terrie says, "now."

She grabs Krissy by the arm and pulls her from the cave. The two women sprint to the raft, surprising Tony while he still crawls along the ground.

"I didn't know we could run to the raft," he says as he joins them in getting the cart free from the mound of supplies.

Terrie pops the cart open while Krissy and Tony gather the supplies and begin the desperate dash to transfer everything they can from the raft.

Biscuit's growls turn to open barking before anyone can stop him. The hybrid rushes the ooze creatures, the ooze creatures rush the hybrid.

"Biscuit! NO!" Terrie yells.

"That's everything!" Krissy shouts and yanks on Terrie's arm. "Come on!"

"I have my radio," Tony says, patting the pack on his back. "We can go now."

"BISCUIT!" Terrie roars, and the dog-wolf skids to a halt just before it leaps at the ooze creatures.

What looks like it was once maybe a sea lion snaps at Biscuit, which forces reality back into the canine's brain, and it whips around and sprints to Terrie's side.

"Good boy," Terrie says and puts her whole weight into pushing the cart across the rocky and wet ground.

Krissy and Tony join her, and they're able to get up to a hobbling sprint, which the ooze creatures soon match.

"Which way?" Terrie asks Tony, her eyes constantly darting to the horde of ooze creatures moving parallel with them.

"What do you mean?" Tony asks.

Terrie and Krissy share a look.

"The better boat," Terrie says. "You said it's on the opposite side of the island."

"Yes," Tony says. "It's an island. There's no 'which way.' You go forward and you end up where you need to be. It's like a circle."

"You sure I can't smack him?" Krissy asks.

"That'd be assault," Tony says, "and rude."

"So we just keep going until we find the boat?" Terrie says.

"It's as good a plan as any," Tony says. "Unless you want to cut across the island. But then we might run into one of the big monsters."

"No, we won't be cutting across," Terrie says. "We just keep going this way. Maybe the disgusting things will tire of chasing us."

"Really?" Krissy asks, the sarcasm back once more.

Terrie ignores her and also ignores the pain in her legs, simply focusing on pushing the cart.

"You have a hole in your undies," Tony says to Krissy. "I see your butt."

"How about you try kissing it then?" Krissy snaps.

Terrie decides to let the teens just bicker. They have to get it out, and it provides the perfect distraction to her pain and exhaustion.

———

"A door," Lowell says with a level of relief he isn't sure he's ever felt before. "Hallelujah!"

"You praise your dead god for finding shelter?" the Ebony

Man asks, crouched down by Lowell's feet as the man studies the door controls. "No wonder this world is over."

"That's enough out of you, Mr. Licorice," Lowell says. He presses a couple of buttons but nothing happens. He'd sigh in frustration, but he's shivering so hard that sighing isn't even physically possible. "You gonna help me open this or what, asshole?"

"Why?" the Ebony Man replies. "I cannot be killed by the thermal extremes like your pitiful primate body can."

"You can be killed by me ripping you to shreds and feeding you to the fucking penguins," Lowell says. "Or maybe that won't kill you, but it'll be fun as fuck to try. I just hope I live long enough to see you become penguin shit."

"You threaten me with flightless avian mistakes?" The Ebony Man chuckles. "Your desperation is showing, Anson Lowell."

"That does it," Lowell says, "prepare for the insertion of my boot into your ass region."

"Stop with the threats," the Ebony Man says. "Help me up so I may open this portal into the facility."

"Now we're talking," Lowell says and lifts the Ebony Man up onto his feet.

The being wobbles slightly, then establishes its balance. A tendril of black extends from one of the Ebony Man's fingers and works its way into the keypad.

Just as Lowell thinks he's going to end up frozen in place, the door to the facility slides open and he hurries as fast as his freezing body can move, shoving the Ebony Man inside before him.

The door slides shut, and Lowell feels relief wash over him. He's not even close to being warmed up yet, but at least he's no longer out in the frozen hell of Antarctica.

Lowell looks about and frowns.

"Is this an elevator?" he asks.

"It is," the Ebony Man says. "This facility is completely subterranean. The only portion of it above ground is the single entrance."

"Works for me," Lowell says and eyes the elevator controls. "Which level?"

"You don't know?" the Ebony Man asks with a chuckle.

"You know what? Fuck you," Lowell says and places his hand on the elevator controls.

Several images flash through his mind, and it takes him a moment to sort through them before deciding where their next stop is.

"Level Seventy-Five it is," Lowell says and presses the corresponding button.

The elevator groans, creaks, then starts to slowly descend.

"Well, this is gonna take forever," Lowell says just before the elevator rockets downward.

Lowell is almost lifted off his feet, and he reaches out to steady himself.

That's when the Ebony Man attacks.

"Motherfucker!" Lowell yells, suddenly fending off blow after blow from the being. "Get the fuck off me, Licorice!"

"Tiny primate!" the Ebony Man roars. "You think to control me? Never!"

Lowell is backed into a corner of the elevator and manages to keep his head protected with his arms, but the rest of his body is wide open and the Ebony Man takes full advantage. Punch after punch, kick after kick, all slam into Lowell's legs, abdomen, sides, and arms.

"Only a brain as insignificant as a human's could conceive of enslaving a being as magnificent as myself!" the Ebony Man shouts, his fists jackhammering into Lowell's rib cage. "I allowed this! It was by my will alone that we have traveled to this facility! You are my puppet, ape! MINE!"

In that moment, Lowell finds it hard to disagree. He finds it hard to do anything except slump to the elevator's floor and curl up tight into a ball. The hammer blows continue, the kicks continue, the Ebony Man's constant barrage of disparagements continue.

For a split second, Lowell is a child again, imprisoned in a dank basement, completely alone and waiting for the door at the top of the stairs to open and the horror to begin again.

"Stop," Lowell croaks.

"Stop?" the Ebony Man howls with laughter that pierces straight into Lowell's mind. "I will never stop! They put me here because I refused to stop for them! Do you think I would stop for a gnat such as you?"

"I'll... kill... you," Lowell says before the air is knocked from his lungs by a brutal kick to his diaphragm.

"They have all tried to kill me and they have all failed!" the Ebony Man says. "You are no different."

The violence stops with an eerie finality.

Lowell waits.

And waits.

Lowell slides his fists from his face and peers through his arms at the Ebony Man's silhouette standing before the elevator doors. The doors open and the Ebony Man turns back to Lowell.

"Eventually, I will have a use for you," the Ebony Man says. "So, for now, you live. But I advise you make peace with your god or gods or whatever you worship, for when I return, you and I will have our last interaction, Anson Lowell."

Lowell is about to respond, but the Ebony Man moves in a blinding rush and the last thing Lowell sees is a pitch-black foot stomping on his face.

NINE

"Tell me something good, people," VanderVoort says from a couch that has been set between the conference table and the main bank of monitors. "Any word from the kid with the radio?"

"No, ma'am," a tech replies.

"What about Dr. Probst?" VanderVoort asks.

"They're still trying to break through the concrete," a different tech says.

"And Anson Lowell? Did the convict make it to Antarctica? Do we have any idea what he's doing?" VanderVoort asks.

No one responds.

"Great," VanderVoort says. "We're on the razor's edge of survivability as a species, in what should be the most powerful place on the planet, and we're stuck in sit-and-wait mode."

"I think that's the new normal now," Director Miles says. "Until we can communicate with the refugee ships and work out how to get everyone into the facilities, we don't have much to do but sit and wait."

"For aliens," Dr. Hall interjects. "Sit and wait for aliens."

"Thank you for reminding us, Dr. Hall," VanderVoort says.

"It's not like you haven't been talking about aliens nonstop for the past day."

VanderVoort yawns and stretches.

"What time is it?" she asks. "I've lost all sense of day and night."

"It is almost 2 pm, eastern time," Alvarez says. "I propose we make lunch."

No one responds.

"I'm serious," Alvarez continues. "After a particularly hard op, all of us agents would get together for a meal to destress and unpack what happened."

Alvarez nods at the many empty chairs and stations where personnel had once been before the Ebony Man's psychic attack.

"I think some destressing would be appropriate at the moment," Alvarez states.

"He's not wrong," Director Miles says. "We should all eat. Not snack, but actual food. Let the techs rotate in and out so we have systems monitored. But there's not much for us to do right now."

VanderVoort shifts and pulls herself more upright so she can see over the back of the couch.

"Charles?" VanderVoort asks.

"It seems wholly inappropriate considering what we've all been through," President Nance says, "but it's not a bad idea. A meal can do wonders to heal the soul."

"That's the folksy shit I was hoping you'd say," VanderVoort replies. "Great. Who's cooking?"

"I can," Alvarez says.

"I'll help," Director Miles says. "Especially with the drinks."

"May I?" Joan asks. "I could use some kitchen time."

"Grab as many people as you need, Agent Alvarez," President Nance says.

"And while we wait, someone get me Sergeant Bolton," VanderVoort says. "We haven't heard from him in a day."

―――――

"Yes, ma'am," Bolton says, the sat phone to his ear, his eyes scanning in all directions as he stands tall in the Stryker's turret. "Again, my apologies for not reporting in regularly."

There's a far-off wail from one of the monsters, but Bolton doesn't panic. He's gotten good at gauging the level of threat depending on the strength of the wails and their proximity. The one he hears isn't even close to them.

"We've been fighting our way mile by mile," Bolton continues. "Been pissing in bottles so we only have to stop to refuel."

Bolton nods a few times.

"Understood, ma'am," he says. "We will continue to try to contact Terrie and the kids as well." He listens, then pulls the phone away from his mouth. "How much farther, Joshua?"

"We'll be there by sundown," Joshua calls from the Stryker's driver's seat.

"That close?" Bolton asks, surprised.

"We've pushed this thing to its limit every inch of the way," Joshua replies.

"We'll be there by sundown," Bolton relays. "I'll report as soon as I have more information. Yes, ma'am, you as well."

Bolton closes the sat phone and tucks it into a pocket on his vest, making sure the pocket is closed tight against the constant and continual jostling.

"They're in a holding pattern until they have comms up and more actionable intel," Bolton calls down to Joshua before he can ask. "Any word from the island bunker?"

"Nothing," Joshua replies. "I just checked and still no answer."

"Let's hope they're on the move and okay," Bolton says. "I need to rescue Terrie, or Lu will kill me and we need that boy's tech to redirect the refugee relocations."

"With ships dead in the water," Joshua says.

Bolton takes one last look around, then descends back inside the Stryker. He takes the passenger seat and sighs.

"Maybe some ships didn't get taken out by the EMP," Bolton

says. "If even a couple are operational, then we may have a chance."

"We?" Joshua asks.

"Humans," Bolton replies.

Joshua snorts.

"You don't think we have a chance?" Bolton asks. "Then why are you bothering to help me?"

"I think a few of us will have a chance," Joshua says. "Myself included."

"So this is purely for self-preservation?" Bolton asks.

"Isn't it always?" Joshua responds.

"I swore an oath to God and country," Bolton says.

"That's not why you're doing this."

"Oh? And why am I doing this?"

"To save family," Joshua says. "Your words, not mine."

"That's not self-preservation," Bolton replies.

"Depends on how you define self," Joshua says.

Bolton begins to respond but keeps his mouth closed.

Joshua is right. Bolton defines himself by the people he cares for. Always has. It's why he's stuck by Lu for decades even without knowing Kyle was his son. Now that that particular cat is out of the bag, Bolton can't imagine a self without the Morgans.

They ride in silence for several miles before Joshua sighs and curls up a lip.

"One last refuel," he states. "Eyes out for viable stops."

"With intact convenience stores," Bolton says. "We're low on water and food."

Joshua nods. Despite the fact they'll be to the Diamondback facility by sundown, both are professional enough to know that shit goes south fast. Provisions are always a good idea to have on hand.

Bolton clambers up into the turret and begins the slow process of scanning the surroundings for not only threats but signs showing exits where fuel and food might be found.

Six miles later, Bolton sees both.

"Shit," Bolton says and ducks down inside the vehicle. "You see them?"

"Yeah," Joshua says, his eyes staring out the windshield at the far-off monsters lumbering across the mountainous landscape ahead. "That's a herd."

"There's an exit that looks workable a mile up ahead," Bolton says. "If the things keep moving, then we may not cross paths."

"Unless they catch wind of the diesel we're about to pump," Joshua says.

Bolton doesn't respond. No need. They'll deal with the situation as it unfolds, just as they have been the entire journey.

In the distance, the herd of monsters navigates its way from the rolling plains and foothills up into the Rocky Mountains. Bolton spies the exit and points. Joshua navigates the destruction and drives the Stryker down the twisting, broken exit and toward a surprisingly intact row of truck stops, smaller gas stations, and fast food restaurants.

"Jackpot," Joshua says as he drives the Stryker through a Burger King parking lot that's more a theory than an actual space still usable for cars.

The Stryker plows over a row of scorched bushes and into a well-preserved truck stop. He ignores the pumps and drives to the fuel tank hatches set into the broken asphalt.

"I'll refuel. You see what provisions are available," Joshua says as he jumps out of the Stryker.

Bolton has gotten used to Joshua's solo operator demeanor. He doesn't argue, grabs an M4, and jumps out of the vehicle, weapon up and aimed at the doors to the truck stop store. The smell of death is in the air, but that's no longer unusual. Bolton proceeds cautiously.

Two of the many windows are shattered, but both front doors are still intact.

And locked.

"Doors are locked," Bolton calls to Joshua.

Joshua pauses at the rear of the Stryker and looks about the area.

"Be careful," he says. "Might be survivors inside."

"That's what I'm thinking," Bolton says. "I'm going around back. Stay alert."

"Always," Joshua says, then is lost from sight as he carries the siphon gear around the Stryker to the fuel hatches.

Bolton moves away from the front doors and slowly circles the large building until he finds the rear entrance. He also finds the source of the death smell.

A pile of human corpses is neatly stacked over by the dumpsters, each carefully positioned so if they shift they'll fall against the fencing surrounding the dumpsters.

Deliberate care for the dead. Bolton is certain there are survivors inside the truck stop store.

He tries the door handle. Locked.

Instead of taking a risk and ending up in a fire fight, Bolton retreats from the store and works his way to Joshua.

"Locked up," Bolton says. "And the dead are stacked behind the building. Someone's inside and I say we leave them alone."

"Probably safest," Joshua says. "There's another store across the street. Try that."

"Copy that," Bolton says and is off again.

He glances briefly at the truck stop store, doesn't see any signs of movement or threats, and quickly crosses the shattered pavement to the convenience store across the street.

Like the truck stop store, the convenience store's windows are pretty much intact. But only one door is locked. Bolton opens it and moves slowly inside, his M4 sweeping back and forth.

"If anyone is in here, I'm not a threat," Bolton calls loud enough that anyone inside will hear him, but not loud enough to draw outside attention. "I'm going to grab some water and food and I'll be gone in a couple minutes. I'm only taking enough for myself and my buddy and only a couple days' worth. I won't clean you out, and if you're not cool with what I'm doing, then say so with words and not violence."

No response.

Bolton keeps moving, his eyes adjusting to the gloom. The fact that he isn't having to step through a debris field of busted soda cans and smashed chip bags tells Bolton that his instincts are correct and the store is occupied. Or at least was recently.

With senses on high alert, Bolton makes his way around the counter and grabs a couple of plastic bags. He then dumps the small bottles from an energy supplement display into one of the bags. Before leaving the counter, Bolton notices that the under-the-counter rack that would have held a shotgun is empty.

Carefully, Bolton moves to the drink cooler and snatches out two gallons of water and a couple of fruit drinks. Then he turns and surveys the snack racks and fills a bag with pretzels and trail mix.

"You can leave that right there," a voice says from behind Bolton. "That ain't yours to take."

Bolton sets the bags down and slowly turns around with one hand up and the other still holding the M4.

A woman is staring out through one of the drink cooler doors, the missing shotgun aimed directly at Bolton's midsection.

"I only need a little," Bolton says. "Can I take half of what I've gathered?"

"Leave it all," the woman says. "No more deliveries. Everything here has to last."

"Understood, ma'am," Bolton responds. "May I take two water bottles and the trail mix? My buddy and I are heading to Colorado Springs and can use the supplies for the last stretch."

"Last stretch?" The woman laughs, but the shotgun doesn't waver. "There is no last stretch. The roads are gone between here and Colorado Springs."

"The roads are pretty much gone everywhere," Bolton says. "We can make it."

"Not unless you're driving a tank," the woman says with

another laugh. When Bolton doesn't respond, her eyes go wide. "Are you driving a tank?"

"Something like that," Bolton says.

The woman could be in her late forties or early fifties, but Bolton's not sure due to the bad lighting and the fact that survivors tend to look a lot older than they are. Her hair is pulled back into a ponytail and threaded through the back of a Broncos cap. Her clothes are flannel and denim and look clean.

"Are you by yourself?" Bolton asks.

The woman gives Bolton a condescending look.

"Right. Stupid question," Bolton says. "You shouldn't tell me either way."

They stand there for a full minute.

"Ex-military?" Bolton finally asks.

"Could be," the woman says. "Doesn't matter. You don't need training with a hinge buster."

Hinge buster. Definitely ex-military.

"If it's just you, then we have room," Bolton says. "You can come with us."

"That's a very nice offer of rape," the woman replies.

Bolton smiles and nods.

"Understood," he says. "May I please take some supplies? Two water bottles and a couple bags of trail mix is all I'm asking for."

The woman sighs and nods.

"Thank you," Bolton says and crouches slowly to remove everything except for two water bottles and a couple bags of trail mix.

He loops the bags around a wrist and stands up just as slowly.

"Listen," he says as he moves toward the front doors. "I can't give you details, but I can give you coordinates. I'll write them down at the counter. If you decide to leave, then go toward those coordinates. There's a government bunker north where we need everyone to evacuate to."

"Everyone? Who's everyone?" the woman asks as she emerges

from the drink cooler's main door. "You mean the assholes across the street?"

"I don't know who's across the street," Bolton says. "The doors were locked, so I came over here."

Bolton sets the bags on the counter, grabs a pen, and writes the coordinates directly on top of the counter.

"It'll take you a few days to get there, and there's not much time left, so if you're going to leave here, then do it today," Bolton says. "If you wait, then it'll be too late."

"I have no idea what you're talking about, and I appreciate the offer, but I ain't leaving my store," the woman says.

"Totally understand," Bolton says, snags the bags, and walks backward to the entrance and out the door. "Good luck, ma'am."

Bolton keeps an eye on the store until he's safely out of shotgun range, then turns and jogs back to the Stryker. He tosses the supplies into the passenger's seat, then loops around the vehicle.

No Joshua.

"Shit," Bolton says. "He better be pissing."

Less than a minute later, Joshua comes walking out the front doors of the truck stop store, his arms heavy with bags of food and water.

The man is also coated in fresh blood. Bolton can tell by how Joshua is walking that none of the blood is his.

Joshua stows the bags of supplies in crates in the rear of the Stryker, then walks around to the driver's side. Before hopping in, he cracks open a water bottle, dumps it over himself, then rips into a roll of paper towels so he can blot himself dry and somewhat clean.

"They jumped me about a minute after you left," Joshua states as he takes his seat, slams the door, and starts the vehicle. "I warned them, but they didn't listen. I let them march me inside."

"Did you warn them a second time?" Bolton asks.

Joshua gives him a pointed look, then pulls the Stryker away from the truck stop.

"Try the kid again," Joshua says.

Bolton nods and grabs the radio handset.

———

The water is choppy, but not worrisome.

Not that Terrie worries about Puget Sound's waters. It's what's in the water that has her knuckles bone-white and cracking as she grips the boat's wheel.

Even with the sun up, the world outside the boat's small bridge is a hazy, gloomy nightmare of shadows and uncertainty.

"I need to connect my device to the boat's radio," Tony says from behind Terrie, causing her to jump and cry out. "I scared you."

"Yes, Tony, you did," Terrie replied after taking a deep breath and letting it out slowly. "Maybe announce yourself next time?"

Tony shrugs and sets his backpack down by the ship's radio.

"You can't use your radio?" Terrie asks.

"It'll be easier to use the boat's radio," Tony says. "It's already connected to an antenna array. This boat is mostly wood, so not enough metal to create a strong enough signal. When we reach the mainland, we'll look for an even larger antenna array, which will allow the White House to piggyback on the device and communicate with others."

"If they have a way to communicate," Terrie says.

"That is a needed component of success, yes," Tony says as he begins his work.

There's a low whine at Terrie's feet, and she looks down at Biscuit curled up close to her.

"You okay, boy?" Terrie asks.

Biscuit whines again, but a little louder.

Terrie glances at Tony and he's staring at the hybrid. Then he meets Terrie's eyes.

"Krissy!" Terrie calls.

In seconds, the girl is up from below and staring out the windows of the bridge.

"What's wrong?" she asks, picking up a pair of binoculars. "Did you see something?"

"The dog whined," Tony says, returning to his work.

"Great," Krissy says and begins searching back and forth with the binoculars. "It's fucking soup out there."

Once again, Terrie ignores the curse. She's just glad that the three of them have reached a point where she doesn't have to give orders. After their flight from the bunker, their race around to the far side of island, where luckily there was a small boat docked that hadn't been taken out by the monsters' tsunami, then their harrowing escape, they have developed a shorthand based on tone of voice and each other's strengths and capabilities.

"Any movement in the water?" Terrie asks.

"Not that I can see," Krissy says, then angles the binoculars upward. "Plenty of flying assholes though. But it looks like they're staying up by the clouds."

"Let's hope they stay there," Terrie says. "Tony? How is the radio coming?"

"I'm finalizing the connections now," Tony replies. "We will be able to speak to the White House soon."

"And Connor," Terrie says. "Maybe we can connect with the bunker where Lu and Kyle are at if the signal is strong enough."

"Big 'if' there," Krissy says. She stiffens. "Port bow."

Terrie's eyes snap in that direction.

"What am I looking for?" Terrie asks.

"A very large shadow that's moving," Krissy says. "It's keeping ahead of us."

"I don't see it," Terrie says and rolls her eyes. "Not that I see much out there at all."

"It's there," Krissy says, "trust me."

"I do," Terrie replies.

A loud squelch of static makes them both jump.

"What?" Tony asks as he receives glares from both women. "I was already in the room. I didn't need to announce myself."

"Cute," Krissy says and returns to scanning the water. "Still there. I don't think it's a monster."

"It could be an escort," Tony says as he starts up his device and checks settings. "They do that."

"What are you babbling about?" Krissy asks without looking in Tony's direction. Her binoculars are locked onto the water.

"Whales," Tony says. "They have been known to escort ships in distress to safer waters."

"The last whales I saw weren't whales anymore," Terrie says. "They'd been changed by the ooze."

"If you're referring to the warped killer whales, then I must say that those are not whales," Tony says, still fiddling with his device. "Those are orcas and in the dolphin family."

"Yes, I know that," Terrie says, "and thank you for the information, but classifying marine life is not a priority right now, Tony."

"If there's something in the water that's big as a whale, then classifying marine life is the only priority right now," Tony replies. "Or it is your priority. Mine is getting my device up and running ASAP."

"Dude," Krissy says. "Please chill."

"I see it," Terrie says before Tony can respond to Krissy. "That's a large shadow."

"Bigger than an orca," Krissy says.

"I don't know," Terrie replies, "maybe. Keep an eye on it."

"That is my one and only job right now," Krissy says.

"My job is done," Tony states. "Connections are made. Now I will test the signal."

He fiddles with the device and the radio simultaneously until a consistent hum issues from the radio's speakers.

"I will call the White House now," Tony says as he places the handset up to his mouth.

"Thanks for the play by play," Krissy says. "It's cutting in front of us."

"I see it," Terrie says.

"Hello? This is Tony Rochester calling the White House, over," Tony says.

"We are receiving you loud and clear," a voice replies. "Please hold for Ms. VanderVoort."

"I find that humorous," Tony says. "Please hold for Ms. VanderVoort…"

"Tony? Good to hear from you, kid," VanderVoort's voice booms from the speakers.

"Turn it down," Krissy says. "Damn…"

"Hello, Ms. VanderVoort," Tony says. "We have escaped the island and are heading to the mainland, where we will travel a long distance then rendezvous with Sergeant Bolton."

"Bolton? You haven't spoken to him yet?" VanderVoort asks.

"I was just now able to get my device operational by connecting it to the boat's antenna array," Tony says. "Should I have called Sergeant Bolton before calling the White House, Ms. VanderVoort?"

"I should probably be on this call," Terrie says.

"I think it's better if you pilot the boat," Krissy says. "You can call back after we safely get to land."

"That's why I haven't asked Tony for the handset," Terrie says.

"Could you repeat that, Ms. VanderVoort?" Tony says.

"Sergeant Bolton is completing his mission and going to the Diamondback facility in Colorado," VanderVoort says. "Then he is coming to get the three of you."

"Four," Tony says.

"Four? I thought it was only you, Ms. Morgan, and the girl?" VanderVoort says.

"The girl? Really?" Krissy grumbles.

"I was counting Biscuit," Tony says. "In case there's limited room in the vehicle Sergeant Bolton uses to rescue us with. I want to make sure that all members of our party are accounted for. No dog left behind."

Terrie and Krissy share a quick look, then start laughing. Tony frowns at them but keeps his attention on the radio.

"Ask her why the change in plans," Terrie says.

Tony relays the question.

"Let Ms. Morgan know that you can contact Sergeant Bolton directly as soon as we are finished speaking," VanderVoort says.

"I will do that," Tony says.

"I heard," Terrie says before Tony can repeat the message that all of them heard.

"How soon will your tech be fully operational?" VanderVoort asks. There's a voice in her background. "Yes, I know I sound like Star Wars, Gordon. Go back to making sandwiches, alright?"

"A sandwich sounds delicious," Tony says.

"I could go for a sub," Krissy says. "With extra pickles and piled high with cheese."

"Stop," Terrie says, her stomach rumbling. "Focus on the shadow."

"Starboard bow," Krissy says. "It moved to the other side."

"It's not a monster," Terrie says. "Otherwise, it would have attacked by now."

"An escort, like Tony said," Krissy says and lowers her binoculars.

"Do you think it's the only thing in the water, young lady?" Terrie asks. "Binoculars up, please."

"I need to pee," Krissy complains.

"As do I, but we'll both hold it until I'm certain we're out of danger," Terrie responds.

"Have you seen the world? We aren't gonna be out of danger anytime soon," Krissy snaps.

"Then we aren't peeing anytime soon," Terrie says. "Binoculars up, please."

"Whatever," Krissy says, but does as she's told and returns the binoculars to her eyes. "Yep, the shadow is still there and every-thing still looks like shit."

"Thank you for the report," Terrie says with a smirk.

She glances behind her and points her chin at a stool tucked off to the side.

"Could you get that for me?" she asks. "My legs are killing me."

"Can I lower the binoculars, or do I need to blindly shuffle backward?" Krissy asks.

"The stool, please," Terrie says.

Krissy decides to shuffle backward with the binoculars still held to her eyes. She slaps behind her for a minute until her palm smacks the stool, then she shuffles forward and pushes the stool into the backs of Terrie's legs.

"Multitasking," Krissy says.

"Appreciated," Terrie says and sits down with a loud sigh.

Biscuit whines and everyone freezes. But nothing happens. No eruptions in the water. No tentacles shooting toward the bridge. No signs of the winged monsters diving down at them.

"Call Connor," Terrie says to Tony.

"I'm going to disconnect my call with you and call Sergeant Bolton now, Ms. VanderVoort," Tony says.

"Let me know the second you find a large enough antenna array to connect everyone together," VanderVoort says.

Terrie does not miss the slight desperation in VanderVoort's voice.

"I will, Ms. VanderVoort," Tony says. "Goodbye."

He cuts the call and then taps at his device.

"Now for Sergeant Bolton," Tony says.

"I'll want to speak to Connor," Terrie says. "You take the wheel, Tony."

"I would prefer not to," Tony says. "I would prefer to operate my radio device."

"Tony, you know how to operate this boat better than Krissy," Terrie says. "You should take the wheel."

"I do not believe—"

"Tony. Take the wheel," Terrie insists.

"Don't look at me," Krissy says to Tony. "I have binocular duty."

Tony mumbles complaints but doesn't argue and replaces Terrie at the wheel. She takes the stool with her to the radio.

"May I use the stool?" Tony asks.

"No," Terrie replies.

Tony shrugs as Terrie puts the handset to her mouth.

"Connor? This is Terrie, over," Terrie says.

"Terrie! Thank God!" Bolton's voice calls out. "I was starting to worry!"

"We had to escape the island," Terrie says. "The bunker was breached and no longer safe."

"Escape the island? You're out on open water?" Bolton asks, the fear evident in his voice. "Please be careful, Terrie. Water isn't any safer than land."

"We are very aware of the dangers, Connor," Terrie says. "We have spoken to Ms. VanderVoort. What's this about you completing your mission instead of coming to rendezvous with us?"

"Completing the mission might be a half-truth," Bolton says. "We're almost to Diamondback. My hope is we will find an aircraft that's not only large enough for us to come get you but still operational."

"Do you believe you'll find a working aircraft there?" Terrie asks.

"I think so," Bolton says. "If the rumors I've heard are true, then they were working on some silent infil/exfil vehicles, aircraft being the main focus."

"Silent? Why does that matter now?" Terrie asks.

"It's how they stay silent that I'm thinking about," Bolton says. "No engines, instead something to do with using the Earth's magnetic field. But we'll know for sure when we get there."

"What's your ETA?" Terrie asks.

There's a pause.

"About two hours," Bolton says. "I'll contact you the second we know what we're dealing with. Keep your radio on this time."

"Shouldn't be a problem now," Tony says from his place at the wheel.

"We will," Terrie says to Bolton. "Connor? Have you told Kyle and Lu that I'm alive?"

"Shit!" Bolton snaps. "I'm an idiot."

"Don't worry about it," Terrie says. "You've been busy. We've all been busy. I'll call VanderVoort and have her relay the message."

"No, I'll do it," Bolton says. "You focus on getting to land safely."

"Alright. Thank you," Terrie responds. "Stay safe out there, Connor."

"Yes, ma'am," Bolton says. "Out."

The radio goes silent.

"How is it looking?" Terrie asks, returning her focus to the world outside the boat. "Shadow still there?"

"It is," Tony says, "and it's been joined by two more."

"What?" Krissy exclaims, her head whipping back and forth. "Where?"

"There's a second shadow just beneath the first one," Tony says. "The third shadow is on the other side. We have three escorts."

"Three is better than one," Terrie says. "We'll take the help."

"Why do you think they're helping us?" Krissy asks.

"It's been a while since a boat has been in the water, is my guess," Terrie says. "They were used to them being about. It was familiar. Now they see a boat and want to get that familiarity back."

"No shit," Krissy says. "We all do."

"Very true," Terrie says. "Tony? Could you dial in the White House again, please?"

"I'm busy at the moment," Tony says.

"Smartass," Krissy says.

"That applies to both of you," Terrie says.

"Am I the captain if I'm piloting the boat?" Tony asks.

"No, I'm captain and you're the pilot," Terrie says. "Or helmsman. Or something like that. But I'm still captain, which is why I am ordering you to dial in the White House."

"Okay," Tony says and lets go of the wheel. "Look. No hands."

Krissy reaches out with one hand and grabs the wheel.

"Don't worry, I've got it," she says.

"Thank you, Krissy," Terrie says as Tony dials in the White House.

———

The jackhammer is silent as Lu crouches on the ground, tears streaming from her eyes, her body wracked with sobs of happiness and relief.

Dr. Probst stands close by, fidgety and uncomfortable.

"Uh… this is good news, right?" Dr. Probst asks.

Lu only nods.

It takes her a couple of minutes before she's finished letting go of the grief she'd been hiding deep down inside.

"I'm good," Lu says, standing and wiping her eyes and cheeks. "I'm good."

She grabs the jackhammer once more.

"You want to take a break?" Dr. Probst asks. "That was a lot to take in."

"No, what I want to do is get through this fucking concrete to whatever it is Lowell has you hunting for," Lu says. "Can we do that?"

"Please," Dr. Probst says, "I'd love nothing more."

Lu fires up the jackhammer and shoves it against the wall once again. Concrete chips fly in a flurry of industrious demolition.

"It's starting to smoke!" Dr. Probst shouts after about twenty more minutes of jackhammering.

Lu doesn't stop.

"Lu? The jackhammer is starting to smoke!" Dr. Probst shouts, waving a hand at Lu. "It'll overheat and seize up! That's bad, Lu!"

Lu continues hammering.

"LU!" Dr. Probst yells.

Lu doubles down, pushing even harder.

"LU! STOP!" Dr. Probst shouts.

The jackhammer groans and thick, black smoke pours from the motor vents. Then it does exactly as Dr. Probst said it would: it seizes tight.

As soon as the machine locks up, Lu is flung backward from the sudden jolt of metal parts fusing together. The tripod topples and the jackhammer lays on the concrete floor of the tunnel, a scorched, useless hunk.

"Are you alright?" Dr. Probst asks Lu, helping her to her feet.

"I'm fine," Lu says.

"Yeah, I'm not so sure about that," Dr. Probst says. "I'm also not so sure there's a backup jackhammer."

"In this place? There're probably six backup jackhammers somewhere," Lu says. "We just have to find them."

"What the hell is going on?" Kyle shouts from down the tunnel. "I smell smoke, and not the good kind!"

He reaches the two women, a food-laden box in his arms, sets it down, and surveys the damage.

"Well, you killed the jackhammer, Mom," Kyle says. "Good one."

"Your grandmother and Biscuit are still alive," Lu says.

Kyle stares and blinks for a second, then rushes to his mother's arms. They both burst into tears, leaving Dr. Probst to shuffle her feet and wait.

There's a loud scraping noise, then a tumble and crash, and Dr. Probst whirls around to see a good portion of the concrete wall slough off onto the floor.

"Uh… guys?" Dr. Probst says.

Kyle and Lu are still crying and hugging each other.

"Hey!" Dr. Probst shouts. "Sorry to interrupt, but look! Look!"

Annoyed, Lu pulls away from her son and turns on Dr. Probst. She's about to unleash on the woman for being so insensitive, then stops as she sees what Dr. Probst is staring at.

"You found the vein," Kyle says.

Kyle moves forward, his hand out.

"Kyle, no!" Lu exclaims.

"It's alright, Mom," Kyle says. "I can touch this. You shouldn't, but I think I can."

"You think?" Dr. Probst asks. "Don't do anything until I grab the laptop."

Dr. Probst rushes over to the cart and snags the laptop and several leads. She plugs the USB end of the leads into the laptop, then slowly approaches the vein of blue crystal.

"Give her room," Lu says to Kyle. He balks. "Kyle. Give her room."

Kyle steps back.

Dr. Probst carefully places the four leads against the vein of blue crystal, then studies the readings on the laptop.

"It's... doing nothing," Dr. Probst says. "No... that's not true. There's something happening, but it's like it won't show me."

"Here," Kyle says, and before anyone can argue again, he places a fingertip on the vein.

Kyle's body stiffens and Dr. Probst gasps.

"Kyle!" Lu shouts, hurrying forward.

But Dr. Probst's hand shoots out and grabs her arm before Lu can drag Kyle away from the vein.

"Look," Dr. Probst says with awe. "Lu, look."

Lu looks at the laptop and frowns.

"What does it mean?" Lu asks.

"It's communicating," Dr. Probst says. "Those wave forms? That's language or something like it. One time, while I was studying the rock formations deep in the jungle of..."

The look on Lu's face stops Dr. Probst's story.

"Sorry," Dr. Probst says. "This is astounding. There's more than just communication going on…"

"It's looking," Kyle says. "It's trying to connect to the other facilities. It has been for… millennia."

"Yes, but what is this?" Dr. Probst asks, pointing at her screen. "The resonance being created is too strong. What else is it doing?"

"A conduit," Kyle says. "Is that the right word?"

"You mean like a tube?" Dr. Probst asks.

"No, no… more than that," Kyle says.

"A passage?" Dr. Probst asks and looks at Lu.

Lu shrugs a why-are-you-looking-at-me shrug.

"Yes," Kyle replies, "a passage."

"That's not possible," Dr. Probst says and laughs. "Which means it's probably true."

"It needs help," Kyle says. "Come on. We have to find where this starts."

"What do you mean?" Lu asks her son.

Kyle reluctantly disconnects from the vein. He shakes his hand and takes a deep breath.

"If it's a passage, then there's an entrance, right?" Kyle says. "Somewhere in this facility is the entrance." He closes his eyes and tilts his head. "I think I know where. Come on!"

Kyle takes off running.

"Kyle! Wait!" Lu yells.

"No time, Mom!" he yells back. "We have to hurry!"

"The cart!" Lu shouts. "We can take the cart!"

Kyle stops and turns back to them.

"Oh… right," he says sheepishly. "That'd be a lot faster."

TEN

For most of Anson Lowell's life, he's known fear.

Not many psychiatrists and psychologists, therapists and analysts, were ever fooled by his bravado, his sarcastic confidence act. They saw his jokes and nonchalant attitude as covering up his trauma. They said it was Lowell's way of deflecting the truth away from what happened to him.

With every "amazing" diagnosis, Lowell nodded and smiled. He allowed the educated pricks and twats to patronize him and he allowed the condescension to flow over him. Yes, he'd be defiant and deny the findings, but he only did so half-heartedly.

And there was a simple reason Lowell allowed the doctors and professionals to come to their conclusions: they were so wrong that to let them in on what was really going on would have terrified them to death.

The truth was that Lowell wasn't hiding from trauma or trying to mask his pain. No, he was using it as a wall for something so much worse.

Rage.

Real rage. Not the rage he'd used on the people he'd killed. That was kids' stuff.

The rage Lowell hid was of a power that could destroy planets, annihilate galaxies, and end the universe.

Metaphorically, of course.

But that was before the Substance changed him. That was before he became attuned to alien technology and biology.

That was before. This is now.

Lowell picks himself up off the floor of the elevator, wipes the blood from his face and eyes, and presses a single button.

The elevator doors open wide.

"I'm in the mood for some licorice," Lowell says as he lifts his head and sniffs the air.

The Ebony Man's trail is easy to follow. Lowell can physically see the being's footprints on the Antarctica facility's floor. Breadcrumbs of corruption that lead down one corridor, then the next and the next and so on.

They lead to another elevator. An elevator that goes down to where the facility connects with the Substance.

Lowell stares at the elevator.

If he follows, he may be able to stop the Ebony Man in time. But Lowell knows that time isn't what he has. And the odds are that the Ebony Man is already at the Substance.

Lowell comes to the conclusion that he has been played and that's that. Get over it and move on.

"You want a fight, Mr. Licorice?" Lowell says to the closed elevator doors. "Oh, you're about to get one serious fight."

Lowell turns away and closes his eyes. He reaches out a hand and touches the facility's wall.

"Come on, come on," he mutters. "Give me more than elevator control. Give me access."

Lowell can feel the facility fight against him, desperate to keep its secrets hidden.

"Oh, he trained you good," Lowell says. "I hate to break it to you though, but Mr. Licorice is a fucking asshole and doesn't care about you. He cut you off from the others. He isolated you and is responsible for all the eons and eons of loneliness you feel."

The lights in the corridor brighten.

"Mr. Licorice will ditch you again as soon as he gets what he wants," Lowell says, and a thought strikes him.

The most important thought that has ever entered his mind.

"And what he wants is off this planet," Lowell says. "He set all of this up so whatever is coming would come. He doesn't care about the war, only about himself. He'll use the whatevers that are coming to escape, make it look like the war destroyed the planet and it isn't his fault. But I can tell you, he's gonna bail from here once he destroys it all."

The lights brighten even more.

"That means you'll be destroyed too," Lowell says, pressing his palm harder against the wall. "All facilities will be destroyed. And the Substance that has grown and lived on this planet will die as it floats into the nothingness of space."

Lowell laughs.

"I watched way too much *Cosmos* in prison," he says.

The lights shut off, plunging Lowell into pure darkness. But he doesn't panic or worry.

When the lights come back on, Lowell is granted full access to the facility.

He can see that his instincts were correct and the Ebony Man is currently stepping into the Substance. That isn't good, but it isn't the worst. There's still a way to stop the Ebony Man.

"Two floors up and six corridors down," Lowell says and backtracks to the main facility elevator.

He steps in, tells the facility the floor he needs, and whistles "Sweet Caroline" while he waits for the elevator to ascend two floors. He isn't even to the chorus when the doors open.

Walking as if he hasn't just recently gotten his ass kicked by a pitch-black alien being, Lowell makes his way down the six corridors until he comes to a door. He places a hand to the door, frowns, then steps back.

"What's the problem?" he calls out.

A flash in his mind.

"Cute," Lowell says and knocks on the door.

It slides open to reveal yet one more elevator. This one is much smaller than the others, meant for two people maximum. Lowell walks in and the door slides shut behind him.

But instead of a feeling of being moved up or down, Lowell is jolted to the right as the elevator moves suddenly sideways.

"Aren't you full of surprises," Lowell says.

The elevator races along for several minutes, and Lowell's eyebrows rise higher and higher with each minute in astonishment at the size of the facility. Close to thirty minutes later, the elevator stops and the door opens.

Lowell is facing a room with two chairs, similar to dentist or salon chairs. Other than the chairs, there are small pedestals, each with a control console on top of them, on the far side of each chair.

"Not how I'd decorate, but it'll work," Lowell says. "Let's see what this room can do."

Lowell plops into one of the chairs and places his hand on the control console. It comes to life and a million holographic images float around the room before coalescing into a single, bright-blue orb.

The bright blue of the crystal veins.

The orb hesitates.

"Come on," Lowell says, "I can take it."

The orb bobs up and down, then slams into Lowell's chest. His eyes widen and he gasps, then slowly starts to take deep, even breaths.

"I got it from here," Lowell says and closes his eyes.

Lowell taps into the power of the blue light as his consciousness descends deep within the facility, diving lower and lower until he leaves the facility and is immersed in nothing but rock.

Rock containing the vein of blue crystal.

"Still cut off," Lowell says to himself. "But I can feel you working on it. There's a signal far off and growing stronger. Come on, Cheryl, do your geologist magic and get these veins talking to each other again."

A bright flash distracts Lowell from the almost connection. He pauses then decides to follow the flash, bringing his mind up out of the rock and back into the facility.

Lowell traverses the facility's systems until he reaches a space so gigantic he can barely comprehend the size. And if he thought comprehending the size of the space was hard, it's doubly hard to comprehend the size of what is contained within the space.

"Shit," Lowell says. "I knew it'd be big, but not that big."

Lowell doesn't try to connect with the body of the massive monster—a kaiju so large that it could devour the former Wyoming monster in only a couple of bites. Lowell knows there's no point in connecting. The mind he'll find won't be a blank slate waiting for a pilot. No, the mind he'll find is that of the Ebony Man.

As the gargantuan creature stirs and starts to uncurl its massive body from a slumber millions of years old, Lowell just can't help himself.

Speakers set throughout the Antarctica facility come to life with the strains of Elton John's "Tiny Dancer."

The monster starts to shake then full-on quake as it awakens to the sounds of Bernie Taupin's lyrics come to life.

The behemoth is not happy.

"Not an Elton fan, Mr. Licorice?" Lowell bellows over the facility's PA. "Come on, dude. Who doesn't love this song?"

The monster roars and stands upright, its head crashing through concrete, steel, and then layer after layer of earth and ice until its torso is free of the facility and facing the frigid winds and weather of the frozen continent.

"Dude!" Lowell shouts. "Just open the door next time!"

The thing is almost a mile high and built like a reptilian gorilla. Scales cover its body from the tips of its fingers to the top of its head. Simian eyes blink several times and it shakes itself, showing the scales to be loosely joined together, not too tightly overlapped. It shakes once more and the true deadliness of the scales is revealed: the edges of the scales are finely honed blades.

The song switches to Frank Sinatra's "I'll Be Seeing You." Lowell laughs at the rage it causes the gigantic beast.

"Hey, Mr. Licorice?" Lowell shouts as the monster climbs up out of the space and onto the Antarctic tundra. "You and me? We ain't done, dude. I'm coming for you."

The beast pauses before lumbering off, turns its head to look down into the space it had just vacated, then lets loose with a roar that causes an avalanche of dirt, rock, and ice to plummet down inside, filling a quarter of the space before the monster lifts its head back up and walks off.

"Oh, yeah, dude," Lowell continues, his voice echoing throughout the facility, "I am so coming for you."

———

"Not looking good," Joshua says as the Stryker comes to a stop before a mangled chain-link gate.

It's only the first stop on the gauntlet of security that fronts the government's Diamondback military research facility, but from what Bolton can see through the vehicle's windshield, none of the other security checkpoints fared much better.

The same can be said of Schriever and Fort Collins, but those bases were much, much worse. The bases were devastated, leaving zero survivors. Worst of all, Bolton and Joshua saw the return of the ooze creatures, and neither were happy about having to deal with the warped things, as well as the giant monsters, still stomping the landscape. Worst of all, evidenced by the state of the corpses they did find, the ooze creatures are more aggressive than ever.

Bolton shoves the images out of his mind.

"Keep going," Bolton says. "Might as well drive up to the front door."

Joshua puts the Stryker in gear and drives them past the destruction of guard posts, more gates, and even a few machine gun nests. Then they're passing burnt-out buildings. Blood stains can be seen here and there, as can signs of ooze, but no bodies.

"Someone cleaned up," Joshua says as he drives the Stryker directly up to a wall of metal set into a cliff face. He parks the Stryker, grabs his M4, and looks at Bolton. "Let's knock."

He and Bolton hop out of the vehicle and approach the wall of metal.

"Single bulkhead," Joshua states. "Not double doors."

"There has to be a way in," Bolton says. "There."

A small, man-sized door stands impotently next to the wall of metal. Bolton walks up to it, notes that the security camera above the door is shiny black and not coated in ash, and slings his M4. He pulls out his sat phone and waves it at the camera.

"I'm Sergeant Connor Bolton," he says, "and I've been sent here by the President of the United States. We need to get inside so we can see what aircraft you have available that might still be operational. It's a matter of the planet's safety and humanity's survival."

"If that doesn't do it, then we're screwed," Joshua says, facing back the way they came, eyes checking for threats. "We aren't getting inside unless they let us in."

Bolton waits, then waves the sat phone again.

"If your systems are working, then you can use face-rec to see that I am who I say I am," Bolton shouts. "This phone is a direct line to the White House Situation Room. If you won't let us in, then at least send someone out."

"We have movement," Joshua says.

Bolton turns to face him then follows his sightline to a collapsed personnel barracks about two hundred yards off.

"People?" Bolton asks, bringing his M4 around and up to his shoulder.

"I'm not sure," Joshua responds. "I don't think so."

"Shit," Bolton says. "Back in the Stryker."

"Retreat?" Joshua replies.

"Regroup," Bolton says. "We'll be safer inside the Stryker."

"We'll be safer inside this mountain," Joshua says but doesn't argue and walks briskly to the Stryker, his eyes never leaving the demolished barracks.

Bolton follows closely behind, and they both hop up into the Stryker then lock it down.

"I'll take the turret," Bolton says. "I can keep an eye on the door too from up there."

"Watch yourself," Joshua says. "I think it's big."

"They all are," Bolton says and climbs up into the turret.

The higher vantage point doesn't reveal any new sights, but a sound does reach Bolton's ears and he puzzles over it.

"Do you hear that?" he calls down into the Stryker.

"Claws," Joshua replies.

"That's my thought too," Bolton says. "None of the diesel junkies sound like that when they walk."

"That's because it's not a diesel junkie," Joshua says. "Look."

From out of the rubble comes a beast on all fours. It raises its snout, sniffs, then turns and faces the Stryker. The beast rears up onto its hind legs and roars. Bright green ooze spittle streams from the thing's mouth.

"A bear," Joshua says.

"Not anymore," Bolton says, taking aim. "Fire when you have the shot. Let's drop this bitch."

Probably close to a dozen roars answer the ooze bear.

"It has friends," Joshua says.

Bolton reassesses the damage and destruction all around the base. Diesel junkies didn't do this; not all of it, at least. Not even close.

"Fucking ooze bears," Bolton mutters.

"Fucking ooze bears," Joshua echoes.

The roars continue until fifteen more ooze bears join the first. As one, they race toward the Stryker.

Without saying a word, Bolton and Joshua open fire, sending a hail of bullets at the charging ooze bears.

Bolton can see his rounds hit the beasts' flesh, but not one of the ooze bears even slows or pauses from the impacts.

"This isn't working!" Joshua yells.

Bolton considers switching to the .50 cal, but he doubts that will make much difference.

"Button up!" Bolton shouts and drops down from the turret.

He secures the hatch, then turns to face the rear of the vehicle. A rear that is wide open after the diesel junkie yanked the hatch off hundreds of miles back.

"They'll get in," Joshua says as he joins Bolton in the center of the vehicle.

Joshua faces the front where the windshields will certainly be broken out despite their reinforced material. Bolton faces the open rear, his M4 to his shoulder and a stack of loaded magazines piled between him and Joshua.

Bolton turns his head and watches the ooze bears get closer and closer. He turns back to the hatch when the monsters are only ten yards out.

"Sorry you couldn't complete your mission," Joshua says.

"Me too," Bolton replies, then slowly starts to squeeze the trigger as the first ooze bear hits the rear of the Stryker.

But before Bolton can open fire, a deafening klaxon fills the air, driving the ooze bears back a couple of yards. The beasts shake off their surprise, regroup, and come back in for another attack. Flames engulf the Stryker, and both Bolton and Joshua instinctively drop to the floor and cover themselves with their arms.

The heat is intense. Almost as intense as the roars of pain and rage coming from the ooze bears. Roars that die away until only the crackling of slowly dwindling flames is heard.

"You alive in there?" a voice calls out.

Bolton and Joshua scramble out of the red-hot vehicle and face a group holding flamethrowers and dressed in fire-retardant suits. A tall figure steps forward.

"Sergeant Bolton? I'm Lieutenant Commander Banks and I'm

in charge of this base," the figure says. "Come with us and we'll explain what happened."

"Thank you, Lieutenant Commander, but I think we have an idea of what happened," Bolton says. "It's a similar story to what's been going on out there."

"Then come inside, get cleaned up, and we'll talk," Banks says.

"You need to talk to the White House," Bolton says and produces the sat phone. "Now."

"He means inside now," Joshua says as another round of roars fill the air.

"Hurry," Banks says and motions for them to follow.

The group quickly get inside the facility through the small door. Once they're inside and the door is closed, a secondary, then a tertiary metal door slide into place to seal off the facility from the outside.

The group strip off their suits and gear and stow everything in lockers that have been placed by the entryway. Bolton can tell the lockers aren't normally located there and had been put in place recently. The fresh scratches and gouges in the concrete floor make it obvious.

"Sergeant," Banks says and holds out a hand. "Welcome to Diamondback."

Bolton shakes and nods at Joshua.

"This is Joshua," Bolton says and smiles at the lieutenant commander's quizzical look. "Just Joshua. He does, or did, wet works for the agencies."

"Which agency?" one of the group asks.

"All of them," Joshua says.

"If you say so," Banks says. "This is Corporal Hines, Corporal Denz, Corporal Rowan, and Private Quint."

Hines and Rowan are male and Denz and Quint are female. They all nod to Bolton and Joshua.

"What's the command structure?" Bolton asks. "Is this a call for you to make or for your superior officer?"

"This is it," Banks replies. "We're what's left of the Diamond-back's personnel."

"Shit," Joshua says.

"Three of those things got in here," Denz says, "along with about two hundred chipmunks."

"Damn Disney rats are all over this mountain," Hines says. "When they went bad, it was like a flood of death pouring down on us."

"By the time we realized we could take them out with fire, we'd lost two-thirds of the personnel inside here," Banks says.

"And the surviving third?" Joshua asks.

"Most slipped out in the night. Deserted. We're what's left," Banks said. "It's all clear now, but the wildlife outside hasn't stopped trying to get in."

"Why not leave?" Joshua asks.

"And go where?" Banks replies. "You're the first evidence we've seen that anyone in the government is left alive."

"This place should be shielded," Bolton says. "Why haven't you answered when the White House calls?"

"Most of the systems are out due to the ooze," Banks says. "The EMP took out only a quarter of our capabilities, but once that ooze got into the systems, they started going offline one by one, their components melted into noxious piles of shit."

Bolton swallows.

"Tell me there's aircraft here that's still operational," Bolton says.

"We have something that might fit what you need," Banks says.

"Manned or unmanned?" Bolton asks, hope constricting his chest like a sudden heart attack.

"Both," Banks says. "Follow me." He holds out his hand. "I'll make the call on the way."

Bolton gives him the sat phone. Banks nods then gestures for the group to move out. Bolton and Joshua follow the others as they make their way through several checkpoints that show evidence of the battles that have taken place inside Diamondback.

By the time they reach the command center, Bolton is amazed anyone lived at all.

"Water?" Rowan asks.

"That'd be great," Bolton says. Joshua nods.

Waters are handed out all around.

Banks ends the call and hands the sat phone back to Bolton.

"I spoke with a VanderVoort," Banks says. "She's different."

"Understatement," Bolton says.

"She told me what the original mission was but said you have the call on the ground," Banks says. "I'm to do what you say and give you what you need. Not exactly following the chain of command, but VanderVoort didn't sound like she cares too much for chains and prefers solid results instead."

"That's her," Bolton says. "So? What have you got for us?"

"Where are you going?" Banks asks.

"Seattle," Bolton replies.

"Long way," Banks says. "How fast do you need to be there?"

"Yesterday," Bolton says.

"I figured as much," Banks says. "I think we can make that happen."

"How many seats does the craft have?" Bolton asks.

"Seats? Two," Banks says. "Two benches also. They're in the small cargo hold and can seat eight operators. You have to hunch over, but the craft will get you where you need to go and back. Do you need bigger? We have bigger, but..."

"No, the smaller aircraft is perfect," Bolton says. He raises an eyebrow. "But, this other aircraft? How much bigger are we talking?"

"That's a conversation I can only have with the President," Banks says. "Or VanderVoort now, I guess."

Bolton nods. "I get it. I do. The smaller one will be fine."

"Do you fly?" Banks asks.

"I do," Joshua states.

"He does," Bolton says.

"Then no time to lose," Banks says.

"I should make a call first," Bolton says then sighs. "We left the radio in the Stryker."

"Relay a message through the White House," Joshua says.

"Good idea," Bolton says and activates the sat phone.

The tech that answers understands Bolton's message and says he'll relay it to Terrie and the kids.

"Hopefully they make contact and get us an exfil point," Bolton says.

"What's so important about these people?" Banks asks.

"One is basically like my mother-in-law," Bolton says. "Former U.S. Marshal Terrie Morgan. Then there's a kid who built a device that should get all comms back online. The third is a teenage girl who's been with them for a while now."

"And the dog," Joshua says.

"There's a dog too," Bolton says.

"So, family with advantages," Banks says.

"The device is the mission," Bolton says. "But, yes, this is about family."

"Copy that. Say no more," Banks says and nods at a door on the far side of the command center. "Come on. You're gonna like what you see."

––––––––

Soaked to the bone as gray rain pours down on them, Terrie, Krissy, Tony, and Biscuit skulk through the gloom, dashing from one hiding spot to the next in their desperate flight away from the battle that rages in the harbor behind them.

The mutant orcas finally appeared when the boat was close to a semi-intact marina. That was when the shadowy escorts revealed themselves to be humpback whales.

Terrie barely got the boat to a half-collapsed dock and everyone out before one of the mutant orcas attacked the vessel, shredding its hull and sending it sinking to the bottom of the harbor.

As the humpbacks breached the surface of Puget Sound, slamming down onto the mutant orcas, Terrie and the rest raced away from the marina as fast as they could. All of their gear—except for Tony's radio and device, the Barrett strapped to Terrie's back, a duffel of ammunition, and a backpack with very little water and food on Krissy's back—was lost when the boat went down.

As Terrie motions for Krissy and Tony to hustle over to a school bus on its side, Terrie is kind of glad they aren't encumbered by too much weight. They need to move as fast as possible, and even the Barrett is almost too much for Terrie's legs to handle.

A far-off screech emphasizes why they have to move fast.

Ooze creatures of all types stalk the cracked and broken roadways, hunting, searching.

They reach the fallen school bus and rest for a few seconds against the ash-stained yellow metal. Terrie studies the skyline, searching for what Tony says will be the perfect antenna array.

The Space Needle.

"There," Terrie says and points into the gloom.

Fog-shrouded and almost impossible to see without its iconic red light blinking on top, the Space Needle can just be made out far off in the distance.

"That's miles away," Krissy whispers. "It'll take us all day to get there."

"We'll look for a working vehicle," Terrie says.

"EMP," Tony says. "There are no working vehicles."

"This is Seattle," Terrie says, "there are bikes everywhere."

"Biscuit can't ride a bike," Tony says.

"Stop being a bummer," Krissy snaps.

A screech fills the air, much too close for comfort.

"Shhh," Terrie warns, then gestures for them to move.

They leave the shadow of the bus and hurry around a mangled Starbucks, then down the street to an open storefront, where they duck inside and stay in the shadows as their ears hunt for threats.

After a minute of silence, Terrie leads them away from the store and down the street once more. They navigate Seattle for most of the day, hiding and running from the constant hunt that dogs their heels. Finally, after searching for hours, and a lot of zigzagging and backtracking, Terrie spots what they need.

"That," Terrie says and points at what look like oversized tricycles with covered backseats.

"Rickshaws?" Krissy asks.

"They're called pedicabs," Tony says. "Rickshaw is an antiquated and possibly racist term."

Two of the pedicabs lean against a shattered brick wall, but both look operational with fully inflated tires and chains still attached. Terrie cautiously moves toward them, a pistol in one hand, her eyes checking every shadow, every nook and cranny where an ooze creature can hide and ambush her.

She makes it to the pedicabs, inspects them closer, and smiles. Then she gestures for the others.

Krissy and Tony hustle over with Biscuit right behind. The teens get the pedicabs upright and each go over them to make sure they truly are operational.

"I'll ride back here with Biscuit," Terrie says and pats one of the pedicabs. "Krissy can drive. Tony, you'll drive the other one with all the gear."

"That is an acceptable plan," Tony says. Krissy nods and shrugs.

"Then we execute the acceptable plan," Terrie says.

Tony and Krissy hop into their respective pedicabs, wheel around the street for a few seconds, then both stop and get everything loaded into Tony's pedicab while Terrie and Biscuit climb into the back of Krissy's.

Then they're off.

The journey is difficult, to say the least.

The fact that most of the streets are destroyed, along with the buildings surrounding them, coupled with the fact that Seattle is an extremely hilly city, make the going rough. Not to mention that several times they have to abandon the small vehicles and hide to avoid being caught by packs of ooze creatures.

Hours go by before they get to the outskirts of the expansive Seattle Center park that houses the Space Needle.

Terrie's face falls as she sees what lies before them.

Once a thriving center of activity and entertainment, the Seattle Center is now overrun by ooze creatures and covered in mounds of ash.

"Great," Krissy whispers.

Terrie pats Biscuit, making sure he doesn't start barking and give them away to the ooze creatures.

"What do you need, Tony?" Terrie asks quietly.

"I need to connect the radio to the Space Needle's frame," Tony says. "It should act as a huge antenna, giving us range enough to communicate with most of the Western Hemisphere. Possibly the entire world, if my calculations are correct."

"Shoulds and ifs are gonna get us killed," Krissy says.

"None of us are getting killed," Terrie says and points to a few intact maintenance buildings. "We move quickly and quietly from building to building. The last stretch will be wide open, but we can make it."

"Then what?" Krissy asks.

"Then we do whatever it takes to get Tony's device hooked up and working," Terrie says. "After that, we do whatever it takes to keep the device working so we can help save the world."

"What's left to save?" Krissy asks.

Terrie fixes her gaze on the teenagers.

"I'm looking at it," Terrie responds. "Enough questions. Let's go."

ELEVEN

"Ma'am! Ms. VanderVoort!" a tech shouts. "A satellite picked up movement in Antarctica! We have a kaiju on the move!"

"Show me, don't tell me!" VanderVoort replies, setting her plate of food down and hauling herself up off the couch.

She moves closer to the main monitor and gasps at the sight. She's not the only one. Others either set their plates down or cease loading their plates from the buffet line set up on the conference table. The Situation Room goes deathly silent.

"What's the scale of that thing?" VanderVoort asks.

"Um…about point-eight-five miles, ma'am," the tech replies.

"Fuck me…" Director Miles says.

"I'll second that thought, Gordon," President Nance says. "Where did it come from? Was there an eruption in Antarctica?"

"No eruption," Dr. Hall says, his head turning back and forth from an array of monitors. "It came out of here."

A secondary monitor shows the massive chamber the kaiju had crawled out from.

"This kaiju was prepped and ready," Dr. Hall continues. "Look at the space. It's like a stasis chamber. To use government speak, this kaiju was off books."

"So is that Lowell?" VanderVoort asks. "It had fucking better be Lowell. Has anyone heard from him?"

Everyone responds in the negative.

"Of course not," VanderVoort says. "Why would a convict report in and let us know he's walking away from the South Pole in a giant gorilla suit? That'd be too convenient."

"What is it?" Alvarez asks. "It looks like a cross between an ape and some sort of lizard."

"More a cross with a snake," Dr. Hall says. "See the scales? They're shaped and overlap like a snake more than a lizard. Except..."

Dr. Hall fiddles with the controls and most of the room starts shouting at him as he zooms in on the kaiju, distorting the main monitor's view.

"Relax!" Dr. Hall yells. "You're going to want to see this!"

The sharpened edges of the scales become terrifyingly large and the complaints come to a full stop.

"That'll mess up your day," Alvarez says.

"No shit," VanderVoort says. "How do you fight something like that? Another kaiju can't get in close."

"To defeat it, the other kaiju would need to have a projectile ability," Dr. Hall says. "Fire or flying spikes or the sonic blast the Wyoming kaiju had. If you get in close, then that thing will shred you fast."

"Where is it going?" President Nance asks. "What is there to fight in Antarctica?"

"It's leaving the continent," Dr. Hall says. "Don't ask me where, I know as much as you do, but it's for sure leaving. Look at it. The kaiju is limbering up, stretching its arms and legs."

"For what?" Alvarez asks.

"A swim," Dr. Hall states as if that should have been obvious to everyone. "He isn't going to fly off the continent."

In minutes, the kaiju proves Dr. Hall right as it dives directly into the ocean and is lost from sight beneath the ice shelves.

"Can we track it?" VanderVoort shouts.

"Yes, ma'am," a tech replies. "We have a lock on it and are tasking all satellites to track it as it moves."

"Good," VanderVoort says. "Wherever that thing pops up, all hell is going to break loose."

"Ma'am? Sergeant Bolton is calling in again," a tech states.

"Tell him we still haven't made contact with Terrie Morgan or the kids," VanderVoort says. "And I'm sorry I can't talk. We're a little busy."

"He says he's ready to leave Diamondback, ma'am," the tech relays.

"Put him through," VanderVoort replies. "Bolton? What ya got for me? Make it quick."

"Quite a lot, Ms. VanderVoort," Bolton replies. "The aircraft is operational and we'll be leaving Diamondback within the hour with several drones in tow."

"Great," VanderVoort replies. "You couldn't have told the tech that?"

"I could have, but we do have an issue," Bolton responds. "We need you to authorize weapons-free on the aircraft and the drones."

"Authorize?" VanderVoort says. "Why are the weapons on lockdown?"

"Ms. VanderVoort?" a voice interrupts. "This is Lieutenant Commander Banks again, ma'am. While I am the acting officer now for the Diamondback facility, I was not the senior officer in charge of these projects. I don't have the clearance to unlock the weapons."

"You're authorized to go weapons hot at your discretion, Lieutenant Commander Banks," President Nance says. "We'll have a tech send you the authorization codes now."

"Thank you, Mr. President," Banks replies.

VanderVoort glances over her shoulder and nods at the president. He nods back.

"Is that all, Sergeant?" VanderVoort asks.

"That's all, ma'am," Bolton replies.

"Then get your asses in the air and go get us that kid and his device," VanderVoort says. "Good luck."

"Godspeed, soldiers," President Nance says.

"Okay, back to Grape Ape," VanderVoort says.

"Huh, the scales do have a purple sheen to them," Dr. Hall says.

"Ma'am? We have another call coming in," a tech says.

"Jesus jumping up and down on a pogo stick while twirling fire batons!" VanderVoort exclaims. "Who else is there? Tell me it's the kid!"

"No, ma'am, it's Anson Lowell," the tech replies. "He says he could have overridden our protocols and forced the call through to the main monitor, but he wanted to be polite."

"How nice of him to finally give us a report," VanderVoort says and twirls her fingers. "Put him through."

"Hey," Lowell says as his image comes up on a secondary monitor. "Whoa. How come I'm not the main attraction?"

"You can tell from where you are that you're not on the main monitor?" VanderVoort asks, her eyebrows raised. "Neat trick."

"It is, isn't it?" Lowell responds. "This facility has way more bells and whistles. Once I'm fully attuned to its workings, I think I'm going to have fun here."

"Good for you, Mr. Lowell," VanderVoort says. "As long as you're having fun. Were you calling in to tell us about the new kaiju?"

"Well, yeah," Lowell says. "I thought I should since I didn't want you to think it was me. Because obviously it's not."

Reality slams into everyone at once. VanderVoort steps back and lowers herself back onto the couch, her hand across her swollen belly.

"Wait… what…?" is all VanderVoort can say.

"Yeah, that's an appropriate response," Lowell says. "Mr. Licorice pulled a fast one on me. Looks like he was just hitching a ride to Antarctica and sorta set things up so he could take control once he got here."

"Then the kaiju currently swimming away from Antarctica is controlled by the Ebony Man?" Dr. Hall asks.

"Correctamundo, Doc," Lowell replies. "The guy gave me a serious beat down, then jacked my ride."

"Where's he going?" VanderVoort asks.

"Fuck if I know, lady," Lowell says. "Maybe he's hitting the Dunkin' in Patagonia because he has a hankering for a Boston creme and a macchiato? Mr. Licorice didn't give me his day's itinerary."

"Do they have Dunkin' Donuts in Patagonia?" Dr. Hall asks.

"Maybe. Maybe not," Lowell says with a shrug. "But the guy's going somewhere. I have no idea where, but I'll keep tracking him."

"Track him? How?" VanderVoort asks.

"Oh, I got the hook up to all the satellites down here," Lowell says. "Seriously, I'm really liking the Antarctica facility. Why didn't anyone tell me about this place before?"

"Because we didn't know about it," VanderVoort says. "That facility has been hidden from us."

"Then I call dibs," Lowell says. "And we all know that dibs is binding during an apocalypse. When the world goes to shit, dibs rules."

"Mr. Lowell, can you please be serious?" VanderVoort pleads. "Tell me you know how to stop the Ebony Man."

"I don't have a fucking clue," Lowell says. "But I'm working on it. I made Mr. Licorice a promise I'd come for his ass, and Anson Lowell keeps that kind of promise. My record stands for itself."

There are more than a few shivers in the Situation Room at the statement.

"Bringing up your record may not be the best move, Mr. Lowell," VanderVoort says.

"Just keeping it real, VanderVoort, just keeping it real," Lowell says.

"How about you just keep me posted when you figure out

how to stop that thing, okay?" VanderVoort says and rubs her face. "If that's all, Mr. Lowell—"

"Oh, fuck no, that is not all," Lowell says. "Has no one there noticed that a really big spider with some serious acne just climbed out of the ocean and is heading my way?"

"What?" VanderVoort exclaims. "Get me an image now!"

"Let me," Lowell says, and the main monitor switches to a view of the freezing landscape of Antarctica.

Through the constantly blowing snow, a giant form can be seen.

"That's Africa!" Dr. Hall exclaims. "It did swim from the Cape to Antarctica!"

"Well, this guy has a doctorate in obvious," Lowell says. "Africa, huh? Anyone care to tell me what's on its back?"

"Villages," Dr. Hall says. "It spun webs and wrapped entire villages up, then affixed them to its back."

"Seriously?" Lowell asks.

"Seriously," VanderVoort says. "Someone get me a better image of that thing!"

"Hold on," Lowell says. "No need to yell."

"I wasn't talking to—oh. Thank you," VanderVoort says as the image clarifies. "See those white lumps, Lowell? Those contain people."

"We believe the kaiju trapped the villages and is keeping them as food for later," Dr. Hall says.

"Food for later?" Lowell shakes his head. "You're an animal doctor, right?"

"I'm not a veterinarian, if that's what you mean," Dr. Hall says. "I am a zoologist, though."

"A shitty one," Lowell says.

"Excuse me?" Dr. Hall snaps.

"How many fucking villagers do you think it would take to fill this guy's belly, Doc?" Lowell asks, then smiles, leans back, and waits.

Dr. Hall sputters for a couple seconds, then deflates into his chair.

"You're correct," Dr. Hall admits. "Fatigue has clouded my thought processes."

"Good of you to own up to it," Lowell says. "There aren't even close to enough snacks on spidey's back to tackle the energy needs of a creature that large."

"Then what *are* you saying, Mr. Lowell?" VanderVoort asks.

"I think it's trying to save those people," Lowell says, "by bringing them here."

"Bringing them there?" VanderVoort pauses, then nods up and down. "It knows the only safe places are the facilities and it brought people to you. But why not use the facility it climbed out of? Why not use Africa?"

"Maybe it was compromised," Dr. Hall says. "Or it's too small."

"Or the facility isn't built for long-term use," Alvarez adds.

"Lots of good brainstorming there, folks," Lowell says. "Doesn't really matter. What does matter is I'm about to have company, so I think I'll get off this call and go prepare some snacks. Maybe mix up some Country Time lemonade. Is that still a thing? I've been in prison a long time, so maybe it's not a thing anymore."

"It is a thing," VanderVoort says. "And I could really go for a glass right now. Gordon?"

"On it," Director Miles says.

"Mr. Lowell?" VanderVoort says.

"Ms. VanderVoort?" Lowell responds.

"Figure this out," VanderVoort orders. "Do that, and I'll make sure you're granted a pardon."

"A pardon? Well, gee whiz, Ms. VanderVoort, you sure do know how to take care of a fella." Lowell laughs. "We're kinda past pardons at this point, don't ya think?"

"I suppose we are," VanderVoort says with a sigh.

"I will figure this out though," Lowell says, suddenly very

serious. "I kinda have to so the planet doesn't get destroyed. You know, the planet I'm on too? We're all in this together, Vander-Voort, old sport."

"You are infuriating," VanderVoort says. "Good luck."

"Thanks," Lowell says and cuts the connection.

"Anyone care to see if the Wyoming facility will answer now? Might as well do the full round," VanderVoort says.

"I'll try to reach them, ma'am," a tech says.

"Super duper," VanderVoort replies as she sinks into the couch cushions. "Maybe they have some boring news. I could go for boring right now."

————

"I almost have the connection," Dr. Probst says, her eyes glued to her laptop screen. "Push a little harder, Kyle."

"He's going to get hurt if he keeps pushing," Lu snaps, her eyes glued to her son.

All three of them are in a room extremely similar to the one Lowell is occupying in Antarctica. Two chairs, two pedestals, and blank walls.

Kyle is seated in one of the chairs, his hand on a pedestal. The air in the room crackles with electricity.

"He's strong, Lu," Dr. Probst says. "He can do this."

"I know he's strong, Cheryl!" Lu snaps. "That's not what I'm—"

"Mom," Kyle says through gritted teeth. "I got this. Back off and let us work, please."

Lu's eyes widen and she takes a step back. Then she nods and smiles at her son.

"Okay. Okay," she says. "Just be careful."

"I am," Kyle says.

"There, Kyle! There!" Dr. Probst says.

A million holographic images explode into the air then coalesce into a single, blue orb. Before anyone can say or do anything, the orb slams into Kyle's chest.

Lu screams and Dr. Probst almost drops her laptop.

"I'm good," Kyle says, holding up his free hand. "Like… really good."

"Kyle? What just happened?" Lu asks.

"I'd like to know that too," Dr. Probst says, her attention back to her laptop. "These readings are off the charts. What are you seeing, Kyle?"

"Everything," Kyle says. "I can feel the entire facility." He pauses and his face scrunches up tight. "And I think I can see another facility. Maybe if I try…"

Kyle goes silent, then his entire body arches and stiffens.

"Kyle!" Lu cries. "Disconnect him! Cheryl! Disconnect him now, god damnit!"

"I don't know how!" Dr. Probst says. "I helped make the connection, but now I'm locked out!"

"Kyle!" Lu yells.

"I'm okay, Mom," Kyle says, but his voice comes from speakers set into the room's walls and ceiling. Then he opens his eyes and speaks with his mouth. "We're in, Cheryl. I'm connecting to Antarctica now."

"You are?" Lu asks.

"That's brilliant," Dr. Probst says.

The wall in front of the chairs comes to life with a very large image of Lowell.

"Oh, shit! Hey, guys!" Lowell exclaims. "Kyle, my man! Way to go, kid. Good job."

"This is nuts," Kyle says. "Like really nuts."

"Want to see nuts?" Lowell says.

Images stream across the walls of the room.

"What is that?" Dr. Probst asks.

"Big spider," Lowell says. "I think it's friendly."

"You have to be shitting me," Lu says. "How can something like that be friendly?"

"We're friends, right?" Lowell says.

Lu laughs. "Point taken."

Lowell fills them in on everything. Lu and Dr. Probst share a frightened look. Kyle only nods.

"I can keep working on connecting all of the other facilities together," Kyle says. "You focus on that kaiju."

"Took the words out of my mouth, kid," Lowell says. "Let me know if you need anything. I have to leave this room, but I think I can maintain a link. I think."

"You can," Kyle says. "The orb is the connection, the room is control. Does that make sense?"

"Totally," Lowell says.

"It does?" Lu asks.

"It does," Kyle says. "Trust me, Mom."

"Not like I have much choice," Lu says.

"Hey, Lowell?" Kyle says.

"Yeah?" Lowell replies. "What's up?"

"There's another facility," Kyle says. "It's in the…"

"Mariana Trench," Dr. Probst says.

"Mariana Trench," Kyle says with a nod. "It's not connected to any of the facilities at all. I'm not sure what it is, but I'm pretty sure we don't want the Ebony Man to get there."

Lowell doesn't respond, only stares out from the wall.

"Lowell? You good?" Kyle asks.

"Sorry, I was trying to see if this facility knows what's up," Lowell says. "I see hints at the facility, but no info. Try to connect to the other facilities first, then see if you can dive into Bikini Bottom."

"Is that a SpongeBob reference?" Kyle asks.

"You watch what's on in prison, kid," Lowell says.

"Gotcha," Kyle says. "I'll see what I can do."

"And what are you going to do?" Dr. Probst asks Lowell.

"Me? Gonna get the Country Time ready," Lowell says. No one responds. "Sorry. Inside joke with VanderVoort. We're tight."

"That's a scary thought," Dr. Probst says.

"It is what it is," Lowell says. "Listen, I gotta go. I think I heard the doorbell."

"That facility has a doorbell?" Dr. Probst asks. Everyone stares at her. "Sorry. I'm so tired."

"The motto of the day, Doc," Lowell says. "Keep at it, kid. You all stay safe."

Lowell's image disappears and the walls go blank once more.

Kyle lets out a deep breath and pulls his hand away from the pedestal.

"What are you doing?" Dr. Probst asks. "We still need to connect to the other facilities."

"I have to pee," Kyle says. "Is that okay? Or should I see if this chair also has a toilet?"

"No, no, go pee," Dr. Probst says, her face red. "That'd be best."

"I think so," Kyle says and gets up from the chair. He wobbles a bit but holds up a hand before his mother can say anything. "I'm good. Just getting used to not being everything. Bodies are small and fragile, did you know that?"

"Yes, Son, I know that," Lu says.

"I hope it goes alright for Lowell," Kyle says. "This shit is nuts."

"Big nuts shit," Dr. Probst says, then rubs her eyes. "Sleep. I think we all need sleep."

"You two sleep," Kyle says. "I'm not tired. The orb, or whatever it is, is like a jolt of adrenaline."

Dr. Probst and Lu share a look.

"I'll keep an eye on that," Dr. Probst says.

"Thank you," Lu says. "But first, you get some sleep. We'll take shifts. Kyle? The second you feel like this is too much, you tell us. You need to rest too."

"I know, Mom," Kyle says. "So do you."

"I'll rest after Cheryl," Lu says.

"Can I go pee now?" Kyle asks.

"Oh, sorry. Yes, of course," Lu says.

Lu and Dr. Probst watch him leave.

"Tell me not to worry," Lu says.

"Don't worry," Dr. Probst replies instantly.

Lu laughs. "You're getting good at that."

"At what?" Dr. Probst asks.

"Bullshitting," Lu says.

Dr. Probst sighs. "These are bullshit times."

"Go find a bunk," Lu says.

"Thank you, I will," Dr. Probst replies and shuffles out of the room.

————

Lowell moves from what he calls the "Meth Room" due to the connection to the blue crystal, to a massive observation deck set against the gigantic chamber where the Ebony Man's new kaiju crawled out from. Not that the chamber is empty. Far from it.

There's a giant spider inside, easily two thousand feet across at its thickest point, meticulously clearing out all the debris that fell in upon the Ebony Man's exit. Chunk by chunk, the spider cleans the chamber until there's barely any dust left inside. Then it settles down, tucking its legs up underneath itself, and turns its head to face the observation deck.

"Hey there," Lowell says, raising a hand in greeting.

The spider kaiju nods.

"Whoa. That's fucking cool," Lowell says. "Can you talk to me?"

The spider shakes its head, then cocks it to the side.

"No, but...?" Lowell says.

One leg slips out from under the kaiju's body and taps one of the observation deck's windows.

"You can talk to me once you're in here?" Lowell asks.

The spider nods.

"Hate to break it to you, buddy, but I don't think you'll fit," Lowell says.

The spider shakes.

"Ha. Made ya laugh," Lowell says. "Then how are you going to talk to me in here?"

The spider stares.

Lowell smacks his forehead.

"Of course!" he shouts and holds up a finger. "Hold on! I'll be right down!"

Lowell races out of the observation deck and finds the closest elevator. The Antarctica facility has a lot of elevators, according to the facility map in Lowell's head. He finds it's easier just to take the closest one and get off on a level that connects to the one he needs.

"Hoppin' elevators," Lowell says to himself. "Ol' Lowell's just hop hop hoppin' elevators."

He pauses, glances around the elevator, and cringes to himself.

"Yeah, that's enough of that," Lowell says.

He gets off at the lowest level the elevator goes, then jogs to the next one and rides that all the way to the very bottom.

Lowell can feel the pull of the Substance even before the elevator doors open. When they do fully open, it's like a hot breeze from the beach hits him square in the face.

"Beer," Lowell says. "I really want a beer."

His stomach grumbles.

"And nachos," Lowell says. "But, first, let's see what crazy shit comes walking out of the Substance this time."

There is no cart hold with ready and waiting vehicles, but Lowell doesn't really need one. Unlike at the Wyoming facility, the bulkhead covering the Substance area in Antarctica is only about fifty yards from the elevator doors. He crosses the distance and places a hand on the outside of the bulkhead.

A grating noise fills the air and the bulkhead slowly rises.

Waiting on the other side is a being. Lowell blinks a few times, then shrugs.

"Not sure what I was expecting," Lowell says. He holds out a hand. "Anson Lowell. Welcome to Antarctica."

The being is humanoid in shape, but that's about as far as the similarities go to anything even remotely human.

With two long, thin legs holding up a torso that looks like it's made of bright orange cotton candy, the being extends one of its many arms and clasps Lowell's hand with a three-pronged claw. A bulbous head at the top of the torso blinks all one hundred of its eyes and nods.

"It is good to meet you, Anson Lowell," the being says, a mandible-dominated mouth clicking out the words. "My name is…"

A name shoots into Lowell's mind and he grins.

"No way I'm going to be able to pronounce that," Lowell says. "I don't think human vocal cords can tackle that one. How about I call you Trey? That cool."

"Trey will do nicely," the being says.

"Cool," Lowell says. "Call me Lowell. Everyone does."

"Thank you, Lowell," Trey says. "I can tell from your aura that you have integrated with this facility nicely. That is good. A native should be connected to all of the…facilities. Not a word that conveys the depth of these structures, but it will do nicely."

"You're big on that word, aren't you?" Lowell says.

"I do not understand," Trey responds.

"Nicely," Lowell says, then shakes his head. "Never mind. Not important."

The two beings stare at each other, although Trey has the advantage in that activity.

"What's next?" Lowell asks.

"Next, we free the refugees I was able to rescue on my journey here," Trey says. "I would appreciate your assistance."

"Works for me," Lowell says. "I'm still working out how I'm going to kick Mr. Licorice's ass, so I have some time to kill until then."

"Mr. Licorice?" Trey asks. "I do not understand this name."

"Oh, right, sorry," Lowell says. "The Ebony Man is what we've been calling him. It translates as…"

Lowell thinks the being's true name and Trey nods.

"He still lives," Trey says sadly. "I had hoped you had dispatched him."

"Nope. No dispatching yet," Lowell says. "Come on. I'll show you around and we can go free some refugees. I'll also fill you in on everything that's gone down here on little ol' Earth."

"That will do nicely," Trey says. "Thank you."

"You're a polite bunch of floss, aren't you?" Lowell laughs. "Kinda refreshing. All us humans have been snapping and biting at each other like caged dogs."

"Why would you cage a dog?" Trey asks. "How very cruel."

"I can relate to that sentiment way too much, Trey, my man," Lowell says. "Come on."

Lowell fills Trey in on everything as he leads the being to the elevators. Once back above, they take a circuitous route to a hatch that leads directly into the kaiju chamber where the resting and waiting giant spider sits, its many webbed pods hanging tight to its back.

"So this facility is not integrated fully into the network yet," Trey states, repeating out loud what Lowell has told him. "This must be fixed immediately. You must integrate with Quetzalcoatl in order to stop the Ebony Man from reaching the Core."

"Couple things you just said I'm going to have to unpack after we get all these good folks out of your web condos," Lowell says. "Where do we start?"

"Place your hand to that panel there first, if you will," Trey says. "We need to close and seal the chamber. Your body is considerably more hearty than most humans due to the Substance and you have adjusted to the cold. They will freeze to death within minutes if they are left exposed to the elements."

"Close the moonroof. Got it," Lowell says. "Uh, how? Mr. Licorice sorta ripped the top off when he went bye bye."

"Use your connection to the facility," Trey says. "You will see."

Lowell connects with the facility.

In seconds, a million small bots swarm up out of the chamber's walls and quickly stitch the top of the chamber back together.

"That is so cool," Lowell says and snaps his fingers.

The chamber seals off from the outside elements. Despite being more hearty than the average human, Lowell is glad the top is closed. Fucking cold is still fucking cold, even if his body can survive it.

"Nicely done," Trey says. "Now, please activate the extraction platforms."

"That's what those are?" Lowell responds, pointing to the sides of the chamber. "I couldn't figure them out."

Lowell does as asked and several platforms extend from the chamber's wall and over to the spider's back. Arms that appear to be both organic and robotic extend from the platforms and slice into the webbing, then hold the material open, allowing thousands upon thousands of traumatized people to walk slowly and groggily onto the platforms.

"For their own safety, I needed to sedate them while traveling," Trey says. "You understand."

"Been on both sides of that scenario before," Lowell says. "Now what? That's a lot of people. What do we do with them? How the fuck do we feed them?"

"Let me take care of that," Trey says. "You should get some sleep."

"Sleep?" Lowell laughs. "Trey, my new friend, I don't think sleep is in the future."

"You must rest, or you will not have the fortitude needed to take the reins of Quetzalcoatl and defeat the Ebony Man," Trey says. "If that being reaches the Core, then all is lost and your planet will be destroyed. He has made a pact."

"A pact?" Lowell asks.

"A pact," Trey says with a nod.

"Oh, right. A pact." Lowell sighs. "He's gonna let the big aliens take Earth in exchange for a ride off this planet, isn't he?"

"Of a sorts, yes," Trey says.

"Shit."

"Yes. Shit."

"Care to explain the sorts part?"

"I will once you rest," Trey says. "Let me facilitate the settling of my ward while you sleep, then we shall prepare you for your transference to Quetzalcoatl the second the connection to that facility has been made."

"About this quesadilla thing…" Lowell says.

"Quetzalcoatl," Trey corrects.

"Yeah. That," Lowell says. "Why does that sound familiar?"

"You do not know Quetzalcoatl?" Trey asks. He pauses. "Ah, yes, humanity's intentional separation of cultures for the purposes of greed and selfishness. A species with so much potential wasted."

"Preaching to the choir, brother," Lowell says. "Quetzalcoatl?"

"When you have rested," Trey says. "Go, go. You have done nicely, but I have this under control."

Lowell glances up at the thousands of confused people standing on the many platforms.

"Yeah, I think I will let you handle this," Lowell says. "I'd probably get in the way. Wake me if something big happens or Earth gets invaded by aliens."

"Earth has long been populated by aliens," Trey says.

"The big ones. The ones coming to destroy us," Lowell says.

"Oh, there will be much fighting before they arrive, do not worry," Trey says. "And you will be part of all of it."

"Awesome," Lowell says and yawns. "Need me to show you where the cafeteria is?"

"There are three dozen feeding areas in this facility," Trey says. "I know the locations of all of them."

"Then you're all set," Lowell says and claps his hands together. "Gonna go sleepy time. Chat with ya later."

"Yes, Lowell, we will most definitely chat later," Trey says as Lowell leaves the kaiju chamber.

———

"You good?" Bolton asks Joshua. The two are seated in the small cockpit of the experimental aircraft with Joshua in the pilot's seat and Bolton in the co-pilot's. "You want a jolt?"

Bolton holds up a canned coffee.

"I'm fine," Joshua says. "How are the drones?"

Bolton sets the canned coffee down and checks the readings on the screen in front of him. The aircraft is flanked by a dozen drones on each side as they fly over what was once Utah but is now just a landscape of broken earth blanketed by ash.

"All systems looking good," Bolton reports, then leans forward and peers outside. "Visual check shows the same." He taps at the headset he's wearing. "Diamondback? This is Bolton, how are the drones looking from your end?"

"Bolton, this is Diamondback," a voice responds. "Corporal Denz here. Zero connectivity issues. All readings are nominal."

"Copy that," Bolton says. "We're about three hours out from the target."

"Be careful," Banks interrupts. "Don't push the bird too hard. This is only the fourth field flight it's taken."

"No need to remind us," Bolton says. "But I gotta say, for its fourth flight this bird is smooth as butter."

"Magnetic propulsion is vibration-free," Banks says. "Air turbulence is all you need to worry about, and even that is minimized by the bird's connection to the Earth's magnetic field."

"It really is a bird," Joshua says.

"Sounds like it," Bolton says. "How are your eyes? We'll need cover once we reach Seattle and start hunting for Terrie and the kids. There are some big bastards in that area."

"Eyes are clear," Corporal Denz says, taking back the comms. "It'll be good to have ears up too once you find that kid. Hopefully everyone is alright and his device is still operational."

"That's my hope too," Bolton says. "For many reasons."

A warning klaxon erupts in the cockpit.

"On it," Bolton says to Joshua.

"I assumed so," Joshua replies, his focus fixed solely on flying the aircraft.

Bolton touches a flashing icon on the screen before him and a display considerably more complex than simple radar appears.

"Bogey on our two," Bolton says and looks up and out in that direction. "I see it. Going weapons hot."

"Copy that," Joshua says. "Weapons hot."

Bolton engages the weapons system and a joystick extends from a slot just under the screen. The image on the screen becomes a targeting system that shows a panoramic view of the air in front of the aircraft. Red crosshairs fly about the screen, then lock onto a shape diving in and out of the ash cloud above them.

"One of the flyers," Bolton says.

"Stands to reason," Joshua says.

"Weapons locked," Bolton says. "Firing."

"Just pull the trigger," Joshua says with a smirk.

Bolton squeezes the trigger and a bolt of what looks like lightning shoots from the aircraft directly at the winged monster.

The beast is enveloped in electricity and curls in on itself before plummeting to the ground far, far below.

"Direct hit!" Bolton cheers.

"Not done," Joshua says.

Four more winged monsters dive out of the ash cloud and speed straight for the aircraft.

Bolton opens fire, hitting three of the beasts. The fourth avoids the strike but doesn't engage. Instead, it retreats back into the ash cloud.

"I'll keep an eye out for that one," Bolton says.

"Good idea," Joshua replies and smiles. "Pretty nice bird."

"Yeah," Bolton says. "It is a pretty nice bird."

TWELVE

Having made the arduous climb from ground level all the way up to the famous rotating restaurant at the top of the Space Needle, Terrie is exhausted.

But her job isn't done yet.

"How's it coming, Tony?" Terrie calls out, the Barrett aimed at the barricaded stairway doors, waiting to see if any ooze creatures, or worse, have followed them up. Biscuit lays nearby, fast asleep. "Any luck?"

"I'm very close," Tony says as he and Krissy work at stripping away wall paneling in order to get directly to the Space Needle's frame. Tony glances at Krissy. "We are very close."

"I think we've got it," Krissy says, pushing past wires and pipes to pry a piece of metal open. "Got it!"

"That's exactly what I need," Tony says, smiling at the exposed piece of steel girder. "Here. Take these leads and attach them to the frame."

"Does it matter where?" Krissy asks.

"No," Tony says. "I'll do the hard part from my device."

Krissy attaches four alligator clips to the Space Needle's frame, then sits back on her butt and sighs.

"I'm fucking pooped," she says.

"We sleep when we're dead," Tony says.

"Jesus," Krissy exclaims.

"Roy used to say that," Tony says.

"Oh," Krissy responds. "Sorry."

"Me too," Tony says and pauses his work. "I miss my mother."

Terrie takes her eyes off the stairway doors and watches the two teenagers.

"I miss mine too," Krissy says quietly. "I miss my dad and my little sister."

Krissy sniffles and wipes at her eyes. She pauses and laughs.

"I miss my face most," she says.

Tony studies her.

"I like the bandages," he says. "You look scary and mysterious. Like an Egyptian mummy queen."

"Thank you…?" Krissy responds.

Terrie returns her attention to the doors. Something gnaws at her guts.

"How long do we need to be here?" Terrie asks. "Once you connect your device, how long until we can leave?"

Tony shakes his head. "I don't understand."

A chill runs up and down Terrie's spine, adding to the unease her guts are already dealing with.

"What's not to understand?" Krissy asks. "You hook that up, turn it on, and we go, right?"

"No," Tony says. "I'll need to maintain the connection. The device is new and there could be bugs. I'll need to be here to fix the bugs."

"Shit," Krissy says.

"I reluctantly agree with Krissy," Terrie says. "Tony? Connor is coming to get us. The plan wasn't to stay here."

"This structure is the most efficient way to send the signal and connect all communications across the globe," Tony says.

"I know," Terrie says. "But we need to get to the Wyoming facility where my daughter and grandson are. We all need to get there and take shelter, because we cannot survive on the surface much longer."

Tony frowns at Terrie, looks to Krissy, then looks back at Terrie.

"A bunker is below ground," Tony says. "My device needs to be above ground."

"We can figure that out later," Krissy says. "But we can't stay here forever."

"Then why are we here?" Tony asks.

"So we can connect everyone's communications systems until we're rescued," Terrie says. "Then once we're settled in the Wyoming facility, we can reconnect your device and restore communications again."

"We should have discussed this plan in greater detail," Tony says. "I agree with being rescued, but the second part is unacceptable. My device will not work underground."

"I'm sure the place has some type of big antennas you can connect to," Krissy says. "It's a government facility that may have been built by aliens."

"I'm not familiar with alien technology," Tony says.

"I doubt anyone is," Terrie says. "But we'll figure it out."

"I will be the one to figure it out, and I'm not happy about that," Tony says.

Biscuit wakes up and whips his head around to face the barricaded doors. Terrie gulps.

"We'll settle this discussion later," Terrie says. "Focus on the now and get your device working."

"This is highly inefficient," Tony says, returning to his work. "To connect here, calibrate the device, then dismantle it and reconnect underground with possible alien technology is just not efficient."

Terrie keeps her mounting annoyance in check. She can tell Tony is getting worked up into one of his episodes. Not quite a tantrum but just as unreasonable.

"We do not have time for this," Terrie says. "Connect your

device, get it working, then we'll discuss what to do once we're rescued."

"I would prefer to plan—" Tony begins, but he doesn't get a chance to finish.

Terrie is about to explode at him, her exhaustion making it impossible to think straight, but she doesn't get the chance to rage at Tony.

Krissy opens her mouth to add sarcasm to the mix, but her chance is lost too.

Everything comes to a stop when Biscuit leaps to his feet and unleashes furious barks at the barricade.

"Tony," Terrie says calmly, instinct kicking in as she relaxes her body and positions the Barrett so the recoil doesn't shatter her shoulder. "They're here. Connect the device."

A keening wail can be heard over Biscuit's barking.

"Uh… okay," Tony says, the fear that fills his eyes driving him to reason. "But I'm not happy."

"No shit," Krissy says. "Terrie?"

"Focus on the job," Terrie says. "I'll focus on what's on the other side of the doors."

Terrie knows the .50 cal rounds can explode the ooze creatures into a million pieces. She also knows the ooze creatures have the ability to reassemble. Personally, she's hoping one of the non-ooze monsters comes for them. She's considerably more confident with the Barrett's abilities against real flesh and blood.

Biscuit's hackles are fully on end and saliva sprays from his muzzle as he snaps and barks at the barricade. Terrie does nothing to calm him down. She'd be doing the same thing if she were the hybrid dog-wolf.

The keening wail intensifies.

Then it stops.

"Keep working," Krissy says without Terrie saying a word.

Tony nods and continues working.

"I'm almost finished," Tony says.

The doors behind the barricade shudder once, then still. Biscuit's barks intensify.

Terrie slows her breathing, preparing herself for what's coming. If that's possible.

"Almost," Tony says.

The doors do more than shudder. They crack and shatter, sending debris flying over the barricade directly at Terrie.

She's forced to roll out of the way and let go of the Barrett so she can cover her head. The doors were metal, and pieces of shrapnel pelt Terrie's body. She feels the gashes in her scalp and along her cheeks start to bleed instantly.

She also hears the barricade being torn apart as the creatures fight their way into the restaurant.

"Tony! Krissy! Run!" Terrie yells.

"Done," Tony says.

"Come on!" Krissy shouts, grabbing Tony's shoulder.

Tony shakes her off and points at the device.

"It's connected," he says.

"We have to go!" Krissy yells.

"Let me turn it on first," Tony says.

"Run! Now!" Terrie yells as she gets herself together, retrieves the Barrett, and levels it at the multitude of ooze creatures that were once birds, squirrels, chipmunks, dogs, cats, and various other types of animals that have been morphed into nightmarish simulacrums of their former selves.

Terrie is ready to open fire, but there's a serious obstacle in her way: the still-barking Biscuit.

"Biscuit! Move!" Terrie shouts. "Biscuit! Here, boy!"

Biscuit does not move.

Ten feet, five feet—the ooze creatures are about to overwhelm Biscuit, and Terrie has to make a hard decision of whether or not to open fire.

Then a vibration starts to work its way through Terrie's body. From the tips of her toes all the way to the couple of fillings in her teeth, Terrie feels a sort of electricity flow through her.

Biscuit must feel it too because he stops barking, lets out a loud howl, and retreats behind Terrie's legs.

"Good boy," she says, her voice taking on a tinny quality to her ears.

Terrie is about to open fire, but she hesitates. So do the ooze creatures.

Every last one of the abominations are frozen in place.

Although, as Terrie stares at them, frozen isn't accurate.

The ooze creatures are vibrating. Vibrating and beginning to come apart.

Terrie watches in fascination as the ooze creatures slowly break into smaller and smaller pieces until all that is left is a huge puddle of greenish ooze seeping out from under and around the barricade.

"Terrie," Krissy calls, her voice tinny too. "Come here."

Terrie's eyes are locked on the ooze puddle. "What is it?"

"You have to see this," Krissy says.

"I'm watching the doors," Terrie replies.

"I don't think you need to anymore," Krissy says.

Terrie frowns but slowly backs up until she's standing next to Krissy and Tony.

"What am I looking at?" she asks.

"Outside," Krissy says.

Terrie looks over her shoulder. At first, she doesn't know what she's looking at. Then it hits her that ooze creatures by the hundreds are streaming out and away from the Space Needle until they're about one hundred yards away.

"The device? Is it repelling them?" Terrie asks.

"Yes," Tony answers. "They do not like the resonance the signal creates."

"Yeah, well, it's not just repelling them," Krissy says and points toward the perimeter of Seattle Center. "It's also calling them."

"Attraction and repulsion," Tony says. "Strange."

Terrie doesn't say a word. She's too busy worrying about how in the hell Connor will be able to get to them if all of Seattle Center is filled with ooze creatures. She returns her attention to the ooze puddle.

"Tony, are we in communication with anyone yet?" Terrie asks.

"Yes," Tony says and turns up the volume on the radio.

A thousand voices explode out of the tiny speaker, all talking over and around each other.

"I need to tweak the filtering protocol," Tony says and sits down next to his device. "Then the system will be more stable."

"Do that," Terrie says. "As soon as you have it stable, then you connect with the White House so they can do what they need to in order to save people."

Tony doesn't respond. He's already lost in his work.

"We aren't getting out of here," Krissy states, reaching the same conclusion as Terrie.

"We'll get out of here," Terrie replies. "Just not through the front door."

———

"Ma'am!" a tech shouts.

VanderVoort is getting tired of everyone yelling that, but she hasn't figured out a better way for them to address her. She just wishes it wasn't such a jolt each time they bark out "ma'am."

"Yes?" she replies.

"I think…" the tech begins.

VanderVoort's patience nearly hits its breaking point.

"You better finish that sentence," VanderVoort says.

"I think we have comms, ma'am," the tech says.

"You think? Either we do or we don't," VanderVoort says. "Which is it?"

The tech types at his keyboard and chaos erupts out of the Situation Room speakers.

"Volume down," VanderVoort says, but the edge is gone from

her voice. "What is that? It sounds like a whole lot of people trying to speak at once."

"I think it's every active comms signal out there, ma'am," the tech says.

"That's a lot of working radios," Director Miles says.

"No, sir, it's not just radios," the tech says. "I'm seeing cell phone signals, television signals, Wi-Fi routers, landlines, everything." He turns away from his console, his eyes wide. "Every possible way to communicate is now connected."

"The EMP didn't take it all out," Dr. Hall says.

"Why couldn't we hear these signals before?" President Nance asks.

"My guess, Mr. President," General Azoul answers. "The communications infrastructure was taken out by the EMP, but that kid's thingamajig fixed all that."

"Yeah, it did," VanderVoort says and points up at an inset speaker. "And it's great to have full comms back, but how do we navigate that mess?"

The noise stops.

"Hello?" Tony's voice calls out.

"Hey, kid," VanderVoort says. "Good to hear your voice. It sounds, and I mean that literally, that you got us some operational comms. Good job."

"Thank you," Tony says. "It was not easy, but it also was not difficult."

"A little of this, a little of that," VanderVoort says. "What do we need to do on our end?"

"I'm sending you protocols for configuring your communications system so you may utilize all capabilities," Tony says. "Do you have the protocols?"

VanderVoort looks at the tech, who pauses then nods back at her.

"We do," VanderVoort says. "Thank you, Tony."

"You're welcome," Tony says.

VanderVoort detects hesitance.

"What's the matter, Tony?" VanderVoort asks.

"Ms. VanderVoort, this is Terrie Morgan," Terrie's voice calls out.

"Ms. Morgan. Good to hear your voice too," VanderVoort says. "What's your situation?"

"Not ideal," Terrie replies. "We've taken refuge in the Space Needle and Tony is using it as an antenna."

"Understood," VanderVoort responds. "But…?"

"But there's good news, bad news, and probably worse news," Terrie says.

"I'll let you choose the order," VanderVoort says.

"Good news is that the signal is vibrating through the Space Needle's structure, creating a resonance that is driving the ooze creatures away," Terrie says. "We were about to be overrun, but God had other plans."

"Bad news?" VanderVoort asks.

"The bad news is the same resonance is also attracting the creatures, and not just the ooze ones," Terrie says. "There are big monsters down there now too. I think it's drawing every single monster in the Seattle area."

"That's got to be a lot of monsters," VanderVoort says and rubs her forehead. "But they aren't attacking?"

"No, they can only get so close," Terrie replies.

"And worse news?" VanderVoort asks.

"Tony insists we have to stay here and keep the device connected to the Space Needle in order for communications to remain active," Terrie says. "We're sorta stuck, even if Connor is able to get to us through the thousands of things down there."

"Thousands?" Dr. Hall asks.

"Thousands," Terrie replies. "And more and more are joining the horde."

"Alright, Ms. Morgan, my turn for good news," VanderVoort says. "Sergeant Bolton is utilizing an experimental aircraft that will not need to land in order to get you. I assume you are up in that nauseating restaurant. The one with nothing but glass walls and turns all the way around, making it impossible to keep a meal down?"

"Yes, we're at the top," Terrie responds with amusement. "I'm sorry you get motion sick."

"I swear it's just that restaurant," VanderVoort says. "Well, and all other turning things. Is it too much to ask for a fixed focus point while eating an overpriced meal?"

"May we contact Connor directly?" Terrie asks. "It'll be easier to coordinate our rescue that way."

"What about the device?" VanderVoort asks. "We cannot afford for comms to go down again. I have my people attempting to contact everyone we can so they understand that the evacuation plan has changed dramatically. We're going to have to guide hundreds of thousands of people to the different facilities across the globe."

"I understand, Ms. VanderVoort," Terrie says. "But we cannot stay here forever. Connor told us what's coming. We need to evacuate to Wyoming."

"I know, Ms. Morgan," VanderVoort says. "But I need you to hang in there as long as possible."

"We will," Terrie says, "if by as long as possible you mean right up until it's time for us to escape to Wyoming."

VanderVoort doesn't answer. She looks about the Situation Room. There are no helpful faces, only scared and expectant ones.

"Ms. VanderVoort?" Terrie calls.

"I'm here," VanderVoort responds. "We'll work the problem from our end and you work the problem from your end. We'll find a way."

It's Terrie's turn to pause.

"I used to be a government employee, Ms. VanderVoort," Terrie says finally. "I understand what you're saying loud and clear."

"I'm sure you do," VanderVoort says. "Good luck."

"Thank you," Terrie replies and the communication ends.

VanderVoort takes several deep breaths, avoiding the eyes on her. She pretty much just told Terrie Morgan they're sacrifices for the greater good.

"Tell me you have communications established with at least some of the refugee ships," VanderVoort barks. She turns to President Nance. "I'll let you start talking to whatever world leaders are still alive and have access to comms. Everyone sitting at the conference table will help coordinate the evacuation to the facilities."

"And what will you be doing?" President Nance asks.

"I'm pretty sure the kaiju didn't just magically go away, Charles," VanderVoort says. "Someone should probably stay on top of that issue, don't you think? That's what I'll be doing."

She sighs.

"Get me Sergeant Bolton," she says. "I need to make him aware of the situation in Seattle and make sure he's one hundred percent clear on how important it is to keep the comms signal going."

———

Bolton glares out the windshield of the aircraft.

"That wasn't a good call," Joshua says after several minutes of silence. "You going to do what she said to do?"

"You mean, am I going to not rescue Terrie and the kids and also pretty much sacrifice our asses so that comms can remain up?" Bolton replies. "I'm a soldier and I've been given orders."

"Not an answer," Joshua says. "Are you going to execute those orders?"

"You think I shouldn't?" Bolton asks.

Joshua only shrugs.

"There are a million cons to not executing those orders," Bolton says, "and only one pro."

"Might be a few more pros than one, but I get your meaning," Joshua says.

"Jesus," Bolton says and closes his eyes. He presses his fists to his temples. "Jesus…"

"We're almost there," Joshua says. "You should probably get back on the horn and sort this out."

"What does that mean?" Bolton asks.

Joshua shrugs.

"No fucking way. You don't get to shrug this off," Bolton says. "Tell me what you're thinking."

"In my line of work, plans rarely, if ever, work out," Joshua says.

"Same here. Plans are great the second until the op starts," Bolton says. "Then they're out the window."

"Which means you have to use every opportunity to your advantage," Joshua says.

"Like…?" Bolton asks.

"For me, it would sometimes be using local warlords, or drug kingpins, or less than ethical financial institutions as resources," Joshua says. "I've cultivated hundreds of high-level assets that I can call on at a moment's notice to get my objective accomplished or get my ass out of the fire. Some assets are close to as powerful as our own government. But minus the red tape."

"Keep talking," Bolton says.

"Who are your assets?" Joshua asks.

"I don't have any right now," Bolton says.

"Sure you do," Joshua says. "You have the most powerful assets on the planet."

Bolton starts to argue, then realizes Joshua is right.

Tony controls the comms device and he's with Terrie, which means Bolton has influence over Tony, which means he has influence over the device.

"You working it out?" Joshua asks.

"Shut up," Bolton says.

Joshua nods, smiling.

Kyle and Lu and Dr. Probst are in the Wyoming facility, which means he has influence, although how much he doesn't know, over the Substance. At the very least, he has influence over one of the precious few facilities needed to help save humanity.

Then there's Lowell. A man who has survived the Substance, melded with a kaiju, and lived to tell about it. He's in Antarctica in control of another precious facility.

Joshua is right. Bolton has access to every person who truly matters.

Bolton adjusts the aircraft's comms system and picks a frequency. Joshua's smile widens.

"Terrie?" Bolton calls. "Are you there?"

There's a crackle of static, then Terrie's voice comes out over the comm loud and clear.

"Connor!" Terrie exclaims. "How far out are you?"

"Minutes away," Bolton says. "We should be in view of the Space Needle within the hour, maybe sooner."

"That's great," Terrie says, and Bolton can hear something close to defeat in her voice. "VanderVoort has already called you though, right?"

"She has," Bolton says. "I've been given orders."

"Yes, of course," Terrie says. "Protect the device, but do not rescue us."

"That's the gist," Bolton says. "Doesn't really matter."

"Excuse me?" Terrie explodes. "It doesn't really matter? How can you—?"

"Hold on, hold on," Bolton interrupts. "The orders don't matter because I'm not executing them. We're coming to get you and take all our asses to the Wyoming facility, where we'll hunker down and deal with this shit as a family."

"Language," Terrie says with a relieved laugh. "Thank you, Connor."

"Don't thank me," Bolton says, "I had help getting to that realization. May I speak with Tony?"

"Yes, of course. Hold on," Terrie says.

There's a pause.

"Yes, Sergeant Connor Bolton?" Tony says.

"Tony, I need to know if your device can set up a closed channel that can connect just us, the Wyoming facility, and Antarctica," Bolton says.

"Antarctica? You want to speak to penguins?" Tony asks. A sharp girl's voice is heard briefly. "Oh, right, yes, Mr. Lowell. The convicted murderer."

Joshua laughs.

"Is that Joshua?" Tony asks.

"It is," Bolton responds. "He's the one flying the aircraft."

"Tell him hello for me, please," Tony says. "It'll be nice to meet in person."

"Same, kid," Joshua says.

"Oh, he's connected too," Tony says. "Good. He has a perspective I relate to."

"I bet he does," Bolton says. "How soon can you create the closed channel?"

"Right now," Tony says. "I've been working on your request while we've been speaking."

"We're connected?" Bolton asks.

"Yes," Tony says. "Would you like me to hail both facilities?"

"That'd be great, Tony," Bolton says and waits.

"Who is this?" Kyle's voice calls out. "Connor?"

"Hey, Kyle," Bolton says. "How's your mom? And Dr. Probst?"

"Dr. Probst is sleeping and Mom is next," Kyle says. "I'm looking at the connection and it's weird. Which is saying a lot considering my life now."

"Tony connected us all together," Bolton says. "Get your mom on the comms too."

"Hold on," Kyle says. "I'm opening the channel."

"Connor!" Lu almost yells. "How's my mother?"

"I'm fine, baby," Terrie says. "It's so good to hear your voice."

"Mom!" Lu shouts.

"Wait, everyone," Bolton says. "We do the reunion later. We have an op to complete first."

"A couple of them," Joshua says.

"What op?" Kyle asks.

Bolton relays the comms issue.

"Where's Lowell?" Bolton asks. "Why isn't he on the comm?"

"I don't know how to connect to the Antarctica facility," Tony says.

"I'm on it," Kyle says. "There. Try now."

"Hello? To whom am I speaking?" Trey's voice responds.

"You're not Lowell," Bolton states. "Who is this?"

"My name is not comprehendible to your minds," Trey says. "Lowell has named me Trey, which will do nicely."

"Right…" Bolton says. "And you're part of the Antarctica facility's personnel?"

"No, I am not," Trey says. "My position is much more complicated. To simplify, you can consider me a pilot."

"Pilot of what?" Bolton asks.

"I see who you are," Kyle says. "Wow. You were in the Africa kaiju."

Joshua turns and stares at Bolton. Bolton stares back, then shakes his head.

"We deal with that later," Bolton says. "I need Lowell on this call too."

"I will wake him," Trey says.

"While he's doing that, we can talk about—" Bolton starts.

"What the fuck?" Lowell booms over the connection. "I finally get a chance to sleep and you all wake my ass up? Of course it's Bolton. Asshole." He chuckles then yawns. "Just kidding. How's everyone doing?"

Bolton explains the issue to Lowell.

"Not a problem," Lowell says. "If you can get your asses to Wyoming, then Kyle can connect Tony's device to the facility and that'll act as the conduit to—"

"Conduit!" Dr. Probst shouts, interrupting Lowell. "I think I figured it out in my sleep!"

"Cheryl's awake," Lu says.

"You figured it out?" Lowell asks. "Trey! See if we're connected to Wyoming now!"

"I just woke up, Lowell," Dr. Probst snaps. "Let me work first!"

"Trey! Hold that thought!" Lowell shouts.

"Can we trust him?" Bolton asks.

"Not sure if Trey is a him, but sure," Lowell says. "The dude is solid."

"He's not raising any alarm bells on my end," Kyle says.

"I have no idea how either of you can know that for sure, but I'll trust you," Bolton says.

"I appreciate that," Trey says. "Your trust will do nicely."

"He really likes that phrase. And he's now connected to the facility like I am, so he's always listening," Lowell says. "Alright, so we have comms figured out."

"Not quite," Bolton says. "When Tony disconnects from the Space Needle, then all comms across the globe will go down again. Right, Tony?"

"That is correct," Tony says.

"What about this bird?" Joshua asks.

"What about it?" Bolton says.

"Can we connect the device to this bird and use it to amplify the signal?" Joshua asks.

"I thought of that," Bolton says, "but there's very little metal in this aircraft because of the magnetic propulsion drive."

"Magnetic propulsion drive," Tony states.

Everyone waits, but he doesn't elaborate.

"Anyway," Bolton says, "that's the main issue. I have no problem disobeying orders and rescuing Terrie and the kids, but severing the comms for the whole planet is not an option. Tens of thousands could die."

"I gave the solution," Tony says. "Was no one listening?"

"What solution?" Bolton asks.

"Magnetic propulsion drive," Tony states again. "I can connect the device to that and the signal will be even stronger than using the Space Needle. It will piggyback on the Earth's magnetic field, which is everywhere at once."

"Anyone disagree with that theory?" Bolton asks.

"It's not a theory," Tony says.

"Lowell? Kyle?" Bolton asks, ignoring Tony's statement. "What do you think?"

"Trey? Does that sound, uh, sound?" Lowell asks.

"The human adolescent is quite ingenious," Trey says. "It will work."

"Good," Bolton says, "because we're here, Terrie. Show us where you are."

Joshua circles the huge disc-like top of the Space Needle until they see Terrie and Krissy waving at them.

"What's going to be the easiest way to do this?" Bolton asks.

"Let me circle a couple more times," Joshua says.

"Alright, everyone, this is go time," Bolton says. "The comms will go down briefly while we load everyone up and take time to reconnect the device to the aircraft. Ask questions now."

"I have one," Lowell says. "Does anyone know who Quetzal-coatl is?"

"Of course," Dr. Probst says. "It's a mythical creature, I believe a god, of the Toltecs and Aztecs."

"Is that the last kaiju?" Kyle asks. "The one in the Mexico City facility?"

"It is," Trey answers. "It is Mr. Anson Lowell's destiny."

"Look at you, Lowell," Bolton says. "An Aztec god is your destiny."

"Cool," Lowell says. "I'll read up on it before I have to leave."

"You know we're not even close to finishing this conversation," Joshua says. "But we have to. I'm going to land on the roof. There should be space right there. We'll have a limited window."

Joshua looks up at the ash clouds covering the entire area. There are obvious shadows and shapes inside the ash cloud.

"Folks, we have to go," Bolton says. "Terrie, we'll see you shortly."

Bolton disconnects as Joshua puts the aircraft down on top of the Space Needle. It's a precarious landing spot, but the aircraft's landing gear locks onto the roof like massive raptor talons.

"Handy," Bolton says. "Ready?"

"I'm not going anywhere," Joshua says. "My hand stays on the stick the whole time."

"Good idea," Bolton says and grabs gear from behind his seat. Especially a small flamethrower like the ones the personnel at Diamondback used. "We'll be back in ten minutes tops."

"I'll be here," Joshua says. "Good luck."

Bolton nods and jumps out of the aircraft, careful of his footing as he slowly makes his way to an access hatch. He has to pull his sidearm and fire at the lock three times before he's able to open the hatch. Bolton is very aware of the keening wails that answer the noise of the gunshots.

Dropping down the ladder inside the hatch, Bolton slides to a maintenance catwalk, then navigates his way to a door that leads to a maintenance corridor followed by another door that leads into the kitchen.

The sidearm put away, Bolton readies the flamethrower. Despite the sight of the ooze creatures and other monsters keeping clear of the Space Needle, Bolton isn't taking any chances.

"Terrie," Bolton calls quietly as he moves quickly past the kitchen equipment to the wait station, then out into the restaurant. "Terrie?"

"Here!" Terrie exclaims.

The woman rushes over as fast as her body will allow and wraps her arms around Bolton, squeezing him hard enough that he has to grunt to get her to let go.

"I never thought I'd see you ever again," Terrie says, wiping away tears.

"Same here," Bolton says. "Except Kyle actually thought you were dead, so we had a pretty good reason to give up on seeing you."

There's a quiet woof, and Bolton looks past Terrie to the huge hybrid.

"Biscuit," Bolton says. "You're the only dog I've seen in weeks."

"Dogs sense danger and hide," Tony says from where he's crouched over his radio and device. "That's a smart thing to do."

"That's what we're about to do," Krissy says. "Go run and hide in a giant bunker."

"It's really a little more than just a giant bunker," Bolton says. "You must be Krissy. And you are the famous Tony."

"I'm not famous," Tony states.

"Oh, that's not true, kid," Bolton says. "You've got a huge fan base right now."

"How do we do this?" Terrie asks Bolton.

"I was about to ask Tony that same question," Bolton says.

"I disconnect the leads," Tony says, "then we get to your magnetic propulsion-driven aircraft and I reconnect the leads. That's all."

"How long will it take to reconnect the leads?" Bolton asks.

"I will not know that until I see the magnetic propulsion-driven aircraft," Tony says. "It would be best if there were schematics."

Bolton grins and presses a finger to his ear. "Joshua? Call Diamondback and see if the aircraft has schematics in its system. If not, then see if they can send them over the comms."

"They can," Tony says. "My device works for data too."

"Did you hear that?" Bolton asks.

"Loud and clear," Joshua says.

Bolton frowns at Joshua's tone. "What's wrong?"

"Did I say something's wrong?" Joshua replies.

"No," Bolton says.

"Then don't worry about it," Joshua says. "Just get back here."

"We're on the way," Bolton says. "Are you all ready?"

"You have no idea," Terrie says.

"Tony? You'll be in charge of your device," Bolton says. "There's some climbing involved, so you may—"

Tony holds up his backpack. "It's also a wet bag so it'll keep the radio dry."

"We aren't planning on going swimming, so I think we're good," Bolton says.

"It's Seattle," Tony says. "There's always precipitation." He pauses. "Although weather patterns have been severely altered."

"No shit," Krissy says. "Are we unplugging the super phone and going or what?"

"She fits right in," Bolton says to Terrie with a smirk.

"At times," Terrie says.

Krissy rolls her eyes.

"Do it, Tony," Bolton says.

Tony nods, kneels, and disconnects the leads from the Space Needle's frame.

Instantly, a hum Bolton hadn't noticed before is gone.

Then a thousand screeches fill the air all around the Space Needle.

"BOLTON!" Joshua shouts. "I gotta move! They're dropping out of the clouds!"

Then they all see the aircraft plummet past the windows, lost from sight in less than a second. That sight is then filled by the nightmare view of several winged monsters plummeting after the aircraft.

"No," Bolton says, just before a winged monster slams directly into one of the windows, shattering what should have been shatterproof glass, sending shards everywhere. "Get down!"

THIRTEEN

"What the fuck just happened to the comms?" VanderVoort shouts. "Get me that Tony kid now!"

"We've got a bigger problem," Dr. Hall states, staring up at the main monitor where he transfers a satellite feed he's been watching. "The Chile kaiju is leaving Mexico City."

"Of course it is!" VanderVoort shouts. "Why the fuck not?"

"Ma'am, we have another kaiju!" a tech yells.

"I'm standing right here," VanderVoort says, only a couple feet from the tech.

The startled man looks over his shoulder and grimaces. "Sorry, ma'am."

VanderVoort stares at the tech. "You were yelling…?"

"Yes, ma'am, the Antarctica kaiju is now moving up Argentina," the tech says.

Dr. Hall spins around in his chair and locks eyes with VanderVoort.

"They're going for each other," VanderVoort says.

"It looks like it," Dr. Hall says. He spins back around and studies a screen. "At the current rate of movement, they'll meet in Venezuela in less than an hour."

"Sure would be nice to have one of those things on our side for a change," VanderVoort says. "They could pick up all the refugees and just drop them… off…"

"Someone get Lowell!" Director Miles yells and smiles at VanderVoort. "I saw where you were going with that one."

In seconds, the Antarctica facility is up on the screen.

But it isn't Anson Lowell everyone sees.

"Hello," Trey says.

"Sweet mother of the Elephant Man, what are you?" Vander-Voort blurts out. She holds up both hands. "My apologies. That was rude. We're in new times and I need to adjust accordingly. Hello, I'm Adrianna VanderVoort. I'm in charge. And you are?"

"Trey," Trey says. "I am a pilot."

"Of what?" Dr. Hall mutters.

"An easy question to answer," Trey says, and the view instantly changes to the Antarctica facility's kaiju chamber. "I have been in stasis within this living vessel for millions of years. To me, it is like a home. To it, I am simply a pilot."

"Fair enough," VanderVoort says. "May I speak with Lowell, Trey?"

"I am afraid not," Trey says. "He is currently busy working with a Dr. Probst in order to fulfill his destiny."

"Lowell has a destiny?" VanderVoort asks.

"That he does," Trey responds. "Every host planet needs at least one pilot of its own. The Substance believes Anson Lowell will do nicely."

"Didn't the Wyoming kaiju die?" Alvarez asks. "What's he going to pilot?"

"Quetzalcoatl," Trey states.

"No way," Dr. Hall says.

"There is a way," Trey says. "Which is what Anson Lowell and Dr. Probst are working on now. The way. Since Anson Lowell is currently occupied with his destiny, perhaps I could be of service. What may I assist you with?"

"You're a pilot?" VanderVoort asks.

"I am," Trey replies.

"And you pilot the Africa kaiju?" VanderVoort asks.

"I do," Trey replies.

"How would you like a job going around and picking up refugees and taking them to secure facilities around the globe?" VanderVoort asks.

"I already have that job," Trey says. "I rescued many villagers from the African continent. Unfortunately, I could not gather them all, but I did my best. Who else would you like me to rescue?"

"Charles, you're up!" VanderVoort shouts. "Trey, I'm going to let you speak to the President of the United States."

"I do not know who that is, but it sounds like it could be a great honor," Trey says. "Is this president a human of great action and know how?"

"He sure as shit is," VanderVoort replies.

"Then he will do nicely as a partner on this mission to rescue more refugees," Trey says.

"Great," VanderVoort says. "I'll transfer you over to him and his team."

VanderVoort twirls her fingers and the image on the main monitor returns to tracking the Chile kaiju.

"That went well," VanderVoort says. "Weird, but well. Is it a bad thing that I'm really not affected anymore by aliens and giant monsters?"

"Depends," Director Miles says. "It could be that you're accepting reality. Or you could be going into minor shock, which would be a bad thing. Knowing you? Just good old acceptance."

"Thanks, Gordon," VanderVoort says. "Anyone have Tony on comms yet?"

No one answers.

"Then get me Bolton," VanderVoort says.

A minute passes before a tech informs her that Bolton can't be reached.

"You tried that new aircraft and the sat phone?" VanderVoort asks. The tech nods nervously. "Shit. Okay. Not good, but not going to panic. All chill." She rubs her belly. "Hey. You in there. It's all chill, so stop kicking the shit out of my guts, will ya?"

VanderVoort turns to see President Nance and his people gathered around a monitor all talking at once, while the placid, alien face of Trey looks on patiently.

"Wait a second," VanderVoort says. "What was that shit about Lowell and Dr. Probst fulfilling some destiny? Dr. Hall!"

"Yes?" Dr. Hall replies. He shakes his head and yawns. "I haven't been up this long since I binged *Twin Peaks* non-stop."

"Jesus, man, that had to mess with your head," Alvarez says.

"I think I had mild hallucinations for weeks after," Dr. Hall replies.

"Are you two done?" VanderVoort asks. "Dr. Hall. What did Trey mean by Lowell fulfilling his destiny with Quetzalcoatl?"

"I have no idea what he means," Dr. Hall says. "At least the destiny part. But if what we know now about the kaiju needing pilots is correct, and what Trey said about each planet needing its own pilot, then it stands to reason that what lies beneath Mexico City is Quetzalcoatl, waiting for Lowell to pilot it. It explains why Chile went to protect that site and the kaiju below never entered the fight."

"Does it make sense?" Director Miles asks.

"It does," Dr. Hall replies. "As much as any of this makes sense."

"But Lowell is in Antarctica," VanderVoort says. "And Dr. Probst is in Wyoming. Neither of which is anywhere close to Mexico City. How the fuck is he getting there? He doesn't have a shuttle anymore."

"We could call Dr. Probst," Dr. Hall says.

"Make it happen!" VanderVoort shouts to the room. The Wyoming connection comes up instantly. "Thank you."

"Ms. VanderVoort," Lu says. She rubs her eyes. "What now?"

"It's good to speak to you too, Marshal Morgan," VanderVoort says.

"Can we skip the niceties?" Lu responds. "What do you want?"

"I need to speak to Dr. Probst," VanderVoort says.

"She's busy," Lu says.

"Interrupt her, please," VanderVoort says.

"No," Lu says. "She's helping Lowell, and that's more important than anything you need her for."

"I'll be the judge of that," VanderVoort says. "Need I remind you that you work for me, Marshal Morgan? As a law enforcement officer of the Federal government, you—"

"I quit," Lu says. "Anything else?"

"Ms. Morgan," VanderVoort says. "That facility you are in is under my jurisdiction. It's one of the few refuges left in the world. If you'd like to remain there, then I suggest—"

The connection ends and the monitor goes blank.

"She hung up on me," VanderVoort says. "She fucking hung up on me."

"She sure did," Director Miles says. "Ballsy."

The monitor comes back to life and Kyle is sitting in front of the screen.

"Kyle," VanderVoort says. "I need to speak to Dr. Probst."

"That can't happen," Kyle says and holds up a hand before VanderVoort can protest. "Do you want to know why?"

"Because everyone has gone rogue?" VanderVoort replies.

"I'm going to explain this once, then I need to get off the comms and help Dr. Probst," Kyle says. "No questions afterward, so listen up. Ready?"

"Kid, you and your family are really pushing it today," VanderVoort says. "When this is done and we sort this all out, you better hope I'm in a good mood."

Kyle rolls his eyes as only a teenager can.

"First, all governmental authority is over," Kyle says. "You folks get to help save people and oversee the organization and administration of the new unified civilization when this is over. But you're no longer in charge. Lowell is. Then Trey. Then me.

Sort of. I'll be more in control than in charge. Dr. Probst will be too, but not the same way at all. That part's complicated. I'll write it all down later."

"Gee. Thanks," VanderVoort says.

"Don't get upset," Kyle says. "You're going to be glad you aren't in charge. Can I keep talking now?"

"Little shit," VanderVoort mutters under her breath, then smiles wide at the monitor. "Keep talking, Kyle."

"Lowell and Dr. Probst are reestablishing the blue crystal conduit network," Kyle says. "This will allow instantaneous travel between the facilities. Kinda like teleportation but not. It's very hard to explain. So I won't."

"I'd really like to hear the explanation," Dr. Hall says.

"Later," Kyle says. "The BCCN—which is what I'm calling it because who has time to keep saying blue crystal conduit network, right?"

VanderVoort only glares.

"Right," Kyle says. "Lowell will transport to Mexico City and take control of the Quetzalcoatl kaiju and use that to stop the Ebony Man before he reaches the Core."

"I'm sorry, what's the Core?" VanderVoort asks.

"Still talking," Kyle says. "The Core is what powers all of the facilities."

"I thought the Substance did that?" Director Miles says and looks at VanderVoort. "Hasn't that been established?"

"The Substance comes from the Core and travels through its own network between the facilities," Kyle says. "Or it did until the Ebony Man messed it all up. He was supposed to be isolated, but things broke at some point and the entire network got messed up."

"Which is why Dr. Probst is fixing it," Dr. Hall says. "What else does the Core do?"

"Still still talking," Kyle says. "But good question. The Core is the main facility. It's what controls and powers the defense system for Earth. Which is currently offline. We need it online. But the

Ebony Man is heading toward the Core to destroy it, which will also destroy all the facilities, and then the big aliens heading our way will rip the planet apart and rebuild it as their military outpost for the intergalactic war that's raging out in space."

No one says a word.

Then Dr. Hall raises a hand.

"Go," Kyle says.

"Where is the Core?" Dr. Hall asks.

"The Mariana Trench," Kyle says.

Dr. Hall raises his hand again.

"Just talk, bro," Kyle says.

"If the Ebony Man is in the Antarctica kaiju, then why is he heading to engage with the Chile kaiju?" Dr. Hall says. "That's the wrong direction. It would have been much faster if he crossed the Antarctic continent and swam over to Australia instead of going to South America."

"He's an asshole," Kyle says with a shrug.

"That isn't helpful," VanderVoort says.

"No, seriously, the guy is an asshole," Kyle says. "There's a reason he was imprisoned here. He's a fucking psycho asshole. Even aliens think he's a fucking asshole. I think he's going to kill Chile just to prove something. Or he could be hungry. The Antarctica facility let loose some smaller kaiju early on, but they took off after Wyoming fell. Antarctica was supposed to eat those just like Wyoming did. The Ebony Man has to fuel the kaiju he's piloting or he won't make it to the Core. If he doesn't make it to the Core, then he's as good as dead when his new pals show up."

"Whoa," Dr. Hall says. "Cool."

"No, not cool!" VanderVoort snaps. "None of this is cool! I'm going to ignore the bullshit about not being in charge anymore and focus on this alien war and the aliens coming to Earth. Tell me about them."

"That'll take too long," Kyle says. "But if the Ebony Man gets to the Core and shuts it down, then we're all dead. All life on this planet will be adios. Getting Lowell to the Core first is how we win this. He can defend it against the Ebony Man while we activate the planet's defenses."

Kyle blinks a few times and shakes his head.

"We… that's the first time I've said that out loud," Kyle says. "I guess I'll be going to the Core. Shit… I should probably tell my mom."

Once again, a Morgan hangs up on VanderVoort.

Dr. Hall raises a hand.

"I'll fucking cut that hand off," VanderVoort snaps.

"I'd like to volunteer to go to the Wyoming facility," Dr. Hall says. "I have to experience all of this firsthand."

Before VanderVoort can explode at the scientist, President Nance speaks up.

"We're all going to the Wyoming facility," President Nance says.

"Oh, cool," Dr. Hall says.

"Well, shit, good to know," VanderVoort says. "Talk to me, Charles."

"Trey will be coming for us so he can move us to Wyoming," President Nance says. "We've decided it'll be better for us to be safe there so we can coordinate the rescue of as many people as possible."

Before VanderVoort can respond to the latest bombshell, a tech shouts, "Antarctica and Chile are nearing each other!"

VanderVoort sighs, takes a deep breath, then turns with everyone else to face the main monitor.

————

With zero regard for the destruction it's causing, the Ebony Man stomps Antarctica across the Amazon rainforest toward the Chile kaiju that is just cresting the horizon in Venezuela. The two behemoths pause as they come within sight of each other.

Then the pause ends, and they rush across the landscape at a speed that causes the earth beneath their feet to ripple. Swaths of rainforest are obliterated. Entire rivers are cut off, diverted, turned into apocalyptic lakes instead of arteries of life.

Chile rears up on its hind six legs, raising the fore six legs before it, claws extended, strange stone mouth open in a wide roar of rage and anticipation.

Antarctica flexes, and all the sharpened scales covering its arms and torso curve and extend, turning the monster into a charging slice-and-dice nightmare.

The two monsters cover the remaining distance between them in a matter of seconds then come together in a collision of violence.

One of Chile's forearms is severed instantly as it tries to strike Antarctica, the limb falling to the ground and crushing a long line of oil derricks, sending black crude spewing high into the air.

Antarctica lifts its right fist into the air and brings it down hard and fast on top of Chile's head. The Ebony Man's kaiju is much taller than Chile, so the blow obtains a good deal of momentum before connecting.

The smaller kaiju collapses to the ground, its legs buckling under it. It shakes off the blow quickly and blocks the next blow once again aimed for its head. Its spindly forearms shake and shudder as it presses up against the strength of Antarctica.

Antarctica roars down at Chile and gives it a shove, putting distance between the two again. The larger kaiju lifts its upper lip in a snarl, revealing a set of canines, each bigger than a city bus. All the sharpened scales lift and lock in place.

Antarctica sprints forward, then launches itself into a spinning leap.

Chile cries out as four of its remaining forearms are sliced to ribbons. Bits and pieces of the monster's appendages litter the trampled landscape and it scuttles backward on its hind legs, desperate to get away from the walking food processor.

Then it does something that seems to take Antarctica aback.

Chile shoves its single good forearm into the vast lake of crude oil that now covers a good portion of Venezuela. Two of the severed limbs begin to regenerate immediately. The rest grow too, but much slower.

Antarctica roars and throws itself at Chile, the scales still locked into place, their sharpened edges aimed directly for Chile's body.

Chile screeches, ducks, and rolls away from Antarctica's attack, just missing having its weird Easter Island head sliced right off its body.

Antarctica lands in the oil, splashing the crude hundreds of feet into the air. It slips and slides, finds some traction, and turns to attack again.

But Chile is waiting.

Trees that were hundreds upon hundreds of years old, that once provided needed oxygen to not just the continent they grew upon but the entire world, are now massive batons gripped in four of Chile's claws.

Antarctica narrows its eyes and watches Chile closely as it slowly moves sideways, trying to flank the smaller kaiju, but Chile turns and counters the maneuver, making sure it's facing Antarctica at all times.

Then they move at the same time and collide in an explosion of giant flesh, wood, crude oil, and blood. The roars and screeches are powerful enough to knock down what few trees had still been standing.

Chile scrambles away, cuts and gashes covering its body, two of the newly formed forearms once again nothing but nubs. Yet the huge head has an unmistakable grin on its face.

Antarctica growls and lunges, then stumbles and goes down on one knee. The monster looks down at its abdomen and bellows with rage and pain at the two trees sticking out from under two sharpened scales. Blood pours from the wounds.

Keeping its distance, Chile circumnavigates the wounded kaiju and returns to the lake of crude oil. It plunges into the fossil fuel, rolling over and over to coat its entire body. The gashes turn to cuts and the cuts seal up. Then regeneration begins again and fresh limbs start to form. Chile wastes no time and extracts itself from the oil to hunt down more trees.

While Chile heals, Antarctica tends to its own wounds and snaps the trees off just under the scales. It doesn't remove the trunks that penetrate its body, leaving them there to act as agonizing stop gaps, maintaining the slow leak of blood instead of creating lethal rivers.

Then Antarctica faces Chile and licks its lips.

Chile pauses, trees held up and ready for battle.

Antarctica takes a step toward Chile, its rage-filled eyes locked onto the smaller kaiju.

Chile takes a couple of steps back.

Antarctica matches the movement, keeping the distance between the two monsters constant.

Chile flings the trees at Antarctica and runs, scrambling toward the Pacific Ocean.

A huge trunk nails Antarctica in the chest, but only sticks to the sharpened edges of a couple of scales, doing no damage. Antarctica's eyes burn with hunger and homicide as it takes off after Chile.

Everything in the beasts' path is destroyed. All that's left is a trail of churned earth.

On Chile races, scurrying as fast as its intact legs will carry it, Antarctica on its ass the entire way.

The monsters reach the coastal range and clamber up over the mountains, then Chile leaps out into the air, its legs propelling it toward the ocean and possible safety.

But Antarctica leaps as well and manages to catch hold of one of Chile's back legs, sending the two monsters into a diving spin, then a brutal collision with the rocky coast.

Ancient lava rock is turned into gravel as the kaiju slam into the ground.

Chile cries out in pain as it's impaled by one of its own legs. The limb is twisted around backward and embedded in the kaiju's right side. Sticky blood oozes from the wound, and Chile desperately tries to drag itself out from under and away from Antarctica.

The larger kaiju is having none of that.

It grabs the twisted limb and shoves it deeper into Chile's body. Chile screams and flails, but it's too weak to fight off the superior weight of Antarctica as the monster shoves and shoves and shoves until the leg snaps and stabs all the way through Chile's body.

Antarctica slowly gets to its feet and stands over Chile in triumph as the smaller kaiju thrashes impotently in the surf. The huge monster glares down at Chile, watching it perform its death throes. Then it snorts, lifts a leg, and stomps down on Chile's head, cracking the stone-like skin down the middle so giant brains leak out into the water.

With a roar of triumph, Antarctica grabs Chile's corpse and drags it up out of the water and back onto land. Then it settles down on its haunches and attacks the corpse, cracking the dead kaiju's body like a tourist digging into a Dungeness crab.

Antarctica scoops flesh into its mouth, letting the blood and juices slop down over its scaled torso. After a few seconds, the kaiju pauses in its gluttony and yanks out the two tree stumps still embedded in its body. It flicks the wood to the side and smooths down the scales, grinning at the already healing wounds.

After feasting for hours, making sure it strips the dead kaiju's corpse entirely of all flesh and edible components, Antarctica stands and walks into the water. It washes itself off, rinsing the blood and offal, the dirt and oil from its scales before it stands fully upright and stares out into the ocean.

Then it fills its lungs, turns to the north, and roars, a single fist thumping its chest before it turns back to the ocean. Once more, the kaiju fills its lungs, then dives into the water, lost from sight in seconds.

————

"Something just happened," Dr. Probst says. "Lowell? Are you alright? I saw a spike in energy in the blue crystal, then it went away."

"Yeah, I'm good," Lowell says, standing in a space about the same size as the kaiju chamber but nowhere as technical looking.

In fact, to Lowell, it's like standing in the middle of a geode the size of a massive football coliseum. All around him are nothing but stone walls veined with blue crystals.

Antarctica's BCCN terminal.

"Are you sure?" Dr. Probst asks, her voice echoing around the huge space. "That spike makes me nervous. Maybe we should wait to try—"

"We can't wait," Lowell says and closes his eyes. "Other than Trey, I think I'm all that's left."

"So the spike was…?" Dr. Probst asks.

"I'd say it was Chile going down hard," Lowell says. He shakes his head. "Man, I really hope all this shit gets easier to process. It's like thoughts and images get shoved into my head anytime anything major happens. Kinda like text messages going straight into my brain."

"Kyle feels the same way," Dr. Probst says. "But I don't think he's at a level you are."

"Not yet," Lowell says, then regrets the response instantly.

"What does that mean?" Dr. Probst asks. "Lowell?"

"Never mind," Lowell says. "We don't have time to get into it. Are you ready on your end?"

"I guess," Dr. Probst says. "It's not like I know what the hell I'm doing. How will I know when it's time to make the connection?"

"You'll know," Lowell says. "It'll be like that spike of energy you just saw except more like a wall or wave. It'll just keep coming, and when it takes over everything I need you to open the bulkhead doors so the Substance is exposed to the facility. Can you do that?"

"Is that going to be safe for us?" Dr. Probst asks.

"Doc, baby, we've been through this," Lowell says with a sigh. "You and Lu are already so exposed it'll feel like a fun little tickle."

"You lying sack of shit," Dr. Probst says. "It's going to suck, isn't it?"

"Totally," Lowell says. "Did you go pee before hooking the sensors up?"

"What? Am I going to piss myself?" Dr. Probst cries. "Lowell!"

"Just fucking with you, Cheryl," Lowell says. "I think…"

Lowell takes a deep breath, closes his eyes, and lets his body become attuned to the vibrations of the terminal. He nods to himself, then opens his eyes.

"Here it comes," he says and pushes his consciousness into that vibration. "Here I come!"

Lowell is gone.

He isn't gone gone. He still maintains that sense of self. But the sense of place he had inside the terminal is no more. Lowell is a passenger along for the ride. He bought the ticket, now he has to take the journey.

Despite being attuned to the crystal, to two of the facilities, Lowell is not prepared for the stress of the travel. His Substance-altered body handles the transformation from solid matter to pure energy without a problem, but his mind struggles.

Thoughts he's kept buried for most of his life claw their way to the surface. Memories of violence and torture fill his mind's eye, and he cringes away from them as if they're happening to him right now. Phantom pains stab and cut, slice and whip at him, causing him to cry out.

The cry is metaphorical only. He has no throat or vocal cords in his current state. The only sounds made are strictly in his mind. But since Lowell is nothing but mind at the moment, the cries double, treble, quadruple in strength until the sounds echo and reverberate so powerfully that Lowell is afraid his currently non-existent brain will explode as soon as it becomes flesh again.

Which doesn't happen.

Lowell stumbles and falls to the ground, his hands out to catch him, but not quite fast enough. He cries a real cry as his elbow turns to road rash when one arm collapses under his weight.

"Ow," Lowell says and slowly picks himself up.

He isn't surprised that he's in a terminal almost exactly like the one in Antarctica. The only difference is the terminal he's standing in is smaller. What really surprises him is there's a Dr. Probst standing by the entrance with her eyes wide, mouth open, and laptop precariously balanced in one palm.

"Hey, Doc," Lowell says. "This isn't Mexico. I've seen pictures, and it doesn't look anything like this."

Dr. Probst continues to stare, then shakes her head and turns away.

"Could you wear clothes next time?" Dr. Probst says.

"What?" Lowell responds and looks down at himself. No jumpsuit. "Huh. We'll need to prep for that. Maybe keep a few extra outfits in a locker or something."

"You're saying you had a jumpsuit on when you left Antarctica?" Dr. Probst asks. "Interesting."

"Not as interesting as why I'm here in Wyoming and not in Mexico," Lowell says. He waves a hand at Dr. Probst before she can reply. "Don't worry, Doc, you did everything right. I screwed up somehow. I was thinking of you and this place when I left Antarctica."

"So you need to think about Mexico instead?" Dr. Probst asks. "How do you do that when you haven't been there before?"

"I haven't been here before either," Lowell says. "Or not in this terminal before. It's not about physical location so much as it is about mental focus. I gotta keep my mind on the margarita. Focus on some delicious salsa verde. That should get me south of the border."

"Oh. Okay," Dr. Probst says. "Do you want to take a break? Come up for something to eat and maybe touch base with Kyle?"

"No time, Doc," Lowell says. "If Mr. Licorice killed Chile, then that means the fucker is already taking a long swim toward the Core. I have to beat him there or we're royally fucked."

"Yes, that's what Kyle says too," Dr. Probst says. "I still don't fully understand it all."

"Me neither," Lowell says. "I just sorta get it. If I try to really think on it all, then it becomes muddled. Human brains aren't built to comprehend everything that has been shoved into mine."

"Again, Kyle says the same too," Dr. Probst says. "So... what now?"

"For you? Nothing," Lowell says and closes his eyes. "You already activated the terminal here, so all I need to do is concentrate."

"Oh, alright. I'll just stand here and be quiet," Dr. Probst says.

Lowell concentrates then frowns.

"Maybe step out of the terminal for a second?" Lowell suggests. "Your quiet is really, really loud."

"What does that mean?" Dr. Probst asks.

"I can feel you wanting to rip everything apart and study it," Lowell says. "It's kind of distracting."

"Right. Sorry," Dr. Probst says. "I'll leave."

"All good," Lowell says. "No need to apologize."

Lowell waits until Dr. Probst's presence barely registers in his consciousness.

Then he thinks about fresh masa and street tacos and he's gone.

When he opens his eyes a millisecond later, there's no stumbling, no tripping, and thankfully not another bloody elbow.

"Now this is what I'm talking about," Lowell says as he looks about the Mexico BCCN terminal.

The space is even larger than Antarctica, which bodes well for Lowell. He's figured out from mental impressions and good old deduction that the size of the terminal is in direct relation to the size of the kaiju the facility houses.

"Let's go find the big boy and see how I turn it on," Lowell says.

He moves to the closest wall and places his hand directly against the blue crystal. Instantly, he's attuned to the facility and a map of the place fixes in his mind.

Lowell exits the terminal and walks the length of a massive tunnel for what feels like forever until he comes to a set of bulkhead doors that are a couple thousand feet high. He'd make some *Lord of the Rings* joke, but he's in too much of a hurry and only places a palm against the bulkhead doors.

Instead of moving apart as a single unit, the doors break into segments and quickly retract one by one into the tunnel's walls. Lowell smiles at the massive kaiju chamber before him.

He smiles even wider as he sees what the chamber holds.

"Well, ain't you gorgeous," Lowell says and steps up to the huge kaiju that slumbers inside the chamber.

Since the kaiju is coiled around itself like a serpent, which it is, Lowell isn't completely sure how long the body is. But some quick calculations give him an estimate of around three thousand feet from snout to tail.

The monster is a deep, iridescent blue on top with a blue-gray underbelly. All across the body are scales as well as feathers in a rainbow of colors that brighten the chamber, even though there's no actual illumination that Lowell can see. The head rests on two arms that look more like wings, the creature's chin atop feathers that look to be the softest ever created.

"Alright, baby," Lowell says and quickly works his way around the kaiju's body to a set of bulkhead doors opposite the ones he'd just come through. "Time to wake up and get to work. We've got a Mr. Licorice to kill and a planet to save."

Lowell gets to the bulkhead doors and places his palm against them, then steps back as they do the same segmented opening process as the other doors.

Once open, Lowell is faced with another massive tunnel and another long walk.

"Jumpsuits and carts," Lowell says. "Gotta remember to set that up for all the facilities. This walking shit is getting old."

But Lowell does walk, and eventually he's standing in front of another set of bulkhead doors, these considerably smaller than the ones to the kaiju chamber.

"Open sesame," he says, and the bulkhead doors open up to reveal the Mexico facility's portion of the Substance. Lowell takes a step back from the heat. "Mmmm, spicy."

He lets the warmth wash over him until his body feels attuned to the specific vibrations of the Mexico Substance.

Then Lowell walks into the chamber and directly into the Substance.

The orange glow becomes a brilliant flash and Lowell is gone.

Minutes pass by and nothing happens.

Then a huff of breath and a stirring is felt in the kaiju chamber.

Quetzalcoatl's eyes open and blink, the slitted pupils narrowing and widening, narrowing and widening until they stabilize. The head lifts and glances around.

"Oh...fuck," Lowell thinks as his consciousness takes over the massive monster. "Wyoming was like a shitty Ford Pinto compared to this baby. Q, my new best friend, you are the Cadillac of kaiju, no doubt."

Lowell raises his serpent head and roars up at the top of the kaiju chamber. The ceiling obeys and begins to retract. Lowell lifts his entire body and stretches as far as he can in the confined space.

Then he looks down.

"No legs? Well, this should be fun," Lowell says.

As soon as the ceiling is wide open, Lowell narrows his wings and raises them directly over his head. Then he whips them downward and lifts into the warm, inviting Mexican air.

In less than a couple of seconds, Lowell is away from land and flying over the Pacific Ocean, his shadow surfing the waves below him as he aims his new body straight for the South Pacific.

He's got a Mr. Licorice to find and kill and exactly zero time to waste.

FOURTEEN

The flamethrower sputters and dies in Bolton's hands.

So he throws it at the fourth winged monster that's tried to clamber inside the Space Needle's restaurant to get at him, Terrie, Tony, Krissy, and the perpetually barking Biscuit.

The scorching hot metal of the flamethrower's nozzle singes the winged monster's snout but doesn't do any real damage.

The beast's shriek, though, nearly bursts Bolton's eardrums.

"Joshua? How are you holding up out there?" Bolton calls. "Any progress?"

"I'm alive and still flying," Joshua responds.

Bolton waits, but there's no other response.

"Connor!" Terrie shouts from her spot by the stairwell doors. "They're going to be up here any second! We have to do something or we'll be trapped!"

Bolton holds his tongue. The joy of finding Terrie Morgan alive is beginning to wear off, and memories of the domineering and imposing woman he's known since he was in high school with Lu come flooding back.

"Work the problem, Terrie!" Bolton shouts and grabs a grenade from his belt. He pulls the pin and chucks it at the winged monster, knowing the explosive won't even come close to killing the beast. "Fire in the hole!"

But like with the other monsters that had breached the restaurant, Bolton uses the explosion as a distraction to disorient the beast. He grabs the last magazine of M4 ammunition from his vest and waits for his opportunity.

The flames and smoke clear and the winged monster roars as Bolton.

With a quick snap of his wrist, Bolton flings the magazine underhand into the beast's open mouth.

Its jaws snap closed and it gulps instinctively.

"Gonna have more foam!" Bolton yells and retreats back to everyone huddled close to the barricade by the demolished stairwell doors.

The winged monster belches, then shrieks just before gray foam bursts from its esophagus.

"Joshua!" Bolton yells over the comm. "You have to pick us up!"

"Not up top," Joshua replies. "They're swarming over the needle."

"Shit," Bolton says. "Wait. What about the drones?"

"Banks and his team are doing what they can to take out as many of these assholes as possible," Joshua says. "But the lasers are only wounding them, not killing them."

"Exactly! The lasers!" Bolton shouts. "Can Banks zero in on my signal?"

"I'll ask," Joshua responds, sounding like that's the very last thing in the world he wants to do. A few seconds later, he's back. "The comms system with this bird isn't strong enough for him to lock onto you. It's taking everything they've got to stay connected to the drones and fight these bastards off."

"He's much more talkative with you," Tony says to Bolton.

"You can't clam up during an op," Bolton says. "Communication is key."

Bolton pauses and looks about the restaurant. He gauges the size of the interior and smiles.

"Okay, I have a very bad idea," Bolton says. "But it may be our only chance."

"I do not like bad ideas," Tony says.

"Do you like being eaten by fucking monsters?" Krissy snaps.

"Not particularly," Tony says.

"What is your idea, Connor?" Terrie asks, her eyes never leaving the stairwell.

"I'll explain it to Joshua," Bolton says. "You all listen."

Bolton explains his idea to Joshua.

"That's a very bad idea," Krissy says. "Probably the worst idea I've ever heard."

"I warned you," Bolton says.

"We don't have a choice anymore!" Terrie screams as the stairwell fills with the unmistakable noise of thousands upon thousands of ooze creatures. "They're here!"

"Joshua! Tell Banks to start now!" Bolton yells, then waves for the others to get down. "Duck and cover, people!"

Everyone hits the deck as a swarm of drones strafe the restaurant with their lasers, systematically slicing a full bay of the restaurant's windows into bits and pieces until an entire side of the restaurant is wide open to the elements.

Tony starts to get up, his eyes wide with fear and amazement at the destruction, but Krissy yanks him back to the floor.

"Stay down!" Bolton yells at them both.

"I was!" Krissy yells back. "Tell him!"

"They'll all get in now," Tony says.

"Nope," Bolton says. "Here comes Joshua!"

The aircraft drops below the window, out of sight, then reappears almost instantly, its body spinning around one-hundred eighty degrees so that the small cargo hold is facing the restaurant. Joshua flies the aircraft backward into the open space and the cargo ramp drops open.

"Get in!" Joshua shouts.

They don't need his urging. All of them are already sprinting toward the aircraft. Behind them, a multitude of ooze creatures lumber, scuttle, scurry, and slither after the retreating party.

The cargo door slams shut as several dozen ooze creatures swarm up over the aircraft.

"Strap in," Joshua says but doesn't wait for anyone to do so.

The aircraft shoots out from the restaurant and plunges straight down, ooze creatures streaming out after it.

Just above the Space Needle, half a dozen winged monsters catch sight of the aircraft and dive.

Bolton gymnastically falls his way into the co-pilot's seat while Terrie, Tony, Krissy, and Biscuit scream, shout, complain, and bark in the cargo hold.

"You got this?" Bolton asks, fighting gravity as he straps in.

"Maybe," Joshua says, then pulls up, and the aircraft skims the tops of the few remaining outbuildings dotting the immediate area around the Space Needle.

Thousands of ooze creatures had poured out of the restaurant after the aircraft. Now they splat against the outbuildings and the ground, coating everything in greenish ooze.

The half-dozen winged monsters fare only slightly better. Two manage to abort their attacks and lift back up into the air. The other four can't manage the maneuver fast enough and crash and collide with the ooze-coated outbuildings, ground, then each other.

"Now what?" Joshua asks as he flies the aircraft away from the Seattle Center. The Diamondback drones flank him on either side, firing laser bursts anytime a winged monster from above gets too close.

"Wyoming," Bolton says, then turns in his seat. "Tony! You're up!"

"Yes," Tony says, untangling himself from the safety netting he'd clung to as the aircraft was in free fall. "I'll need some help."

Bolton makes eye contact with Terrie and she nods.

"Show me what you need," Terrie says.

As those two work at connecting Tony's radio device to the aircraft's magnetic drive, Krissy moves carefully to the front and leans in between Bolton and Joshua, her eyes staring out the windshield.

"It's…" she starts and shakes her head.

"A lot, I know," Bolton says.

"There are so many of them," Krissy says as they fly over a thick patch of ooze creatures that stretches on for miles. "They're like ants."

"A fungus," Joshua says.

Krissy frowns at him. "What do you mean?"

"I watched it happen," Joshua says. "Most of the ooze things to the east have started to melt and just be ooze, not creatures. But the ooze is working to break down whatever it melts on."

"Terraforming," Bolton says. "They're helping to turn the planet into something else, for something else."

"Aliens?" Krissy asks. "Are there really aliens?"

Joshua and Bolton both give her a look. She holds up her hands.

"Okay, whatever," Krissy says. "There are aliens."

"How's it coming back there?" Bolton shouts.

"Slowly," Terrie replies. "This aircraft is confusing Tony."

"It is not confusing me!" Tony shouts. "I am simply unfamiliar with the technology utilized to power this vehicle!"

"Can we get Banks and his folks on the horn?" Bolton asks Joshua.

"I told you comms are weak," Joshua says. "They're using everything to maintain control of the drones."

"We'll need to risk it," Bolton says and activates the aircraft's comms system. "Banks? Come in!"

"Banks here," Banks replies, his voice staticky. "What's your sit?"

"All accounted for and unharmed," Bolton says. "Tony is trying to connect the device to the aircraft, but he's having problems."

"I am not having problems," Tony protests. "I am unfamiliar with the technology."

"Which is a problem," Bolton says. "Who can answer his questions?"

"Probably me," Banks says. "Connect me to him and I'll see what I can do."

Bolton grabs a headset and tosses it back to Terrie, who catches it easily and positions it on Tony's head.

"This better work," Joshua says.

"It will," Krissy says. "Tony is a huge pain-in-the-ass weirdo, but he makes shit work."

"Sit down and strap in," Bolton says to her.

"Why?" Krissy snaps. "I want to see outside."

Bolton points at several dark shapes dropping out of the ash clouds and heading their direction.

"Oh," Krissy says and quickly retreats into the cargo hold to strap in.

"Hang on tight," Bolton yells back to Terrie and Tony.

"Tony has the comms occupied," Joshua says. "We can't coordinate with Diamondback."

"Let's hope they see what's coming for us," Bolton says and brings up the weapons system. "You fly, I'll shoot."

"I figured," Joshua says.

Joshua punches it and the aircraft races toward the incoming monsters.

Biscuit lets out a long yowl as Krissy begins scream-cursing from the sudden acceleration.

Bolton squeezes the trigger. Nothing.

"The lightning gun is out!" Bolton shouts.

"Then shoot them with something else!" Joshua shouts back.

Bolton studies the weapons system, then targets the winged monsters and lets fly a battery of small missiles. The monsters easily dodge the missiles, letting the explosive projectiles fly by harmlessly.

"They can't lock on," Bolton says.

"Mmm hmm," Joshua responds, his eyes narrowed and focused on the monsters.

"What's wrong?" Bolton asks.

"They're going to try something," Joshua says. "Watch."

The group of beasts splits apart and the drones break formation to follow, half going up, half going down.

A battle wages that neither Bolton nor Joshua can see as the winged monsters and the Diamondback drones dogfight above and below the aircraft.

Then a laser nearly slices the nose of the aircraft off and Bolton jumps.

"See," Joshua says. "They're trying to use the drones against us."

"Shit," Bolton says as another laser just misses hitting the aircraft. "Tony? How's it coming back there?"

"Progress is being made!" Tony shouts.

"Will it be made soon?" Bolton shouts. "We don't have much time!"

An alarm blares and Joshua hunts about the dash for the source.

"Our right side got clipped," Joshua says. "The aircraft is compensating, but we can't take another hit like that. This is a prototype, not a battle-ready field vehicle."

"Just keep flying," Bolton says, returning his attention to the weapons system. "What do we have that could work?"

"Napalm?" Joshua asks.

"Not on the menu," Bolton says, then smiles. "But there's something close. Phosphorous."

"Flares?" Joshua asks. "I don't know if that's gonna help."

"Not flares," Bolton says and taps the screen in front of him. "This says starbursts."

"Flares," Joshua replies, unimpressed.

"We'll find out," Bolton says. "Get us out of the sandwich."

Joshua banks the aircraft hard to the right, just missing a collision with a dueling drone and winged monster. Bolton catches an explosion out of the corner of his eye as they speed past and he's pretty sure the drone lost the duel.

"Clear," Joshua says. "Fire your flares."

Bolton fires off eight starbursts and the windshield instantly dims to nearly black tint.

"Kinda makes it hard to fly," Joshua growls.

Then the air around the aircraft explodes like the surface of the sun and Joshua is no longer complaining. He's having to use all of his strength and attention to keep the aircraft stable.

"Big flares," Joshua says.

"No shit," Bolton says, squinting at the windshield even with the tinting. He blinks away spots and checks the screen. "Damn…"

"What?" Joshua asks.

"The monsters are gone," Bolton says. "Three are retreating and there's no sign of the others."

"Drones?" Joshua asks.

"Other than a couple lost because of the monsters, they're all there," Bolton says. "They weren't affected."

"Neither was this bird," Joshua says. "We need to find out what this thing is armored with."

"And we need more starbursts," Bolton says. "A fucking lot more."

"Connected," Tony announces from the cargo hold with a bored voice. "Global comms are reestablished."

"Banks?" Bolton calls.

"Here, Sergeant," Banks replies. "That kid is a genius. We're now connected to everyone, everywhere. Anyone seeing a lag?" Banks pauses. "No? Damn. Sergeant Bolton?"

"Yes, Lieutenant Commander?" Bolton replies.

"Drop off your people at the Wyoming facility, then get that bird back here," Banks says. "If that bird can be that strong of a relay, then we've got something even better to connect the device to."

"Is it portable?" Bolton asks.

"Very," Banks says. "Why?"

"Because after Wyoming, we're coming to get you for good," Bolton says. "Diamondback won't be sustainable. You want to be in the Wyoming facility. See what you can do to make that whatever portable."

"And more starbursts," Joshua says.

"Right," Bolton agrees. "We'll need plenty more of those starbursts."

"I think you'll be pleasantly surprised," Banks replies. "See you soon."

"Copy that," Bolton says. "Out."

He turns in his seat.

"Great job, kid," Bolton calls to Tony. "You've probably saved several hundred thousand lives."

"I'm not giving my device to the government," Tony states. "I will need to be compensated."

"Okay... I'm sure something can be worked out," Bolton says and looks at Joshua, who just shrugs.

The aircraft races through the sky toward Wyoming as the shadows in the ash clouds keep a wary distance.

————

"Are you sure this is the correct way?" Lu asks Kyle, then glances at Dr. Probst as all three ride in an elevator that Lu hasn't been in before. "How do we know it's safe above?"

"It's not safe above," Kyles says. "Nothing will ever be safe above."

"You know what?" Lu says. "You can stop trying to freak your mother out at any time, Son."

"Sorry, Mom," Kyle says. He rubs his forehead. "It can be hard to remember who I am sometimes."

"Is it painful?" Dr. Probst asks, her eyes flitting across the screen of her laptop to the other two, back and forth. "Are you in discomfort?"

"Painful?" Lu asks, alarmed. "Kyle, are you alright?"

"I'm fine, Mom," Kyle says and gives Dr. Probst an exasperated look. "It feels like after cramming for a final, not getting any sleep, then taking the final, cramming for another final, and still not getting any sleep."

"Oh, I know that feeling," Dr. Probst says.

"It's called exhaustion," Lu says. "Kyle, you need to sleep."

"Later," Kyle says as the elevator comes to a stop. "We get this process going, then I'll see if I can rest."

"We get this process going and then you will for sure rest," Lu says. "That's an order from your mother."

"Okay, Mom," Kyle says and steps off the elevator into a huge observation deck that looks out onto Wyoming's own kaiju chamber.

"Holy crap," Dr. Probst says. "Is this where the Ebony Man had his kaiju?"

"No," Kyle says. "He should have, but he figured out a way to grow it and all the others, the cattle, in the Yellowstone caldera, which started all this fucking mess."

"Oh," Dr. Probst says. "So what now?"

"That," Kyle says and points to the ceiling of the kaiju chamber.

The ceiling irises open and a strange aircraft hovers briefly, then descends to the chamber's floor. As it lands, Lu presses against the observation deck's window. Then she cries out when she sees her mother, Tony, Krissy, and Biscuit climb out of the aircraft's cargo hold. Then she cries out again as the aircraft lifts off and shoots out of the chamber.

"Mom, you know where they're going," Kyle says. "Connor told us they have to get to Diamondback."

"I know, I know," Lu says, wiping at her eyes. "But he could have said hello."

"Your mom is waving at you," Dr. Probst says. "Oh, and we need to get them out of there fast."

"Is Trey here?" Kyle asks, glancing at Dr. Probst's laptop. She nods. "Okay. I have to help with this. Mom, you go down and get Grandma and the others up here. Dr. Probst, wait here for them, then be prepared to help coordinate this."

"What do I do?" Dr. Probst asks.

"Set your laptop there," Kyle says as a small pedestal rises from the floor. "It should connect you seamlessly. You can also talk to me while I talk to Trey."

"You can communicate with Trey while he's a kaiju?" Dr. Probst asks. "How?"

Kyle spreads his arms. "Gotta love alien tech."

Lu frowns. "Do we though?"

"It's all that will keep the human race alive," Kyle says, his voice sounding much older than his age.

He returns to the elevator, leaving Lu and Dr. Probst in the observation deck.

"I'll be right back," Lu says and spins around, searching for the way out and down.

"There," Dr. Probst says and points to a recess in the wall.

Lu rushes over, and as soon as she's close enough the recess opens and reveals a set of stairs connected to a catwalk, which is in turn connected to another set of stairs and more catwalks that encircle the entire chamber.

It takes Lu a few minutes, but she makes it to the ground floor and runs to embrace her mother.

The two women slam into each other, crying and laughing as they hug fiercely.

"You were dead," Lu sobs. "Kyle said you were dead."

"I should have been," Terrie says. "So many times. But I found some good folks, lost some good folks, and made it here with these two amazing young people."

"You sound so old when you say young people," Krissy says and gives a shy wave. "Hi."

"Lu, this is Krissy and Tony," Terrie says as Lu finally lets her go. "I'd be dead without them."

Biscuit yowls and barks.

"And you too," Terrie says.

"Biscuit!" Lu cries and crouches down to give the dog-wolf a huge hug and fur ruffle. She kisses the hybrid's snout, then looks up at Krissy and Tony. "Thank you for helping my mother."

"She saved our butts too," Krissy says.

Tony just shrugs.

"Lu! You need to get back up here now!" Dr. Probst calls, her voice echoing throughout the kaiju chamber.

"Does she need to yell?" Krissy asks, her hands to her ears.

"Sorry," Dr. Probst replies. "I'm still figuring the system out. But get out of the chamber now! Trey is here!"

"Trey?" Terrie asks.

"You'll see," Lu says. "Come on."

She leads them all up the stairs, across the catwalks, and into the observation deck.

"Hey," Dr. Probst says with a wave. "Dr. Cheryl Probst. Call me Cheryl."

"Hello, Cheryl, it's good to meet you," Terrie says. "Thank you for helping keep my family…"

Terrie trails off as a shadow is cast over the open top of the kaiju chamber. All eyes turn in that direction and mouths drop open.

"Uh… should we run?" Krissy asks, her hand clamping onto Tony's arm.

"Ow," Tony says and pries her fingers apart. "I am not an emotional support animal."

"Neither is he," Krissy says and nods at Biscuit, who's backed himself up against the far wall of the observation deck.

"I hear you, boy," Terrie says.

The Africa kaiju climbs down inside the kaiju chamber with several large, long lumps attached to its back. As soon as the creature settles onto the chamber's floor, platforms extend and extract the contents of the lumps.

Ships. Dozens of ships. Military ships, cruise ships, commercial liners, and even some smaller, personal craft, are systematically removed from the Africa kaiju's back.

"Cheryl? Do you read me?" Kyle asks, his voice coming from the observation deck's PA system.

"I'm here, Kyle," Dr. Probst replies.

"Kyle!" Terrie shouts.

"Hi, Grandma," Kyle says. "I'll come see you in a minute. I'm helping Trey right now."

The platforms lock onto the many ships, each taking one to the chamber's walls so it can be secured into place and stabilized for the refugees' departures.

"Trey?" Terrie asks Lu.

Lu points at the Africa Kaiju.

"There's a person in that?" Terrie asks, her mouth open wide.

"Not exactly," Dr. Probst says. "Kyle, everything looks good from here. How are you doing?"

"Most of it is automated," Kyle replies. "But since the facility and the ships are of different tech, I'm helping them talk to each other when needed. Trey says hello."

"Oh…uh… hello back?" Dr. Probst says and shrugs at Lu. She shrugs in response.

"An organic battle vehicle," Tony says, moving closer to the observation deck windows. "I would like to study it and have one of my own."

"You and me both, kid," Dr. Probst says. "The study part. I have no desire to be in one of those things."

"It's not as easy as just hopping into a cockpit," Kyle says.

Tony looks up at the ceiling. "Why?"

"Long story, no time," Kyle says. "Mom? Cheryl and I have it from here if you want to take everyone down and get them settled. I have the quarters closest to the main control room sectioned off for all of us. It'll get cramped in this facility before this is all over, so I made us a little extra room."

"Kyle, I taught you better," Terrie says. "You share your bounty with others. We don't need extra room."

"Trust me, Grandma," Kyle says, "it's not that extra. You'll see."

"Come on," Lu says. "You have to be starving."

"And we stink like sewage," Tony states.

"He says it like he sees it, huh?" Lu says with a laugh.

"You have no idea," Krissy says.

Lu nods at her. "We can get your bandages changed too. This facility has several medical bays we can use. One is out of order because of, well… we'll talk about that later."

Lu leads them to the elevator and they all step on.

"You sure you're good, Cheryl?" Lu asks, looking to Dr. Probst.

"Huh? Me? Oh, yes, of course," Dr. Probst says. "Take care of them. We'll call if we need you."

"Alright," Lu says and presses the button.

The elevator doors close, and Krissy and Tony lean back against the wall as Terrie leans on her daughter. Lu just smiles.

"We have so much to talk about," Terrie says.

"Yeah," Lu says. "But we'll get you all fed and cleaned up first. Then we talk. We won't have much time though. There are thousands of people on those ships, and they'll need help. We'll coordinate from the control room."

"I can coordinate from where I am, Mom," Kyle says, making everyone jump. "Sorry."

"Warn us next time," Lu says. "What do we do?"

"Shake hands, give hugs, and assure people that this place is safe," Kyle says. "You'll also need to handle the officers that will think they're in charge."

Lu laughs. "Oh, is that all?" She smiles at her mother. "I think between the two of us, we'll be able to take on any brass that think they'll be running the show."

"There *is* a chain of command," Terrie says, uncertain.

"And they aren't the top, Grandma," Lu says. "Not anymore."

———

Lowell studies the ocean, hunting for signs of Antarctica.

"You have to come up for air sometime, fucker," Lowell says out loud, which is instantly translated into a Quetzalcoatl roar.

A dot on the horizon gets Lowell's attention, and he shifts his focus. The kaiju's vision is incredible, and Lowell realizes it must be what raptors experience as he dials in his vision closer and closer until he's able to see the dot clearly.

Or dots. A string of islands on the horizon.

"Islands?" Lowell thinks. "Hawaii? Guam? Where the shit am I?"

An image slams into his mind, and he instantly has a sense of exactly where he is. Hell, he has a sense of where everything in the Pacific Ocean is.

"Damn," he thinks. "That's handy as shit."

Lowell contemplates seeing if he has the entire map of the world in his brain, but he doesn't want to push it since he's flying over open water in a kaiju that's supposed to be a god of some sort, and his body may be huge and powerful, but the Pacific Ocean is even larger and even more powerful. He tucks the idea away for later.

If there is a later.

"Oh, there'll be a later!" he shouts, sending a roar rippling across the waves. "Coming for you, Mr. Licorice!"

Lowell catches sight of something, a shadow, ahead of him just under the water's surface. He dives hard and fast, straight down, then folds his wings and plunges into the ocean.

A heavy film instantly covers Quetzalcoatl's eyes, and the underwater world is as clear as the air above. On instinct, Lowell spreads his wings and is pleased to feel them act as flippers, the feathers binding together to help trap the water.

Lowell sees the Antarctica kaiju swimming furiously about a mile in front of him and says, "Hello, Mr. Licorice! Your ass is mine!"

Lowell panics for a minute as the air escapes his massive mouth, sending waves of bubbles bursting out before him. Just before the panic overtakes him, Lowell realizes he's not drowning and can actually breathe underwater.

Yeah, Quetzalcoatl, you and me are gonna be best buds, he thinks.

Then he sees that Antarctica has stopped swimming and has turned to face him, the kaiju's huge simian arms and legs pumping up and down, treading water.

Lowell puts on a burst of speed by whipping the lower half of his long, serpent body back and forth.

Antarctica roars. Just like with Yellowstone, rippling rings of sonic power erupt from the kaiju's mouth and head straight for Lowell.

"Shit!" Lowell yells and dives deep, angling Quetzalcoatl's body straight toward the ocean floor miles below.

The sonic blasts shred the very molecules the ocean water is made of, and Lowell barely manages to get clear of the blasts. But he doesn't get clear of the aftereffects and loses control of his rapid descent. The kaiju spins and tumbles, twisting this way and that as water around him turns a murky brown from the thousands of fish and other aquatic creatures that weren't lucky enough to avoid Antarctica's attack.

Lowell struggles to regain control, and as the water becomes darker and darker, to the point of near impenetrable blackness, the panic from before returns. He can feel the pressure weighing on the kaiju's body, and he wonders if the giant monster can actually make the dive down into the Mariana Trench before being crushed.

He snarls and watches bubbles burst the moment they're formed. "Stop being weak."

Digging deep, Lowell rights the kaiju and points its snout up toward the faint light above. He stretches his wings out to their fullest and whips them downward, sending the kaiju's body rocketing up toward the surface. There is a moment where Lowell wonders about depressurization, but then he's suddenly erupting out of the ocean and into open air, his wings taking him high up above the rippling waves.

The fact that rapid depressurization doesn't break the kaiju heartens Lowell. He's pretty confident that Quetzalcoatl will be able to handle the crushing depths of the Mariana Trench and, if the time comes, the total lack of pressure in open space.

But first, he has an Antarctica kaiju to stop.

Lowell aims for Guam, the island where the Ebony Man has taken Antarctica.

Even from the distance Lowell is at, his kaiju ears pick up the sounds of destruction as the Ebony Man stomps onto shore and begins grabbing up anything and everything edible.

Which is mostly people.

Guam was never evacuated because it was well away from the Yellowstone caldera. The island was to be a staging area, as well as a command center, for the Pacific Fleet's refugee evacuation missions. None of the refugee ships reached the island, but there are plenty of residents and U.S. military personnel still there for the Ebony Man to feast on.

And he does.

The beach is littered with mangled bodies, detritus made up of arms and legs and heads, the bits and pieces that fall out of Antarctica's mouth as it makes its way across the island with wild abandon, stuffing handfuls of screaming human beings into its wide-open maw.

Lowell shivers at the crunching and chewing noises that echo across the island.

Finding an area clear of corpse parts, Lowell sets down, coiling the kaiju's body under him for support since Quetzalcoatl doesn't have legs, only wings.

"Hey!" Lowell roars. "Mr. Licorice! How about you don't massacre all the nice people of Guam?"

Even though the sounds coming out of Quetzalcoatl's mouth are roars and shrieks, not words, Antarctica pauses, turns, finishes chewing, and responds with its own roars and shrieks.

Lowell laughs when an instant translation fills his mind.

"You are all food to me!" the Ebony Man roars. "Even you,

Quetzalcoatl! I'll wipe this island clean, then kill you and use your bones to pick my teeth!"

"Oh, Mr. Licorice," Lowell replies. "Haven't you learned yet? You're dead. You're so fucking dead. And there isn't a goddamn thing you can fucking do about it."

There's a slight pause, then the Ebony Man replies, "This is my planet, primate. I took it, I shaped it, I created new life under its crust, life that only exists for my needs, for my plans, for my triumph! You pitiful apes are fleas on the surface of my kingdom!"

"Fleas on the surface…? That's gotta be the shittiest metaphor I've ever heard," Lowell says. "Dude. Just give it the fuck up."

Antarctica snatches up two fistfuls of screaming Guamanians and crams them into its mouth like peanuts, making a show of chomping up and down as the people continue screaming then go silent.

"God, you are such an asshole," Lowell says and shakes his huge head back and forth. "And that's saying a lot coming from me."

"You should eat too, Quetzalcoatl," the Ebony Man roars. "You will need all the energy you can get before I kill you!"

"Jesus Christ, dude…" Lowell shakes his head again. "Did a jellyfish sting you in the head? Because you sound like you're trippin' balls. And why the fuck would you want me to have more energy? That'll just make your beat down even worse. Honestly, Mr. Licorice, it's time for you to call it quits. You just aren't thinking straight, dude."

Antarctica roars and all of its scales stand on end, the sharpened edges glinting brightly in the South Pacific sunlight. The Ebony Man flexes the kaiju's muscles and stomps both legs, crushing buildings, people, and everything underfoot. Then it charges.

"Fucking hell," Lowell says and uncoils Quetzalcoatl's body.

Lowell takes to the air just as Antarctica reaches the beach, a double swath of destruction going and coming behind it. The

Antarctica kaiju shoots out a huge fist and just misses snatching Quetzalcoatl's tail.

But Lowell makes sure the Ebony Man still gets a piece of that tail as he whips it down across the kaiju's skull. Pain erupts all the way up Quetzalcoatl's body, and Lowell has to concentrate hard in order to keep flapping his wings so he doesn't get caught by Antarctica's other fist.

Once up far above Antarctica, Lowell takes a moment to assess the damage to his kaiju.

The bright blue skin and feathers at the tip of his body flap and flutter in the air like gory strings, dark red blood dripping from the flaps and shreds of skin.

"Fuck. That hurts," Lowell says.

"You will know agony a million times worse!" the Ebony Man roars up at him.

"Fuck off," Lowell replies.

Lowell rises farther and farther into the air, making sure he's well out of reach of Antarctica, even if the Ebony Man makes the kaiju leap up at him. Then he hovers for a minute to check the damage to his tail again.

"Shit," Lowell says. "That's a design flaw."

He hunts through his mind to find a solution, but for some reason he has almost limitless knowledge of the facilities, the aliens, the everything happening to Earth, except for the abilities of the kaiju he's currently occupying. Lowell puzzles at this, then does what any wounded animal would do—he licks his tail with his huge forked tongue until the bleeding stops.

"Hey, Mr. Licorice!" Lowell shouts down at Antarctica. "My spit heals! I'm like a punk Jesus! Got a boo boo you need me to fix? Here! Have some!"

Lowell hawks up a giant kaiju loogie and bombs the Ebony Man with it. The bloody phlegm splats on Antarctica's forehead, sending the kaiju into a fit of rage that results in a quarter of the coastline being destroyed as the Ebony Man thrashes around, kicking and punching at the island's once-beautiful beaches.

"I wonder what else I can do?" Lowell thinks. He risks closing his eyes and tries to push his mind through the kaiju's body, but it doesn't work. He just gets kind of dizzy. He snaps his eyes open. "Fuck. Not doing that again."

"You cannot defeat me!" the Ebony Man roars up at Lowell. "I had this kaiju created in order to defeat all kaiju! Quetzalcoatl is a weak creature! You have no powers, Anson Lowell! Only flight by those sad wings! You cannot win against me!"

"You know what?" Lowell roars down. "Fuck off! I don't need powers to kick your ass, bitch!"

Then he dives with all his strength and speed directly at Antarctica.

The collision sends shockwaves across the island, leveling any and all buildings more than a story tall. Lowell doesn't have time to regret the repercussions of his attack, even as sirens wail and the cries of Guamanians fill the air; his only thought is to keep Antarctica down.

The Ebony Man has different plans.

Even though the impact drives Antarctica a hundred feet down into the island's soil, the Ebony Man still manages to wrap an arm around Quetzalcoatl's neck and get the kaiju into a headlock.

"Shit!" Lowell screams as he realizes that he's about to be decapitated by the sharpened scales lining Antarctica's arm and torso. "Get the fuck off me, asshole!"

"It is you who are upon me!" the Ebony Man shouts. "You get off of me, for you are the ass-a-hole!"

Lowell responds by clamping his entire jaw over Antarctica's chin. He feels the insides of his mouth turn to tatters from the scales, but he doesn't relent. He bites down harder, putting all of his energy into his jaws.

There's a satisfying crack, and the Ebony Man shoves Lowell off and away from Antarctica.

Quetzalcoatl rolls across the coastline for half a mile before coming to a stop. Lowell stares up at the bright blue sky that's able to peek out from the ash clouds. He marvels at the sight, happy to see sun again, even if it is only in brief snatches. It's a hell of a lot better than the thick ash hell that blankets North America and most of the rest of the world.

"Get your shit together," Lowell mutters before flipping his body over and rising up on the lower half of his serpent body.

Lowell spits gallons of blood out onto the remnants of the beach, splashing blood up over the mangled trees that were also felled by the kaiju impact. After a couple more tries to clear his mouth of blood, Lowell begins licking his wings, then wipes the wings across his neck and upper chest, sealing the wounds caused by Antarctica's scales.

Even during the self-care, Lowell never takes his eyes off Antarctica, watching as the other kaiju slowly gets to its feet. Lowell can't help but smile as he sees the kaiju wobble slightly and favor its left leg.

"Looking gimpy there, Mr. Licorice," Lowell says, continuing the healing process by slathering more and more of his kaiju saliva across his battered body. "You sure you don't want to call this quits? We can head down to the Core, get you out of that gorilla suit, and you can be imprisoned for eternity. Better than the alternative."

"There is no alternative!" the Ebony Man roars. "There is only my triumph!"

"Man, somebody hurt you bad," Lowell says. "I'm not judging, because I totally get that. But instead of destroying my planet, maybe we can find you a good therapist and about six hundred kilograms of Diazepam. I'm not one for benzos, but I think a heavy dose of chill would do you some good."

The Ebony Man responds by charging Quetzalcoatl, covering the distance in seconds despite the kaiju's limping gait.

This time, Lowell is ready for the attack.

Instead of launching into the air out of reach, Lowell sends Quetzalcoatl diving under Antarctica's rage-filled swipes, coming up behind the kaiju.

Lowell braces for the pain and clamps his kaiju's jaws down on the back of Antarctica's neck, forcing the other kaiju face down into the sand and soil. With a powerful thrust of his wings, Lowell lifts Antarctica up a few feet and drags the kaiju out into the surf. Then with another wing thrust, Lowell shoves the Ebony Man into the water, covering the kaiju's entire head in roiling seawater.

Antarctica thrashes, fighting desperately against Quetzalcoatl's hold on its neck and the continual flapping of wings that maintains enough force to keep the kaiju's head submerged.

"That's right, fucker," Lowell thinks. "Just fucking drown, bitch. Just fucking drown."

Antarctica's fight lessens, lessens, then the kaiju goes completely slack and its body relaxes into the ocean water.

Lowell has been in enough prison fights to know that you only let go if you're sure the other party is unconscious, dead, or you start getting beat upon by a dozen guards and their batons. He counts to a hundred, gives the back of Antarctica's neck a good shake, then lets go and eases back, his eyes never leaving the still kaiju.

Which is a good thing, because the second Lowell has Quetzalcoatl a couple dozen meters away, Antarctica's left foot snaps out and clocks Quetzalcoatl across the jaw.

"Son of a bitch!" Lowell yells just as the Ebony Man dives into the ocean and is lost from sight. "Right… space kaiju probably don't need to breathe… fuck!"

Shaking off the kick, Lowell dives after him, but the destruction the two kaiju caused to the island of Guam has churned up tons upon tons of sand and soil so that visibility is almost zero, even with Quetzalcoatl's superior vision.

"God damnit," Lowell says with a gigantic kaiju sigh.

He tunes into the planet and orients himself, then sets off blindly into the depths again, aimed for the Mariana Trench and the Core facility.

FIFTEEN

"Okay," VanderVoort says, her eyes on the main monitor as a satellite tracks the progress of the Africa kaiju across North America down to the Gulf of Mexico, where it can retrieve more refugee ships. "We got this."

Behind VanderVoort, the Situation Room is alive with the raised voices of all present as they try to help coordinate the evacuation to the Wyoming facility. Mostly techs and those left of the Cabinet are forced to use their powers of persuasion to keep the captains of those ships from total panic as a giant monster crawls over the country to their locations.

"Adrianna?"

VanderVoort turns and is face to face with President Nance.

"Charles," VanderVoort responds. "What can I do for you?"

"You aren't listening to the comms," President Nance says with an amused smile. He looks up at the main monitor. "Understandable, considering."

"What? Oh, shit," VanderVoort says and taps at her earpiece, increasing the volume. She recognizes the voice. "Bolton?"

"There you are," Bolton responds. "And here we are. Time to go."

"Go?" VanderVoort replies. She turns and takes in the chaos of the Situation Room. "We still have work to do here, Sergeant Bolton. We cannot—"

"Adrianna, it's time to leave DC," President Nance says.

"How do we coordinate the evacuation?" VanderVoort asks. "We're still talking to other countries, trying to get everyone to work—"

"Ma'am, we have a space all set up where you can coordinate everything from here," Bolton says. "But we don't have much time. The winged assholes are tracking us. They're also heading for the Africa kaiju. Trey will need backup really soon, so we need to return to the air as fast as possible."

Before VanderVoort can ask what Bolton's talking about, she remembers what else was being developed and housed at Diamondback.

"It's operational?" VanderVoort asks, surprised.

"Banks and his team got it up and working," Bolton says. "That's pretty much been their focus since the EMPs took down the country."

"Good for Lieutenant Commander Banks," VanderVoort says. "We'll be right up."

Then she panics and blinks at President Nance.

"Can we get up top?" she asks.

"We can," President Nance says. "We managed to get one elevator operational, and Bolton has already assured me that the area is cleared above."

"Then let's do this and get out of this shit hole," VanderVoort says, then shrugs at the hurt look on President Nance's face. "No offense meant. I'm sure it'd be ideal under other circumstances, but personally, I could use some fresh air."

"I'm not sure how fresh the air is," Director Miles says with a couple of bags thrown over his shoulders. "All packed. Come on."

"Listen up, everybody!" VanderVoort shouts. The noise only lessens slightly. She takes a deep breath and bellows, "SHUT THE FUCK UP AND LISTEN!"

The Situation Room goes quiet.

"Gather your personal belongings and head to the exit," VanderVoort orders. "You each have about one minute to get your shit together before we leave. Tell whoever you're talking to that we'll call them back once we're onboard the... shit. What's it called again? Fuck..."

"Joan?" President Nance asks.

"The codename is Valhalla," Joan replies.

"Seriously?" VanderVoort asks. "That's a bit much. Let's just call it V."

"Now that we have that settled, can we go?" Director Miles asks.

"Time to leave!" VanderVoort shouts.

The room's chaos quadruples as everyone jumps up from their stations, grabs what they can, and hurries to the corridor that leads to the working elevator.

It takes two trips to get everyone up top, and VanderVoort waits in the ruins of the White House, making sure the head counts match before she lets Director Miles lead her to the gigantic airship that hovers a few feet off the ground. The vehicle is the shape of and at least the size of an aircraft carrier, if not larger, but instead of floating in the water, it floats over the ruins of the White House grounds via its own magnetic drive, with several ramps extended down so the surviving members of the Situation Room's personnel can climb aboard quickly and efficiently.

VanderVoort takes her turn to ascend one of the ramps and is surprised at the utilitarian look of the corridor she steps into.

"Two trillion dollars, and they couldn't paint some lines or something on the walls to break up the gray?" she asks.

"This is the ship's maiden voyage, ma'am," Bolton says as he hurries down the corridor to greet the woman. "Banks assured me it's one hundred percent operational, but I could see the doubt in his eyes. So far, this baby has performed flawlessly, so let's focus on that."

"Did you just lecture me, Sergeant Bolton?" VanderVoort asks.

Bolton's eyes widen and she laughs.

"Just fucking with you," VanderVoort says. "Sorry. Take me to the bridge and let's get on our way."

"Yes, ma'am," Bolton says. "This way."

They make their way through the carrier's many corridors, up several flights of stairs, and finally arrive at the airship's bridge. President Nance, General Azoul, and National Security Advisor Joan Milligan are already on the bridge and speaking to Lieutenant Commander Banks.

"Ma'am!" Banks announces and gives VanderVoort a quick salute. "Welcome aboard the Valhalla!"

"V for short," VanderVoort says. "Valhalla is a bit much, Lieutenant Commander."

Banks frowns for only a brief second, then smiles and nods. "V it is."

"Sir? We need to go now," Corporal Rowan says from the airship's helm.

"Take her up, Rowan," Banks replies. "Everyone brace themselves. We're still working out the finer points of flying V. It has its… quirks."

"So do I, Banks," VanderVoort says and lets Director Miles guide her to a seat up against the wall of the bridge.

She eases her pregnant bulk down into the seat and sighs.

"You good?" Director Miles asks, leaning in close so only she hears the question.

"For now, yeah," VanderVoort says and rubs her belly. "This little fucker and I have an understanding. He stays in his room until I tell him he can come out."

"Uh… are we getting that close to showtime?" Director Miles asks.

"Gordon, I've been that close to showtime for a good week now," VanderVoort says. She catches President Nance looking at her and nods. "Go mingle. Charles is getting suspicious."

Before Director Miles can walk away, President Nance moves

carefully over to the two of them and crouches down, looking VanderVoort directly in the eye.

"How close are you?" President Nance asks.

"This is not a topic up for discussion, Charles," VanderVoort says. "Everything is under control."

President Nance chuckles and stands up. He places a hand on VanderVoort's shoulder and gives it a warm squeeze.

"You keep telling yourself that," President Nance says. "Just know that I will step in the second I have to and get our people through this." He glances out the bridge and his focus softens. "As we get all of Earth's people through this."

VanderVoort begins to respond with a sarcastic quip, then swallows the words and only nods. President Nance walks away and VanderVoort turns to Director Miles.

"Thoughts?" she asks.

"About Nance?" Director Miles replies.

"Yes, Gordon, about Nance," VanderVoort says.

"He's being sincere," Director Miles says. "I think reality has set in and the concept of borders is beginning to leave the President's head."

"Good," VanderVoort says. "We'll be dealing with nationalistic tendencies from a lot of world leaders soon enough. I don't want to go head to head with Nance if I don't have to."

"I have a feeling we can count on him," Director Miles says.

"That's what I want to hear," VanderVoort says. She narrows her gaze. "But...?"

"But you know his record," Director Miles says with a shrug. "Personalities like his don't just change."

"Agreed," VanderVoort replies.

Then her attention is drawn to the view outside the bridge. She slowly stands up and makes her way to the windows.

"It's different when you see it firsthand instead of on a monitor," Dr. Hall says, coming up beside her. "It's even worse than before."

VanderVoort studies the destruction that lies below the airship.

"DC is gone," she says. "It's all just… gone."

"The ooze creatures took care of that," Dr. Hall says and points to certain buildings. "See how it's dissolving the structures down to their frames? I have a feeling in a few days even those frames will be part of the sludge that's covering everything."

"How do we come back from this?" VanderVoort asks, then shakes her head, knowing she should have kept that thought to herself.

"We don't," Dr. Hall replies. "There is no back, only forward. It's a whole new world now."

"What's left of it," VanderVoort says, then clamps her hands over her ears as a klaxon splits the air.

"Bogies!" Corporal Denz yells. "And they're coming in hot!"

"Release the starbursts!" Banks orders. "Joshua! Hines! Get airborne and do what you can!"

The bridge's windows tint to almost black, then flashes of sun-bright light explode in all directions.

"What the fuck was that?" VanderVoort asks, shielding her eyes despite the windows' tinting.

"We have some very effective countermeasures," Banks replies. "We had lightning guns, but they seized after their first firing. We're working on that. So far, though, we've been able to keep the winged monsters away. But they're starting to get bolder, so we're sending two of the smaller aircraft up to make our point."

"Which is?" VanderVoort asks.

"Fuck with us and you're gonna get burned," Banks replies with a sly grin.

"Good point," VanderVoort says.

"How many aircraft does this carrier have?" President Nance asks. "I thought there was only one prototype."

"We have fifteen, Mr. President," Banks replies. "They're all prototypes, each slightly different, but only six are truly operational and I trust only four of those six, sir. My team hasn't had time to go over the others yet."

"Let's send a couple techs to the hangar and start on that, Banks," President Nance says then looks at VanderVoort. She nods in agreement.

"Lieutenant Commander Banks? Kyle Morgan is on comms," Denz announces.

"Open the channel," Banks says.

"Channel is open, sir," Denz replies.

"Excuse me," Banks says and moves closer to Denz. "Kyle? What is it?"

"Trey is under attack," Kyle replies, his voice loud and clear in everyone's ears. "Africa needs your help or the winged bastards are going to pick those ships apart."

"On our way already," Banks says.

"Hold on a second there," VanderVoort says. "We aren't going to Wyoming?"

"Wyoming? No," Banks says. "We have to go help Trey and the Africa kaiju immediately. We'll let you all disembark once we've escorted Africa safely back to the Wyoming facility."

"This has all been coordinated without me," VanderVoort states. "Kyle Morgan was right that it's out of my hands."

"It won't be for long, ma'am," Banks says. "I've been around teenagers my entire career. We get a few in the armed forces."

VanderVoort chuckles. "I bet."

"As strong as the young man sounds now, he can't maintain that strength," Banks says. "Once we have everyone we can reach secured in facilities, I have a feeling he's going to take a thousand steps back and let the adults take over."

"Yes, but take over what?" VanderVoort asks as Banks returns to his conversation with Kyle.

————

Kyle holds his head in his hands as he sits in one of the chairs in Wyoming's blue crystal control room. He can't bring himself to call it the "Meth Room" like Lowell.

"I know, Banks, but we need more aircraft covering Trey!" Kyle exclaims. "The Valhalla has firepower, but it doesn't have maneuverability. I can already tell that the winged monsters are catching on to that. Look at their attack patterns! They're testing you!"

"Kyle, I've been at this a lot longer than you and am well aware of our current needs," Banks replies, his voice strained over the comms. "But right now, only Joshua and Hines know how to fly the aircraft! Rowan is flying the V and Denz is handling everything else when what I need is about ten times that many manning the stations on this bridge!"

"You just picked up a whole bunch of people from the White House!" Kyle yells. "There have to be pilots there!"

"Let me get us a couple states away from Virginia before I start recruiting," Banks snaps. "I'll see what I can do."

"We need all the birds in the air, Banks," Kyle responds. "Have you seen the images from the gulf? The ships are being attacked from below too!"

"Kyle, I know," Banks says, his voice trying to express calm and confidence. "We're all doing what we can."

"DO MORE!" Kyle shouts. He takes a shuddering breath. "Sorry, sorry…"

"That's all for now," Terrie says from the room's doorway, a tray of food in her hands. "Let the man handle his situation so you can handle yours."

Kyle whips his head around. "This is all my situation!"

Terrie raises an eyebrow and Kyle cringes.

"Open the comm," Terrie orders.

"Grandma, now is not the—"

"You will do as I say, Kyle Morgan," Terrie snaps.

Kyle swallows, then nods.

"To whom am I speaking?" Terrie asks.

"This is Lieutenant Commander Banks, ma'am," Banks replies.

"And this is former U.S. Marshal Terrie Morgan, Lieutenant

Commander," Terrie says. "I assume you can handle your end of things for a few minutes without my grandson?"

"Yes, ma'am," Banks says. "I have everything under control as much as anything can be controlled."

"Good to hear, Lieutenant Commander," Terrie says. "I will have Kyle back to you as soon as I can."

"Take your time, ma'am," Banks says. "The young man has earned a break."

"Thank you, Lieutenant Commander," Terrie says. "Wyoming out."

Terrie stares at Kyle until he severs the comm.

"Now, grandson, you will eat," Terrie says. "And do not even think of arguing. God gave Earth a bounty so that human beings might nourish themselves. Understood?"

Kyle understands all too well and nods again. Terrie smiles and hands him the tray.

"Good. Eat," she says and sits down in the other chair.

"Are you going to watch me?" Kyle asks as he picks up the sandwich and takes a bite.

"I am," Terrie says. "You can eat while I talk."

Kyle frowns. He doesn't like the sound of that.

"Your mother tells me you're going to leave this facility and somehow transport to a different facility," Terrie states. Kyle starts to respond, but she holds up a hand. "Didn't I say I was going to do the talking?"

Kyle grins around a mouthful of sandwich. He'd missed his grandmother.

"I will be going with you," Terrie says.

Kyle chokes on his bite mid-swallow and coughs. Once he's able to get himself under control, he shakes his head and says, "You can't right now. You have to be attuned. Later, maybe, once we—"

"Then let's get me attuned," Terrie interrupts.

"It's not that simple," Kyle says. "I became attuned when a representation of the aliens that built these facilities touched my forehead. I think it was a one-time thing, because I can't find a trace of the alien anywhere in this facility's system anymore."

"Then how did Lowell become attuned?" Terrie asks.

Kyle laughs. "He was sucked into the Substance, became one with a kaiju, and touched the blue crystal vein directly just before dying."

Kyle waits for a look of shock to overcome his grandmother's face, but the look never appears. Instead, Terrie leans forward and smiles at Kyle.

"That isn't very efficient, and I believe the beings that made these facilities are probably more prepared than that," Terrie says. "You now have a new task, grandson. Find out how I become attuned to the blue crystal and travel with you."

A realization hits Kyle. He was going to have to solve this problem anyway if refugees are to travel back and forth from facility to facility once the places become humanity's permanent homes. He knows that the surface will no longer be viable as soon as he activates the Core's planetary defenses.

"Okay," Kyle says, which does surprise Terrie. Kyle laughs again. "I kinda have to anyway."

"Ah," Terrie says and nods, then points at the sandwich. "Finish up. We have work to do."

"Yes, ma'am," Kyle says and devours the rest of his sandwich, all of the chips, an apple, and then a pint of orange juice. He belches loudly and stands up. "We'll need to go to the basement."

"There's a basement?" Terrie asks, amused.

"You'll see what I mean," Kyle says and motions to the door. "Come on."

Kyle leads Terrie out of the blue crystal control room and down the corridor to an elevator. From there, they descend several floors before having to switch to a different elevator. When the doors finally open onto the bottom level, Kyle can see that his grandmother is trying not to look overwhelmed.

"The place is big," Kyle says when the doors open and he steps out into the huge tunnel.

"There are better words to describe this facility than big," Terrie says.

"Big works," Kyle says and shrugs. He smiles at the cart that sits a few meters from the elevator. "I was hoping that'd be here."

He hops in the cart and Terrie hops in beside him. Kyle drives them the length of the tunnel to the spot where the blue crystal is exposed. Long, thick cables snake away from veins of crystal and connect to a bank of servers Dr. Probst set up. Kyle parks next to the servers and gets out.

"Come on," Kyle says. "Let's test it."

"Test?" Terrie asks. "When I said I should be attuned, I meant after the tests are done."

"The tests won't ever be done, Grandma," Kyle says with a sigh.

Terrie frowns. "Maybe we should come back when we have Dr. Probst or a different scientist with us."

"I know more than they do," Kyle says. He navigates the coils of cable and points to the wall. "Give me your hand."

"What?" Terrie asks.

"Give me your hand," Kyle says. "I have an idea."

Terrie hesitates, then steps around the coils and takes Kyle's hand. Before she can protest, Kyle places his other hand on the vein of blue crystal.

The feeling that rushes through Kyle, while intense, is mild compared to his previous experiences with the blue crystal. And definitely milder than when the alien apparition shoved a lifetime's worth of knowledge into his head.

Kyle waits for the feeling to level out, then he sorts through the images in his mind.

There.

"Okay," Kyle says, his eyes closed, his hand still gripping his grandmother's. "Close your eyes and empty your mind."

"I'll try," Terrie says. She closes her eyes.

Kyle waits until he can sense that his grandmother is as close to an empty mind as the woman can get. Then he opens a connection to the blue crystal, using himself as a buffer.

Terrie's body stiffens. "Kyle…"

"Just go with it, Grandma," Kyle says quietly.

A minute, two minutes, three, four, five minutes pass by before Kyle removes his hand from the blue crystal vein.

"Well?" Kyle asks Terrie. "Feel different?"

"I feel…" Terrie takes a few short, slow breaths. "I feel… larger? Does that make sense?"

"Yes," Kyle says. "Any new thoughts or images in your head?"

"No," Terrie says, her eyes narrowed. "But something is there…"

"Alright. We can work with that," Kyle says.

"HEY! WHERE'S THE DAMN CART?"

"Cheryl," Kyle says to Terrie.

"You mean Dr. Probst," Terrie says. "She worked hard for that title."

"We're kinda past being formal, Grandma," Kyle says. "We should take the cart back to her."

"Hold on," Terrie says. "When are you transferring to the other facility?"

"When Lowell calls me," Kyle says. "He has to get there first and activate it."

"He's racing this Ebony Man thing, right?" Terrie asks. "What happens if the Ebony Man reaches the…?"

"Core?" Kyle finishes for her.

"Yes," Terrie says. "What happens then?"

"We all die," Kyle says. "He'll keep the defenses inactive and let this planet be destroyed and changed into something else for monsters a million times worse than the ones we've been fighting."

"KYLE!" Dr. Probst yells from down the tunnel. "I NEED THE CART!"

"We should go," Kyle says.

They hop back into the cart and drive to the elevator where Dr. Probst is waiting with a large group of refugees.

"There you are," Dr. Probst says, exasperated. "We need more carts down here."

"I'll get someone to do that," Terrie says immediately without being asked.

"A Morgan taking charge," Dr. Probst says with a smile. "What a surprise…"

"What's going on?" Kyle asks, checking out the members of the group.

"I found scientists," Dr. Probst replies, excited. "An astrophysicist. A quantum physicist. Two chemical engineers. An ethnobotanist. And even two more geologists!"

The members of the group smile and nod at Kyle and Terrie. They all introduce themselves, but Kyle forgets the names almost as soon as they're spoken. His focus is on Dr. Probst.

"Be careful, Cheryl," Kyle warns. "Don't push it."

"Trust me, Kyle, I'll be the most careful human being on this planet," Dr. Probst says. "The last thing I want to do is mess with the crystal. We're simply going to monitor and study it. No pushing or prodding."

"Uh huh," Kyle replies, seeing some of the looks on the other scientists' faces. "Still…"

"It's all under control," Dr. Probst says with a laugh. "As much control as we puny humans can exert on this insanity." She turns and does a head count. "It'll take three trips to get us and the equipment down there. I say start with the equipment; that way, we can be setting up while everyone is ferried to the breach."

"Breach?" Kyle asks.

"We did jackhammer a hole in the wall," Dr. Probst says. "I call that a breach."

Kyle shrugs and smiles at the group, then walks into the elevator. Terrie is right on his heels.

As soon as the doors close, Terrie turns to Kyle.

"What's wrong?" Terrie asks.

"Nothing," Kyle says. "For once, nothing is wrong."

They ride back up in silence.

———

"This is probably a bad idea," Bolton says as he sits in the pilot's seat of one of the magnetic drive aircraft. "But it's not like we have a choice."

A tech is seated in the co-pilot's seat, her dark skin blanched to a terrified gray. Her head turns to Bolton, her eyes wide with terror.

"You can fly this, right?" the tech asks.

"We're about to find out," Bolton says and activates the drive.

As the platform the aircraft sits upon rises to the carrier's flight deck, Bolton ticks off everything in his head. He mentally runs over the controls again and again.

Then they're exposed to the world and the tech gasps.

"No," the tech says and starts to fumble at the straps holding her secure to the seat. "Let me out. I don't want to die."

"Sit down and calm down," Bolton says tersely. "We don't have a choice."

With that, Bolton lifts off and aims the aircraft for what he can only describe as a flock of winged monsters that are in pursuit of Joshua's aircraft.

The tech screams, but Bolton barely hears the noise. He's focused solely on keeping control of the aircraft.

Which, to his amazement, he's able to do with surprisingly little difficulty. The aircraft wobbles for a moment, but the controls are fairly intuitive and basic enough that Bolton punches the acceleration without hesitating. The aircraft rockets at the flock of winged monsters.

"Prep starburst release on my mark," Bolton says. When the tech doesn't respond, he slams his fist on the dash. "Listen up!"

"Yes, sir," the tech says.

"I'm a sergeant," Bolton says. "I'm no officer. I work for a living."

The tech smiles but doesn't laugh. Bolton takes the smile as a win.

"Starbursts are prepped and ready," the tech says.

"Good," Bolton says. "As soon as you fire the volley of starbursts, you immediately fire missiles. Do not wait for my order. Loose the starbursts, then launch missiles. We have to hit them unawares."

"But missiles don't kill them, right?" the tech asks. "Isn't there some lightning gun? I heard people talk about—"

"Only on the main prototype and the V. And they only worked once," Bolton says. "Just hang on and do what I tell you."

Bolton banks down and to the left then levels out, his eyes looking up toward the winged monster flock. One of the beasts breaks from the flock and circles lower, obviously checking the aircraft out.

"The missiles will do what we need them to do," Bolton says. "That's all that matters."

The tech gulps and nods.

With his eye on the winged monster that's scoping them out, Bolton banks right then dives straight down. He checks a screen on the dash for a view from the rear camera. The winged monster is still circling below the flock, but it didn't pursue.

Bolton smiles, pulls up hard on the stick, and stares straight out of the windshield as he races the aircraft right at the center of the flock.

The circling monster shrieks in alarm and dives for the aircraft.

"Sergeant?" the tech squeaks.

"On my mark," Bolton says.

He works out the timing in his head, then shouts, "Three! Two! One! Mark!"

The tech fires the starbursts just before the winged monster collides with the aircraft. Bolton yanks the stick right, avoiding a collision with the monster, then immediately yanks left, bringing the aircraft's trajectory back in line with the flock.

Even with the windshield fully tinted, Bolton can see the outlines of the monsters as they rage at, then flee from the starbursts.

"Missiles, god dammit!" Bolton shouts.

The tech cries out in surprise, then fires all missiles.

Winged monsters scatter in all directions as the missiles impact with their bodies. The explosions send many tumbling out of control toward the surface, but Bolton knows the chaos is only temporary. Unless the things eat ammo, the monsters will continue to be a threat.

But for the moment, the threat is anything but coordinated, which gives Joshua the space he needs to dive down and strafe the winged monsters trying to attack Trey and the Africa kaiju.

"Sergeant, they're regrouping," the tech announces. "We're out of starbursts and missiles."

"That's fine," Bolton says and angles the aircraft back toward the V. "Reinforcements are coming."

"Nice flying, Sergeant," Director Miles calls over the comm from a different aircraft just leaving the carrier's flight deck. "Land and get loaded back up. We'll take it from here."

The other aircraft whips past Bolton.

"You feeling comfortable with the controls?" Bolton asks.

"I used to do some crop-dusting for the agency back in the day," Director Miles replies. "Once you've flown a single-engine airplane only ten meters above the ground while an army of guerrillas empty AK47s at your ass, you tend to get the hang of flight controls quickly."

"I'll bet," Bolton says. "Good luck."

Bolton carefully pilots the aircraft back to the flight deck and lands with only a couple of bumps. He waits until the aircraft is lowered into the hangar before he unbuckles his straps and hurries from the seat.

"Come on," he orders the tech. "There's no flight crew. We're reloading ourselves."

The tech nods and gets up, then braces herself against the back of the chair.

"You good?" Bolton asks.

"We're going back out there?" the tech asks.

"Yes," Bolton says. "As many times as we have to."

"Okay," the tech says, takes a deep breath, steadies herself, and follows Bolton out of the aircraft and over to where racks upon racks of starburst cartridges and missiles are secured.

They get to work and reload the aircraft as fast as possible, then both hustle back inside and take their seats.

"Here we go again," Bolton says and waits as the aircraft is raised back up to the flight deck.

The other aircraft is coming in to land just as Bolton lifts off and accelerates straight for the monster flock.

Bolton risks a glance out of the window on his left and shakes his head at the impossible sight of a giant spider creature carrying webbed pods containing actual ships filled with refugees.

"Ready?" Bolton asks.

"Yes, Sergeant," the tech responds, and Bolton smiles at the steel that's formed in her voice.

"We just have to keep these things off Joshua and Hines," Bolton says. "So they can keep the things off Trey. Chaos is our objective."

"Not a problem," the tech says, causing Bolton to laugh.

Bolton aims for the monster flock. "On my mark."

SIXTEEN

While the pressure of the ocean depths presses in on Quetzalcoatl, Lowell prays that Antarctica isn't equipped to handle the weight of the planet's water and is quickly being turned into giant monkey pulp.

"Mr. Licorice go squish," Lowell mumbles. Tiny bubbles escape the kaiju's mouth and are lost in the darkness.

A darkness that has gone from cloudy, to murky, to downright all encompassing. If it wasn't for the kaiju's ability to see clearly in almost all conditions, Lowell would be descending blind to the Core facility. Luckily, the darkness has a blue-green tinge to it, sort of like night vision goggles but without the distorting contrast. Combine that with the internal map of everything that he holds in his head, and Lowell isn't too worried about the total lack of surface light.

He's not too keen on the things that are brave enough to come investigate the intruder into their unseen ocean world. Lowell has nothing against fish, but there are some freaky beasts trailing in his wake. And not all of them are little.

A giant squid rushes by the kaiju, its tentacles flashing with bioluminescent lights in what Lowell believes is some type of communication. He laughs inside at the fact he is now fluent in kaiju but not giant squid, even though the latter is actually part of his home planet.

Then the squid darts directly in front of Quetzalcoatl, forcing Lowell to come up short quickly and bring the kaiju's descent to a sudden halt.

And a good thing too, because the water all around Lowell becomes a swirling maelstrom of churning chaos.

Then Lowell feels the sonic pulse slam into Quetzalcoatl, and the kaiju is sent twisting and tumbling through the ocean.

Lowell is fairly certain that if the squid hadn't stopped him, he would have been seriously injured by a direct hit from that pulse.

Motherfucking Aquaman here, Lowell thinks.

Lowell gets Quetzalcoatl under control and righted, then races back down toward the Core facility. Unfortunately, he's confirmed that the Ebony Man is ahead of him and will more than likely reach the facility first, but that doesn't slow Lowell down. He uses that realization as motivation to dive even faster.

Not that he has a choice any longer. As he gets closer and closer, he can feel the pull of the Core. A thought slams into Lowell's mind that even if he wants to, he can no longer resist that pull. Lowell has passed the point of no return, and it's do or die.

Lowell prefers do.

On he dives, the water becoming so cold that Lowell is reminded of his harrowing hike across Antarctica to reach the facility there. But even with temperatures dropping well below lethal levels, Lowell knows Quetzalcoatl can handle it. The kaiju seems to be able to handle anything.

Then Lowell sees it. The Mariana Trench.

It's a deep, dark slash across the ocean floor. There isn't a single sign of life along the edges of the trench when Lowell knows there should be. The Ebony Man has already passed into the trench and scared off the locals.

Why you gotta be such a dick, Mr. Licorice? Lowell thinks.

Then he pulls up and pauses just at the lip of the trench's ridge. Something isn't right…

A huge hand grabs one of Quetzalcoatl's wings and yanks Lowell over the lip and down into the trench. The kaiju is flung down hard, then slammed against the wall of the trench. Boulders the size of skyscrapers break free from the wall and tumble into the pitch-black waters.

"You will fail!" the Ebony Man screams.

Lowell flinches.

"Jesus, Mr. Licorice," Lowell replies. "If you're going to psychically talk shit, can you turn the volume down?"

"Your inability to take your situation seriously will be your downfall!" the Ebony Man shouts as he launches Antarctica onto Quetzalcoatl's back.

"Now you sound like my last warden," Lowell says, twisting his kaiju around so he can clamp Quetzalcoatl's jaws onto one of Antarctica's arms, filling his mouth with blood.

But Lowell is surprised that not all the blood is a result of his mouth being shredded yet again by the sharpened scales covering Antarctica's arm. He tastes the other kaiju's blood as well and is very happy about that. He's also slightly disgusted that he can taste the difference between his blood and another kaiju's. Not exactly an ability he would have put on the super powers wish list.

The Ebony Man roars and the sound fills Lowell's brain. He doesn't know how to block the psychic communication connection yet. He tries to shove the Ebony Man's voice from his mind, but all he manages to do is barely lower the volume.

But the inconvenience of having the being psychically berate him is tempered at the joy Lowell feels when he bites down even harder and the scales between his teeth crack, then break off.

"No!" the Ebony Man screams before yanking his arm free from Quetzalcoatl's jaws.

The monster kicks out, connecting with Quetzalcoatl's snout, sending Lowell spiraling down into the trench. Lowell regains control after only a few seconds and quickly launches himself at the Ebony Man.

Lowell can taste Antarctica's blood in the water and he stretches Quetzalcoatl's mouth into a satisfied grin.

"You better give it up, Mr. Licorice!" Lowell mentally shouts. "I got a taste for you now, bitch!"

A fist flies out of the pitch-black water and just misses Quetzalcoatl's temple. Lowell rears back then slashes in the direction of the punch with both wings. Bubbles burst all around Lowell as Antarctica lets out a physical scream this time.

The pitch-black water is thickened with kaiju blood.

Lowell races into the blood cloud and whips his wings back and forth ahead of him, trying to catch the Ebony Man by surprise and maybe spill more of that sweet, sweet kaiju blood.

But Quetzalcoatl's wings find only empty water.

Lowell spirals about, hunting, searching for his prey.

"Oh, Mr. Licorice!" Lowell calls. "Come out and play!"

Nothing.

Fuck, he thinks and dives.

He's only a few meters down when pain erupts from his tail and he feels his entire body stretch, then recoil as Antarctica yanks, then throws Quetzalcoatl against the trench's wall again.

Actual stars explode inside Lowell's brain. Seriously. He sees galaxies, constellations, swirling nebulas from parts of the universe that are trillions of light-years away. Then everything becomes a heavy, distorted jumble and he feels Quetzalcoatl start to float freely down into the trench.

Lowell shakes off the concussion and forces his mind to clear. The stars and nebulas fade away and all Lowell can see is the impossible blackness of the trench.

No Ebony Man.

"Fuck," he thinks again.

He checks his surroundings, careful not to get ambushed again, then points himself back in the direction of the Core facility.

This time, Lowell doesn't slow or stop. He pushes the kaiju's body to its limits and races with all his strength to the very bottom of the ocean.

Seconds pass, minutes pass, and finally, after almost an hour of swimming at full speed, Lowell feels then sees the facility reveal itself from the very center of the trench.

Rage fills him as he sees a primate-shaped splotch clambering across the facility's smooth, orb-like surface.

And it is smooth. Nothing clings to the outside of the Core facility. A couple hundred meters away, Lowell can just make out the tubes of giant sea worms, but none inhabit the space within the Core's influence. Not even the many forms of blind sea life dare swim close to the Core.

Lowell can feel the danger the facility exudes as he gets closer and closer.

The dark splotch that is Antarctica is lost from sight as the Ebony Man finds an entrance and disappears inside the facility.

Lowell swims even faster until he almost collides with the surface of the Core. He brakes hard and pulls up short, his eyes hunting for the way inside. Lowell starts to get frustrated as he finds not a single sign of an entrance. The surface of the Core remains smooth and unblemished.

"Chill yourself before you kill yourself," Lowell thinks. "Mr. Licorice got in. So can you."

He mentally closes his eyes and hunts through his knowledge for anything on the Core. Bits and pieces reveal themselves but nothing that helps him get inside. Lowell panics, thinking the Ebony Man has figured out how to lock him out. But he shoves that panic aside and gets back to basics.

You've spent most of your life in prison, Lowell thinks. *You know locked doors like the back of your hand. You got this.*

Lowell relaxes and lets Quetzalcoatl settle to the ocean floor, right at the base of the orb. He stares at the facility, dialing in Quetzalcoatl's vision until he spots what he's looking for.

If he had hands, he'd smack his kaiju forehead.

An orb at the bottom of the ocean wouldn't have an entrance on top. It'd be underneath.

Lowell presses a wingtip to a specific point on the facility's surface and is deeply satisfied when part of the orb irises open to reveal a kaiju chamber to rival all kaiju chambers. Lowell climbs inside the facility, grateful to be up out of the water, in open air, and away from the constant pressure of the ocean depths.

Before the entrance closes, Lowell spins Quetzalcoatl around and pukes up a thousand gallons of seawater. He sighs with satisfaction, then lets the entrance iris closed.

Lowell turns the kaiju and glares at what is locked into place against the chamber's wall.

Antarctica.

Lowell knows instantly that the kaiju is empty and in stasis. What he doesn't know is where the Ebony Man has gone. The Core facility is not like the other facilities. There's no Substance hidden behind a bulkhead that the Ebony Man will emerge from. The Core is one with the Substance.

"I guess we'll find out how you eject from these babies soon enough," Lowell says and moves Quetzalcoatl over to one of a dozen empty stasis bays that ring the kaiju chamber.

He climbs his way up to a set of clamps, spreads his wings, and watches in amazement as the facility takes over. The clamps secure the wings to the wall of the chamber before a series of locks hold the entire body in place.

Nothing happens for a moment, then a sharp pain pierces the back of Quetzalcoatl's head and Lowell grunts.

Lowell's no longer merged with a kaiju but standing naked in a room not much bigger than a shower stall. Mist floats down about him from the ceiling and three of the four walls glow orange like the Substance. Before Lowell can get too curious, the non-glowing wall in front of him irises open.

The Ebony Man is waiting outside and lunges at Lowell, knocking him back against the wall of the small room. Pitch-black fists pummel Lowell about the head, and he's barely able to get his arms up to block the blows that are trying to beat him into unconsciousness.

"Get the fuck off me, Mr. Licorice!" Lowell shouts and shoves the Ebony Man away.

"Stop calling me that!" the Ebony Man roars, doubling his attack.

Lowell flashes to his years in prison, and that rage he's kept deep inside explodes out of him.

"I'll fucking call you whatever I want!" Lowell roars as he slams his fist into the Ebony Man's throat.

The being stumbles back to the room's entrance and Lowell presses the attack, landing a kick dead center in the Ebony Man's chest.

"Now, Mr. Licorice, you and I are gonna get a few things straight," Lowell says, wasting zero time as he rushes from the small room, his feet continuing the assault on the pitch-black alien. "This place? The Core? Mine. Not yours. Mine. If you think you're going to take control of this place, you are so fucking wrong I'm amazed you can even walk and talk. My Core. Got it?"

Lowell stops the attack and crouches down close to the Ebony Man's approximation of a face.

"Now, Mr. Licorice, what should I do with you?" Lowell asks.

"I warned you not to call me that," the Ebony Man croaks.

"Whatev—" Lowell starts to say, then stops suddenly as he looks down to see a thin, black strand of the Ebony Man protruding from his abdomen. "You... little... fucker..."

Lowell falls back on his ass and yanks the piece of the Ebony Man free from his guts. He grunts and winces but doesn't cry out, despite the good amount of blood that begins to seep out of the wound and coat his naked legs.

The Ebony Man stands and stares down at Lowell.

"Pathetic," the Ebony Man says. "You are what your species sends to stop me? It is no wonder that your planet's time is over. Not one of you sad little monkeys deserves to survive. And none of you will once I fully activate this facility."

The Ebony Man looks about and sighs, then returns his attention to Lowell.

"But, first, I have to make sure I am not interrupted," the Ebony Man says. "I will clear this and all facilities of the pests that infest them."

Lowell, still sitting on his ass, grins up at the Ebony Man.

"Bitch, you fucked up," Lowell says. "You have no idea."

The Ebony Man snorts, shakes his head, and walks away, lost around the far corner of the corridor. Lowell watches him go, then takes a deep breath and lies back.

"Okay, dumbass," Lowell mutters to himself. "You screwed that up. Now what?"

He rolls his head to the side and looks into the small room he'd just come from and wonders if he should just crawl inside and merge with Quetzalcoatl again. But he has no idea if that will help him or harm Quetzalcoatl. Lowell chuckles at the thought of worrying about a giant, feathered snake monster while he slowly bleeds out on the floor of an alien facility.

"Anson Lowell," a voice says, and Lowell almost ignores it, thinking that maybe blood loss is messing with his brain. "Anson Lowell?"

Lowell rolls his head away from the view of the small room and looks down the corridor.

"Huh," he says as he sees a figure standing there. "Trey?"

"Anson Lowell, this is a projection," the image of the alien being says. "Interaction is minimal, so please pay attention. You must not die."

"No shit, Trey," Lowell says.

"Trey... ah, confusion is understandable," the alien projection says. "But I am not the one named Trey. This is a representation of a being you are already familiar with in order to instill trust. Please listen."

Lowell gives the projection a thumbs up. He can't think of what else to do at the moment.

"The one you call Mr. Licorice is currently on its way to kill the…" The alien projection cocks its head then continues, "Staff. The word is not sufficient, but it will serve to describe our duties and responsibilities."

Lowell groans. "Staff. Got it."

"Anson Lowell, please pick yourself up and follow me," the alien projection says.

Lowell laughs. The alien projection flickers, then moves a few feet closer to Lowell.

"There is no humor at this time," the alien projection says.

"Again, no shit, Not Trey," Lowell replies. "But you have to be joking if you think I can stand up and follow your hologram ass."

"Please only listen," the alien projection says. "Your strange colloquialisms are hard for the emergency system to process and only slow down our interactions."

"Complicated way to say shut the fuck up, but I hear ya," Lowell says.

"Get up and follow," the alien projection orders.

Lowell shakes his head, laughs again, then rolls over onto his front so he can push up onto his hands and knees. Pain explodes from his abdomen, but Lowell literally pushes through it and struggles up onto his feet. Blood streams down from his wound.

The alien projection nods, turns, and walks away.

"Follow," it says.

"No problem," Lowell mocks, placing a hand against the corridor's wall for support.

He does as ordered and follows the projection down the corridor, around the corner, down another corridor, and another, and another until he's forced to stop and put his back against the wall. He slides to the floor, his entire lower half coated in sticky blood.

"No, Anson Lowell," the alien projection says. "You have not reached your destination."

"Oh, I think I have," Lowell says. "Because this is as far as I can go."

"No, Anson Lowell," the alien projection repeats. "You must return to your feet and follow."

"Buddy, I'm bleeding like a stuck pig," Lowell replies. "If you know anything about human anatomy, then you know that blood is kinda important to us. Sorta helps us live and shit."

"Your scatological needs are unimportant at the moment," the alien projection replies. "Stand, Anson Lowell. It is not far."

"Fuck me." Lowell moans, then takes a deep breath and barely manages to get back up on his feet.

He staggers through three more corridors before the alien projection stops.

Next to a blank wall.

"Kinda anticlimactic," Lowell says.

"Your flesh is needed," the alien projection states.

"Whoa, pal, I'm in no shape for sexy time," Lowell says.

The alien projection points to the wall. "Your flesh is needed."

Lowell frowns, then places a bloody palm to the wall. Instantly, a door appears and dissolves open, nearly causing Lowell to fall inside the room it reveals. That's when Lowell realizes that none of the corridors he's struggled through have had doors. Nothing but smooth walls.

"This is an auxiliary control center," the alien projection says. "There are many throughout the facility so that the Core can be maintained, no matter how much of the facility is damaged during an attack."

"You expect an attack to get to the bottom of the ocean?" Lowell asks.

"Unfortunately, you will understand soon," the alien projection says. "I am sorry. Please enter the room and take a seat at any of the eight stations. They are uniform and will adapt to your needs. Which is currently medical assistance. Once you are stable, I will return."

The projection disappears, leaving Lowell alone to stare in at the new room.

He stumbles inside and collapses into the closest chair. The moment his ass makes contact with the chair, the wall closes behind him, sealed completely as if it doesn't exist. Lowell waits for something to happen.

"Hello? I could go for that adaption shit now," he calls out.

The room is pure white, including the chairs, which are stationed in a circular pattern about the room, each facing a part of the blank walls. Lowell would be frustrated with the lack of response, but he's so tired that he can't even muster that emotion.

"Fucking… fix me…" he says with a sigh, his eyelids drooping closed.

Before Lowell's eyes can fully close, the wall in front of him comes alive with what looks like a holographic interface and monitor. The blank wall is still there, but projected across it is a series of boxes and images with lettering from a language he can't even begin to comprehend.

Then the language transforms into English, projecting, "Please remain still."

"No problem," Lowell says.

The chair enwraps Lowell, but he doesn't even flinch. That would take too much energy.

But in seconds, he does flinch, and even screams, when a million tiny needles penetrate his wound and the flesh surrounding it.

To Lowell's credit, he doesn't struggle against the intense searing pain that has enveloped not just his abdomen, but his entire torso and within seconds, his entire body.

Lowell endures the agony for an eternity. Then the pain ends as if it had never happened.

Waiting for the punchline, which he assumes will be a giant needle aimed for one of his eyes, Lowell remains still even after the chair reverts to its original form.

"You have been fixed, Anson Lowell," the words on the wall projection state.

The door to the room dissolves open and the alien projection returns.

"Please hurry," the alien projection says. "The one you call Mr. Licorice is about to purge the facilities."

"He's about to fucking what now?" Lowell snaps, jumping up from the chair. He slips in a puddle of his own blood that has started to congeal on the floor, steadies himself against the chair, then points at the alien projection. "Take me to Mr. Licorice. And maybe a pair of sweatpants, if they're on the way."

There's a whispering sound, and a drawer extends from the wall in front of Lowell's chair.

Inside the drawer is a pair of sweatpants, just as Lowell had asked for. He snags them and slips them on quickly, then sees what's written on the legs.

"Juicy? Seriously?" he says.

"These are a representation of a popular clothing style on your planet," the alien projection states. "Now, follow, please."

Lowell does, and they quickly make their way through three more corridors before arriving at what Lowell assumes is an elevator. A door dissolves open to reveal something straight out of Star Trek. Lowell shrugs and steps inside.

The moment the door solidifies, the alien projection disappears and the elevator races to the side. Lowell barely feels the movement other than a slight shove to the right and realizes that the Core facility is considerably more advanced than the other facilities, even Antarctica.

The door dissolves again without Lowell even feeling the elevator stop. The alien projection reappears as Lowell steps out into a massive atrium that has to be ten stories high. Balconies and walkways line the sides of the atrium all the way up to the top, where a massive skylight domes the space. Instead of sky, or even seawater, the dome glows bright orange.

"Substance," Lowell mutters.

"Correct," the alien projection says. "Follow. Quickly."

"Thanks to that acupuncture chair on steroids, I can do that," Lowell says. "Where to now?"

"There," the alien projection says and moves to where a small platform is descending from the top of the atrium. "Step on."

"Stepping on," Lowell says.

He does, and the platform moves rapidly back up to the top of the atrium. The railing on a balcony dissolves and Lowell steps off the platform and onto the balcony. The wall before him dissolves and he faces a corridor that instantly gives him the creeps.

The corridor is bathed in blood-red light that pulses slowly like a heartbeat.

"Uh, it looks alive," Lowell says.

"Correct," the alien projection says. "Follow."

Lowell notices that the projection has lost some of its solidity and is flickering in and out.

"What's up with you, Not Trey?" Lowell asks.

"Cannot answer," the alien projection says. "Follow."

Reluctantly, Lowell follows.

Halfway down the corridor, Lowell feels a tremor in the floor, then a deep humming reaches his ears.

"Do I want to know?" Lowell asks.

"The purge process has begun," the alien projection states. "You are almost out of time."

"Then hurry it the fuck up!" Lowell shouts and starts running, which forces the alien projection to speed up and run ahead of him.

They make it to the end of the corridor and a blank wall. Lowell doesn't even pause and places both palms to the surface.

The wall dissolves and a startled, then enraged, Ebony Man turns to face Lowell.

"How?" the being shouts.

"I told you that you fucked up," Lowell says as he stalks into the room.

Lowell has to ignore the many control stations and the large observation window that lines the front of the room. He really wants to check it all out, but he knows he has one task to tackle first.

The Ebony Man's right arm extends across the room and tries to grab Lowell, but he ducks under it, then comes up fast and throws a solid right hook into the Ebony Man's face. The being's head rocks to the side but recovers quickly and the extended arm snaps back, wrapping around Lowell, pinning his arms to his torso.

"Nope," Lowell says and flexes.

The Ebony Man's stretched arm shatters like it's made of plastic. Hunks and chunks fly in all directions where they smack against the control stations, the walls, the floor. Instead of sliding back to the Ebony Man, the hunks and chunks remain where they are, then slowly fade into nothing.

"No..." the Ebony Man gasps. His attention turns to the flickering alien projection. "You cannot win. They are already coming."

"That's nice," Lowell says and slams a fist directly into a spot on the Ebony Man's chest where his sternum would have been if he was human.

Despite not having a sternum, the blow has the same effect.

The Ebony Man collapses to his knees, his remaining arm clutching at his chest where a fist-sized crater has formed.

"I'm so done with your ass," Lowell says.

He moves in closer and towers over the cowering being.

"Most of all, I'm done with all the assholes like you," Lowell says. "Human or alien. I'm. Fucking. Done."

He clasps his fists and raises them above his head, then brings them down in one hard blow to the top of the Ebony Man's skull.

The being's entire body shatters.

Lowell doesn't bother to avoid the pitch-black shrapnel. He stands there and waits for the pieces to fall off his body, hit the floor, then fade away into nothing.

The room is empty except for Lowell and the flickering alien projection.

"How do I stop the purge?" Lowell asks after a couple of seconds.

"There," the alien projection says and points to a specific control station.

Lowell rushes to the station, studies the interface, then presses his right palm to a glowing red panel. Without saying a word, the panel interprets Lowell's needs and in seconds turns from red to green.

"Did that do it?" Lowell asks the projection.

"The purging of the facilities has ceased," the alien projection states.

"What about the staff you were talking about?" Lowell asks.

"Safe," the alien projection replies. "Stored and secure."

"Awesome," Lowell says and turns from the observation window. "Now what?"

Then he notices that the corridor outside the room is still bathed in blood-red light.

"Shit," Lowell says. "What's wrong?"

"The purge of the facilities has ceased," the alien projection states.

"But...?" Lowell asks.

"But the planetary purge cannot be stopped," the alien projection replies. "Those of your kind that remain on the surface will be destroyed before one full rotation of the planet has been completed."

"What the fuck?" Lowell shouts. "What does that mean?"

"It means you will need to use this facility's full capabilities to help your fellow humans survive," the alien projection says. "Direct them to the other facilities with much haste so you can prepare for the battle."

So many questions fill Lowell's mind, but none reach his lips.

He takes one huge, deep breath, then turns his attention back to the control stations.

"What do I do?" Lowell asks.

SEVENTEEN

Lu collapses into a chair and stares at the image of Lowell projected before her. The sudden shock from him appearing in the control room has worn off and given way to the shock from the news Lowell just told her.

"What do you mean purged?" Lu asks when her voice returns to her.

"Fucking purged, Lu," Lowell says. "Basically, the surface of the planet is going to be wiped out and all that will be left is the mantle and the conduits connecting the facilities. Earth is about to look like a dirt clod with spikes sticking out."

"Good God," Lu says. "How do we stop it?"

"We can't," Lowell says. "The process began as soon as Mr. Licorice emerged from the Substance. Earth is dead, Lu."

"But you killed him, right?" Lu asks. "The Ebony Man?"

"Oh. I fucking killed him," Lowell says. "But this purge was meant to happen. Just a few millennia in the future. Ideally, when humanity was on its last legs."

"We kinda are now," Lu admits.

"Yeah, no shit," Lowell says. "Listen, I'll do what I can from here, but now it's up to everyone still outside. They have to get to a facility, and fast. Anything left outside will be obliterated. And I mean fucking obliterated."

"Christ. Okay," Lu says. "I'll get on the comms and let everyone know…"

"Good," Lowell says and frowns.

Lu has been around the man long enough to know the frown.

"What are you about to ask for?" Lu snaps.

"Where's Kyle?" Lowell asks.

"No," Lu says. "No, Lowell. Kyle stays by me so I know he's safe."

"I get that, Lu, but I need him here," Lowell says. "He's attuned. I need his help. We can run all the facilities from the Core. All you and everyone else will have to do is get people inside and secured. We'll do the heavy lifting."

"No," Lu growls. "Kyle is staying here. I don't care if he's the only other person on this planet that's attuned to these fucking facilities!"

"Language," Terrie says as she walks into the control room, Kyle right behind her. "And he isn't the only other person attuned."

"Mom? What do you mean?" Lu asks.

"Well, shit," Lowell says. "Welcome to the club."

"I'm not as all-knowing as Kyle and Lowell," Terrie says, which gets a sarcastic snort from Lowell, "but I understand the basic mechanics of this facility."

"What is going on?" Lu asks.

"Grandma is coming with me," Kyle says. "She isn't taking no for an answer."

"Yeah, well, I say no," Lu says.

"Honey, you can't get in the way of this," Terrie says. "God put us all on this Earth for a reason. Mine is to be with my grandson and help protect him. Like I have done since he was born."

Lu starts to argue, but the logic of what her mother is saying hits her hard. Terrie has always been there to protect Kyle. More so than Lu has.

"What does Kyle have to do?" Lu asks Lowell, her voice resigned to reality.

"Honestly? I don't really know," Lowell says. "But I need him here to handle things while I get back in ol' Q and try to keep this planet from being destroyed."

"I thought you said there was nothing that could be done to stop the purge," Lu snaps. "Which is it, Lowell?"

"Sorry. The purge can't be stopped," Lowell says. "The surface is going bye bye. That's not what I'm talking about. I'm talking about the real threat coming to wipe us all out."

"The other side of the war," Kyle states. "The aliens that want Earth as their own."

"That's still happening?" Lu nearly shouts. "But you killed the Ebony Man! You have control of the Core! That should have stopped it all, right?"

"War is hard to stop, Mom," Kyle says. "And Earth is in the middle of a war."

"So, you guys are saying that even if we get people into the facilities and safe from the surface purge, that we could all die anyway?" Lu sighs. "I'm not a fan of aliens."

"Right there with ya, Lu," Lowell says.

Everyone stands in silence until Terrie claps her hands.

"Let's get this show on the road, shall we?" Terrie says. She looks around. "Where's Biscuit? I need to say goodbye."

"He's asleep in my room," Lu says. "You can see him when you get back."

Terrie shoots a sad look at Lu, then nods.

"I suppose you're right," Terrie says. "When I get back."

"Mom…?" Lu asks.

Terrie shakes her head and smiles at her grandson.

"Ready to go?" Terrie asks.

Kyle nods. He closes the distance between himself and his

mother and gives Lu a huge hug. Lu is taken aback at first, then commits to the hug with all her soul.

Terrie steps up when Kyle lets go and she gives Lu an even stronger hug.

"You have to come back," Lu whispers in Terrie's ear.

"It's not up to me, honey," Terrie whispers in return. "God's will be done."

Lu chokes back a sob and nuzzles her head into her mother's neck then breathes deeply, taking in a scent she's known since birth.

Then she coughs and pushes Terrie back.

"Keep him safe," Lu says.

"You know I will," Terrie says.

"We have to go," Kyle says, eyeing his mother and grandmother.

"I'll see you when you get here," Lowell says and is gone.

Lu watches her mother and her son leave the control room, then waits a full minute before she collapses onto the floor and sobs uncontrollably.

When she's able to get herself together, she gets up and activates the comm.

"Connor? We need to talk," Lu says. "Now."

————

"Not a problem," Bolton replies as he flies the aircraft straight for the Wyoming facility.

Five other aircraft are in formation behind him, which is followed closely by the Valhalla. Winged monsters flit in and out of the ash cloud above, but they've learned their lesson and stay a good distance back.

Bolton grins at their caution.

"Open the kaiju chamber," Bolton calls. "We can land the V in there and get everyone off before going out for another rescue run."

He sees the massive chamber iris open and banks the aircraft out of the way so the Valhalla can get in position.

"You need to land too," Lu says. "We all have to talk."

"That doesn't sound good," Bolton says. "Shit. Lowell failed, didn't he? Fuck! I knew that—"

"Lowell didn't fail," Lu replies. "Land on the V and I'll join you all there."

"Lu? What is it?" Bolton asks.

"Just land, Connor…"

The comm goes quiet. Bolton frowns, then looks at his co-pilot.

"Relay that message to the other aircraft and the V," Bolton says as he preps to land.

He brings the small aircraft inside the kaiju chamber, aims directly for the V's flight deck, and manages to land without much jarring.

By the time Bolton has powered the aircraft down, unstrapped from his seat, and climbed out onto the flight deck, Lu is there waiting.

"Where's VanderVoort?" Lu asks.

"This way," Bolton says. "You're freaking me out, Lu."

"Yeah, well, you need to be freaked out," Lu says. "Show me the way."

"What's going on?" Director Miles asks, having emerged from his aircraft. "What's with the power down? We need to get back out there."

"Change of plans," Bolton says.

Bolton catches Joshua's eye as he climbs out of his own aircraft. He nods for him to follow and Joshua gets in line behind Director Miles as Bolton leads Lu to the V's bridge.

"Hello, Ms. Morgan," VanderVoort says as she struggles up onto her feet and extends a hand to Lu. "A pleasure to meet in person."

Lu takes VanderVoort's hand and shakes it, but Bolton can tell she's only going through the motions.

"I doubt you're going to find pleasure in what I'm about to say," Lu says. "We're all fucked."

"We've kinda been fucked for a while," Director Miles says. "Care to be more specific?"

Lu relays what Lowell has told her. The small amount of joy that comes from hearing that the Ebony Man is dead is quickly gone when Lu explains the purge.

"May I ask from what point, start to finish, does this alien consider the beginning of Earth's rotation?" Dr. Hall asks, breaking the stunned silence. "The international date line? Eastern Time? Greenwich Mean? Knowing that will help us calculate the amount of time remaining for rescue attempts."

"You don't get it," Lu says.

"No, but I do," VanderVoort says. "There are no more rescue attempts, are there? The people in the facilities are the people who will be the last people left alive on Earth. Am I correct?"

"Yes," Lu says. "We have to lock down the facilities now. No more in, no more out."

"Christ, Lu," Bolton says. "There are still millions of people out there."

"You think I don't know that, Connor?" Lu snaps. "It's not my fucking fault! I have no control over any of this!"

"I know, I know," Bolton says. "I'm sorry."

"And there's nothing we can do?" President Nance asks. "This Anson Lowell can't stop the purge from the Core?"

"No," Lu says. "The purge process began when the Ebony Man escaped his prison. It started a chain reaction that can't be undone."

VanderVoort stares at Lu for a long few seconds.

"Come with me," VanderVoort says to Lu, then looks at President Nance. "You may join too."

"We don't have time for this," Lu snaps.

"We'll make time," VanderVoort says. "Gordon? Will you and Sergeant Bolton make sure everyone is off the V and it is secured inside this chamber appropriately?"

"Fuck," Director Miles says. "You scare the shit out of me when you get all formal."

"Gordon?" VanderVoort asks.

"We have this under control," Bolton says. "Go talk."

"This way," VanderVoort says and slowly makes her way off the bridge to a side room. She gestures for Lu and President Nance to sit down. She waits until the door closes, then focuses on Lu. "Okay, Lucinda Morgan, now tell me the real bad news."

"What can be worse than this purge?" President Nance asks.

"A war," Lu says. "The one between the aliens that built the network of facilities and the ones headed this way now."

"Oh," President Nance says. "That."

"How much time do we have?" VanderVoort asks.

"Lowell didn't know," Lu says. "But not long. The purge will happen, then we wait."

"We'll do more than just wait!" President Nance snaps. "I'm President of the United States of America! I'll launch our full nuclear arsenal at these aliens that think they can take our planet!"

"I highly doubt nukes will work, Charles," VanderVoort says. "They didn't work on any of the kaiju, so why would they work on even worse monsters from outer space?"

"So we sit on our hands and do nothing?" President Nance snarls. "Unacceptable, Ms. VanderVoort! I ceded authority to you because you were making rational decisions in the heat of the moment and you were right pretty much every time. But now? I'm sorry, Adrianna, but I relieve you of your duty. You may go rest and take care of that baby. I'm back in charge."

"No one is in charge except for Lowell," Lu says. "Get pissy all you want, Mr. President, but pretty soon there won't be a United States to be president of. There'll only be the facilities and the Core. The Core runs the facilities, and Lowell runs the Core."

"Then what do we do?" President Nance asks, his voice shaking with barely controlled rage.

"We get to work settling everyone in, then we help coordinate between the facilities," Lu says. "We have to all work together because this is a network. Countries are about to be nonexistent, so borders mean nothing. We can travel back and forth between the facilities through the BCCN, but the system is barely up and running and we need people to be attuned. Don't ask. First, we establish ground rules amongst us while we strengthen the BCCN. Then we put those ground rules into effect and wait for what comes next."

"Is that all?" President Nance laughs. "I'm guessing you've never been to a UN Council meeting, Marshal Morgan. By the time the aliens get here, we'll probably only have agreed on what time to eat lunch."

"But you're forgetting the first ground rule," Lu says. "Lowell runs things. It may go smoother if we explain that, if we don't get basic ground rules in place, then a convicted cop killer will be in charge. And as far as I know, there isn't a damn thing we can do to stop him."

"Then let's not waste time," VanderVoort says. "I do have one point that needs making."

"What?" Lu asks.

"The comms," VanderVoort says. "Without Tony's device in the air, we can't speak with those who are still on the surface."

"I already thought of that," Lu says. "Tony is hooking his device to this facility now. If by some miracle people do survive the purge, we'll be able to speak with them. In the meantime, he's sending out an emergency warning to all ears."

"And what does this emergency message say?" VanderVoort asks.

———

"Well, at least you already sorta sound like one of those automated computer voices," Krissy says as she and Tony listen to the emergency message he's just recorded. "And you're to the point."

They both stand in the Wyoming main control room as Tony plays the message one more time.

"Attention all residents of Earth," the message booms. "Seek shelter within one of the alien facilities immediately. The surface of the planet is about to be destroyed and all left outside the facilities will die. Thank you and goodbye."

"I love that last part," Krissy says. "Thank you and goodbye. Classic."

"Do you have an alternative message you want to record?" Tony asks.

"Nope. I'm good," Krissy says and scratches at her bandages.

"Stop that," Tony says, pulling Krissy's hand away from her face. "You won't heal if you keep disturbing your dressings."

Krissy looks down at her hand, which Tony is still holding, before looking up and into Tony's eyes. She clears her throat.

"Thank you," she says and leans in to kiss his cheek.

Tony lets go of her hand and shrinks back.

"Well, fuck you," Krissy snaps. "It's my face, right? Fucking great..."

"I'm sorry," he says, his face bright red. "It is not your face. I don't... I don't know how to... I don't kiss."

"Oh," Krissy says and laughs. "I wasn't gonna French you or anything. It's just a thank you peck on the fucking cheek. You think you can handle that?"

"I don't kiss," Tony says and looks down at the ground. Then he gives a barely perceptible nod.

If Krissy hadn't spent so many days with the boy, pretty much twenty-four-seven, then she would have missed the nod. She smiles, leans in slowly, almost cruelly drawing it out, and kisses Tony's cheek.

"My first kiss," he whispers.

"Dude, that doesn't count as your first kiss," Krissy says. "That has to be on the lips. We'll work on that some other time."

She gets a considerable amount of joy at watching Tony's skin go from beet red with embarrassment to bone white with fear.

"This is it?" VanderVoort asks from the control room's doorway. "Pretty small time considering the size of this place."

Both the kids jump and spin around.

"Hey," Lu says, pushing past VanderVoort. "Did you send the message?"

"Yu... yu... yeah," Tony says.

Lu looks back and forth between the teens, then catches Krissy's eye and smiles.

"Where is this device?" President Nance asks, coming in behind Lu.

Dr. Hall and Alvarez are right behind him, followed by General Azoul and Joan Milligan.

"That table is like only a quarter the size of the one in the situation room," Dr. Hall says.

"Just like with everything else in life," VanderVoort says, "size doesn't really matter. Take a seat, folks. Joan? Will you have Tony get you connected to the global comms and start playing damage control?"

"Gladly," Joan says and waits for Tony. When he doesn't move, she snaps her fingers. "Where do I sit?"

"There," Tony says and points to a seat behind him without taking his eyes off the others. He clears his throat. "You're President Charles Nance."

President Nance raises an eyebrow and nods.

"And you are Tony... Rochester? Is that it?" President Nance replies. He offers his hand. "You have an exceptional mind, son. You're an asset to your country."

"She helped," Tony says and points to Krissy.

President Nance nods. "Then thank you as well, young lady."

"Yeah. Sure. Cool," Krissy says, embarrassed.

"Happy fun time is over," VanderVoort says from the table. "Lu? You're up. What's next?"

Lu sits down and waves a hand over the table. A holographic image of the Earth comes up and begins to rotate.

"Holy shit, that's cool," Dr. Hall says, taking his own seat and leaning as close to the hologram as possible.

"According to Lowell," Lu begins, "this is what will happen to the planet when the purge starts."

The surface of the rotating planet cracks and massive gouts of flame shoot into the air. By the scale of the holographic model, the flames have to be several miles high. Then the fire spreads over the entire surface of the planet and large chunks of earth break off and slowly drift away from the planet, leaving only a naked mantle and a series of crystalline spikes that stick out from areas that correspond to each facility.

"How is that possible?" Dr. Hall asks. "The Earth is still rotating. There's no way anything can break apart and defy gravity like that."

"Aliens, man," Alvarez says and pats Dr. Hall on the shoulder.

"Wait a minute," General Azoul says and points at the hologram. "Look at the debris. It's stopped drifting and is forming a... shield?"

"Yeah," Lu says. "Part of the defenses are that the purge expels the crust so that it can be utilized as a framework for the protective shield."

"I like the sound of that," General Azoul says. "But there's a lot of space between that debris? How big are these aliens coming for us?"

"Damn huge," Lu says. "But small enough to get through the gaps, which is why the Core will add an energy shield to protect the open space."

Dr. Hall starts to speak, but VanderVoort holds up a hand and shakes her head.

"Nope," she says. "We're moving on. None of us can fully understand any of this, so let's get to the part that saves our asses. If this is the defense, then what is the offense?"

Lu sighs and closes her eyes, then opens them wide and smiles at VanderVoort.

"Lowell. Trey," Lu says. "And my family, apparently."

———

"You made it," Lowell says as Terrie and Kyle walk into the Core's control deck. "It's a trip, isn't it? Any side effects?"

"A headache," Terrie says.

"I'm good," Kyle says.

"You have your clothes," Lowell says.

"Yeah," Kyle replies. "I fixed that glitch."

"Nice," Lowell says. "No side effects? Really?"

"Nope," Kyle says. "I feel fine."

"Oh, to be young again," Terrie says. "Mr. Lowell. Nice to see you. Now what?"

"Hold on," Lowell says as a hologram of Trey appears in the center of the room. "Hey, pal, where you at?"

Trey cocks his head, then nods.

"I am at the Africa facility, Mr. Lowell," Trey replies. "I have initiated lockdown procedures in anticipation of the purge. Unfortunately, I was not able to rescue as many human beings as I had hoped I would. Millions remain on this continent, and I am sorry for their loss of life."

"You did what you could, Trey, my man," Lowell says. "Try to get some rest and eat something." Lowell swipes the air and a new image appears. It shows the Earth, then zooms out and focuses on a small dot racing past Mars. "We're gonna be up sooner than we thought."

"Up?" Trey asks.

"Needed," Lowell says. "Ready to fight."

"Oh. Of course," Trey says. "I will rest and find sustenance. Then I will await your call to arms."

"Talk soon, pal," Lowell says and swipes the images away, leaving only empty air and Terrie's wide-open mouth.

"You're catching flies, Grandma," Kyle says with a grin.

Terrie's mouth snaps shut. She coughs.

"You'd think after teleporting to the bottom of the ocean, nothing would surprise me," Terrie says.

"Oh, shit will still surprise all of us," Lowell says and taps his temple. "What I have in here only scratches the surface of things. People will be studying these facilities for lifetimes."

"Not like we'll have anything else to do," Kyle says. "Can't really go outside for a hike."

"You ain't wrong there," Lowell says and gestures to the open chairs. "Sit down and let's get this shit coordinated."

"May I ask that we keep the language to a minimum, Mr. Lowell?" Terrie responds, taking a seat.

"You can ask, but I won't listen," Lowell says. "Self-censorship isn't my thing. Cool?"

"I'll try to be cool, yes," Terrie says. "What do you have for us?"

"This," Lowell says and swipes again, bringing up the view of the Core's kaiju chamber. "Or these. Antarctica and Mexico. I don't know what the Antarctica one is called, but—"

"Grape Ape," Kyle says. "I overheard someone from the White House call it that."

"I'm not calling it that," Lowell says. "Antarctica it is. The other one does have a name. Quetzalcoatl."

"I know," Kyle says.

"I think I do too," Terrie says, frowning. "I can't be certain."

"What can you be certain about?" Lowell asks. "I mean that. Not trying to be sarcastic. What got transferred to your head? Kyle and I both had very different experiences, so we seem to understand different shit. Right, Kyle?"

"Yep," Kyle says. "Grandma?"

"It's not like a ton of knowledge was given to me," Terrie says, looking thoughtful. "It's more like… ability. I feel like I can do… something. I just don't know what it is."

"Take a guess," Lowell says.

"Alright…" Terrie thinks. "It's similar to after being in the field for a few years. I don't have to think to act, my body simply knows. Like I already have muscle memory for something I haven't done yet. Does that make sense?"

Both Kyle and Lowell nod.

"I was hoping you'd say that," Lowell says. "Because I need Kyle to take the reins here while you and I join Trey and get our hands dirty."

Terrie nods, and Lowell suddenly realizes she's been acting doubtful for her grandson. He can see the look in her eyes and he knows instantly she's completely aware of what her fate will probably be. Her eyes narrow, and Lowell sees that she knows he knows. He nods back to her in acknowledgment.

"Wait a damn minute," Kyle says and points at the image of the kaiju chamber. "I'm younger, stronger, and in better shape than my grandma. I should be the one fighting with you, not her. She has tactical and management experience. She'll be way better at coordinating things than me."

"But I have the combat training," Terrie counters. "You both have been given insight into different parts of the whole. Parts that play to your strengths. I believe the same has happened to me, Kyle." She shrugs. "I'm a Morgan. I know how to fight when it comes time."

"Your grandmother doesn't have the right connection to the facilities, kid," Lowell says. "You do. You can manage everything faster than most people can think. When you have to act, and I mean for all the facilities, you'll be able to. I need you up here."

"So you two can go brawl with alien kaiju?" Kyle snaps. "Fuck that. I want in on the fight."

"Kyle Morgan!" Terrie snaps.

"Sorry, Grandma," Kyle says.

"I feel ya, Kyle, I do," Lowell says. "Personally? I'd rather be safe here in this facility than flying a giant snake-bird out into space to fight off alien monsters. I'd trade places in a heartbeat. But your grandmother nailed it. We've each got our strengths and our parts to play. My strength has always been whupping some ass when that ass needed whupping. Sounds like your grandmother is the same. Add in an experienced pilot like Trey, and we might have a shot."

"Bunch of BS," Kyle mutters.

"How many are coming for us?" Terrie asks.

"Fuck if I know," Lowell replies. He brings the space image up next to the kaiju chamber image and points at the incoming dot. "They're on a whole other wavelength. I can't even get close to that knowledge."

"Other attacks across the galaxy have usually been conducted by two to four interstellar kaiju," Kyle says. His eyes go wide and he blinks with surprise. "Didn't know I knew that."

"Which is why you get to park it here," Lowell says, sweeping his hand out at the control room. "You're going to get snatches of insight like that that will helps us win this shit."

"I guess…" Kyle says, but most of the protest has left his voice. Most of it.

"Alright, so how do we—?" Terrie begins to ask, but her voice is drowned out by the loudest klaxon ever conceived.

"Kill the noise!" Lowell shouts, and the klaxon ceases instantly.

"What's happening?" Kyle asks.

"I think we all know," Lowell says. "The world is ending."

EIGHTEEN

"Hold on!" Bolton yells as the Wyoming facility shakes and shudders.

It's nothing like when the outer bunker was destroyed after the last Yellowstone eruption, but the violence is bad enough that he has to help several people keep from falling flat on their faces as the footing in the facility becomes tenuous.

Dust rains down on everyone as Bolton helps the refugees brought in from the V get to the cafeteria level. While it freaked him out at first, Bolton is glad the Wyoming facility seems to sense the increase in population and is taking steps to expand areas where refugees can congregate.

At least a dozen more cafeterias suddenly became open and available as more and more people were dropped off to shelter in the facility.

A thought hits Bolton.

Not sheltering.

Living.

They are there to live, not shelter. Wyoming isn't a temporary refuge. It's now their home.

Bolton coughs out some dust and Director Miles claps him on the back.

"Better than the ceiling collapsing on us," Director Miles says as he looks up, making sure he's right. "See? Not a crack in sight."

"Let's hope it stays that way," Bolton says and opens the elevator doors.

Again, he's not surprised by the changes. Where the elevators were once only slightly larger than a normal elevator, with maybe a bit more space so a cart can be driven inside, now the elevators are freight-sized. Bolton could drive half a dozen carts into one if he wanted.

What does surprise him is the fact that the elevator now has multiple cars to a single shaft. Somehow, he can't wrap his mind around the engineering it takes to make that happen.

"Aliens," Bolton mutters.

"What was that?" Director Miles asks, herding a group of two dozen refugees into the elevator before the doors close.

"I said aliens," Bolton replies as, two seconds later, the doors open onto an empty elevator.

"No more explanation needed," Director Miles says.

The two men look at each other in confusion and fear as they both feel a tension build in the air.

"Oh, shit!" Bolton says and drops into a crouch, instinctively covering his head with his arms.

Director Miles does the same, as does every single person in the corridor waiting for their turn on the elevator.

A nearly eardrum-shattering thunder crack echoes through the facility and people scream. Some collapse onto the floor, having fainted from the shock of the noise.

When Bolton is sure there won't be a repeat, he slowly gets to his feet and gestures for everyone else to do the same.

"No time to waste, folks!" Bolton says. "We need to get centralized and secured now!"

Bolton motions to the elevator, but no one steps on.

"People!" Director Miles shouts. "This facility was built by aliens! The elevators are perfectly safe! I doubt they gave the job to the lowest bidder like we do here on Earth!"

There are more than a few government employees mixed in with the refugees, and nervous laughter is heard in response to Director Miles' comment.

It eases the fear just enough that people start to slowly enter the elevator.

Bolton steps away for a second and presses the comm in his ear.

"Lu? You copy?" he calls.

"I copy," Lu responds.

"What was that?" Bolton asks. "That thunder crack? Is the facility alright?"

"Yeah, it's fine," Lu replies. "The crack wasn't from the facility."

"Then where'd it come from?" Bolton asks.

"Most of North America," Lu says. "The country is gone, Connor. It broke off and is floating up into the atmosphere."

Bolton sees Director Miles turn to face him, his eyes wide with shock. Bolton's very glad only he and the director have active comms. The panic that news would have set off wouldn't have been pretty.

"Copy that," Bolton says and gets back to work.

———

For those left on the surface of the planet, the end is both terrifying and merciful.

As the Earth shatters and cracks and massive chunks begin to ascend into the sky, the many pockets of survivors are lifted with the debris. The debris chunks are the size of entire states, so multiple survivor pockets are lifted together.

For the unfortunate few that literally fall between the cracks, death is swift. For the rest, they have each other to cling to until the temperature becomes too cold and the atmosphere disperses out into space.

Millions upon millions of human beings, all across what was

once a globe, take their last few breaths while staring at what is possibly the greatest view ever, a view that only a handful of trained astronauts have seen in person.

Then it's simply over.

The Earth as it was no longer exists.

What remains is fully exposed to space, leaving a not-quite smooth mantle and the crystalline spikes that tower over the rocky surface.

No atmosphere. No oceans. No planet.

An alien base of gargantuan proportions is revealed.

And it waits.

––––––––

"From sea to shining sea," President Nance says, staring at the holographic image of the new Earth floating over the table in the main control room. "God bless America."

"God bless the world," VanderVoort says.

"Praise Jesus and pass the ammo," Director Miles says as he joins the group in the control room. "What? Just trying to lighten the mood."

"The mood is perfectly appropriate as it is, Gordon," Vander-Voort says. "Ms. Morgan? Lu?"

Lu turns in her seat and stares at VanderVoort for a second before her eyes focus.

"What? Oh, sorry," she apologizes and points at her earpiece. "I was listening to the other facilities report in."

"May we all listen?" VanderVoort asks.

"Yes. Of course," Lu says and opens the channel. "This is Australia."

A woman's voice echoes about the room as she reports on the number of people who have been able to take refuge in the Australia facility. Close to four hundred thousand. There are appreciative whistles and comments on the amount.

"Amazing," President Nance says. "These facilities are

incredible."

"They're built to be," Lu says, then instantly goes quiet as the Australian woman reports on the estimates of those who could not be saved.

The math isn't hard. Around four hundred thousand saved out of a total population of about twenty-five million.

President Nance doesn't comment on that number.

Next, Italy reports in. About two hundred thousand. France has five hundred thousand.

Iceland took in a good amount of Northern Europe, as well as many from Canada. Three hundred fifty thousand saved.

Japan reports almost five hundred thousand, with China reporting nearly a million.

Chile is next with three hundred thousand, followed by an astonishing million in Kenya. But Trey has taken over reporting the numbers now, so no one is totally surprised since he could help directly. Then he reports Antarctica's numbers.

"Two million?" President Nance gasps. "Good Lord…"

"We'll want to keep an eye on that," General Azoul says. "Those numbers could be an advantage for them."

"No!" Lu shouts and gets right in General Azoul's face. "There are no sides here. Once we win this fucking battle, Lowell will help us move people around so that the facilities are more balanced and are utilized to their best potential. Each region has different attributes. We have to work together to survive!"

"I think he gets the point, Lu," VanderVoort says. "Don't you, General?"

"I understand the sentiment, yes," General Azoul replies.

VanderVoort shares a look with Lu.

"That'll be all, General," VanderVoort says.

"Excuse me?" General Azoul barks.

"No excuse needed," VanderVoort says. "You are dismissed."

"Ms. VanderVoort, he's the last member of the Joint Chiefs of Staff," President Nance says. "He has every right to be here."

"Charles? Shut the fuck up," VanderVoort says and points at

Lu. "She understands. I now understand. And if you want to apply your years of public service to helping all human beings survive, then I'll assume you understand too. But General Azoul is a man who only understands borders and wars—"

"And we are in a war!" General Azoul shouts.

"Not your kind of war, General," VanderVoort says. "You are dismissed. Now."

General Azoul doesn't move. He stubbornly leans back in his seat and crosses his arms over his chest.

"Lu? Does this facility have a way to get rid of his ass?" VanderVoort asks.

General Azoul's eyes go wide and he stands up immediately.

"Oh, never mind," VanderVoort says. "I think he's getting the picture."

Without another word, General Azoul stomps out of the control room.

"He's the one who's gonna need to be watched," Dr. Hall says and frowns at the looks he gets. "I'm just saying…"

"Can we play back the reports we missed?" VanderVoort asks.

One of the techs assigned to the control room stares at the station in front of him.

"Here," Lu says and waves her hand over a blue square. "Don't think too much about it. The interface sort of intuits what you need."

"Cool," the tech says and nods appreciatively as the reports back up and start from where they left off.

Mexico City managed to save eight hundred thousand.

"And Wyoming?" VanderVoort asks.

"Six hundred thousand," Joan responds from her seat at a station. "We tried."

"We're all fucking tried," VanderVoort says. "And we're lucky we have this many. It's a lot more than we thought would fit. Now for the fun part. Lu?"

"What?" Lu responds.

"What's Lowell's plan?" VanderVoort asks.

"I, uh…" Lu looks about the room at the expectant faces. "I'm not totally sure."

"Which is reasonable considering the circumstances," Vander-Voort says. "But still not an adequate answer. Maybe call him?"

"He might be busy," Lu says.

———

"Yes, I'm fucking busy!" Lowell yells as he and Terrie make their way down a brilliantly white corridor that houses their respective interface rooms. "I'm literally about to launch a fucking kaiju out into a world that not only no longer has water but doesn't even have atmosphere! You want to know what's in my pants right now, Lu? Shit! A fuck ton of shit!"

"The language, Mr. Lowell," Terrie says, but Lowell waves her off.

"Are you getting where I'm coming from, Lu?" Lowell continues. "The bureaucrats will need to suck it up and just wait until everything plays out. Because if we don't win this fucking fight, then what comes next won't fucking matter, will it?"

"You're open wide, Lowell," Lu responds. "Everyone heard you."

"Good!" Lowell shouts. "Then you don't have to repeat it! Hey, everyone! Fucking deal and let me do my job! Cool? Cool!"

Lowell pauses before his specific room and waits.

"Just us," Lu says over the comm. "I told them you hung up and that I have to go pee."

"Do they realize what we're about to do?" Lowell asks. "You gotta tell them, Lu. We may not win this."

"We will win, Mr. Lowell," Terrie says. "God won't abandon us."

"You're assuming God is on our side, lady," Lowell says. "It's a big fucking universe, and maybe he's disappointed in us and that's why we have space kaiju coming to finish the job."

Terrie frowns but doesn't respond.

"Did you just give a religious smackdown to my mother, Lowell?" Lu growls.

Lowell closes his eyes and shakes his head, then opens his eyes and grimaces at Terrie.

"Sorry, Terrie," Lowell says. "Sorry, Lu." He sighs. "Look at what you've turned me into, Lu Morgan. I'm apologizing as I'm about to fight space kaiju."

"That sounds like progress to me," Terrie says. "Now, which one is my room?" She looks up and down the corridor. "Where are the rooms?"

"Mine's here," Lowell says and waves at the wall. A door irises open. "Yours is there."

He hooks a thumb over his shoulder to the opposite wall. Terrie steps up and copies Lowell's movement. A door irises open for her as well.

"Mom? What are you doing?" Lu asks.

"My duty, dear," Terrie says. "No. My calling."

"She's gonna suit up and whup ass with me," Lowell says. "Kyle has control of the Core while we go beat the shit out of some space kaiju."

"Mom, no…" Lu says, but that's all the argument she offers.

Terrie smiles and looks over to Lowell. "We all have our parts to play, remember? Mine is to protect our boy, which is exactly what I'm going to do. Turns out I'll also be protecting not just Kyle, but everyone else who has survived."

"Your mom is pretty badass, Lu," Lowell says. "You're no slouch either, but she's told me a few stories while we got ready for this." Lowell snaps his fingers. "Shit, Terrie, I forgot to tell you you have to go in naked."

"Did you just tell my mother to take her clothes off, Lowell?" Lu shouts.

"When she's alone in the room, Lu," Lowell replies. "Jesus. Calm down. I'm not a perv. She can leave her clothes on the floor for if she gets back."

"When she gets back," Lu insists.

"That's what I meant," Lowell says.

"That's enough talking about me like I'm not here," Terrie says. "Lucinda?"

"Yes, Mom?"

"I love you. Know that always," Terrie says.

"I know, Mom. I love you too," Lu says, her voice cracking.

"We gotta go, Lu," Lowell says. "We'll talk to you when this is all over."

"Good luck," Lu says, and the comm goes quiet.

"You still there, Kyle?" Lowell asks.

"Yeah," Kyle replies quietly.

"You good, kid?" Lowell asks. "Holding it together?"

"I'm not a baby, Lowell," Kyle snaps. "I'm connected too. And I'm getting more and more connected the longer I'm here at the Core. I know what's going down."

"Cool. Just checking," Lowell says, then faces Terrie and smiles. "It was short but meaningful, Terrie. Good luck."

"We can still communicate when we're in the kaiju, right?" Terrie asks, confused.

"Oh, yeah, I forgot," Lowell says. "So much shit in my head…"

"Are you holding it together?" Terrie asks.

"We'll find out, won't we," Lowell says and laughs. Then he steps into his room and the door irises closed behind him.

Lowell strips down and kicks his clothing to the side, then stands in the dead center of the room. He doesn't have to say or think anything for the three walls to turn from white to the glowing orange of the Substance.

Before Lowell can smile, he's no longer in the room.

———

Terrie doesn't strip down immediately. Instead, she kneels in the center of the room, places her hands together, and bows her head.

"Dear Heavenly Father," she says, "please see me through this ordeal You have set before me. I am not asking You to spare my life, for I know that may not be a part of Your plan. All I am humbly asking for is that You allow me to complete my part of Your plan and defeat these demons that are coming to kill the ones I love. I know I always have Your grace, but I pray I also have Your protection for as long as it takes to make sure Your flock is safe."

She takes a deep breath and sighs. Then she removes her clothing and places it all neatly in a pile close to where the door is.

"Amen," she says as she takes her spot and the walls turn Substance-orange.

————

"Welcome back," VanderVoort says as Lu returns to the Wyoming main control room.

Lu gives her a weak smile, then takes her seat.

"It's starting," Lu says and plays at the station for a minute, then spins in her seat and makes a throwing gesture, which brings up a new holographic projection.

"This place is so cool," Dr. Hall mutters.

"It'd be a lot cooler with a bar," Director Miles says.

They are both ignored as the hologram solidifies once again into an image of the Earth.

"We'll take a look at the Core first," Lu says and dials in the image to show where the Core facility sits just above what remains of the mantle. "We should see Lowell in the Quetzalcoatl kaiju and my…mother in the Antarctica kaiju emerge soon."

Lu ignores the pointed and confused stares from most everyone in the room.

"We'll tackle that tidbit later," VanderVoort says, rolling her hand in a get-on-with-it gesture. "How soon are we talking, Lu?"

"Does now work for you?" Lu asks.

The image zooms in closer to show the massive form of Quetzalcoatl climbing out from under the sphere-like facility.

"It really is amazing," Dr. Hall says.

"Giant monsters tend to amaze, Doctor," VanderVoort says.

"No, I mean that we aren't supposed to be afraid of that thing," Dr. Hall says. "It's here to help us, not destroy us."

"Well, yeah, I guess that is amazing," VanderVoort agrees. "Good call."

A second kaiju emerges, and the amazement turns to apprehension at the sight of Antarctica, which most everyone had just watched less than a day ago fight Quetzalcoatl.

"That one has your mother piloting it?" President Nance asks. His voice is calm, even, soothing. "How is she capable of doing that?"

"It's complicated," Lu says. "But she connected to the blue crystal vein with Kyle's assistance. Touching the crystal imparts knowledge or skills or whatever that help a person to attune to the facility. But I think the facility attuned her to being a kaiju pilot."

"So all anyone has to do is touch the crystal?" President Nance asks. "Interesting."

Lu sends a worried look to VanderVoort, but VanderVoort only gives her a blank stare, giving away nothing. Lu really hopes the woman is as worried as she is over President Nance's interest in the blue crystal and is simply hiding the worry behind a poker face.

"Ma'am?" a tech calls.

"Yes?" Lu and VanderVoort reply at the same time.

"Uh…" the tech stammers at the sudden confusion, then continues. "The Africa kaiju is emerging."

"Oh, quick question!" Dr. Hall blurts, his hand shooting into the air. He looks at VanderVoort and quickly drops his hand. "Uh, how are the kaiju getting out of the facilities without depressurizing the kaiju chambers? Or do they just not depressurize?"

Lu blinks then smiles. "Dr. Hall? Have you met Dr. Probst yet?"

"Not in person, no," Dr. Hall says. "I've interacted over the communications system before all the—"

"Hey, Cheryl?" Lu interrupts, calling over the comm. "How are you doing down there?"

"Hey, Lu," Dr. Probst replies. "Everyone is safe down here. Got a little dicey when, well, you know... but stable now."

"Can I send Dr. Hall down to you?" Lu asks. "He has a billion questions I can't answer."

"I don't have time for a billion questions," Dr. Probst protests.

"I'll keep the questions to a minimum if it means I get to see this blue crystal up close," Dr. Hall says, the look on his face like a kid begging a parent for a puppy. "I promise."

"I may join you later," President Nance says. "Once we're safe, of course."

"We'll all go on that field trip, Charles," VanderVoort responds. "Once we're safe, of course."

The two leaders smile at each other. Lu suppresses a shiver and wonders what all has gone down between the two of them before they got to the Wyoming facility.

"Can we see the Africa kaiju?" VanderVoort asks.

Lu dials in the image, spinning it so it shows where the continent of Africa used to be but is now only a crystalline tower jutting up from the empty mantle.

The massive spider-like kaiju crawls out of what had once been Mt. Kilimanjaro. It moves at a speed that only the alien technology can keep up with and, without landmasses or oceans in the way, soon joins Quetzalcoatl and Antarctica as those two move closer to the Australia spire.

"They're big, but are they big enough?" President Nance asks.

No one responds.

"What are they doing?" VanderVoort asks.

Everyone watches as the Africa kaiju spins its webbing into a sort of parachute form. Then it spins a webbed harness around itself and Antarctica as Quetzalcoatl takes to the sky on its own. Africa flings the web parachute toward the encircling shield of

Earth, and it and Antarctica are lifted off the mantle and up into the sky.

"I think I want to stay here now," Dr. Hall says as he turns from the control room's doorway and sits back down, his eyes locked onto the image. "I'll learn about the crystal later."

No one responds to him.

———

Lowell lands Quetzalcoatl on a chunk of floating earth. He doesn't even try to play "What part of the planet did this used to be?" Thinking about what has happened to Earth will be too much of a distraction, and as he rises up onto his back end and stares out into open space, he knows distractions can be deadly.

"We can survive without breathing," Terrie says as Antarctica and Africa land next to Quetzalcoatl. "My Lord, this creature is amazing."

Africa disposes of the webbing, sending it floating out into space in the general direction of Venus.

"It took millions of your Earth years to develop this technology," Trey says. "It is most unfortunate that these marvelous living machines were immediately utilized for warfare purposes."

"It'd have been a lot better for us if they'd just formed a football league instead," Lowell says. "Or hockey. Kaiju hockey would be cool."

No one laughs, not even Lowell.

"They are coming," Trey says after several hours pass.

Despite the amount of time that has passed, it feels like only seconds to the kaiju and their pilots.

Lowell nods Quetzalcoatl's head.

Far off, just beyond the moon, a dot blacker than deep space can be seen.

"I'm not one to wait around," Lowell says. "I say we take the fight to them. You guys with me?"

"Yes," Terrie says.

"A wise strategy," Trey responds.

The three kaiju tense, then leap from the chunk of earth, launching themselves out into open space.

NINETEEN

The dot is, of course, not a dot, but a fully formed orb made of a crystal similar to obsidian but without the shine. This orb is so black it absorbs all light that hits it. Nothing reflects from the surface, all spectrums trapped forever.

The black orb races toward Earth, having left Mars far behind. It's passing the moon when it pulls up short. No deceleration. The orb just stops.

Three shapes are flying up from the broken planet. Large shapes. Dangerous shapes.

Fighting shapes.

There is a quick discussion amongst the orb's occupants, but a conclusion is quickly reached. Without translation, the word would be unpronounceable. With translation, it is easily recognizable.

Kaiju.

The black orb splits down the middle and opens wide.

Inside is not some nebulous, alien nightmare, but a rather mundane-looking docking bay.

Four massive kaiju are secured to the inner surface of the orb by a series of clamps and locks.

One by one, the clamps release and the locks pop open, freeing the huge monsters from the restrictive positions forced on them during their multi-light-year journey.

The orb kaiju shake themselves, loosening their bodies from the kinks and constrictions of travel. Two lift their heads and roar while the other two clamber to the edge of the orb and stare down at the approaching Earth kaiju.

They talk to each other in a language older then Earth itself, commenting on the sad state the planet is in but what good fortune they have since now they only need to conquer the kaiju. The planet itself is ready to be transformed into an outpost with very little terraforming.

Yes, they will need to create a surface atmosphere that their kind can breathe, but Earth is a tiny planet and the generators will have ammonia gas flowing in no time.

The other two orb kaiju join them at the edge and study the Earth kaiju.

One of them says a name and the other three shake their heads or shrug or do whatever their bodies consider a noncommittal answer.

The one that said the name growls. It is looking for the Ebony Man, but even from the distance it stands, it can tell that none of the three Earth kaiju are the prisoner, traitor, spy. The kaiju shakes its enormous head and barks orders to the other three.

There is some slight hesitation at the orders, but it's barely noticeable, and the three other orb kaiju scramble back deeper into the orb, returning with weaponry that's the size of skyscrapers.

There's a bark of contempt from the lead kaiju and the other three return their weaponry. None seem pleased, but they do not hesitate and all four converge on the edge of the orb one last time.

Then they leap, ready to get the battle started.

———

"Holy shit," Lowell says. "Look at those things!"

"This is less than ideal," Trey says. "I know of these kaiju. They are fearsome warriors, having conquered countless planets across the galaxy."

"Well, that fucking sucks," Lowell says.

"What are they?" Terrie asks. "They're so strange looking. Is that one a... tadpole?"

"The one on the far right is Nachaza," Trey says, naming an orb kaiju that is made up of four massive, heavily muscled arms connected to a small torso. The beast has no legs but does have a face in the center of its torso. The face is grinning wide to reveal a mouth full of nothing but sharp canines.

"The one next to it is Grongu," Trey says. "Yes, Terrie, it does look like a tadpole. Just be aware that the mouth holds an infinite number of razor-sharp teeth. It will saw you apart and devour you in a single gulp if given the opportunity. Avoid the teeth."

"Avoid the teeth," Terrie replies. "Sound advice."

"And that one?" Lowell asks. "It looks like Satan's doily. If a doily had a billion barbs all over it and was as large as Long Island."

"Kesil," Trey says. Lowell almost thinks he sees the Africa kaiju shudder.

"I'm guessing it's a lot more dangerous than a doily with a skin condition," Lowell says.

"It will wrap itself around you and slowly dissolve you with radioactive digestive fluids," Trey says.

"So if the gut juices don't kill ya, then the cancer will, huh?" Lowell replies.

"You will not survive to develop cancer," Trey says.

"Yeah, I got that," Lowell says.

"The last one is Isk," Trey says. "It is of a race that has been with the universe since its creation. The oldest of all races."

"Looks like that Lovecraft dildo's Mary Jane monster. You know... Cthulhu. That's it," Lowell says of the one that has two arms, two legs, two wings, and a whole lot of tentacles dangling from its chin. "Lovecraft. That guy. What a racist prick. Did you know he literally named his cat Nig—?"

"I know who Cthulhu is, Lowell," Terrie says. "I'm an educated and widely read woman. Although that type of fiction is not my preference."

"It is possible that some of Isk's race have visited your planet before," Trey says. "They can travel vast distances even without an interstellar orb. They slip through the cracks in reality and appear wherever they desire."

"Then why didn't this one just appear?" Terrie asks.

"The energy it takes would leave it too weak to do battle," Trey says.

"Glad it's rested," Lowell says. "I'd hate for this fight to be unfair. Like, you know, four on three. Oh, wait…"

"You seem to know these kaiju, Trey," Terrie says. "What are their weaknesses?"

"They have none that I am aware of," Trey replies.

"Not even a guess?" Lowell asks.

"At their weaknesses? No," Trey replies. "To guess would be folly. We must fight what we see and what we know."

"Special powers?" Terrie asks as the three Earth kaiju get closer and closer to their foes.

"They do not need them," Trey says. "Teeth and claws are sufficient."

"Don't forget deadly gut juices," Lowell says.

"Yes, but that is not special," Trey says. "It is only anatomy."

"What's our strategy?" Terrie asks. "How do we win this?"

"I am not sure we can," Trey says. "Now that I see who has been sent to defeat and commandeer Earth, I am uncertain of how we survive. The other side has sent their best."

"Have they?" Lowell says. "The problem with the best, Trey, is they get overconfident. The overconfident make mistakes. I'm pretty damn good at taking advantage of mistakes."

"I do hope you are correct, Anson Lowell," Trey says. "If you are not, then the young Kyle Morgan may be Earth's only chance at survival."

"You hear that, kid?" Lowell calls. He waits, but there's no answer. "Shit. I thought we'd be able to communicate."

"I'm here, I'm here," Kyle replies, sounding out of breath. "There was a feedback issue in the interface. The Core kept trying to reroute my thoughts to a section of the facility that's at the very bottom. It's a spike that drives deep into the planet's actual core. But I was able to override and get my thoughts back to you three."

"Oh, dear," Trey says.

"Not liking that," Lowell says.

"Me neither," Terrie says.

"Kyle Morgan, you must follow that route," Trey says. "The Core is telling you there's a problem. You must fix the problem."

"Ten to one the problem is with the defensive shield," Lowell says.

"I believe it is," Trey says. "A solid guess, Anson Lowell."

"Shit will always find fan," Lowell says.

"Is that an old Earth proverb?" Trey asks.

"Yep," Lowell says.

"Kyle, is the shield holding?" Terrie asks.

"Yes," Kyle replies. "It powered up as soon as you three left the land ring. As far as I can tell, it's working perfectly. I don't know how it will hold up to an attack, but everything the Core is telling me is that the shield is fine."

"But?" Terrie asks.

"But I definitely saw an image in my head of a shield failing," Kyle says.

"Then get down there and fix it," Terrie says. "You do what you have to."

"I will," Kyle says.

"And be careful," Terrie says.

"I will, Grandma," Kyle replies with teenage exasperation. "I gotta go. The Core is pushing hard and I can't maintain the connection."

"Go," Terrie says.

All three of them feel Kyle disconnect.

The orb kaiju are close enough that Lowell can easily make out facial expressions. At least on the kaiju with faces. He has no idea what the doily kaiju's mood is. But a quick guess probably puts the mood at kill, kill, kill.

"Strike hard, fast, and don't stop," Lowell says. "It's like being jumped in the yard. You thrash and do whatever you can to cause as much damage to the other person as possible. You do not stop causing damage until you're dead or someone drags you off and restrains you."

"I've seen my share of yard fights, Lowell," Terrie says. "And their aftermath."

"Good, then you know what I'm talking about," Lowell says. "Do that. No mercy. Kill or be killed."

"Kill or they kill the ones we love," Terrie says.

"Love's a little mushy for me, but yeah, whatever motivates your boat," Lowell says.

"I do not understand the idiom," Trey says.

"Neither does Lowell," Terrie says. "Here we go!"

The orb kaiju suddenly spread out, then launch their full attack and rush at the Earth kaiju even faster.

———

"Everybody not named Kyle Morgan or Cheryl Probst should shut the fuck up right now!" Dr. Probst shouts over the clamor that the group of excited, confused, terrified scientists are making as the Core facility's elevator lowers rapidly to the bottom-most level. The scientists quiet down. "Thank you. Kyle?"

"No one touch a thing," Kyle says. "Just stand still and watch. If we need your help, we'll ask for it."

"We're to listen to a teenager?" a short, squat man asks with a sneer.

The elevator comes to a sudden stop and the doors open.

"Get off," Kyle says to the scientist.

"I will do no such thing," the man protests.

"Okay," Kyle says and steps off the elevator and into the corridor. "Come on, Cheryl."

Dr. Probst doesn't even hesitate. After having teleported from facility to facility, not to mention the fact she lives an existence where mile-high monsters are real, following the teenager out of an elevator without explanation is about the most normal thing she can do.

Kyle moves a few meters down the corridor, then waves a hand over the blank wall. A new set of elevator doors appear and open. Kyle steps on. Dr. Probst is right behind him.

Before the doors can close, three of the other scientists race inside, desperate not to be left behind.

The squat man tries to get on as well, but Kyle places a hand against his chest and shoves him across the corridor.

"Teenager says no," Kyle says, smiling at the rage on the man's face as the doors close.

Dr. Probst opens her laptop and balances it on one hand as the elevator descends once again. But instead of the screen lighting up, a holographic image appears above the keyboard. The Core facility was able to make some alterations to her computer, and she is very pleased with the results.

"This is amazing," Dr. Probst says, studying the image of the part of the Core they're descending toward. "We'll be almost dead center inside the Earth."

"How is that possible?' a woman asks. "Nothing can survive that kind of heat and pressure."

"Nothing from this planet, maybe," Dr. Probst replies. "Please, everyone, try to stop being so Earth-centric, okay? If I have to remind you that the rules don't apply anymore every time something new and unusual pops up, then we'll never get anything done."

"Yeah, you don't want me to kick you off this elevator now that we've left the facility," Kyle says, nodding at the image hovering over Dr. Probst's computer. "No more corridors left. Just magma."

"The Earth's core is actually made up of—" a man starts to say but stops when he sees the looks on Dr. Probst's and Kyle's faces.

"So, Kyle, what is the Core telling you to do?" Dr. Probst asks.

"I'm not sure," Kyle says. He closes his eyes. "I know it's about defenses."

"So it *is* the shield," Dr. Probst says.

His eyes still closed, Kyle shakes his head.

"I don't know," Kyle says. "I keep getting flashes of fighting and war. Then I see a shield covering some old planet, not Earth, followed by the shield collapsing."

"That doesn't sound good," Dr. Probst says.

"It isn't our planet," Kyle says. "It's just an example of something that already happened to a different planet."

"Keep working it out," Dr. Probst says. "I'll help however I can."

"As will we," one of the three scientists says.

"No, you'll stay back and zip your lips," Dr. Probst says. "How was I not clear on that?"

The scientists shuffle their feet awkwardly but don't argue.

The elevator stops and the doors open.

Two of the three scientists squeal like frightened toddlers. The third faints and collapses onto the elevator floor.

"This isn't about the shield," Kyle says as he steps out into an atrium the size of the Roman coliseum. The Earth's actual core swirls and flows around the atrium but doesn't penetrate the structure.

"Nope," Dr. Probst agrees. "What are they?"

Kyle closes his eyes once more.

Lining the atrium are half a dozen stasis pods. Stasis pods that hold twenty-five-foot aliens. They look nothing like Trey. Each one is identical and closer in approximation to a bullfrog. If bullfrogs were nearly ten meters tall, wore thick, dark brown robes cinched at the waist with cords made of pure energy, and had four arms and four legs.

"Kyle?" Dr. Probst asks when Kyle doesn't open his eyes.

She waits, but Kyle doesn't respond.

She reaches out and touches his shoulder. Kyle's eyes snap open.

"What did you see?" Dr. Probst asks. "What are we supposed to do here?"

Kyle takes a deep breath and shakes his head, then stares at the huge aliens.

"We're supposed to wake them up," Kyle says.

"Oh… goody," Dr. Probst replies.

———

While Lowell knows that the Isk kaiju is probably the ringleader and he should go straight for that bastard so he can chop the proverbial head off the proverbial snake, Lowell's time in prison taught him that you always go for the biggest guy first. Drop that son of a bitch, and everyone else starts to second-guess their role in the fight.

Not that Lowell thinks any of the orb kaiju will second-guess their attack on Earth. They came all this way, after all.

But prison training is hard to let go of, and the strategy always served him well before.

So he gives a tilt to his right wing, feeling the solar winds under his feathers, and aims for the four-armed Nachaza freak. The kaiju is the largest of the four, but the truth is Lowell really, really just wants to punch that ugly torso face.

"Do not let it grapple with you!" Trey warns, his kaiju aimed for the Grongu tadpole kaiju. "Its strength is unbreakable!"

"Now you tell me!" Lowell shouts just before he's in reach of the orb kaiju.

Nachaza roars and swipes at Quetzalcoatl with all four fists.

Lowell barely flies out of the way of the quad-strike, diving down under the kaiju and around to face its back.

Sort of.

"The motherfucker has a mouth on this side too!" Lowell yells. "What the holy fuck?"

Then a thought hits Lowell. A foreign thought from outside his mind.

"Shit," Lowell says. "I heard it roar. Did you all hear it roar too?"

"We can hear you banter, Earthling," a voice echoes inside Lowell's head. "Your pitiful, secret strategies are not secret."

"Oh dear," Terrie says and ducks her kaiju under a swipe from Isk's spiked tail.

"While I applaud your instant grasp of our language," Lowell says, "I have to deduct points on gameplay. You probably should have stayed silent about hearing us talk. That would have been a serious advantage."

"We do not need an advantage," Kesil hisses. "You are inferior foes. We will play with you until bored, then kill and devour you."

"Cocky much?" Lowell replies.

Nachaza spins like a dervish, all four arms extended to their full lengths, and flies straight for Lowell. He tries to get out of the way, but the orb kaiju moves way faster than he anticipates and Lowell finds himself being pummeled repeatedly by the whirling fists.

Then exactly what he needs to avoid happens. The four arms wrap themselves around Quetzalcoatl, pinning its wings to its body, immobilizing Lowell and his kaiju.

"Fuck!" he shouts.

The orb kaiju all laugh.

"Bunch of smug assholes," Lowell growls.

"Focus!" Trey yells.

Lowell has a few choice responses ready, but he doesn't get time to shout them as he feels Quetzalcoatl's body start to crack under the pressure of Nachaza's strength.

"Unbreakable?" Lowell thinks. "Nothing is unbreakable."

Pain radiates up and down the length of his kaiju and he winces inside, suffering along with it.

Nachaza squeezes harder and Lowell starts to panic. He tries snapping and biting at the Nachaza, but the orb kaiju has perfect position, its arms just out of jaw reach. And with no head, there's nothing sticking out for Lowell to focus on.

More pain shoots through Quetzalcoatl, streaking from its snout to the tip of its tail.

A thought occurs to Lowell. It's not a pleasant thought. Certainly not one that will keep him from being harmed. But sometimes you have to push through the pain to get the win.

"Nachaza, right?" Lowell gasps.

"Quiet, pig," Nachaza replies. "Let me enjoy your death in silence."

"Yeah, silence isn't my thing," Lowell says, feeling what might be about a dozen ribs start to crack. "Oh. Damn. Ow." He takes a deep mental breath. "So, where do those mouths go?"

To Lowell's surprise, the pressure eases up.

Nachaza is easy to distract. All brawn, not so much brain.

"Do you have a giant kaiju asshole?" Lowell asks. "An alien sphincter that is air tight so you can fly around space without leaving a trail of kaiju pellets behind you?"

The pressure returns, increasing considerably.

"You would be called a funny guy in your language," Nachaza states. "Is death funny to you?"

"Depends on whose death it is," Lowell replies and gasps even harder. Shit is hurting bad. "So, about that poop chute of yours? It's not, like, one of your mouths, is it?"

"You are ignorant," Nachaza says. "We absorb all we eat. We do not defecate like you primitives."

"That's a relief," Lowell says. "For a second there, I thought I was going to have to shove this up your ass."

The pressure increases.

"But… I'll… do… this… instead," Lowell barely manages to say right before he whips Quetzalcoatl's tail up and jams it inside the mouth on Nachaza's opposite side.

"Ha!" Nachaza cries. "I have two mouths, you fool! You will now lose that—"

The end of Quetzalcoatl's tail explodes out of the mouth facing Lowell, spraying flesh and blood all over both kaiju. Nachaza's grip loosens immediately.

"What goes in, always comes out," Lowell says, then flexes as hard as he can, breaking Nachaza's grip on Quetzalcoatl. Lowell also screams a little as broken ribs grind against each other.

Nachaza floats limply out into open space, its body leaking fluids everywhere in a gory trail of blood and guts.

"Nachaza!" Kesil cries, then turns its attention on Lowell. "You will pay for that, slug!"

"Slug? Bitch look at these feathers!" Lowell yells. "I'm pretty as fuck!"

"No more restraint," Isk says. "Kill them now. Be quick and erase the shame of Nachaza's death."

"Bring it, bitches!" Lowell yells.

"Lowell!" Terrie snaps. "Stop taunting them!"

Lowell doesn't get the chance to respond as Grongu dives at him, then turns around suddenly before impact and gives Quetzalcoatl a hard smack with its huge, flat tail. Quetzalcoatl tumbles across open space until it slams into the surface of the moon.

"One giant leap…" Lowell gasps. "Christ…"

With excruciating pain, Lowell wriggles Quetzalcoatl up onto its tail end and is able to dive to the side before Grongu's direct attack smears him across the moon's surface. The orb kaiju skids through the lunar dust for a couple of kilometers before coming to a stop.

"Flee all you want, bird snake!" Grongu shouts. "You cannot escape my teeth!"

"Or your breath," Lowell responds and waves a wing. "I can smell that fish funk from here, man!"

"Lowell!" Trey yells. "Focus!"

Lowell's sarcastic response is turned to one of alarm as he sees that the Africa kaiju is unable to avoid Kesil's swift attack from behind.

"TREY!" Lowell shouts before having to duck under another of Grongu's tail swipes. "Terrie! Help him!"

"I'll try!" Terrie yells, diving under Isk's attack with its spiked tail.

Pain erupts from Lowell's left wing and he sees blood spurt in a slow, low gravity spray away from him. Without thinking, acting only on Quetzalcoatl's instinct, Lowell whips his head down and bites into Grongu's skull as the orb kaiju chomps down even harder on his wing.

Both kaijus roar in agony as teeth press deeper and harder into kaiju flesh, neither willing to let go and attempt escape.

Lowell barely registers Trey's screams as Kesil begins to dissolve and devour the Africa kaiju. He only has time to register two things: his wing being torn off and sent floating out into space, and the satisfying crunch as Quetzalcoatl's jaw crushes Grongu's skull.

For a brief, peaceful second, Lowell savors the win. Then the agony of his severed wing and the continuing screams from Trey slam him back to the now. Once more, Quetzalcoatl's instinct takes over and suddenly a massive burst of plasma energy streams from the kaiju's mouth, washing over the nub that was once a majestic wing. Flesh sears and cauterizes even in the almost zero atmosphere of the moon.

"Looks like Mr. Licorice was wrong," Lowell says. "Q's got a gun."

Unable to accurately maneuver without both wings, Lowell reverts to his prison skills again and assesses the situation. It helps he now has some serious firepower.

Trey is wrapped in Kesil's death hug while Terrie is barely avoiding Isk's constant attacks. The leader of the orb kaiju has

Antarctica on the permanent defensive, a position Lowell knows only delays inevitable defeat.

This is gonna suck so hard, Lowell thinks, then coils Quetzalcoatl's body into a tight spring.

He launches directly at the spot where he anticipates Terrie to be. Despite her decades of combat training, even Lowell can spot her patterns. He just hopes she keeps to the pattern for just a moment longer.

An Isk claw comes dangerously close to decapitating Quetzalcoatl, but Lowell manages to dip his head just in time. He shoots past Isk and collides directly into Antarctica.

"Terrie! Spread those scales!" Lowell shouts as he shoves away from Antarctica. "All of them! NOW!"

Terrie doesn't question the order and pops every single sharpened scale into an extended position. The sunlight glints off the edges, and Lowell smiles right before Antarctica slams into Kesil and Trey.

The orb kaiju screeches and begins to thrash, its body suddenly receiving a hundred mortal gashes from Antarctica's scales. Fluids of all kinds drift and swirl across space, and the Africa kaiju is quickly free from Kesil's death wrap.

"YOU!" Isk roars, and Lowell is yanked backward by a claw to the back of Quetzalcoatl's neck.

Lowell thrashes against the grip, but his focus and attention are on the Africa kaiju, which floats limply down to the chunks of Earth and the defensive shield.

"Trey! Eject!" Lowell yells. "Get back to the facility before your kaiju dies!"

Lowell has no idea if Trey is conscious and hears his cry or if the alien ally is already dead from Kesil's attack. All he sees is the multi-limbed kaiju collide with a part of the defense shield and start to burn up.

"Trey!" Lowell yells again, but then he's forced to focus on himself as Isk rears back its arm and tosses Lowell out and away from the fight.

Suddenly, Lowell is tumbling tail over snout directly toward the sun. Which he decides is not a good direction to be going in, considering the end result would be a very fiery death. He desperately forces his remaining wing to somehow stabilize Quetzalcoatl's body and stop the tumbling.

Lowell manages to get stabilized, which he's more than relieved about, but he isn't strong enough stop his progress, and Quetzalcoatl continues to float quickly away from the fight.

And from what Lowell can see, it isn't much of a fight.

As Kesil's leaking body collides against the shield almost directly on the burning Africa, Terrie is able to twist her kaiju so that Antarctica lands on a good-sized chunk of Earth. She regroups and launches herself up at Isk, but Lowell quickly sees she's made a huge mistake.

Even with the sharpened scales protecting her kaiju's body, Terrie has left herself wide open. From the body language she projects, Lowell can see she's entirely focused on colliding with Isk and turning the space brawl from a one-two punch affair to a grapple fight, hoping to utilize Antarctica's massive muscles against the orb kaiju leader.

Except Lowell knows Isk sees the move as well and is already countering.

"Terrie! Put your fists up!" Lowell screams. "Terrie!"

But he's too late, and so is Terrie.

With combat experience older than the destroyed planet they fight above, Isk doesn't even hesitate. The orb kaiju flaps its wings, twists out of the way, and brings up its spiked tail directly into Terrie's face—the one part of Antarctica that isn't protected by scales.

A bulge appears at the back of Antarctica's skull, and Lowell doesn't need to see the tail emerge to know it's done its job.

Antarctica goes limp and slack around the tail.

"Terrie..." Lowell whispers. He gets no response and doesn't expect one.

Isk flicks the dead kaiju off its tail like it's a squashed bug.

Which, Lowell thinks, to the ancient kaiju, it probably isn't even that significant.

"You're a dead hunk of sci-fi horror bullshit, you squid-faced cunt!" Lowell yells.

But either he's too far away or the orb kaiju is ignoring him, because he receives no hint of a response or indication Isk even heard him.

Lowell turns his head to see that instead of heading for the sun, he's aimed directly for the permanent shadow of Mercury's dark side. A few calculations later, and Lowell expects his impact to be in about fifty to sixty days.

Everyone he's come to care for will be dead long before that.

He needs a new plan.

"Can't fly," Lowell thinks. An image slams into his mind. "Really, Q? Hold the fuck on."

Lowell squirms about and reverses his position so that his head faces Mercury and his tail is aimed for what's left of Earth. He straightens out, his eyes going wide from the pain in his ribs and other assorted areas of the kaiju's body, opens his mouth, and to his surprise, unleashes a burst of plasma.

"I really wish you came with a manual, Q," Lowell thinks. "Could have used some plasma before, you know."

The burst of pure energy does the trick, acting like a rocket engine, and launches Lowell away from his date with Mercury and once more into the fight.

Backward.

Lowell pictures the entire scene and runs more calculations in his head. He'll be close to Isk's last position in only a few seconds. Only problem is, he won't be able to see Isk until the very last moment when he can risk whipping around face forward again without losing his momentum.

But Lowell's calculations are for nothing as he feels claws grip his tail. He's suddenly spinning in a wide circle as Isk rotates over and over again.

The Earth. The moon. The sun. Open space.

All of it is a carousel of images as Quetzalcoatl is whirled around and around.

Then the view is only of Earth, and Lowell knows he's about to find out what it feels like to slam into Earth's new defensive shield.

It isn't pleasant.

"Fuck me!" Lowell roars as fire erupts throughout Quetzal-coatl's body.

He's like an earthworm wriggling on summer pavement, and there's nothing he can do about it. Off to his right are Africa's and Kesil's bodies, both still smoldering and smoking.

Despite his predicament and the agony it brings, Lowell notices that the shield is obviously weakening due to the constant surges of energy produced by the burning kaiju.

"Shit," Lowell thinks.

Then he doesn't have time for more thoughts as he's plucked from his part of the shield and whipped away by his tail.

"You will prove yourself useful, insect," Isk says, whipping Lowell over his head right before slamming him down on top of the other two kaiju bodies.

If space had atmosphere, Lowell would gasp all of it in as Quetzalcoatl collides with the burning kaiju. Pain is a constant eruption, and Lowell is fairly sure something important inside his kaiju has broken. He has no doubt that the Core facility can repair Quetzalcoatl, but he also has no doubt he's in no position to think he'll live that long.

Lowell is whipped back up, then slammed down onto the burning kaiju again and again.

There is a sound like a thunderclap, and even in space, Lowell's kaiju ears ring from the noise.

A noise which signifies the end of Earth's defensive shield.

Lowell's first thought as he tumbles past hunks of the planet, aimed for the surface below, is that the defensive shield really isn't all that if it can be short-circuited by a couple kaiju corpses and some body slams by Quetzalcoatl.

His second thought is how disappointed in himself he is. He thought he could do it. He honestly thought he could pilot a kaiju up into space and whup some alien kaiju ass. He really believed he could do it.

His third thought is about the people he now considers friends, and even possibly family, after all the shit they've been through together. He's obviously the black sheep of the family, but still, it hurts to know he's let them down too.

His fourth thought is a resounding "OW!" as he impacts against the surface of the planet.

Isk lands right next to him, the orb kaiju's feet touching down with an ease that really, really ticks Lowell off.

"Still… gonna… beat… your… ass," Lowell grunts. "Bitch…"

"Poor little worm," Isk says. "There was talk of this kaiju waiting on this planet, and I had hoped it would have been an admirable foe. Perhaps with an experienced pilot it would have been. Unfortunately, all that could be provided was you."

"Blah blah… fuckity blah," Lowell replies. "Just fucking kill me and get it over with."

"Kill you?" Isk laughs, and it is like nails being shoved deep inside Lowell's skull. "Not yet, little bird. You are needed still."

"Fuck… you," Lowell gasps as Isk drags Quetzalcoatl across the landscape, directly for the Core facility spire.

"Your curses have no effect on me," Isk says. "The translation is meaningless."

"I could… describe… the act," Lowell says.

"Silence is preferred," Isk says and bashes a fist into the top of Quetzalcoatl's head, which achieves the desired effect. Lowell groans and goes quiet, his mind a swirling mass of confusion and disorientation.

Then he feels himself being lifted into the air and his eyelids are yanked open. Lowell is staring directly at the entrance to the Core facility's kaiju chamber.

"Command it to open," Isk orders.

"No," Lowell manages to say. That one syllable takes all of his effort.

"Command it and I will make the last seconds of your friend's lives mercifully short," Isk says. "Defy me and they will be tortured for eternity. That is not hyperbole. My kind have the ability to make pain last forever."

"Lowell," Kyle's voice says. "Don't respond. He can't hear me. Only you can."

Lowell barely shakes his head.

"No?" Isk responds. "A wrong choice, but one that merely slows me down. It does not stop me."

"Nod," Kyle says. "Show him you're opening the Core. We need him confident."

Lowell musters the strength and switches his motion from a shake to a nod.

"A change of heart," Isk says. "Sentimental fool. I'll torture your friends anyway. I enjoy doing that."

The Core facility irises open and Isk moves in close but is suddenly sent flying backward across the surface of the planet, covered in half a dozen smaller kaiju.

Unfortunately for Lowell, Isk's grip remains on Quetzalcoatl, and he's wrapped up with the surprise melee, every part of his body bouncing and ricocheting off the planet's surface.

"Mother… fucker," he gasps as the tumbling fight comes to a halt.

Lowell isn't sure what he's seeing, but if he has to guess, his guess would be he's watching a Cthulhu motherfucker get its ass beat by six weasels. He blinks, which is an excruciating event in of itself, and takes another pained look.

Yep. Six really pissed-off weasels are swarming over Isk, biting, scratching and tearing into the orb kaiju's flesh, sending ribbons of skin and muscles flying up into the air, preceded by a mist of alien blood.

Isk roars and struggles against the weasel kaiju and manages to disengage one and tosses it to the ground, stomping on its head before it can attack again. But that's all the progress Isk can make before it's brought to its knees and claws.

"There will be more coming," Isk says.

Lowell struggles to force Quetzalcoatl to slide closer until Isk is within tail reach.

"I'm… sure… there will… be," Lowell gasps and manages to raise Quetzalcoatl's tail over his head. "But at least… you'll be… dead."

Quetzalcoatl's tail strikes Isk's head, piercing an eye and shooting deep into the kaiju's brain. For a moment, Lowell panics and worries that Isk's brain is in its ass instead of its head, but he soon sees Isk's life drain away. He withdraws the tail and the orb kaiju collapses onto its face, dead.

The weasel kaiju clamber away, dragging the corpse of their fallen comrade with them, then form a circle. Lowell hears chanting just before the five standing kaiju and single fallen one explode into flames.

"Kyle?" Lowell calls, watching the kaiju immolation with a stunned and shocked mind. "What the… actual fuck?"

"Can you get inside the facility?" Kyle asks.

"Can you… go… fuck… yourself?" Lowell responds as he lies Quetzalcoatl down with zero intention of moving ever again.

"No problem," Kyle says. "Eject and I'll see what I can do from here."

"Kyle… Terrie didn't—" Lowell starts to say.

"We know, Lowell," Kyle replies. "We know. Trey made it though. And you."

There's a hitch in Kyle's voice, and Lowell is surprised to find himself choked up.

"I'm sorry," Lowell whispers.

"Just get inside," Kyle responds. "It's over."

For now, Lowell thinks. *For now…*

TWENTY

A week of mourning is declared across the facilities, not that anyone has time to mourn as they try to make sense of their new realities.

With 7.5 million survivors spread out haphazardly across twelve facilities, the focus instantly becomes organization and disbursement so that the larger facilities take on as many people as they can, easing the burden on the smaller facilities.

Water doesn't seem to be an issue, but food resources and future production plans quickly take on an air of desperation, despite Trey insisting that the facilities will be able to provide all basic needs, including food.

Fear hangs over the facilities like a net ready to drop and tangle what's left of humanity into a ball of fighting, scrambling animals.

Yet, despite the constant need to be productive and solve all the problems at once, a few survivors are able to take a moment and give one of their own a proper send-off.

Lowell stands just outside the doors to the Substance atrium, ready to enter and pay his respects, but pauses when he sees Dr. Probst hurry by the end of the corridor.

"Cheryl!" Lowell shouts.

Dr. Probst backs up and gives Lowell a wave, then disappears again.

"Cheryl! Wait!" Lowell shouts and heads her way.

"What is it, Lowell?" Dr. Probst asks, not unkindly. "I'm extremely busy and—"

"You're not going to Terrie Morgan's memorial service?" Lowell asks.

"I wasn't planning on it," Dr. Probst replies. "I assumed it was for family only."

"But you got Lu's invitation, right?" Lowell asks.

"I did, yes, but it just doesn't feel right," Dr. Probst says. "I really didn't know Terrie."

"I didn't either," Lowell says. "But I sure as fuck got to know her family and what she meant to them. You've spent as much time with Lu, Kyle, and Bolton as I have. You should really be at the memorial."

"I don't know…" Dr. Probst says.

"Yes, you do," Lowell responds. "Memorials are about the living, not the dead. Come on."

Lowell takes Dr. Probst by the elbow and steers her back to the atrium doors. She resists at first, but gives in and allows Lowell to drag her inside once the doors iris open.

"This place leaves me in awe," Dr. Probst says as they enter the huge space. She looks about and frowns. "It's empty. Why aren't there more people here?"

"Kyle made it known that the atrium is off-limits for the next hour," Lowell says. "Folks are learning to listen to Kyle when it comes to the Core facility."

Dr. Probst leans in and whispers, "Should we be worried? I love Kyle, but he's only a teenager. Can he handle the responsibility now that the Core has chosen him?"

"Jesus Christ, Cheryl," Lowell says with a laugh. "How many adults can you name right now that you'd rather have controlling the Core?"

Dr. Probst pauses and thinks.

"Exactly," Lowell says before she can answer. "Not a mother-fucking one."

"I wouldn't say that," Dr. Probst says.

"Bull and shit," Lowell says with a laugh. "VanderVoort is alright simply because she's an insane badass, but the rest? Fuck that. Plus, the Core hasn't reached out to anyone else. Kyle was picked and it's his fucking burden to bear. We just have to help him."

Dr. Probst regards Lowell for a long time. Long enough that he starts to fidget and get nervous.

"Are you going to eat me or something?" Lowell asks.

"No," Dr. Probst replies with exasperation. "I was just thinking about how much you've grown since I first met you. You've become a leader, Lowell. And you even seem to have gathered a little wisdom along the way."

"Don't get all 'very special episode' on me, Cheryl," Lowell says. "I'm still a hardened criminal and murderer. Can't erase the past."

"No, but I'd say recent events, you know, like saving the planet, may have changed people's perception of you," Dr. Probst says. "Plus, millions of people don't have a clue about your past, they only know your present."

"Oh? And what is my present?" Lowell asks with a sneer.

"Hero," Dr. Probst says.

"Hey! You two!" a voice cries from the top-most catwalk ringing the atrium before Lowell can respond. "Get your asses up here!"

"On our way!" Lowell shouts.

"Are we climbing all the way up there?" Dr. Probst asks.

"No," Lowell says, then gestures toward the atrium wall.

Again, he takes Dr. Probst by the elbow and guides her to a small platform. He steps on with her and the platform instantly begins to rise. The movement is so smooth that neither of them lurch or feel jostled. Although both would like maybe at the very least a handrail encompassing the platform. The open-air vibe is a bit much, especially once at the top.

Lu greets them at the edge of the catwalk, giving both big hugs.

"Thanks for coming," she says. "Kyle says you two were worried you shouldn't be here because you aren't family. Which is bullshit. You are. There are very few people I trust now, and the two of you made the cut."

"Well, do I feel fucking privileged or what?" Lowell says, then stops. "Wait... Kyle was listening?" Lowell turns to Dr. Probst. "I take it all back. The boy must be stopped."

"Ha ha," Lu says. "I asked him where you were and he found you outside the atrium. He wasn't trying to snoop, but he can't really help it."

"Oh, I get it," Lowell says. "Trust me. Which it sounds like you do! Nice. The marshal and the con getting along at last."

"Don't be a dick, Lowell," Lu says. "My mother did just die."

"I know," Lowell says. "I was there."

They stand in uncomfortable silence.

"What's going on over there?" Bolton shouts from the spot on the catwalk where Kyle, Krissy, Tony, and Biscuit wait.

"I'm just killing the mood!" Lowell shouts back. "You know, because I'm a killer!"

"Asshole," Lu says, but there's a small smile playing at her lips. She punches Lowell in the chest. "Come on, shithead."

"Don't call Cheryl a shithead," Lowell says.

"Can I choose a different family?" Dr. Probst asks.

"Nope," Lowell says as Lu leads them to the group. "You're stuck with our asses."

"Yay..." she says and twirls a finger in the air.

Everyone nods to each other, then all eyes turn to Kyle.

"You called for this memorial," Bolton says to Kyle. "It's your show... Son."

Kyle shuffles uncomfortably, whether at having to lead the

memorial or at Bolton's use of the word "son" is unclear, but after a few seconds he nods and begins.

"I was raised by my grandma," Kyle says. "Mom was around when she could be, and I now understand more about the reasons she was gone so much, but it was really my grandma and Stephie that made sure I was clothed, fed, and got all the love a boy could want." He smiled. "Sometimes a lot more than I wanted."

Everyone smiles. Kyle takes a deep breath.

"I thought losing her would be harder, but in a weird way, I already lost her once," Kyle continues. "I thought that Linder guy had killed her and Biscuit back in Montana, and it nearly killed me too. If I hadn't been so angry at that man, I don't think I would have made it."

At the mention of his name, Biscuit lets out a low whine and lays his head down on the catwalk.

"Jesus, dog," Lowell mutters and wipes at his eyes.

"There's so much I can say about my grandma, about Terrie Morgan," Kyle says. "But there's only thing that needs to be said, because I want God, the universe, and any of those aliens out there that might be listening to know that she was a hero. A hero to me, a hero to those she met along the way, and a hero who gave her life to save everyone from extinction."

Krissy sniffles loudly, and Tony hesitates then puts a hand on her arm. They aren't the only ones sniffling, crying, and comforting. The whole group moves closer together in remembrance of Terrie Morgan.

"If I can take one lesson from my grandma, it's this," Kyle says, "Be honest with yourself and always do the right thing, even if it means making the ultimate sacrifice."

Lowell notices a worried glance shared between Lu and Bolton, catches their eye, and gives them a confident smile. He knows the kid is going to be fine. He has a strong family to support him and an alien facility that will do everything it can to keep him from failing. Not bad for a kid who hasn't even graduated high school.

Plus, and Lowell is pretty sure Kyle knows this, there's something called the "staff" waiting in the wings. Whatever that is…

"The last thing I want to say is to all of you," Kyle says and turns to everyone standing around him. He clears his throat. "I have no idea what's coming for us. I don't think the Core even knows. But what I do know is that with the lessons my grandma taught me, and with your help, we'll be able to do our very best to keep everyone alive and thriving. Like my grandma, I have faith in that."

"Jesus, kid," Lowell mutters and flicks the tears away that stream down his face. "I'm the tough guy here. You're not helping my image."

"No one's fooled, Lowell," Bolton says, dealing with his own stream of tears. "We all know you're a soft touch."

"Bite me, Sergeant Slaughter," Lowell says with a smile. A smile returned by Bolton.

"May I?" Tony asks.

There are puzzled looks, but Kyle nods and steps back. Tony steps forward.

He looks out at the atrium, then up at the Substance that glows down upon them.

Several seconds go by and Tony says nothing, then he nods and says, "Thank you, Terrie Morgan. Thank you very much."

Krissy loses it and starts sobbing, which pretty much sets off a group sobbing jag. Biscuit joins in with a long, mournful howl.

Then a loud beeping interrupts the emotional tsunami and all eyes turn to Dr. Probst.

"Really, Cheryl?" Lowell says, grinning.

"Sorry, sorry," she says and pulls a small radio from her pocket. She wipes her eyes, clears her throat, and answers the beeping. "This is Dr. Probst."

"Hey, Dr. Probst, Dr. Hall here," Dr. Hall calls over the radio. "I have Trey with me and we were wondering if you and Lowell could join us in the main kaiju chamber."

"Isn't this the main kaiju chamber?" Dr. Probst whispers to Lowell.

"They can't hear you unless you press the button," Lowell says.

"Fuck off," Dr. Probst says.

"This is the Substance atrium, which can be used to house..." Lowell stops talking and holds out his hand. Dr. Probst gives him the radio. "We'll be right down, dude."

"Oh, hi, Lowell," Dr. Hall says. "Um, good. Thanks. See you soon."

Lowell gives Dr. Probst the radio back and faces everyone else.

"Duty calls," he says, then lowers his chin to his chest and shakes his head. "I sound like Bolton. Shoot me."

"Shoot to kill or just shoot to wound?" Bolton asks.

"The jokes!" Lowell exclaims. "Now he's trying to sound like me. Maybe the Core had us switch bodies without our knowing."

"That isn't funny," Lu says.

"Tell me about it," Lowell says. "Cheryl? Let's go chat with the über-nerd and the alien, shall we?"

"That's where I was originally heading..." Dr. Probst sighs. "Never mind. Let's go."

There are hugs of varying degrees all around. Awkward ones, desperate ones, and knowing ones. Lowell is surprised at how easily he accepts all of them. He truly never thought he'd ever feel connections to people again.

He just hopes those connections will last. Now that he has them, he's loathe to give them up.

———

"Okay, so what you're saying is that we can make any kaiju we want?" Dr. Hall asks as he, Lowell, Trey, and Dr. Probst stand on a platform and look out at a single kaiju, Quetzalcoatl, which is secured against the chamber's wall. "Like, any kind?"

"He said any kind, dude," Lowell says. "Keep up."

"Don't be a dick, Lowell," Dr. Probst says. "This is a lot to take in for anyone, especially anyone on the periphery like Dr. Hall here."

"I don't know if I've been on the periphery," Dr. Hall complains. "I was in the White House's underground Situation Room, where I was an integral part of coordinating—"

"Dude, unless you were busy fighting for your life every single fucking moment, then you were on the periphery, like Cheryl says," Lowell snaps.

"I killed a man," Dr. Hall says. "Not personally, but it was my fault he died. And I watched men and women die around me."

"Well… shit," Lowell says.

"I believe the word in your language is awkward," Trey says. "May we continue to discuss the process for creating new kaiju? Having our offenses and defenses ready to go will be integral to our survival."

"Defenses!" Dr. Probst exclaims, then cringes. "Sorry. That was loud. I just meant to ask about those other kaiju. The small ones that helped rescue Lowell."

"Hey, Quetzalcoatl and I didn't need rescuing," Lowell protests. "We had it under control."

"Human attempts at humor are puzzling," Trey says. "But to address your inquiry, Dr. Probst, the smaller kaiju were a last-resort defense. The pilots were clones with a lifespan only as long as their services are needed. The same with the small kaiju they piloted. Once the mission was completed, they returned to the molecular framework that is the universe."

"One and dones," Lowell says. "Weasels go poof."

"Badgers," Dr. Hall says. "Yes, they were in the weasel family, but from what I could see on the hologram footage, they were closer to badgers than simple weasels."

"Oh, you're going to be lots of fun to work with," Lowell replies.

"How soon can we get started on making more kaiju?" Dr. Probst asks.

"Currently, the Core facility has six thousand different templates ready for use," Trey says. "However, the majority of those may not be suitable to this planet's new makeup and environment, nor would they handle the rigors of open space."

"Let's not use those," Lowell says. "We ain't got time for wussy kaiju."

"I am unfamiliar with that word," Trey says. "But, when narrowed down to only kaiju that can accomplish all that we need of them, eighty-five templates remain."

"Sweet," Lowell says. "That's still some good variety to choose from."

"Does this facility have the resources to make eighty-five different kaiju?" Dr. Probst asks.

"This chamber can make a dozen kaiju, right?" Dr. Hall asks. "And, if I'm not mistaken, new kaiju chambers are already being built?"

"Told ya," Lowell says to Dr. Probst.

"Shut up," Dr. Probst responds. "No, what I mean is that matter is finite. Does the Core facility have the materials needed to actually build new kaiju while also sustaining all the lives that are slowly, but surely, moving here?"

"You're asking if we can both eat and fight," Lowell says.

"Pretty much," Dr. Probst says.

Trey, with his many eyes, looks annoyed.

"I have expressed to all of you that the Core facility will provide everything we need," he says and points up to the Substance. "It is finite, too, but it would take the entire population of this planet trillions of years to deplete the Substance to a point where you would need to worry. Your sun will devour this galaxy long before that."

"Good to know," Lowell says. "Cheryl? You cool?"

"I am cool, Lowell," Dr. Probst says. "So… what now?"

"Now, we work," Trey says. "Dr. Hall is a zoologist and cryptozoologist, so his knowledge will be invaluable in the creation of appropriate kaiju."

"I'm also an ethnobotanist, anthropologist, as well as a xenoarcheologist and senior researcher and fellow at SETI," Dr. Hall says.

Lowell gives him a slow clap then says, "How's SETI doing these days? Any progress on discovering intelligent life out in the cosmos?"

Dr. Probst snorts.

"Humans are tiresome," Trey says with a long, alien sigh.

"I believe my expertise in geology will come in handy with the BCCN, as well as the Substance," Dr. Probst says. "As far as I know, I'm the only human expert on those subjects, right?"

"Correct," Trey says. "And also correct that your expertise will be handy, as you say. My knowledge is considerably more than all humans' combined, but I am still not an expert on all things Substance or BCCN. My role was to wait and pilot the Africa kaiju when the time came. Ideally, I would not have been needed and would have slumbered for eons, but the Ebony Man interrupted that slumber and you all know what followed."

Lowell points a finger at Trey.

"Are more of you coming?" Lowell asks. "You know, good guy aliens?"

"I am afraid not," Trey says. "Or to clarify, not any time soon. We, even I, will be long dead before more can join us. I have sent a message to our side of this war, but I do not expect an answer before the current decade is up. Even with an answer, interstellar travel is not instantaneous. It will take lifetimes for reinforcements to arrive. That is why we needed to secure Earth for our side."

"Then we've got plenty of time before more asshole kaiju show up," Lowell says. "Great."

"That is not what I said," Trey responds. "I was specifically referring to our side. The enemy will have already planned to send more orbs in the unlikely, however completely likely now, event that Isk and its comrades are defeated."

"Doesn't our side have orbs?" Dr. Hall asks.

"No," Trey states.

"Oh… too bad," Dr. Hall replies.

"It is," Trey says.

"And we have no idea when the new fuckers will get here, do we?" Lowell asks, then waves his hand. "That's rhetorical. I know the answer." He sighs and rubs his temples. "Great. So, really, my reward after all this shit is I'm pretty much back in a prison and waiting to get shanked at any second."

"Yeah, but you've got a really awesome shiv of your own on hand," Dr. Hall says and points to Quetzalcoatl. "You literally got to pilot a mythical god."

"Yeah, that part's not bad, I guess," Lowell says.

"Ya think?" Dr. Probst says and smiles.

"For the moment," Trey says, trying to push the conversation along, "we will all work to create a stable environment within the Core facility and the other support facilities."

"Support?" Dr. Probst asks.

"The Core facility is what matters to ultimate survival," Trey says. "The others are here to provide strategical backup for when an attack happens."

"Outposts," Dr. Hall says. "Or as the military says, forward operating bases, or FOBs."

"Yes," Trey says.

"Cookie for the nerd," Lowell says.

"Goddammit, Lowell!" Dr. Probst says. "Enough with the jokes."

Lowell smirks and holds out his arms. "Someone needs a hug."

Dr. Probst doesn't move fast enough to avoid the embrace.

"I hate you," she says, her voice muffled as Lowell presses her face to his chest. "So fucking much."

"Again," Trey says. "Awkward."

————

VanderVoort is having her own awkward moment as she sits uncomfortably in a med bay, having moved from Wyoming to the Core facility. She is dressed in the facility's version of a hospital gown while a half-dozen medical bots whirr around her, taking readings and checking her vitals.

The gown and bots and med bay aren't why she's uncomfortable and awkward.

The many holographs of former world leaders all standing in the med bay, arguing with each other, and a few staring daggers at her, is the why.

"People," VanderVoort says. No one responds.

"They aren't going to listen," Director Miles says from across the med bay. He's fiddling with equipment and trailed by a bot that has to restore everything he's fiddled with back to the original settings. "You can shout all you want, but none of these assholes are going to take you seriously."

"We'll see about that," VanderVoort says, glaring at the images. "Kyle? Do you have a moment?"

"A quick moment," Kyle responds immediately via the facility's comms system. "What's up?"

"Can you turn out the lights to all facilities?" VanderVoort asks.

"You're the best," Director Miles says.

"The Core too?" Kyle asks.

"Nah, we're good here," VanderVoort says.

"Proving a point?" Kyle replies.

"Yes, I am," VanderVoort says and smiles. "I like you, Kyle."

"You're not bad either," Kyle says. "For how long?"

"Ten seconds should do it," VanderVoort says.

"Done," Kyle says. "All facilities just went dark, and the lights will come back on in ten seconds."

"Thanks," VanderVoort says. "That's all I needed."

"Cool," Kyle says. "Chat with ya later."

"Good kid," Director Miles says.

"And a good thing too, because he could boot all of us out of here any time he wants," VanderVoort says.

She turns her attention to the very dim outlines of the former world leaders. Then she counts down and waits for the lights to come back on.

VanderVoort is greeted with looks of fear, anger, horror, confusion, and cold calculation. The latter look is from President Nance, still in Wyoming. And VanderVoort doesn't need words to translate that look.

"Fuck," Director Miles whispers. "He's really gunning for you."

"I pushed him a little too far," VanderVoort says then lifts a hand. "Volume."

A cacophony of voices and languages assault VanderVoort's ears.

"Chill the fuck out, all of you!" VanderVoort shouts. The cacophony lessens but doesn't die away. "I said chill, or I'll have more than the lights turned out!"

The people quiet down and all focus on VanderVoort.

"Thank you," VanderVoort says. "That little demonstration was to prove that I'm not the one who holds the reins to these facilities. That would be a sixteen-year-old boy named Kyle Morgan."

She lets that sink in, then continues, "After that, it's a toss-up between the alien named Trey or the former convict Anson Lowell. Me? I'm support and advice. Some seriously heavy support and advice, but still just support and advice. Those lights going off? I had to ask Kyle to do that. I know all of you cackling numbskulls think you will eventually be able to maneuver into taking some type of control, but you're wrong."

"Cackling numbskulls," Director Miles says and laughs.

"Hush, you," VanderVoort says, then addresses the images again. "Your days as Heads of State are done. My days being the behind-the-scenes puppet master are done. We are now just citizens of this new world. No nations, just survivors. However, our expertise and experience running complex organizations and entire countries will be needed to handle the kajillion details that it will take to keep all people healthy and safe."

"Are you proposing we form a new United Nations?" President Nance asks.

"Oh, fuck no," VanderVoort says. "Talk about a waste of space. No, I'm saying that egos need to be checked at the door so reality can be let in. Nationalities no longer exist. Factions can be formed, but they'll be useless since even if one of you morons wants to try for a coup or revolution, Kyle or Trey or Lowell or shit, who knows, maybe the Core itself, will wipe you off the map in seconds."

"Mutually assured destruction," President Nance says.

"Christ! NO!" VanderVoort shouts. She winces and takes a deep breath. "No. The only assured destruction is all your asses. Maybe mine too. But there's nothing mutual about it. You. Cannot. Win. Against. This. Facility. And. Kyle Morgan. Is. This. Facility."

Director Miles turns and faces VanderVoort. They share a look and a single thought. A single thought that VanderVoort can see every one of the people before her are sharing.

"What if Kyle Morgan is taken out?" VanderVoort voices. "Then Trey and Lowell too? Ignoring the moral issues, I think that's some stinkin' thinkin'. I haven't been in this facility for long, but from what I've learned, we're nothing but ants. There is a universal war happening. Plays none of us can comprehend have already been put into motion. I'm sure of that. If we bicker and act like children, then when the adults get here, we'll be lucky if we're only grounded."

"So, what?" President Nance asks. "Everything all of us have worked for in our lives. All the sacrifices. All the pain and heartbreak we've all endured is for nothing?"

"Again, Charles, a big whopping no," VanderVoort says. "It's all for the good of humanity. Just like it's always been for, right?"

The silence is telling.

"Listen," VanderVoort says with another wince. "I have a baby about to pop out my woo hoo, so let's table this discussion after I meet my kid, okay?"

VanderVoort grins at the shocked faces and quickly, one by one, the holograms fade out, including the smirking President Nance.

"Shit, really?" Director Miles asks. "You're in labor?"

"I've been in labor for about thirty minutes, Gordon," Vander-Voort says. "Want to be useful? Go find me a human doctor right the fuck now! It was nice of Trey to activate these, but I swear I'm going to break every single one of these fucking alien bot things!"

All of the bots freeze for a moment, then jump back into action.

So does Director Miles as he scrambles out of the med bay.

"Gordon!" VanderVoort shouts. "I meant use the comms system! Don't you fucking leave me alone in here!"

———

"This isn't half bad," Bolton says, looking around the rooms assigned to Lu and Kyle. "Plenty of space. A little breakfast nook over there. Nice."

Lu smiles as Bolton moves from room to room, a running commentary never stopping as he points out how nice the place is and how much space there is.

"Connor?" Lu asks, finally grabbing his arm and stopping his rambling and shambling. "Would you like to move in here with me and Kyle?"

Bolton tries to look stunned as if he wasn't fishing for that exact invitation, but he fails spectacularly.

"Yeah," he says, an honest, heartfelt grin spreading across his face. "I'd really like that."

"I thought you would," Lu says, then points to a room. "You can stay in there. It's supposed to be a closet, I think, but you can fit a twin mattress on the floor."

"Oh, that's hilarious, Lucinda Morgan," Bolton says and takes her in his arms. "I think I'll take the master bedroom and put you in the breakfast nook."

"Or, and I'm just spitballing here," Lu says. "Maybe we both stay in the master bedroom? I think I can make room."

"Can you?" Bolton asks. "But before I commit, how's the bed? I tend to toss and turn, so maybe we should try it out and make sure it's big enough for both of us."

"Should we, now?" Lu laughs.

Bolton picks her up and tosses her over his shoulder. He carries her into one of the rooms, quickly retreats, and carries her into a different room. The door irises closed as Bolton and Lu laugh.

A welcome sound after all they've been through…

———

"Hello? Kyle? Are you listening?" Krissy asks as she, Tony, and Kyle sit in front of an impossibly large screen with Biscuit asleep at their feet.

Tony is busy playing some sort of video game that none of them have seen before. It's like a weird kaiju battle simulation. There are no controllers, and Tony's face is scrunched up in concentration as he figures out the hand gestures needed to operate the game. He looks like he's the happiest he's ever been.

"Earth to Kyle," Krissy says and tosses an empty cup at Kyle's head. "Dude!"

"Huh? Oh, sorry," Kyle says and shakes his head. "I was going to ask my mom something, but…"

"But… what?" Krissy asks.

"Um… she's with Bolton," Kyle says. "You know… my dad."

"Are they having intercourse?" Tony asks.

"Fucking gross!" Krissy shouts.

"Never say that again!" Kyle shouts.

Tony shrugs.

"Sorry if you saw anything," Krissy says after an uncomfortable silence. "But I guess it's nice to have your mom and your dad here."

"Shit," Kyle says. "I should be saying sorry. You lost everyone."

"I lost everyone too," Tony says. "She isn't special."

"Most of the planet lost everyone," Krissy says. "So, none of us are special. Jesus Christ. Billions down to millions in days."

"Hours," Tony says.

"Dude," Kyle says. "Play the game so you can show us how it works."

"On it," Tony says.

"Are you really in charge now?" Krissy asks Kyle.

"In charge? I'm a teenager who will be living with his parents for probably a very long time," Kyle says. "So, not in charge. In control...?"

Kyle snaps his fingers, and a panel in the room slides open to reveal an assortment of what look like liquor bottles.

"We're gonna be the best of friends," Krissy says.

"The best of sober friends," Lowell says as he walks into the room. "Kyle?"

"Lowell?" Kyle replies, then sighs. He snaps his fingers again and the panel disappears. "Fine. Happy now?"

"No, because I was going to snag all that booze," Lowell says. He snaps his fingers. Nothing happens. "You'll authorize my booze-making powers later."

"What's up, Lowell?" Kyle asks. "Everything cool?"

"Yeah, totally," Lowell says. "I just wanted to make sure you were okay with me addressing the remaining population of the world instead of you doing it. It's sort of your show."

"It's really not, and I wish people would stop thinking that it is," Kyle says. "I'm like the plant manager, not the CEO. I need you and Mom and Bolton and Trey and Dr. Probst and—"

"Got it, kid," Lowell says. "I just didn't want to step on any toes."

"Thanks," Kyle says. "But making a speech is all you."

"Speech?" Krissy asks.

"Yeah, I kinda need to relay to all the facilities what we're up against," Lowell says. "Bring the mood way, way down. Lower than it is, but then maybe pick it back up with some hope."

"Keep hope alive," Tony says.

"Sure," Lowell says and grimaces. "Any advice?"

Krissy and Kyle look shocked.

"You're asking us?" Krissy asks. "Shouldn't you ask some adults?"

"If you don't know by now, adults are fucked up," Lowell says. "You guys will shoot me straight."

"You're not wrong there," Kyle says. "Yeah. Take a seat and tell us what you've got."

———

Lowell has been through Hell and back, but having to lay it all out there for seven and a half million people might just be worse than fighting Isk.

Well… maybe not that bad….

"You're up," Kyle says.

"I know," Lowell says and taps his temple. "I'm connected too."

He clears his throat and looks down from the catwalk at the thousands of people filling the Substance atrium. Tens of thousands more are listening and watching him across the Core facility, as well as millions more across the planet.

"Maybe someone like VanderVoort should do this?" Lowell says, surrounded by Kyle, Lu, Bolton, Trey, and Dr. Probst.

"She just had a baby a couple days ago," Lu snaps. "Get on with it, Lowell."

"Right," Lowell says and clears his throat again. "Right…"

He takes a deep breath.

"Hi," Lowell says. "I'm Anson Lowell. Some of you know me.

Most of you don't. I'm not going to get into specifics about who I am or why I'm here, except to say I have some insight into the situation we've found ourselves in. I know everyone listening is hurting from this, uh, apocalypse, and I respect that pain, so I won't sugarcoat it."

He pauses and lets that sink in for a moment.

"If you don't already know, these facilities were made by aliens," Lowell says. "Hard to believe, but we're probably all past the disbelief point, right? We've all seen shit that ain't exactly normal."

Lowell glances at Quetzalcoatl.

"Like Q over there," he continues. "That big guy is what the Japanese call a kaiju. I am its pilot. I was put inside that thing through an energy transfer thing that... you know what? Everyone can get details on that later. What's important now is that all of you know that these facilities are safe, that we can't—and let me stress the can't part—that we can't run out of food and water, so no need to get all Mad Max or anything, and that, well…"

Lowell glances behind him and receives encouraging looks from his friends.

"That we're going to be here the rest of our lives," Lowell says. "And so will everyone's children. And grandchildren. And great grandchildren. And—"

"They get it," Bolton whispers.

"Yeah, you get the picture," Lowell continues. "But even though we'll be secure, safe, and well fed, doesn't mean we don't have work to do."

He points at Quetzalcoatl.

"We will be making more of those," Lowell says. "A lot more. Which means we'll need pilots. A lot of pilots. It's going to take some time to get up and going, but when we have shit figured out, we'll let you all know. We'll be asking for volunteers to help start some sort of training program. You know, a training program for kaiju pilots."

Lowell laughs.

"Never thought I'd say that while not on drugs," Lowell says, then grimaces at the disapproving grunt from Dr. Probst. "Anyway, people more qualified than me will be working on the day-to-day operations of the facilities while I, and my good friend Trey here, will be working on the kaiju training program."

Lowell looks at Trey.

"My pilot buddy here has let us know that we need this program because one day in the future, whether next week or next millennium, the war will be back," Lowell says. "And it'll be a lot worse than before. Right now, we're it. The last of the human race. We have to protect what we have left and also do our part to help win this war. Because if we don't, then everyone who has already died will have lost their lives for nothing."

Lowell swallows hard against a lump in his throat.

"And you know what? That's fucking unacceptable to me," he says. "I don't know about you, but I can't live with that thought. No way. If human beings are anything—and trust me, I know from pure experience—it's that we're fighters. Probably some of the best goddamn fighters in this motherfucking universe."

"Jesus, Lowell," Dr. Probst says. "Children are listening."

"Sorry, sorry," Lowell says. "But I mean it. We've been fighting amongst ourselves forever. We now have one shot to stop that crap and focus that ingrained violence outward."

He points up.

"Out against the space jerks that nearly won," he says. "When they show back up, we're gonna be ready. We're gonna show them that if they mess with the human race, then they're going to get so much more than they bargained for. We will not go quietly and we will not go without the biggest motherfucking fight this universe has ever seen!"

Lowell lifts his arms into the air.

Silence.

He lowers his arms.

"Uh, thanks," Lowell says. "And sorry about the cussing."

Silence.

Lowell backs up and turns to face everyone.

"I don't think that went well," he says.

"I wouldn't say that," Kyle responds. "Listen."

A sound slowly reaches Lowell's ears.

A sound like… applause.

Lowell turns back to the crowd below to see cheering, clapping, crying, shouting, but mostly smiling, people.

People who he helped save.

"Fuck me…" he whispers.

Then he's surrounded by the others and they're all clapping too. And hugging and laughing and just… being human.

Except for Trey, who isn't human.

But he joins in too.

They're all in it together now, after all, and will be for a long time.

THANK YOU FOR READING OUT OF THE STARS

We hope you enjoyed it as much as we enjoyed bringing it to you. We just wanted to take a moment to encourage you to review the book. Follow this link: **Out of the Stars** to be directed to the book's Amazon product page to leave your review.

Every review helps further the author's reach and, ultimately, helps them continue writing fantastic books for us all to enjoy.

———

Also in Series:
Out of the Earth
Out of the Sky
Out of the Fire
Out of the Stars

———

Want to discuss our books with other readers and even the authors? Join our Discord server today and be a part of the Aethon community.

Facebook | Instagram | Twitter | Website

You can also join our non-spam mailing list by visiting www.subscribepage.com/AethonReadersGroup and never miss out on future releases. You'll also receive three full books completely Free as our thanks to you.

Looking for more great books?

————

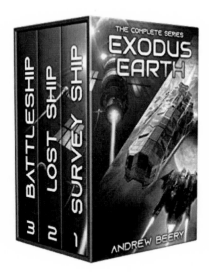

*Earth is a frozen wasteland... The victim of a war we hadn't realized
we were fighting. Opportunities there are few and far between... that
is unless you're willing to put on a uniform. For ace-pilot Deborah
Allen Riker (a.k.a "Admiral Dare"), life had never been easy. She's
defended Earth against countless enemies, both alien and human
alike. Now a civilian and academic living on the fringes of civilized
space, she has committed herself to a life of solitude and studying a
race of long-dead aliens. Everything was great... until she finds
herself dragged into a new conflict. A conflict she never saw coming.
One of the great Arks built to carry the last vestiges of humanity into
the deepest reaches of space goes missing. And she's just the gal to
find it.*

GET THE EXODUS EARTH NOW!

They've plundered their way across the galaxy and just found the score of a lifetime. All they have to do is steal from the most ruthless crime lord in the galaxy. What could possibly go wrong? Yan and his band of rogues are intent on plundering their way to fame and fortune. When they stumble across the score of a lifetime, they quickly go all in for one last job. With everything on the line, there's no way they can fail. At least that's what they're hoping. In the end, they just might have gotten into something bigger than they ever imagined possible.

GET MOST WANTED NOW!

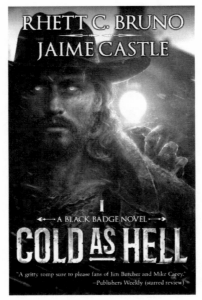

In the West, there are worse things to fear than bandits and outlaws. Demons. Monsters. Witches. James Crowley's sacred duty as a Black Badge is to hunt them down and send them packing, banish them from the mortal realm for good. He didn't choose this life. No. He didn't choose life at all. Shot dead in a gunfight many years ago, now he's stuck in purgatory, serving the whims of the White Throne to avoid falling to hell. Not quite undead, though not alive either, the best he can hope for is to work off his penance and fade away. This time, the White Throne has sent him investigate a strange bank robbery in Lonely Hill. An outlaw with the ability to conjure ice has frozen and shattered open the bank vault and is now on a spree, robbing the region for all it's worth. In his quest to track down the ice-wielder and suss out which demon is behind granting a mortal such power, Crowley finds himself face-to-face with hellish beasts, shapeshifters, and, worse … temptation. But the truth behind the attacks is worse than he ever imagined … **The Witcher meets The Dresden Files in this weird Western series by the Audible number-one bestselling duo behind Dead Acre.**

GET COLD AS HELL NOW AND EXPERIENCE WHAT PUBLISHER'S WEEKLY CALLED PERFECT FOR FANS OF JIM BUTCHER AND MIKE CAREY.

Also available on audio, voiced by Red Dead Redemption 2's Roger Clark (Arthur Morgan)

Wrong crew. Wrong ship. Right Captain. Idealistic navy lieutenant Jacob Grimm just wanted to honor his mother's sacrifice in the last great war. When he's forced to return fire and destroy a squadron of ships to save his own, he thinks he's the hero... Until they discover the ships are full of children. Disgraced and denied promotion, Jacob's career is over. That is until the head of ONI needs a disposable officer to command a battered destroyer on the rim. There's just one problem, Interceptor hasn't had a CO in months and the ship is a mess. Worse, the system he's assigned to is corrupt and on the verge of all-out civil war with the Alliance. However, no one told Jacob he was disposable. Pirates, smugglers, and Caliphate spies complicate the situation and one captain with an old ship can't enforce the law, let alone stop anyone. The single greatest discovery of all time is about to change intergalactic politics forever. If Jacob doesn't find a way to succeed, then it won't just be the end of the Alliance, it will be the end of freedom for humanity.

Get Against All Odds Today!

ABOUT THE AUTHOR

A Bram Stoker Award nominated-novelist, short story writer, independent screenwriter, podcaster, and inventor of the Drabble Novel, Jake is the author of over sixty-five published novels including the bestselling *Z-Burbia* zombie apocalypse series, the bestselling *Salvage Merc One* military scifi series, the bestselling *Roak: Galactic Bounty Hunter* space crime series, the fan favorite hit Team Grendel/Mega thriller series, and his original post-apocalyptic mech/zombie mash-up, the Apex Trilogy. His other novels include the YA zombie novel, *Little Dead Man*, the Bram Stoker Award nominated YA horror novel, *Intentional Haunting*, the middle grade scifi/horror series, *ScareScapes*, and the historical fiction/space opera mash-up series, *Reign of Four*, for Permuted Press, as well as *Stone Cold Bastards and the Black Box Inc.* series for Bell Bridge Books.

Born and raised in the Pacific Northwest, Jake currently lives in Asheville, NC with his wife, two cats, an old dog, and occasionally his college-aged kids. He enjoys the eclectic, outdoorsy attitude of the area and the good ol' Southern hospitality. But, he really, really wishes the tourists would go away.

Subscribe to Writing In Suburbia with Jake Bible for free fiction, audiobooks, news, and the free podcast!